Jane Linfoot writes fun, flirty bestselling romance with feisty heroines and a bit of an edge. Writing romance is cool because she gets to wear pretty shoes instead of wellies. She lives in a mountain kingdom in Derbyshire, where her family and pets are kind enough to ignore the domestic chaos. Happily, they are in walking distance of a supermarket. Jane loves hearts, flowers, happy endings, all things vintage, most things French. When she's not on Facebook and can't find an excuse for shopping, she'll be walking or gardening. On days when she wants to be really scared, she rides a tandem.

🐦 @janelinfoot
📘 www.facebook.com/JaneLinfoot2
📷 @janelinfoot
www.janelinfoot.co.uk

Praise for Jane Linfoot

'Just like the perfect wedding cake, Cupcakes and Confetti is beautifully crafted and wrapped in romance'

Heidi Swain, *Sunday Times* bestseller

'A pure delight . . . fabulous, fun and unforgettable'

Debbie Johnson, bestselling author of *Summer at the Comfort Food Café*

'Simply stunning'

A Spoonful of Happy Endings

'Gorgeous book with characters full of heart, and an impassioned story to make you smile'

Reviewed the Book

'This author packs a punch'

My Little Book Blog

'Loved this book. The main characters are vividly drawn . . . the writing is fast and feisty'

Contemporary Romance Reviews

'With every book I read I fall more in love'

Booky Ramblings

'Jane Linfoot has got out the mixing bowl and whipped up a truly gorgeous story . . . A deliciously scrumptious treat'

Rebecca Pugh

Edie Browne's Cottage by the Sea

Jane Linfoot

A division of HarperCollins*Publishers*
www.harpercollins.co.uk

Harper*Impulse* an imprint of
HarperCollins*Publishers*
1 London Bridge Street
London SE1 9GF

www.harpercollins.co.uk

A Paperback Original 2019

1

First published in Great Britain in ebook format by
Harper*Impulse* 2019

A catalogue record for this book
is available from the British Library

ISBN: 9780008356293

Set in Birka by Palimpsest Book Production Limited,
Falkirk, Stirlingshire

Printed and bound in Great Britain by
CPI Group (UK) Ltd, Croydon CR0 4YY

MIX
Paper from
responsible sources
FSC™ C007454

For Val, with love

epic

ˈɛpɪk/

adjective

heroic or grand in scale or character
particularly impressive or remarkable

achievement

əˈtʃiːvm(ə)nt/

noun

a thing done successfully with effort, skill or courage

Chapter 1

Day 1: October
Five miles east of Salisbury

Epic Achievement: The skydive.

'C'mon, Edie, let's do this.'
We're bumping our way backwards along the fuselage floor and when I screw my head around there's a gaping space where the door used to be. Then the backdraught hits and we're sucked out of the plane.

What happens next is the most crazy thing that's happened in my life so far. There's no lurch of my stomach, no warning, but I'm hurtling downwards. The air rush is wrenching my cheeks off my face, and the blow is so hard I can't breathe. I'm just screaming and falling. Falling and screaming. Somehow I remember to stick my arms and legs out. Then I'm freezing and screaming. And choking. And the flat patchwork of fields below are hurtling nearer and nearer. It's going on forever. We have to stop soon, or we'll definitely die.

Somehow we spin, and I catch sight of the camera guy a few metres below us who almost looks stationary. And bizarrely he's waving at us. It's that weird thing about waving. Without even

1

thinking, I'm waving back. Then we're twisting again, and I'm looking up across the sky at Bella. Her cheeks are distorted, her hair is plastered across her face and she's waving madly too.

Then, just when it feels like it's never going to stop, there's a yank and the air rush stops. Everything slows down and my screams have stopped. Instead of falling we're hanging, suspended on strings, and up above us a broad blue parachute is billowing across the sky. And I can hear Dan's voice again.

'That's the 'chute out. Not long now. Would you like to do some twists and turns on the way down . . . or hold the parachute?'

He has to be joking me, make mine vanilla. 'Straight down is fine . . . thanks all the same.'

It's so relaxed, there's even time to look around. Far below I can make out a tiny tractor ploughing a rectangle of field, cars zooming along a ribbon of road. There's the cream rendered slab of the headquarters, and minutes to admire the logo in shades of blue, painted on the roof. There's even time to see my shiny new Audi, its flinty metallic paint glinting, on its own at the far end of the car park where it won't get bashed. A gleam of sunlight reflects off the driver's window straight into my eyes – that has to be a good omen. Tash acing it as the supportive sister, perched on a straw bale at the edge of the gazebo in her pale blue mac, one arm around her children, Tiddlywink and Wilf, the other holding her phone up to the sky.

Then the ground is rushing towards us; it's close enough to see individual blades of grass, a tree at a wonky angle.

And there's Dan's voice again, as his hand clamps my head onto his chest. 'Okay, and we're almost down, lift up your legs like we showed you.'

One massive bump later we're lurching forwards as Dan lands for us. Then my feet hit the ground too and guys are running in for high fives as they hurry past to sort out the ropes and pick up the crumpled parachute. As I stagger I hear a whoop, and I whip round to catch Bella crashing back down to earth too. There's a needle of pain under my ear as my neck cricks, but a second later it's whooshed away as Dan unclips me.

'Okay? So how was that?' His smile is wide, and the video guy is hurrying over to catch my reaction.

'C-c-c- cold.' I'm back to juddering again, but I'm alive, and the whoosh of happiness bursting up in my chest is like a fountain. 'And f-f-f-frigging a-a-a-amazing.'

And right now there's a rush of thoughts stampeding through my head. How I'm so grateful to Dan I could throw my arms around him. That after this I can do anything. How cool it would have been if Colin Firth *had* been waiting on the ground. Or Marcus even. I strike that one out pretty damned fast. How awesome it is being alive. How I need to do it all over again.

Then Bella's there and she sweeps me into a huge hug. And when we finally break apart Tash is standing on the grass, beaming, passing us a plastic flute each.

I take a gulp of fizz, then gasp. 'I really can take this new job and make it my own. And in two weeks' time I sign for my new flat, and there's no need to worry. After this, every day's going to be *BRILLIANT!*'

Because when you've survived a skydive, whatever comes next *has* to be easy, right?

Chapter 2

Four months later . . .

You could say this all started the day of the skydive. Like a lot of people, I'm obsessed with beginnings. It's as if we have this need to look back and identify the exact moment where things began, as if fixing an exact point in time could help any. But there again, if I hadn't broken up with Marcus, I seriously doubt I'd have done that jump, so possibly it began earlier, with the split. But there again, if I hadn't got my new job, things with Marcus would never have kicked off as they did. So maybe it began with that. But whatever went on before, right now I'm on a journey I didn't choose to make and didn't anticipate either. And the rest of my life will only begin again when I get back to where I started.

*

A hundred and twenty-nine days ago I had a stroke.

At the time no one else believed it either. The Tuesday after my skydive I was still giddy with adrenalin. But when I got into the Zinc Inc office in Bath where I work, my boss, Jake, had to carry my morning coffee and muffin fix to my desk because I had pins and needles in my right arm. By lunchtime I couldn't feel my fingers enough to hold my apple turnover. When I told Jake I could see rainbow halos around his head he took me straight to A&E.

At first they thought I'd slept awkwardly, and sent me home. It took days for them to discover a clot had formed in a blood vessel in my neck, then moved to my brain where it was causing a blockage. The skydive I'd done a couple of days earlier wasn't directly to blame. They can only think it happened when I wrenched my head around to wave to Bella. Or because I'd spent so long staring up at the sky before we set off. Or maybe when I fell over the champagne bucket.

I didn't know then, but the brain has millions of tiny things whose name I can't put my finger on now, all firing messages to different parts of your body. If the blood flow to an area of the brain stops, random bits of your body stop working too. And that's what happened to me.

You'd think if science has come far enough to land rockets on Mars that doctors would know everything about how the human body works. But the brain is so complicated there is still a lot about it even doctors don't understand.

There are some things I do know. I'm actually lucky because it could have been a lot worse. I'm walking and talking, and I couldn't be any more thankful for that. The outlook for recovery is good – most young people who have strokes will return to the job they did before. And that's the hope I'm hanging on to.

My stroke took things away from me. Right now I'm having trouble with words. I can't read. My speaking lags way behind my thoughts, and a lot of words I knew before just aren't there any more. My sensations are all messed up too. Some are heightened, but others have disappeared completely. And I did have a seizure at one point too, so – for now – I can't drive.

The last four months I've grabbed every therapy and

medication on offer; I've improved a lot, and now it's over to me. My car's in the garage at home. My boss, Jake, is paying me a tiny amount until I'm well enough to do my job again. So what I have to do is to find my way back to what I was, one day at a time. It might be slow, and I'll need to be patient. But what I think is, if I can jump out of a plane I can pretty much do anything. So long as I put my mind to it, I'll get there with this too. All I want is to go back to being the person I was before. And so now I'm going to Cornwall for a while – I can always remember the Cornwall bit – because it's my best hope of getting my life back on track. Watch this space . . .

Chapter 3

Day 133: Wednesday, 14th March
St Aidan, Cornwall

Epic Achievement: Finding Cornwall.

'Periwinkle Cottage, first on the left down Saltings Lane – this is the one!'

I'm looking at a rambling stone cottage next to the lane, its shiny slate roof and chimneys etched against the sky, one windy field back from the cliff edge, but the latticed front porch we've pulled up at is just like it looked in the pictures Mum showed me. I've been repeating the address under my breath since we left Bath this morning and my woozy head feels like I've crossed continents not counties. It's the furthest I've travelled in a while, but it was important to hold out and stay independent on this one. Thanks to Dad's mate Hal, an Uber driver, I've dodged the embarrassment of being a thirty-something getting dropped off by my parents. For the first time in ages I almost feel like a fully fledged adult again.

As we drove into St Aidan along the seafront there was time to take in the long stretch of the bay and the strings of lights being blown around between the blue painted lamp posts. As the sea spray lashed across the taxi windscreen and I peeped out at the clusters of random cottages with their pink and white render clinging onto the hillside, the tiny butterfly flutters I'd had in my stomach all the way here turned to flapping. We passed the neat harbourside houses, the lines of boats bobbing along the quayside, the cockle sellers' sheds shut up against the winter winds, then wound up the narrow cobbled roads, where emporiums full of surfboards and neon-coloured T-shirts rubbed shoulders with patisseries and cafés and even a gorgeous upmarket wedding shop. We passed houses with small paned windows and bright front doors, and with every corner the car swung around there was a new glimpse of sea between the rooftops. And then we came out onto the top of the hill to find fields edged with rough stone walls, and as we turned into the lane the narrow tarmac road became a rough track, and the first cottage on the left was *the* one. And now I'm actually here there's an entire flock of seagull wings battering my chest.

As I jump out and wrestle the taxi door closed I can't help notice that the bright Cornish sun my mum promised is missing. When I turn to gasp at the hugeness of the sea over the cliff edge beyond the next field, instead of being blue and sparkly the water is blacker than the wide, stormy sky. But for now I don't give a damn that it's nothing like the azure postcard views in my head – what matters is I'm here, I've done it! And, better still, for the first time since the day I jumped out of that plane, I'm feeling a wonderful lift of achievement. That has to be a good sign.

'My bags will be fine here. Thanks for everything, Hal.'

I know he's rushing off to his next job, so I clamber over the pile of abandoned paint pots and stepladders heaped in the porch, give the ship's bell by the door a loud jangle, then step back to wait.

Ideally I'd like to get off the lane as soon as possible so no one sees how much crap I've brought with me, but also because I try to keep my mum's bags on wheels under wraps at all times. When Marcus and I split he kept all the designer cases, probably because they were all his. Wacky neon luggage might be great at baggage collection for someone my parents' age, but as far as style goes I'm dying here. Not that I'm one of those 'must have every label' people, but a woman has to have some standards.

Hal's already back in the car and I'm still here next to my bag pile, so I give another tug on the bell rope and wave him off. By the time he's pulling out onto the main road again I'm remembering Mum mentioning my aunt and her afternoon naps, and how I had to go straight on in if no one answered. So I turn the door knob, giving it a shove, then, when it doesn't move, I try the bell again but this time I ring it much harder and longer and even louder. Hal said we made good time and my aunt might well have nipped out to get something tasty for tea. Knowing how chatting runs in the family, I could be here all day.

But I'm on a roll here. This is the new, brave, Cornish version of me – I'm not going to let anything as small as a locked door stand in my way. When my mum talked about the fabulous healing sea air in St Aidan she somehow missed out that it would blow my face off. I clamp my hands on my scalp to save the last of my messy up-do, step out into the wind and take in the long stone cottage. I run my gaze along the higgledy row of salt-spattered windows to check for a light shining into the late afternoon gloom, but there's no flowers or plants on the windowsills and most of the blinds are down. My gaze stops at a narrow sash window where the central bars don't quite line up. It's a sure sign that the latch isn't on, and as my fingers close on one of the stepladders on the porch the choice is clear. I can wait down here until I get blown out to sea – which will probably happen in the next few seconds, given the gale – or I can nip in through the window and have the kettle boiling in time for when the cakes arrive. The message was to let myself in, and that's exactly what I'll be doing. The only difference will be that I'll be arriving through an upstairs window instead of the downstairs door. So long as I whip off my shoes the moment I'm through, my aunt won't have anything to grumble about.

The window is at a half level so it's not even that high, and the ladders are light and extendable. A few seconds later I've shimmied up to find it's as I thought – the catch is off, and as I push on the bottom sash it trundles upwards. As I launch myself off the ladder and into the gap it leaves, what I'm thinking most is that I'll have to tell my aunt to be more careful to lock her windows in future. But then something more important takes over.

You know those times when you pick up a pair of jeans in a shop and they look big enough, massive even. Then you get in the fitting room and try to pull them up, but somehow there's a complete mismatch between the size they appear and the size they actually are and, no matter how much you wrench, they'll only come up to your knees. That's what happens with me and the window. As I dive for the hole it looks plenty big enough, but I plunge as far as my waist before sticking fast. There's plenty of room above, so it's my width that's wedged. And right at the moment my ribcage sticks, something else not so good happens too – I look down the wall inside and realise the window's way above the floor in a double height hall, so even if I did flip in like a seal as planned I'd be hurling myself into thin air rather than onto some wonderfully sturdy floorboards.

And just when I'm kicking my legs against the wall in a wild attempt to get free, thinking how things couldn't possibly get any worse, there's a shout from outside.

'WHAT THE HELL DO YOU THINK YOU'RE DOING?'

It's a guy and, unless my aunt arrived out of nowhere, he has to be talking to me. I freeze as I try to think of some words to explain but I've only got as far as a whimper when he starts again.

'BREAKING AND ENTERING. SCARING THE ELDERLY. YOU'RE NOT GETTING AWAY WITH THIS!'

My aunt would be mortified to be called elderly, and she's being so kind having me to stay, so I'm already bristling on her behalf. I manage to screw my head around and catch sight of some shoulders down below, bursting out of a beaten-up denim jacket, and yell down a reply. 'What the hell's it got to do with you?'

'Ever heard of Neighbourhood Watch? Well, I'm from next door.'

I feel my chest implode, although it can't have deflated too much as I'm still stuck. 'Okay, Mr Nosey-Neighbour, thanks for the concern. I rang the bell but no one came, the front door was locked, so I'm letting myself in.'

The deep notes of his voice turn high with disbelief. 'Digging yourself in deeper with every word. EVERYONE knows the front door's round the back – this part of the house is shut up.'

And damn that I didn't work that out for myself. 'But I'm visiting my aunt.' I meant it to be less of a wail.

'Good luck to her with that if this is how you carry on.' There's a moment's hesitation, then he goes in for the kill. 'So *which* aunt would that be?'

'I . . . I . . . I . . .' I remembered the name of the cottage all the way. 'I'll know . . . as soon as she reminds me.'

'Nice try.' There's a loud snort. 'We'll see about that once you're on the ground – let's have you down that ladder NOW, please.'

'There's nothing I'd love more . . .' if only I wasn't squeaking '. . . but I'm stuck.'

'Now I've heard it all.'

There's a scrape of the ladder on the wall, the creak of metal, then a sharp yank on my belt. Next thing, the gale is lashing my ears and my ribs are free, but now I'm being crushed between the ladder and what my bestie Bella would call a 'hard, hot human'.

Strictly speaking, when a woman says a guy is 'hot' it's shorthand for him having eleven key qualities; stuff like empathy and generosity count just as much as looks and muscle definition when it comes to heat. When I grab a quick glance behind me, all I'm taking in is some tousled brown hair, eyes that match and a seriously sexy voice, even if it is coming out with all the wrong words. Enough to say, from what's accidentally pressing against my back, we can mark him down as fit and ripped enough for Bella. Between us, her 'hot' only has about three tick boxes – she's never that fussed about integrity *or* a sense of humour.

As for me, I'm avoiding *every* kind of guy until I get back in touch with my fast comebacks and my 'old' self is as I used to be. In any case this one's just seen my two worst assets – my bum and my luggage – so I'd be a lost cause even if he wasn't out of my league.

So, for my next trick, all I have to do is to work out how to disentangle myself here and reach the ground *without* falling off the ladder and making even more of an arse of myself than I have already. Further down the track I can see a boy kicking the grass on the verge, hands rammed in the pockets of a blue puffer coat. A small dog skittering at his feet. And suddenly there's another figure too, rushing forward, hand shading her eyes, peering up at me as she shrills, 'Edie? Is that you?'

'Aunty . . .?' She doesn't even look like she's dressed and, worse still, there's no sign of any bags of cake at all.

'I'm Aunty Josephine – you remember me, don't you?' If you leave a gap where a word should be, someone will usually fill it in for you. As for remembering her, it's only a couple of weeks since she visited us in Bath, so who knows what she's implying with that. 'What on earth are you doing up there, Edie? And why have you come with a window cleaner?'

'He's not a . . .' The details are too confusing; I need to skip to the important bit. 'When you didn't answer the door, I thought I'd come in through the window.'

I stick my chin out and stare down at the crinkly bits at the edge of those dark chocolate eyes just below me. 'Aunty JOSIE – is that the answer you were looking for? Maybe now you can stop banging on about breaking and entering?'

His hand on the ladder has wide knuckles and broad thumbs and, worst of all, it's still there, making my insides fizz a little when it should be moving downwards. He's staring at me through narrowed eyes. 'Great, so now we've sorted that, what's your status, exactly?'

I might not always remember what my mum's sister is called, but I know the answer to this one. 'I'm happily single and deter-mined to stay that way, thank you. Why?'

'That makes two of us then, but I'm not about to propose.' There's a twist to his lips. 'All I meant was, are you a tourist or a local? You've got a hell of a lot of luggage if you're only here for a weekend. Unless that's your swag pile down there?'

It's good he cleared that up then. No need for the ground to open up and swallow me at all. If he's going to take a life history, I'd rather he did it when my butt wasn't rammed against his chest.

'Actually I'm here to . . . er . . . help with this place.' Three hours of hanging onto the name and now it's gone. 'I'll be here for a while.'

'Wonderful, well, if you're a long-stay prisoner remember there are barns further along and the delivery lorries are extra wide.' He stops to let that sink in. 'So best not park on the lane if your car is shiny or precious.'

'Thanks for that.' I'm not going to share that my car *is* both of those things, but that sadly it won't be here to get in his way. 'You might like to think about yellow lines for next season then?' I'm proud of myself for remembering those enough to toss them in here. Apart from anything, it's a dirt track. The paint would never stick.

He pulls a face. 'Forget yellow, in summer this lane has virtual double reds. You've no idea how much time we waste towing trippers' cars into the yard so they don't get demolished out here.' His eyes narrow again. 'How about I help you into the house with those cases?'

I'd rather expire than accept his help after how aggressively he came on just before. 'Thanks all the same, where I'm from women carry their own bags.' And are red lines even a thing? That's the trouble with mind blanks; they make it harder to sort the truth from bullshit. 'Are we done here – can we get down now?'

He finally shifts, springs to the ground with one jump, gives a whistle, and the dog's legs start to scrabble in the dirt. As I ease my own way down the ladder and step off the bottom rung into the mud I grin at the child, but all I get back is the barest flicker of an eyebrow. I'm ransacking the filing cabinets in my brain for the best way to say 'goodbye and get lost' to someone who accused me of robbing my relative. But he isn't leaving at all. He's off up the ladder again.

'Excuse me, what the eff are you doing now?'

He gives a shrug as he heaves the sash back down. 'Just closing the window so we don't get any more random intruders making opportunist raids.'

I'm shaking my head. 'It was NOT random. I was actually trying to put the kettle on.'

He's down again and swinging the ladder back onto the ground. 'You'll need to lock that from inside. And next time you're at the door and desperate for tea, I suggest you take a look around the back first.' Patronising doesn't begin to cover it. 'If you're here to stay, no doubt we'll be seeing you.'

On balance, I'm thinking totally not. The words 'over my dead body' just popped into my head, and I'm liking the way that sounds. But my mouth is moving all by itself. Lately it has this Tourette's tendency and, even though I try to stop it, I come out with the kind of things that are at best a surprise and at worst downright embarrassing, with no input on my part.

'Love you, bye then.' There you go! I swear that had nothing to do with me. It's a catch phrase from a phone-in I used to listen to in the car driving between building sites. They used it to get the callers off the line. Totally indiscriminate, moderately cringey, but it was worth saying if only for the shock in his eyes as he turns to leave. But if it got rid of him I'll take that as my first result! I'd rather not have an audience as I stagger off dragging Day-Glo bags as big as ponies.

Chapter 4

Epic Achievement: Finding the kettle.

'This way, Edie.'

I'm following Aunty Josie as she pushes through a picket gate at the far end of the house, trundling my biggest case behind me. Round the back of the cottage there are weeds between the stone setts and the pale tangle of last year's grass, but at least we're sheltered from the worst of the wind. I pause to take in the pale grey stone of the cottage wrapping around a pretty courtyard, a walled garden beyond, small paned window frames crying out for paint. As we head past a painted conservatory to a door in the far corner, it's easy to see that the ship's bell is so far away from here I might as well have rung it out at sea. I follow her into the back porch, let go of my bags, then dip in for a hug.

'Well, Aunty Josie, it's great to be here at last.' As I go in to rub my cheek against hers I wonder if she still smells of Nina Ricci.

L'Air du Temps. In pale lemon packages. With the prettiest frosted flying doves on the bottle tops. When we were kids Tash and I used to fight to sit at her dressing table. It was so exotic compared to our mum's, and always rammed with fancy fragrances. That happens when your husband travels for work and heads for the shop in every airport he passes through, and never forgets a birthday or an anniversary. Unlike our dad, who rarely flies and doesn't know what day it is, even though he's great in other ways. Which was a good thing, because I can't ever imagine Aunty Josie buying perfume for herself. As I squeeze her into a hug I can feel every rib through what I'd swear are striped pyjamas.

I smile at her. 'It's a lovely place you've got here.' Or it could be, with some TLC, which is where I come in. I'm looking at the outbuildings beyond the garden wall. 'Are they yours too?'

'Yes, all ours. Or rather, all *mine*.' She gives a sigh. 'Harry had such big plans.' His whole working life Harry dreamed of living by the sea. Him dying within weeks of them getting here was tragic. For both of them.

I pull her in for another hug. 'You were lucky to find it.' In this corner of the world where the coastline wiggles around the harbours and villages, everyone wants outbuildings *and* a view of the sea.

'There's so much to do, I'm holed up in one room.' Which probably explains all those closed blinds and blank windows too.

'Don't worry.' As I squeeze her arm I realise it's a change to be the one doing the comforting. As I drag my bags and follow her inside, the sight of the kitchen makes my mouth drop open.

'Let's have some tea.' As she fills the kettle she disappears against the riot of hydrangeas on the wallpaper. Only her feet, in first position in silver pumps, give away where she's standing.

'Someone liked flowers.' It's what's known in the trade as migraine wallpaper.

She shakes her head. 'The wallpaper was how we managed to buy it – most viewers didn't get past the hall.'

'I'll get the milk.' I'd make a grab for my tinted glasses but I don't want to upset her, so I head for the soothing white of the fridge, hoping to find a sugar hit too. As I swing open the door I realise my double whammy mistake. Not only is there no milk; unless you go for colourless smoothies, nothing in there actually looks edible.

'Will green tea be okay? It's great for your yin and yang.' The set of her mouth tells me this isn't up for discussion. My mum does the same thing, but she'll throw in a smile too. When I think about it, the joking around always came from Harry, but it's a bit late to remember that now.

'Have you gone low-fat?'

'There's a milkman. I'll get him to call again now you're here.' She brushes an invisible crumb off her knee. 'I'm actually eliminating this week.'

Which explains why the milkman lost the will to live. 'That wrecks my plan to cheer us up with a fish supper.'

She pushes a steaming cup towards me. 'I could take off the batter and you could have my chips.'

Chips. Of course. That's what they're called. So far I've reconnected with the words 'chocolate', 'cake' and 'custard' without difficulty. Now she's reminded me, I'm feeling the gap where my stomach should be.

'You've still got your car?' Mum already checked. I know I'm here for the peace and quiet, but this would be a nightmare place to be stranded without one. If we zoom we could be down to the fish shop in no time.

'It hasn't been out for a while.' The corners of her mouth dip even further. 'But when we do get it started, you will do the driving?'

Shit. 'Sorry, Aunty – Aunty . . .'

'Josie.'

'I'm *not* driving. That's why I came in the Uber.' Aunty Josie. I need to get that in my head. As for my licence, we're all hoping I'll get that back in a few months. Or maybe a bit longer. Which reminds me. 'Does the man from down the lane bother you?'

Her nostrils flare. 'It's fine – the delivery drivers all know to leave the lane clear, I don't often see him.' Which is the best news yet.

Deliveries. The alarm bell clanging in my head is louder than the one outside. 'When did you last go out?' I watch her pull her top around her as she works it out.

'I've been up to visit your mum every couple of months, you know that.'

'But you do get dressed apart from that?' She has to.

'I never go without undies.' She drags in a breath and sits up very straight. 'Your mum and I both have a soft spot for Cath Kidston sleepwear. I expect you're the same?'

'You got navy and red stripes from Cath Kidston?' Loungewear used to be my first choice, but lately pyjamas in the day make me feel too much like an invalid. And I might be confused, but I'm damn sure those stripes aren't a colourway I ever saw in the Bath shop.

A flash of guilt crosses her face. 'Actually these are Harry's.' Her hands are in the pockets and as she winds the jacket tight around her hips her nose goes up in defiance. 'They're warm. He had so many pairs I might as well get my wear out of them.'

'Great.' I'm sounding the kind of bright that goes with pretending that her wearing my dead uncle's pyjamas is entirely expected and everyday normal. Considering it's off-the-scale bonkers, I have to ask. 'So, when did you last put your coat on and pop into St Aidan?'

'It was the first meeting at Trenowden's Solicitors, to deal with the will.' She pauses and winds the wedding ring that's loose on her finger. 'George from there has been very good. Since then he's brought things to me.'

'But that has to be ages ago?'

'Only a year and a bit.' Her tone brightens. 'You know what it's like. Harry was the extrovert, I'm hardly going to go out on my own when I don't know anyone.'

This is way worse than any of us thought.

She takes a sip of her tea. 'Anyway, enough about me. You're looking well.'

I don't tell her how often I hear that, or how it makes me feel like a pretender every time. 'I'll show you my magic secret.' I smile and whip out my make-up bag.

She comes in closer. 'Laura Geller Balance-n-Brighten? How does that help with your brain?'

I can't help laughing. 'It's not for my head, just for my cheeks.' My make-up bag's never been so full. When other parts let you down, how you look matters more. That's another reason I'm welded to my pink and black dogtooth coat and my Audrey Hepburn slim tailored slacks.

'You mean for contouring? I'll have to try some of that.' She gives a knowing nod. 'I might not have bothered with proper clothes, but however bad I've felt, I've always put my face on.'

'You didn't run out of powder?'

She shakes her head. 'You must have heard of Amazon Prime? It's well worth the extra, they deliver all the way to the French windows in the day room.'

'Is that where we're going now?' I dump my tea down the sink, then follow her into a space where the giant poppies and ferns furling between black bars on the wall make it feel like being locked in a cage in a hot-house.

She edges onto a cream linen sofa. 'You'll be used to lavish decor like this with your work?'

I didn't ever work on the designs as such, but we never let our statement prints get out of control like they are here. How can I put it without being downright rude?

'Our designs are . . . less in your face.' Less likely to make you gasp for all the wrong reasons.

'A crumbly cottage by the sea was Harry's dream, not mine.' Her frown drives the last of her lightness away. 'I'd swap back to my Harpenden Tudor in a heartbeat if only I could.'

That was nineties mock, not fifteenth century Elizabethan, and Dad insisted the half-timbering was plastic. But the staircase scored a ten on the Cinderella scale, so as kids Tash and I were smitten. It also had a garden so large it could easily have swallowed up our entire cul-de-sac.

'It could be worse.' Ignoring the paper, the place looks sound enough.

'Worse *how?*' Her voice rises to a shriek. 'It's dreary and dirty, it's practically being blown off the clifftop and the nearest John Lewis is counties away.'

'I'm here now, I've got this.' All I need to do is to make the place fit to sell. 'We'll have you back to happy Harpenden before you can say Henry the Eighth.' I only hope I'm not talking bollocks. Me coming through on this is vital for both of us, then we can both move on. But the great thing is, it's not like my real job where everything's too hard. This is stuff I can do, and it's going to be great to feel useful. I'm going to love it here, with the beach and the sea, and no one to judge what I can't do. We're a perfect match – Aunty Jo needs the help and someone to jolly her along. I need a place to stay, some company while I get better. Back to how I was.

'It's very good of you to come.'

She sounds so uncharacteristically grateful there's a lump in my throat. My mum's always been the sister with the less shiny life, and we're used to being the shabby relations who get looked down on, not the ones who come to the rescue. We've never had to help fix things before, because Josie and Harry didn't have disasters like the rest of us. But she can relax now; the cavalry has come to Cornwall. Give me a few months, I'll make sure she's okay again – or at least as okay as you can be when you've lost your life partner.

'I'm happy to help.' Even if I haven't the first idea how I'm going to cope with the sludge in the fridge or how stubborn and snobby Aunty Thing can be at times, it's buying me the time I need to get back to how I used to be, and turning her life around too. 'You know me, I always like a . . .' It's the one word that *always* escapes me. I'm Zinc Inc Interiors' some-kind-of manager for the southeast. How the hell do I not know it?

The worry lines in her brow deepen as she considers. 'A quest?'

'Quest. That'll do. You're my quest.' I let out a short sigh because, like so many things in my life now, it's not quite right. And it's not completely wrong either. But for now it will have to do. 'Shall we phone for a pizza?'

Chapter 5

Epic Achievement: Getting Aunty Josie back out into the world.

There's always a fragment of every morning, as I gently slide into consciousness, when, for the first intake of breath, everything feels like it used to do. And then there's this frantic scramble as my head catches up with my body and, seconds afterwards, I readjust and remember again. I'm Edie Browne. I'm thirty-two. And my life's been turned on its head.

When it came to choosing a bedroom last night I went for the oversized rose and daisy garlands. Waking to giant sprigs was jarring, but the orange birds of paradise next door would have been worse, and it would have been worse again if the sun had been streaming in. As it is, when I realign with reality and look outside today, the sea and the sky are both stony, but it's definitely light enough to be morning.

I still wear the watch Marcus gave me, not because I understand the pointers any more but because it was super expensive and he always used to notice if I didn't have it on. But right now I'm wearing it for me, as my reminder. A promise to myself that I *will* find my way back to who I was, a talisman to help me find my path back to where I should be.

When I get down to the kitchen and peep into the day room Aunty Josie is already up, eyes tightly closed, the tartan of her PJ trousers knotted into some cross-legged position. The funny kind of humming moan I could hear all the way down the stairs and through the jungle-papered hallway is coming from her. If I'd been living here I'm not sure I could have lasted all that time with so many monkeys on the landing. They'll be top of my schedule to go, as soon as she helps me write it. As I cough, her eyes snap open.

'Edie, I'm just finishing my meditation – you might like to join in another day?'

'Woah, I'm not that bendy!' It's the first excuse I come to. There are a lot of spaces in my head, but I'm completely certain yoga puts me to sleep. As for meditation, I'd probably have more laughs in a coma.

The pizza boxes from last night are out on the side, and I help myself to the last piece of my giant Hawaiian.

Aunty Josie's wearing her 'disgusted-of-St Aidan' face as she pokes at her pizza box. 'Help yourself to the rest of mine.' Hers was the smallest, gluten-free with dairy-free cheese and no tomato, and she still only picked at a tiny bit. From the way I wolfed the side salad and both fudge cheesecake slices too, you'd never guess I can't taste things. But I have to keep fuelled, and I'm always secretly hoping that next bite will be better.

'So is it pizza for breakfast too?'

'I've got some delicious juice here, or the milk arrived. There's Oat So Simple if you'd rather?' She gives a disapproving shudder.

'That sounds way better.' Her bean sludge is beyond disgusting. Porridge is beige too, but somehow that's different.

'I'll show you how to make it.' She rips open the packet, then slowly fills it up with milk. 'Then we can watch *Swan Lake* while we have breakfast.'

Crap. 'You don't like Piers then?' Breakfast telly has become a morning ritual for Mum and me, but now I think about it, Josie and Harry only like BBC. As for ballet, I'm not sure I can handle men in tights this early, even if they're fit. Which reminds me, the guy from next door came down the road in his van just as the pizza delivery was blocking the lane last night. What are the chances? I accidentally let out another, 'Love you, bye!' as I scooted off with my stack of boxes, which I minded about less because I could swear I saw him jump.

'I can't get my head round news these days. The great thing about ballet is it gets the day off on the right foot.' As Aunty takes the porridge bowl over to the microwave her unflinching expression tells me we're waving goodbye to any hope of *Good Morning Breakfast*. 'Push this button for three pings, Edie. Will you remember three for tomorrow?'

She's making a big effort to be helpful so I want to say yes, but I have to stay honest. 'I'll try.' Most probably I won't.

It's not that I'm a party pooper, and I'm not a quitter. But by the time I'm in front of the TV with my breakfast, what with ballet, stripes on the wallpaper, checks on the PJs *and* purple poppies, I give in. If I've eaten porridge wearing shades before I can't remember. Maybe I did the time Marcus and I went to those huge mountains near India and had breakfast watching the sunrise. But if not, there's a first time for everything. I jam my sunnies on my nose and settle back to watch the figures in gauzy net leaping across the screen.

'You danced, didn't you?' It's wedged in my head but the details have gone, and I'm half expecting her to tell me off for talking.

'That was years ago.' Aunty Thing's abruptness softens. 'And just once I was on the same stage as Margot Fonteyn.'

'Awesome.' I'm giving the air a mental punch for unearthing that.

'Harry always made more of it than it was.' If we're talking stiff upper lips, Aunty Thing's is made of steel, so I'm guessing her loud sniff has to be down to how much smoothie she's still got to get through.

'Do you watch Margot all day then?' As fast as my heart's sinking, my panic's rising. Cosying up in front of Dad's log-burner with *Bridesmaids* and *Love Actually* on repeat was fine, but I'm not up for all-day *pas de deux*.

She nods. 'Dance is very therapeutic.'

'We should go out.' It's easy to do, I know. The more you stay home, the more you want to. 'There must be some classes. Can you look what's on?' I nod at the laptop even though I'm not that hopeful. As remote places go, St Aidan is at the end of the line. As the gale thrashes sand grains against the window, I'm wondering how I ever imagined I'd be sitting on the beach soaking up a winter sun patch.

'Let's see.' She pulls her laptop onto her knee and scrolls through. 'They do them at the Leisure Centre – there's macramé, or basket-making?'

Surely that can't be it? 'Read them *all* out, please.' I'm using the 'don't-mess-with-me' tone I keep for stroppy builders because, to be fair, the most awkward contractor probably has nothing on Aunty Josie when it comes to heels being dug in. Due to my voice recognition software completely failing to understand my West Country twang, brushing up on reading's what I'll be concentrating on next. In between renovations, that is.

'Fine.' Aunty Jo lifts her eyebrows. 'Woodworking, Car Maintenance, Kick Boxing and Learn Spanish while Making Tapas.' She pulls a face. 'The best ones seem to be run by the Singles Group, but we can't go to those.'

'They might be . . . er . . . friendly?' We are both on our own, in case she's forgotten. It's one of my greatest reliefs that I split from Marcus a couple of months before I was ill, because he wasn't the best with hospitals or looking after people. But in case anyone's wondering – though I can't speak for Aunty Jo – a partner's the *last* thing I'd be looking for right now.

One sniff from her says that's a no to the singles. 'The ones at The Whole Earth Centre are better. Paint your Own Plant Pot, Molecular Gastronomy, How to Make Vegan Dumplings, Hydroponics for Beginners, Breast Painting, Handstand Masterclass, Play the Ukelele in an Hour . . .'

'Breast *what*?' I have to ask.

'From the picture, it looks like you roll on the floor and paint with your boobs. I'm not sure mine are big enough.'

Even if mine are, I still shake my head. 'Keep going.'

'Sew Your Valentine a Pair of Boxers. Oh, no, sorry, that's gone.'

'Damn.' I grin at her, but she doesn't smile back.

'Interior Design . . . Well, that's wasted on you. Creative Writing's not suitable for now. We'd be out of place at Wedding Flowers. Which only leaves Heart Surgeon for a Day, Zombie for an Evening or Goat Rearing.'

I let out a groan. 'Who goes to these?'

'Oh, but there's a Practical page.' She looks more closely. 'Dry-Stone Walling or Plastering. With the buildings to finish, either of those might be useful?'

It's great she's so up for this, but with everything else going on, I'm not ready to drop rocks on my feet.

'What about Cupcake Making?' Cupcake's another word I can always find. Thankfully. Or Cake Icing would do, so long as it's the squishy sort.

'Edie, I'm sugar-free. So we're back to Macramé?'

I'm a stroke survivor, I could have died. I may not be able to tell the time, but I value every second. 'Not things from string. Life's too short.'

'Calligraphy, then? Harry's mum used to do that, she made wonderful Christmas cards.'

In my head it's in the same box as string.

'It says *Modern* so it must be for young people like you. It's drop-in, which is good, so you only pay when you go. Tuesday afternoons at The Deck Gallery.'

'Is that it?' It's vital to get Aunty Jo out again, and it'll be great to sharpen up my writing. But I can't believe I've come all this way to end up doing that.

'You *can* still write?' She knows because Mum talked to her about helping me with my letters.

'A bit.' It's odd that writing's easier than reading. Tash says they're worked from different bits of my head, which is why it's useful having a sister who's a doctor. She also has a house, a husband and two kids and she's older and cleverer. Seriously, she's got all her shit together.

'There you go then.' Aunty Thing looks pleased. 'It says Tasty Treats on offer too.'

Which finally tips it for me, even if it doesn't for her.

Chapter 6

Day 137: Sunday, 18th March
At Periwinkle Cottage

Epic Achievement: Cake on Sunday.

'So, you can see the stables haven't been used in a while.' The bunch of keys Aunty Josie's swinging is too big to fit in her pocket.

However much I'd intended to get straight down to work, it takes a few days to find my way around. I half expect to open the quirky cottage doors and find Red Riding Hood or Hansel and Gretel hiding behind them. It's Sunday morning by the time I get out my clipboard and as we make our way towards the outbuildings I'm so intent on business, all that's missing is my hard hat.

I thought the days might drag here, but since I arrived I'm yawning before it's tea time. It's hard to believe I used to be up at four and rarely went to bed before midnight. At least I'm finally getting my wear out of the navy pinstripe PJs Tash gave me as a 'new job congratulations' present, as a joke to celebrate my new-found 'suit status'.

To be fair, up until I moved out of Marcus's house, the pyjamas stayed firmly in their Net-a-Porter carrier bag because Marcus and

I always slept naked. Out of bed he turned a blind eye to global warming and cranked up the heating so I rarely wore more than a teensy vest and shorts. But I could hardly go around like that when I boomeranged back to live with the oldies. Quite apart from the over-exposure, in a family of women, the thermostat is one of the only places where Dad takes control. After Marcus's, Dad's running temperature is arctic, and whoever invented those damned Smart meters that flash up how much you're spending on gas every minute through the day wasn't thinking of me and Mum.

Aunty Jo is making her way along the horseshoe of stable buildings which border the garden, opening every door and closing them just as fast. Apart from the stiff locks, it's hard to believe it's her first visit since she and Harry colour-coded all the keys the day before he died. On the fourth door, when I've still not seen anything, I barge my way past her, click on the light and kick into professional mode.

'Nice switches.' They're funky and industrial, but best of all, there's not a jungle beast in sight. Looking up at the old hewn timbers is spinning me back to the Zinc Inc sites. 'The roofs are new and the floors feel level, so that's a good start.'

'They ran out of cash halfway. That was how we could afford it.' Aunty Jo gives a sniff of disapproval.

'They probably blew the budget next door on exotic wallpaper.' I come to a halt by a newly installed wood-burning stove. 'So what were they planning here?'

'Holiday accommodation around the courtyard.' She frowns. 'It's not my cup of tea at all. I like a room to have a dado.'

I already know that. Our house didn't have those either, and she reminded us every visit. I peer into a tiny room and spot a drench shower head. 'They haven't got around to tiling, but at least the wet room fittings are in.'

She sniffs. 'Very downmarket – my friends don't look twice if there isn't a Jacuzzi with steam jets.'

I peer out of a tiny window. 'A lot of the groundwork has been done. What's left is the finishing.' That's the time-consuming and expensive bit and, with eight units, it's a good thing she's not counting her pennies. On the plus side, there's loads of space and it's wonderfully airy, even if it is freezing.

'So there could be dados, after all?' As she hugs her jacket closer there's no vestige of the upbeat jovial couple she and Harry once were. I know she's grieving and sad, but I've been here days and I haven't seen a hint of a twinkle. Though if she has any idea how much work it's going to take to transform what's here to luxury accommodation, I can understand why.

It's my turn to pull a face. 'We might give dados a miss but we can certainly get the place done.' It's time not cash that's our priority; once I find a reliable builder who's available, we'll fly to the finish. 'And look at that sea view.' Across the field the clifftop edge is sharp against the grey of the water, which merges in turn with a smoky sky strewn with scudding grey clouds. And the water is the colour of iron, stormy with dashes of cream foam. The truth is, now I'm here scuffing my toes in the building dust, the twang in my chest is about way more than another cloudy day.

I went to Zinc Inc by accident, the summer I was seventeen. I'd fallen out of sixth from after a year of hard partying with an F in every subject, then went to a careers fair because someone told me they were giving away free T-shirts. I ended up at Jake's mass interview with no idea what interior design even was. Apparently Jake wasn't looking for raw natural talent with carpet swatches, he chose me because I had all the nervous kids in the group smiling within minutes, and then went on to talk the tea lady into serving us her private doughnut stash. He said a taste for cake and a friendly smile counted for a lot in the building industry, and he wasn't wrong.

Back then the company mainly worked on upmarket jobs in London. But then loft living took off along with the property market, and every last home owner wanted to rip the guts out of their terraced house and design the arses off their open-plan living spaces. What I loved most was going to see the jobs on site and it turned out I had a natural eye for detail. If Tash's superpowers are being a brainbox and making ill people well again, mine are noticing stuff and being able to persuade reluctant builders to do what I ask. Before long Jake was sending me out to jolly the tradesmen along on the smaller jobs.

As the business expanded I barely noticed I was taking on more. Then one day Jake came in and announced he was giving me a fancy title I can't even remember now and a shedload of extra responsibility, which was amazing but is probably also why I never had time to go to bed. And why now I'm not getting up at stupid o'clock and rushing from site to site, angsting about schedules and quality control and progress meetings and one-off disasters and handover dates, I feel like I've lost every bit of who I am.

Aunty Jo's voice cuts in. 'I know the sea's still grey, but there's no need to look that gloomy, Edie.'

I swallow, resist pointing out that she's in no position to talk about people looking miserable and let out a sigh for everything I'm not doing. It's not just the status and the sense of satisfaction I miss. It's the camaraderie, and the banter, and knowing there are a whole load of tradespeople working their butts off to do their best jobs for you. Most of all, it's the human contact. However much they drove me to distraction on some sites, at the end of any working day I'd have spoken to more people than I could count.

'There's something indoors to cheer you up.' Aunty Josie sounds even gruffer than usual.

'Really?' I rub the dust out of my eye and force myself to think of something that's not Zinc Inc. Not that I'm ungrateful, but please may it not be yet another ballet DVD. I've managed to force her out for a walk every day, down the twisty streets to the shop above the harbour – to be fair, we have had earache from the wind – but other than that it's been wall-to-wall tutus. I never thought I'd be begging to watch *Cash in the Attic* and reruns of *Garden Rescue*, or be desperate to sit and listen to my mum saying Charlie Dimmock has let herself go and could do better with her choice of sweatshirts. I'm not being mean, but if home had been nearer and the Uber less expensive, I'd have gone.

'The *Secret Garden* colouring book arrived this morning. And some Faber Castell felt tips.'

'Thank you.' If she was less sharp I'd say how sweet it was too, but I don't want to risk her jumping down my throat. Colouring is what I turn to when my head feels like it's going to burst. Which is usually straight after I've been working at my puzzles, which are a lot less fun than they sound. Fitting the pieces together is supposed to help, but when it comes to those dimension things, I've totally lost it. At the moment, trying so hard and still ending up with a random pile of plastic bits literally blows my mind.

It's also strangely soothing to colour when the ballet's on. Mostly I do *Hearts and Flowers*. Now and again I use Bella's *I'm Sick of This Shit* book. Mum went storming off when she saw that one. But it was actually great for me because it meant Bella totally gets where I am. It fits, because we've been besties since we met in junior school. Even when she was seven Bella had that same effortless Kate Moss fabulousness. In the least posh part of Bath where we lived, with her purple nails and her denim ra-ra skirts embroidered with sequin appliqué she stood out like some exotic flower. Back then her mum worked at Tammy Girl and provided Bella with a non-stop supply of strawberry lip gloss and lemon sherbets. Bella's heart is so big, she gave the sweets away. Mostly to me. I still run best on sugar, even now.

Lately my tears have a mind of their own. They come gushing down my face and the first I know is when my shirt is soaking. Or my thick woolly scarf that I use to wrap up against the cold. Like it is now.

'Oh, dear, crying won't do, Edie – if anyone knows that it's me.' Aunty Jo is holding me at arm's length, staring at me with an appalled scowl. 'Come on, dry your eyes. I'll show you the big barn where Harry was going to have his main workshop.'

Somehow I'm still holding a handful of her coat sleeve. 'I was going to give you a hug. For the book?'

'There's no need – one click, that's all it took.' She's pulled away.

'It's a nice coat.' I'm not letting her off, if she won't have a hug she can have a compliment. 'It makes you look like Paddington. Or one of those men who save people from the sea.'

She pulls away, frowning. 'Oh, dear, it's my first ever anorak. Don't lifeboat men wear red, not yellow?'

'No . . .' I know this one. 'Fire engines are red, yellow shows up in the sea.' And mostly Paddingtons are blue, but Tash had a yellow one so we could tell them apart and didn't fight. Except she used to steal the wellingtons from mine because she liked the blue ones better than the red ones. She also stole the massive middle chocolate from inside the big doors on my advent calendar one year too. It's lucky for me I can still remember that, because I never let her forget it either.

'The yellow's too much, isn't it?' Aunty Thing's staring down at herself.

I'm kicking myself for making her doubt. So often I can't find any words at all. Then the wrong ones have this awful habit of tumbling out before I can stop them. 'It's great – yellow's big this year. And it's got fur.' I definitely know this one. 'It's a parka. That's good too.'

'You're right there with your colours and your fashion.'

'Too right.' There's no need to panic about the future. I could always try a Saturday job in H&M for a bit. Obviously I'd have to brush up on my cash skills and sort out my numbers first, but whatever.

I follow Aunty Josie beyond the stone-flagged courtyard towards a monumental stone building with huge wooden barn doors with a small door at the centre. As we push through into a vast space I'm pulling my sunnies down off my head.

'Wow, looking at this you can see why people say barns are like cathedrals. I can see why Harry loved it.' In spite of the grey day there's light flooding from windows in the high roof and, with its massive hewn timbers, it's as big as a village hall. So long as you overlook the monster piles of old planks dumped in random places across the floor, it's a lot more finished than the stable spaces even though it's not clear what its use is. I move across to a huge glazed doorway on the other side and take in the next group of buildings beyond a strip of grass. 'Are they yours too?'

'No, thankfully, only the field. Those buildings are let out – there's a caravan factory and a few others.' She's about to turn back when she stops. 'Who's this?' There's a boy hugging himself back against the door frame, staring at us through the glass.

When I push up my shades to get a closer look, the blue jacket is familiar. 'He was on the lane with a dog the day I came, remember?' Kicking the mud, just like he is now. Before I can remind her that he hangs out with Mr Nosey-Neighbourhood-Watch she's turned the key and pushed the door open.

'Can I help you?' Her tone is so stern he shrinks so far into his jacket his face almost disappears. 'Aren't you too little to be out on your own?' If she meant to prod him, it's worked.

'Actually I'm not small, I'm six.' As he stands up straighter he ages inch by inch. 'Have you got any cake at your house?'

'Cake?'

He's wrinkling his nose. 'I'm having some later, but I'm actually hungry now.'

I laugh at how direct he is. 'Sorry, I ate the last piece for breakfast.' I'll pick up more when we finally brave the cold and go down to the harbour later.

His eyebrows shoot up. 'You *can't* have *cake* for breakfast.'

I find myself back-pedalling under his scorn. 'It's not every day. Well, hardly ever. Only because we ran out of oats.'

Aunty Josie clears her throat. 'Actually we have got cake at the cottage.' She wrinkles her nose. 'But you'll have to wipe your feet before you come in.'

'You bought *cake*?' I didn't mean to shriek so loud. But what the heck happened to sugar-free? And where the hell's she hiding it? I might have had some after lunch if I'd known, that's all.

'There's no need to sound so shocked, Edie. It's *Sunday*.'

'So?'

'It's a ballerina thing. If you're careful what you eat every other day of the week, you can eat whatever you like on Sunday.'

'That's what *you* do?' Apart from it being a million years since she danced, I'm not sure if I'm gobsmacked at the deprivation or relieved she's breaking out.

'Of course. I wouldn't have a figure like this if I didn't.'

She's half the width of my mum and me, but we just assumed she had different genes. 'So what have you got?'

She gives a cough. 'Carrot cake – it arrived this morning.' Which explains how it's escaped my cupboard raids. She turns to the boy. 'If you'd like some, we'll be in the cottage next door. You'd better ask your mum first. Or your dad. Or whoever's looking after you.' She gives a sniff. 'Or not looking after you.'

'That's Barney.' He's already running.

She calls after him, 'Come around the back. Tell Barney he can come too. We'll make some tea.' She turns to me. 'That must be the window cleaner.'

I clamp my sunnies firmly back on my nose. 'Barney? *Really?*' If that's the same guy from the lane he's the last person I'd want to serve tea to. Unless it was green. 'And, by the way, he doesn't actually clean windows.'

'Like you say, it's good to get to know people.'

'It is.' Anyone other than him.

Chapter 7

Day 137: Sunday, 18th March
At Periwinkle Cottage

Epic Achievement: Discovering a carrot patch in the vegetable rack.

I'm not sure if it's the thought of guests or the excitement of an all-you-can-eat day, but as soon she's delivered my new colouring book Aunty Thing rushes off and starts crashing around the kitchen. As she clatters the cups and plates onto a tray and gets out a gigantic teapot, she's dancing around so fast her gold pumps are leaving light trails.

She waves at the next room, snaps out another order. 'Get the cake, Edie, it's in the vegetable rack.'

That's not a place I've visited yet, but moments later I'm back in the kitchen sliding a square cake out of the box, eyes popping at the creamy topping and bright orange knobs of icing carrots sprouting green sugar leaves.

She's tutting critically as she watches me unwrap it. 'It's an M&S carrot patch cake – the milkman picked it up for me from Penzance.'

'It's pretty fab.' Even though I'm reeling from being bossed about, I have to hand it to her. In my other life with Marcus I might even have tucked the idea for that away in my mental recipe file and pulled it out later as a cute sweet to take round to his friends' for a weekend barbie. My desserts were the sole trick I had to impress them with. Marcus's mates in creative media – and he had a lot – took male bonding to a whole new level. The kind where, if they weren't away on some kind of wacky adventure, they were incapable of making it through a weekend without meeting up on someone's patio. Mostly they swilled back craft beers with odd names and incinerated choice lumps of cow from the craft burger shops while they tried to channel their younger selves. Even though they'd graduated from flats to houses, due to soaring Bristol property prices and the burst of the dot com bubble, no one had yet made it to the stage of owning a full-blown flower-filled garden. So we chewed on our chargrills in back yards, sitting on stacked-up railway sleepers listening to *Wonderwall* against backdrops of reclaimed brickwork.

At the time it felt like we'd be twenty-something all our life, and be doing that for ever. Then the inevitable happens, someone forgets to take their Pill, someone else thinks 'Why not us?' And, before you know it, baby bumps aren't just trending, they're exploding under every Nicole Farhi silk T-shirt. And whatever people say about not letting kids change their lives, they're kidding themselves. I had an aunt's-eye view when Tash had Tiddlywink and Wilf. It was like a hurricane upended their home and then came back through for seconds. Put it this way, once you shell out more on a Bugaboo Cameleon pushchair combo than a Vera Wang wedding dress – and there were plenty of both among Marcus's friends – nothing's ever the same again.

But, getting back to Aunty Jo's carrot patch, even for a cake-face like me, it's huge. I'm also impressed at how obliging the door-to-door people are around these parts. I'm counting the sprouting carrots in my head and I get all the way to eleven before I falter. It could be the sea air, or Aunty Jo making me count along with her when she does her before lunch Stay Young stretches. But that's the most I've reached for a long time, so in my head I'm giving a silent cheer.

'We could have tea in the conservatory? As we have company.'

'Great plan,' I say. It's warm in the garden room, even on cloudy days, and this way we sidestep the visitors seeing we live in what looks like a rainforest theme park.

By the time the boy is kicking his way across the courtyard we're settled onto basket chairs, marvelling at how the gunmetal paint on the window frames matches the shine of the distant sea. Aunty Jo pushes the door open, points at the mat and, after a frenzied foot wipe, the boy wanders over to where my pens are spread out on the low table next to me.

He's giving my felt tips a hard stare. 'Aren't you too old for colouring in?'

I smile. 'You think so?'

He shrugs. 'I don't like colouring. I go over the lines.'

I get that. 'Same here.'

His hands are deep in his pockets. 'Making up your own pictures is better for your imagination.'

Why didn't I think about that? He could be right. 'Anyway, I'm Edie Browne with an 'e', and this is Aunty—'

She's straight in there, filling the gap. 'Jo. Aunty Jo. Jo like 'joker', because I laugh a lot. Let's see how that one works?' From the look she gives me she knows I'm liable to forget.

I turn to the boy. 'So do *you* have a name?'

'Cam. Except at school I'm Cameron Michael Arnold, but that's *so* long to write.' He sounds despondent. 'I'm *really* slow at writing.'

'Me too.' I'm not actually getting how Aunty Jo is any fun at all, but I can sympathise with the slow part. Even so, I bet if we had a race he'd win. If he's here because he's a sponge fan too we could have a lot in common. 'But I'm fast at eating cake.'

His eyes pull back into focus. 'Barney said to hurry, we're going to see a customer.'

Aunty Joke's tone hardens. 'He *will* still have time for tea?'

'Nope.' Cam's shaking his head.

'That's a shame.' *Not.* I'm mentally punching the air with relief as I reach for the knife. 'I'd better go fast then.'

His brow furrows. 'What are those orange things?'

Do six-year-olds understand irony? 'They're icing carrots because it's carrot cake. They're meant to be funny.'

He wrinkles his nose. 'I don't like vegetables.'

That's another thing we have in common. I prise off a carrot top and pass it to him. 'Try one, they're delish.' Not that I could taste them myself, but if they're M&S they have to be. As I watch him chew, his frown melts. 'Good?'

'Yep.'

Aunty Joke isn't giving up on her teapot. 'Well, you can always have tea another time. Next weekend, maybe?'

I slice through the buttercream. 'One for now and one for later?' I pass Cam the first chunk in kitchen roll, then wrap up the second.

Aunty Jo prompts me, 'Don't forget – do some for Barney too, he's here now. I just hope he doesn't look at how dirty our windows are.'

Damn. People like him don't deserve cake. And I'm giving up on the window cleaner thing.

When Barney finally slides his shoulder up against the frame, he fills the doorway. Then my worst nightmare happens and his eyes lock with mine. I clutch at my stomach as it lurches into some kind of cartwheel, spectacularly fail to stop it as it slips into free-fall and somehow lose my grip on the cake knife, which arcs through the air and clatters onto the tiles next to Barney's feet.

He stoops to pick up the knife and as he stands up his lips twitch. 'Hey there, butterfingers.'

41

I roll my eyes. 'You again? So soon.'

Then, as his eyes slide down to the cake, they widen. 'Nice carrots. Is that homemade?'

Why the hell would I even care he's noticed? As for the pang of disappointment that I can't claim the cake as mine, that's bonkers too because he's the last person I'd want to impress. That little pool of wide-eyed awe of his isn't one I'd want to bask in. Honestly.

I feel my nose wrinkle. 'I guess someone with a home made it.' I have no ideas where that bollocks came from, but I have to come clean. 'It wasn't me.'

He looks half amused. 'In that case I *won't* say great cooking. Or make any mention of *baking* and entering.'

I'm groaning inwardly at that, but I don't flinch. 'And I *won't* say thanks a lot for the compliments, although I might risk an "enjoy".' But that's only for Cam's sake, obviously. Okay, someone please tell my mouth it's time to stop. 'And in case you're thinking of sending the special constables round to interrogate us, it isn't stolen – the person who brings that white stuff in bottles brought it.'

His nostrils flare slightly. 'Any cake is good cake as far as we're concerned. Not that we're desperate or anything.'

'I'll take your word on that.' I swear that's my last word too.

'Ready, Cam?' He cocks his head at the boy, then turns to Aunty Jo. 'I hope it's okay he gate-crashed your afternoon tea?' He's raising an eyebrow at Cam. 'C'mon then, big man, fast as you can, we're already late. What do you say?'

'Thanks.' Cam's clutching his stack of cake parcels, dropping crumbs as he hurries out onto the stone-flagged path.

'You will come again?' There's no time for Aunty Jo to say more because they've almost reached the lane.

So there's 'in a hurry'. And there's 'bad mannered'. And I know where my money is.

As she pulls the door closed behind them her voice has lightened. 'He was nice.'

'He was, I don't see many kids that age.'

Her eyes narrow. 'Not the child, I was talking about Barney.'

It takes me a while to pick myself up off the floor. 'Nice, in *what* way?' All that stubble and on-trend scuffed Timberlands still don't make up for rushing off. Or accusing me of robbery. Even worse, now he's gone my heart is pounding and my pulse is racing. I blame my faulty adrenalin circuits. The slightest excuse, they flood my body so I'm ready to run away. Which is great for survival and outsmarting the Neighbourhood Watch brigade, but leaves me feeling way more jumpy than I'd like.

'Put it this way, if he'd asked me to dance thirty years ago I wouldn't have said no.' Her wicker chair creaks as she settles back into it.

I can't believe what I'm hearing. 'But you're *grieving*.' And she's also my aunt who's into ballet and wheat grass juice and rubs on Estée Lauder Youth Dew body lotion morning, noon and many times later on. Every day. How can a guy whose idea of a meet-the-client outfit is a ripped T-shirt and is hunky enough to have jumped off the pages of *GQ* magazine even register on her radar? He's totally nothing like, you know . . . the one who looks like he wants to snog Margot's face off every time he snatches her out of the air. Or smooth old Uncle Harry, come to that.

'Don't be so frumpy, Edie, I've lost my husband, not my eyes.' It's another one of those times when her snap is so sharp, arguing is pointless.

I fix my gaze on the ferns in the room beyond the door. 'We really need to do something about this wallpaper.' This is me, and I'm taking back control. A few minutes' break from the riot of black and purple has been bliss. At home Dad repainted my bedroom and the pale grey walls and soft light filtering through the muslin nets worked wonders for clearing my head. We've got to make a start somewhere and Edie Browne, site manager, knows the cottage is the place.

'You could be right. If we're having regular visitors we don't want to come across all dark and gloomy, do we?'

If Mr Awful-Neighbour got an upgrade to visitor status, even if it's only in her head, we need to get this quest up and running. The sooner we do, the sooner I'll be back to civilisation. And normality. And after today I could really do with some of that.

Chapter 8

Epic Achievement: Remembering that word I keep forgetting. But mostly getting Aunty Jo down the hill.

'Don't worry, Aunty Jo, it's only a bit of lettering – what can possibly go wrong?'

I'm power walking a reluctant Aunty Jo down the narrow winding streets of St Aidan, hoping I'm not about to answer my own rhetorical question. For starters, I can't remember the name of the cottage let alone the postcode. Worse still, it's going to be like the stroke department revisited, and everyone will be ancient.

It's funny how my life has flipped; when I remember that most days I'd be toughing it out with contractors at site meetings it's hard to align *that* person with the one who's about to sit at a table with a load of dreary people doing loopy writing. Truly, if someone had told me I'd be going to an after-lunch Care in the Community class I wouldn't have believed them either. But this is for Aunty Jo not me, so I'm happy to do it.

We've eaten a compromise lunch of pasta tubes made from split peas, which was way worse than it sounds, with lettuce leaves, followed by prunes. We stopped at the cash machine outside the Spar shop on the way down, where Aunty Jo barked prompts over my shoulder and I punched in my 1111 pin all by myself. I've now got a bundle of notes, so from here on I can pay with cash. As we push our way into the gallery there's a wall of huge paintings of the sea that feel so real I can almost hear the crash of the waves on the canvas. Further down the space there's a group of women around a large table, their laughter bouncing off the high white ceiling.

As their heads all turn I feel Aunty Jo go rigid. She's growling through her teeth at me, 'If we leave now, they might not notice?'

'Hang on.' She's not getting out of it that easily.

The tug I give her is so hard that we speed down the gallery. Then, just before we reach the group, she locks her knees but I keep on going. My body's miles ahead and my legs are running to catch up. As I make a grab for the table edge my thighs crash into it too and set the ink bottles rattling and send a pen rolling off onto the floor. I ignore the gasps around the table and pull out my best sparkly smile. 'We're here for the class?'

Whatever I was expecting, it wasn't someone my age in a daisy print jumpsuit bounding towards me around the table in duck-egg blue Converse.

'Josie and Edie? And I'm Beth – we were hoping you'd come.' Her bleached pixie haircut shows off the cute dents in her cheeks when she smiles. Better still, she's almost as breathless as me. 'It's more of an informal workshop actually, we all work on different projects but we help each other along.'

I make a grab for my sunnies, then push them back up on my head again as I realise there's nothing flashy or jarring about the light. It's seeping in through a series of frosted slit windows and, instead of dazzling me, it's washing the room with softness. It's as if a lot of the places I've walked through in my mind the last few months have come to life again here. As the people sit back in what look like fabulously funky chairs for a backwater and let go of the pens and ink pots they've grabbed hold of, even if I can't read what it says, I have to admit there's some pretty cool work going on.

As Beth's words sink in I whoosh around to Aunty Jo. 'Projects! That's what I was trying to think of – the one I can never get.' It's days ago now, but I can't let it pass. *Projects Manager. For the South-West.* That's my job at Zinc Inc.

Aunty Jo's eyes are open very wide. 'I see why you said getting out would be good, Edie.'

Beth pulls some spare chairs in our direction. 'It's not all hard work – we do a lot of chatting too. Drinks and snacks are on the side, come and help yourselves. Then settle in, and I'll get you some practice sheets.'

I dangle a fruit tea sachet from my fingers in front of Aunty Jo. 'This one for you?' I recognise the strawberry and exotic flowers as the one she has at home when she's not insisting on green. Which would be another good sign if we were looking for them.

Aunty Jo picks up a muffin. 'Are these double chocolate?'

Beth nods. 'And vegan too, homemade in the Little Cornish Kitchen just beyond the harbour. They're great for creativity.' She's talking so fast she could be nervous blurting herself.

By the time I sit down with my mug of hot chocolate I'm definitely warming to community classes. 'Can we pay?'

'Or shall we fill in any forms?' Aunty Jo's slipping her coat onto the back of her chair so I take it we're staying.

Beth hands us a blank sheet of paper. 'Don't worry about cash, your first time is free, so just jot your names and contact details on here. You're at Periwinkle, aren't you? The views are lovely from there. Loella and I are practically your neighbours – we're in the cottages just along the road to Rosehill.'

'Fabulous views,' I agree. Neither of us has a clue where the hell she means, but whatever.

'Best writing.' Aunty Jo might have made a joke there. A moment of scribbling and my name and number are down there too, then she hands them back to Beth. Easy as that. No one even noticed the cheat.

Beth whisks the addresses away then hands us some paper with sets of lines on and a mug of pens and pencils. 'I'll show you some basic letter forms. It's no big deal. Calligraphy is only handwriting but a bit more careful and well thought out.'

Although the little pots of ink, and brushes, and jars of water and scraps of different coloured paper scattered across the table look interesting, this isn't the best place for me right now. I *can* still write, but it usually ends up all over the paper and looks like someone else did it – blindfold, using their wrong hand. Keeping anywhere near the lines is going to take a massive effort. But a few minutes later we've been shown how to hold our pens at the right angle, done a – very wavy in my case – row of little straight lines, then watched Beth tracing out the curves of an 'a', 'b', 'c' and 'd' a few times on our papers.

Now Aunty Jo and I are trying on our own I'm finding it hard to keep my mind on the job. I take one bite of muffin then do a stroke of a letter. A bit of staring at the very white ceiling. Another bite of muffin. In the time it takes me to do my first 'a', Aunty Jo has filled a sheet and is onto the next. She's hitting this with the same high-impact energy she uses for her Keep Fit and Look Ten Years Younger routines in the mornings.

For me, my full attention is going to the sponge. It's so dark and sticky – if I'm going to taste anything, it'll be this. So far I'm not, but you can't win them all. Not straight away. In between times, I feel like I'm back at junior school. I can't say I'd ever have put myself at a calligraphy class, unless I was intending to write my own wedding invitations of course. In which case Bella and I would definitely have pulled in one of those lovely *Pens and Prosecco Workshops for Brides* at Paper Moon in Bristol, and we'd have spent an entire Saturday inhaling our bodyweight of delicious canapés and teensy macaroons. Which I might have dreamed of fleetingly, in passing, maybe one time. Well, maybe a bit more often than that if I'm being completely true to myself. But which definitely won't be happening now, not since Marcus and I had our discussion, where we talked totally honestly and openly for the first time ever about where we saw ourselves going as a couple.

Don't ask me how we got seven years into the rosy land of living together before we had that talk. However it happened, we can't undo it now. And, due to complete fucking mismatch of expectations of the most epic proportions, we had a humungous and hugely fierce argument. Followed by a calm after the storm week of realisation, then a very tearful rethink, where I think I was supposed to back down, but for the first time in seven years, I didn't. Which was the point we both knew we weren't going to agree on some of the most important decisions in our lives. So we realigned our pathways to go in different directions. He kept the house, which was only fair because it was his to begin with. And I headed off, leaving years of heartfelt renovations behind, feeling this was all my fault for not getting things straight to begin with.

As she reaches for her next sheet, Aunty Jo looks up. 'You always had lovely writing on the letters you sent us.'

When we were younger, probably because they didn't have kids of their own, Harry and Aunty Jo never missed a birthday and my mum was a stickler for 'thank you's so we never lost the habit. Marcus always poked fun at my family's obsession with gratitude. All our quirky 'thank you' cards propped behind the toaster and cluttering up the magnetic steel noticeboard drove him wild because they wrecked the minimalist lines of the kitchen. Mostly he saw thanking anyone for anything as sign of weakness.

I smile as I remember school. 'My writing was neat.' That bit was easy. Everything else was where I lost it. For me school was simply a chance to have fun with my friends, and my life only took off properly once I'd left. Put me in a room of people and I'm straight off making besties and having a ball, which is why it's hard to adjust to how I am at the moment. The truth is, with my non-stop chatter on temporary go-slow, even my good friends find me strangely quiet. I don't want to go out with them either, because it's just too weird not being the noisy one. It's fine, we'll make up for lost time as soon as I'm back to my old self. But it's strange to think this afternoon is the closest I've been to a social event in ages.

'So, as a newbie, how are you finding St Aidan?' A woman with a wide grin and a tumble of dark curls falling over the shoulders of her chunky cardigan is pulling up a chair next to me.

I focus on the flowers rioting across her dress, ignore the sweat prickle on the back of my neck and scramble around my brain to find a reply. Any will do, ideally nothing too insulting or unfiltered. 'It's . . . er . . . quiet.' What else is there to say about an empty village where the sand blows in your eyes so hard you can't see the sea, even when you're not on the beach?

From her laugh she finds that funny. 'You won't say that in July. At least when it's not busy we get to meet here.'

Beth chimes in. 'Without us, Plum, the owner here, could go right through the winter and never see another human.'

'So which one's Plum?'

The dark girl nods at the distant staircase. 'She's upstairs painting her seascapes, she lets us put on craft workshops in winter to keep the place alive. I'm Loella, by the way.'

Beth's smile is hopeful. 'There are actually lots of other sessions you might like to dip into.'

'Yes?' They sound great for Aunty Jo.

Loella carries on. 'I do patchwork, quilting and anything creative with fabric.'

I sense Aunty Jo sitting up in her funky chair, so I smile at her. 'You enjoy sewing, don't you?'

Aunty Jo sits up even straighter. 'Actually, life drawing was always popular in Harpenden.'

'WHAT?' I'm picking my jaw up off the floor, desperate to move this onto anywhere that's not here. 'Or how about r-r-rings and things?'

Loella's beaming and jumping to her feet. 'We *do* have an occasional life class, when we can get a model. I'll put you down for that, upcycled jewellery making when we do it, and quilting? I'll email you with the times. You *will* still come to calligraphy?'

Aunty Jo's flicking through her pile of sheets of perfect swirly letters, but she's looking doubtful so I jump in before she can refuse. 'Absolutely.'

Loella turns and nudges me. 'And whatever you said before, what's coming now is going to make you think again about St Aidan being quiet.' She checks her watch. 'Any second the kids will be back from school and all hell will break loose.'

Beth's hurrying round with a tray and what looks like an urgent expression. 'Hand over your ink pots everyone.'

There's a whoosh of air all the way down the gallery as the door opens, then the hammering of feet and the kind of whooping you'd expect from those Americans who ride horses, do cattle drives and shout 'yee haw!' as they wave their ropey things around. There's a blur of colour as more kids than I can count come stampeding down the gallery, waving their coats in the air. Then my stomach sinks because there's a skittering daxi too. And, coming up the rear, with a couple of littlies hanging off each arm, there's a horribly familiar faded denim jacket.

Aunty Jo gives me a very significant nod. 'Not just a pretty face. Isn't it nice to see a man who's good with the small ones?' Then she leans in and her voice drops to a whisper. 'Have you seen how muddy their feet are? I *do* hope he keeps them away from *us*.'

'Me too.' Obviously I love Tash's little ones, but other people's kids in large numbers are on my 'avoid at all costs' list.

I should tell Aunty Jo off for objectifying too, but I'm not up to smart replies right now. Luckily a tug on my elbow saves me. 'Cam . . .?' I'm hoping I've got that right. It's acceptable to forget adult names – kids, not so much.

His frown is accusing. 'Why are *you* here, Edie Browne – you *hate* writing?'

I lift my arm off my paper so he can see my work and hope he's remembered the 'e' on my name.

'*Three!* Is that all you've done?'

I nod. That's three 'a's, not three sheets. It's as if I'm seven again, and I just zoomed straight to the bottom of the class.

'*All* afternoon?'

'Yes siree.' It's my voice, but the accent's unexpectedly American.

'That *is* worse than me.'

'See, I told you. And high fives to that!' I hold up my hand and he smacks his palm against mine before he rushes off.

Then Loella sweeps by with an armful of papers and flashes me a smile. 'Cam's already chatting to you? Well done for that – a lot of us have tried and failed there, so great work.'

It's nothing, but for someone who took all afternoon to write three 'a's it's the high point, so I'm going to grab it and enjoy.

'And we'll see you same time tomorrow for Fun with Fabric?' I'm trying my best to return the wall-to-wall smile Loella's sending me when hers suddenly fades. 'You *do* want to come? I mean you *would* like to try sewing?'

Crap. If I'm bad at writing, needlework will be so much worse, because I could never do that before. 'Errrr –' This is not the moment to run out of words either.

'You look less up for this than your aunt, that's all?'

Damn. 'W-w-whatever g-gave you that idea?'

Her face cracks into a smile again, but this time it's rueful. 'One, the faces you pulled when I mentioned it earlier, two, the way you looked like you wanted to make a run for the door most of the afternoon. Need I go on?'

I have to admit as I take in her hand-knitted cardi that wouldn't look out of place on a catwalk, the stylish knitwear *and* the straight talking have both caught me off guard.

'Two tiny things, you've totally misread.' This time I make sure my smile is dazzling and I'm really over-compensating. 'Don't worry, w-we'll be there. So much fun – how could we not?'

'Don't worry . . .' It's almost an echo and as she cocks her head her laugh is low and dirty. 'Your secret's safe with me, Edie Browne. See you tomorrow.'

Fuck, fuck, fuck. This time I don't even try to hold back my groan.

She's still there grinning at me. 'And I'm so pleased you swear. You're going to fit right in here, I just know.'

And that was calligraphy.

Chapter 9

Epic Achievement: Getting a different view of St Aidan. (It's all about the 'boom'.)

Fun with Fabric? That has to be one of those oxymoron phrases that totally contradicts itself. As for how I still know about those when I can barely remember that my middle name's Sara, that's just another of those pesky anomalies I collide with every day. If I had my way there'd be a law against the words 'fabric' and 'fun' ever appearing in the same sentence. Just saying. So there's no misunderstanding. Even if I can't look at a pin without messing things up, this is for Aunty Jo – she's like my mum, they could sew in their sleep.

Up until we reach the gallery, it's like reliving the last time. Pasta, prunes, lettuce. Speeding Aunty Jo down the hill because, despite the promise of needles and scissors, she's suddenly very reluctant. But today there is a difference because, even before we push through the tall plate-glass gallery doors, we can hear the whirr of sewing machines. As we make our way towards the work table we're faced with an explosion of colourful fabric and then, one by one, the bowed heads look up and we're faced with a sea of waves and smiles, and a chorus of 'hi's and 'hello's.

It takes Aunty Jo one blink to take it in, then she overcomes her shyness. 'Cathedral window patchwork – how wonderful.' A nanosecond later she hurls herself into a discussion about backing fabrics that's so involved I can't even understand it, let alone join in.

I spot Loella brandishing a hissing iron at one of the ironing boards beyond the fabric piles and give her a little wave. 'Hey, this is every bit as mind-blowing as you promised.' I flash her a smile huge enough to reinforce how super-happy I am to be here, but mostly to keep her off my case. Then I sidle into a seat, grab a spare pin cushion and make myself look extremely busy re-arranging the pins. Then Aunty Jo comes and shows me how to draw around a template, and cut out squares for patchwork. But, even though I'm not joining in the chatter, I'm finding it hard to keep on task. It's like calligraphy revisited – Aunty Jo is beaming from behind a huge heap of perfectly cut hexagons, and I'm still struggling to cut out my first square and kicking myself for scoring a total fail. I'm just wondering if swapping to a different pair of scissors might help when there's a cough beside me.

I'm racing to get my excuses together for Loella. 'Actually, I'm just checking out . . .' When I pull my eyes into focus, what I'm actually checking out are some super-hard denim-clad thighs so I take a moment to get over the shock – and take in any details Bella might be asking about later. Then I flash upwards to a familiar stubbled jaw, and a mouth that's not quite twisted into a grin. 'Barney? W-what the h-hell are you doing here?'

He gives a shrug. 'I popped in to drop some tools off for Beth, but if you can spare a minute, I could do with a hand outside.'

Going with Barney, or staying here. Two choices, both of them equally awful in their own way. 'I'm not sure.'

'C'mon Edie, I promise it won't take long.' That direct gaze is so dark it's playing havoc with my insides.

Aunty Jo has somehow torn herself away from her discussion about stitch length. 'Run along now, Edie. I'm sure Loella won't mind.'

My wide eyes are pleading with Loella to insist I stay, but she just smiles. 'If Barney needs you that's good with me.'

'Fine.' It's not at all. On balance, now it's happening, I'd rather sew an entire quilt than go with Barney. If this is my punishment, I'm really regretting not trying harder with the cutting. By the time I've pushed back my chair he's away. By the time I catch up with him he's holding the door open and, as the chilly afternoon air hits my face, he's thrusting an oilskin jacket into my hands.

'Here, have my coat, we're off to the harbour, not that I want to rush you, but you might need to hurry up if we're going to make it back for the end of the class.'

'But . . .' What the hell happened to that minute this wasn't going to take? It's not like I can argue when I'm running to keep up. I'm getting glimpses of the bay in the gaps between the buildings as we cut down through a narrow cobbled alleyway, watching the long lines of the waves rolling in over the shine of the wet sand, seeing figures bending against the breeze, hearing the rush of water in the distance as the waves break on the beach. And for once the iron grey of the sea has lifted a shade and the water surface is silver, hammered like the dapple of fish scales. Then we come out onto the quayside, edged with its neat rows of cottages with pink and blue front doors, and the piles of lobster pots and rope coils, and the blue and red and black boats lined up along the jetties, their masts sharp against the sky.

By the time we leap down the wooden steps onto a very wobbly pontoon my chest feels like it's going to burst from the exertion. 'What are we h-here for?'

'She's rigged and ready, so I'd have thought that was obvious.' He dips down into the low open boat we're standing next to and hands me a padded waistcoat and pulls one on himself too. 'That's your buoyancy aid, slip it on over the waterproof and we're good to go.'

'Go *WHERE?*' As if I'd know one end of a boat from another, let alone know the nuances and implications. If we're talking water I have no objection to paddling, but if the water's any deeper than my ankles I'm not a happy bunny. When I was with Marcus, whenever his family dabbled with boats on holiday, which was a lot, I always did a silent hooray, made my excuses and went off to read on the beach instead.

'No need to panic – we'll be out and back again in no time. I've done some repairs to the rudder in return for a favour. I'm just testing it holds before we deliver it back.'

'Marvellous.' I wedge my jaw shut to stop my teeth chattering. I know from work, it's crucial to set clear boundaries at the outset. 'And h-h-how do I fit in? If you think I'm going to swim to shore for help when the damn thing breaks into pieces, you can bloody think again.'

'Definitely no swimming – I can sail her on my own – but it's better with two people because there's more weight.' He's already jumped down into the boat and he's pulling on ropes.

'So you've brought me along as ballast?' Of all the insults, that has to be the biggest yet.

'Not entirely, it was more a spur-of-the-moment thing. You looked like you were really struggling back there.' He looks like he's agonising. 'I wanted to save you from a crap afternoon.' His hand grasps mine and in one pull I'm in and sliding onto a tiny plank seat, clinging onto the boat side behind me as it lurches, trying to look like I do this every day. As the oilskin's Velcro prickles my chin there's no time to wish that Dayglo orange was more my colour because I'm too busy watching the dark shiny water going up and down as the boat rises on the swell, and holding onto my stomach which feels like it's a washing machine working a full load. If I said I'd rather make a quilt, revise that upwards. I can't count how many quilts I'd have sewn to avoid this. More importantly, if this is being saved, I hate to think what being dropped in it would be like.

Meanwhile Barney's leaping around like bloody Superman doing a million things at once; undoing ropes, pushing us off from the side, hauling up the sail.

'Boom!'

The yell makes me jump so much I almost end up in the harbour. But I'm catching on here, I'd hate to come across as clueless, so I join in too but make sure mine's louder. 'Boom! Back at you!'

From Barney's bemused stare you'd think he was the beginner here. 'Sorry, that means "Mind your head!" – that's the boom there.' He's pointing at this long pole at the bottom of the sail. '*Boom!* is what we shout when it's about to swing across the boat, so watch out.'

'Shucks!' I duck and narrowly miss getting my skull caved in as it skims past my ear and silently thank Christmas it didn't bump my head. Then, as Barney squats down at the back, some kind of stick in one hand, still pulling on a rope in the other, there's this awful creaking, but we start to move away from the jetty and out across the harbour.

'Okay on the side there?'

'Great.' My fake I'm-totally-fine-thanks smile would be way more convincing if my lippy hadn't all just blown out to sea. Even though I look like Mr Blobby I attempt a nonchalant lounging position, but when I lunge slowly backwards there's nothing to lean on. I'm sure I had many clips in my messy up-do, but it feels like the wind wrenched them all away and tossed them into the water, so I push my scarf into my pocket so I don't lose that too. 'Are you sure it's okay going out in this gale?'

He pulls down the corners of his mouth and does a little wiggle on the stick. 'Probably only a force two.'

Which means absolutely zilch, but I'm pretty proud of the way I exclaim about it anyway. 'A *TWO!* Jeez, well, that explains why it's *so* rough and windy.'

'It's like a millpond, Edie. I wouldn't have brought you out if it wasn't.' He's frowning at me. 'Maybe you'd like to let go of the side and hang onto the sheet instead? Get a feel for the wind?'

'Great, you've brought a sheet – I'll wrap myself up in it if it gets any colder.'

He purses his lips. 'The sheet is this rope here, you could pull it and hold the sail in place?'

'Hell no. Thanks all the same.'

If I didn't know better I'd think he was trying to hold back his smile. 'So maybe you can tell me how come you're less in love with sewing than the rest of them?'

'I got off to a bad start at school.' To be honest it's a relief to have something to take my mind off the heaving of the ship. 'The first ever lesson, the textiles teacher caught me holding a pin in my mouth.' That was practically the only useful thing my mum had ever taught me about needlework. 'Apparently teenagers giving sudden whoops and ending up in A&E with pins jammed in their throats is a massive Health and Safety issue.' I know that I'm blurting *and* over-sharing, but I can't stop. My only excuse, I must be a nervous sailor. 'To be honest I'd have thought sewing through your finger with a machine was way worse. That's what Bianca Hill from the other group in our year did. But, whatever, the teacher had a hissy fit and things went downhill fast from there.' A lot like things have in St Aidan, come to think of it.

'Okay, we're going to swing the sail around and change direction in a minute, so hang on tight and duck . . . one two three, BOOM!'

'Jeez, what the HECK . . . BOOM! To you too!' There's so much splashing and heaving and groaning it feels like we have to end up upside down, pitched into the water. I'm digging my fingers in so hard to the boat side I get splinters under my fingernails, but at the end of it somehow we're still afloat, even if we're at a crazy angle.

'Okay, now come and sit the other side of the boat, and this time try to lean back as far as you can to get your weight out over the water.' As he watches me make my way across, inching forwards on all fours through the puddles, I no longer give any fucks. The will to look stylish disappeared somewhere in the harbour car park, and I left my last shred of pride back on the jetty. I get there *eventually*, but he can forget leaning out.

'So much chopping and changing. It's hardly relaxing is it?' He's rubbing his fist over his mouth. 'So, how far downhill did your sewing go?'

'By the time we got to making dresses for GCSE, mine was the size of one of those things that you put your bed quilt inside.'

'What, a duvet cover?'

'That's the one. Then I put the zip in upside down, and somehow stitched the front to the back so, even though it was the size of a house, it was still impossible to climb into.' It's all true, and at least it's a better excuse for why I was completely failing to cut out Loella's patchwork pieces. I'd rather not explain that my fingers won't do what I want them to at the moment.

'I can see why you're traumatised.' He's spluttering into his fist. 'Okay, we're turning again, ready, and BOOM!'

'Surely not? BOOM!' But we are, and the whole damned heaving and splashing thing starts again and, before I know it, I'm on my hands and knees, crawling back across the boat again. Once I get back onto my plank seat with both hands safely clamped on the boat sides, I squint at him. 'And people do this *why?*'

He shrugs. 'Because it's fun.'

That word again. 'Not in my book it's not.'

'I've had more laughs in the last half hour than I have for a long time.' He's tilting his head at me *and* being ridiculous, because he hasn't even broken into a grin. 'I'm not sure you know quite how funny you are, Edie Browne.'

I give that the eye roll it deserves. Funny was how I was before, what he's finding amusing now are my blunders.

With his deck shoes and tousled hair, and the shadows under his cheekbones set against the flashes of the dark water, he could have been parachuted in from a Diesel advert.

He coughs. 'I know we're only going slowly, but listen to the swish of the water as the boat passes across it, feel the rush of the breeze. I mean, look back at the harbour and the shore.'

I only screw my head around because I know if I don't he'll go on about it. Looking back from out here in the bay, I'm getting the familiar postcard view of the town with the higgledy rows of cottages rising above the cluster of masts in the harbour, and the seafront railings that stretch around the bay.

'So, doesn't it give you a wonderful sense that you're escaping?'

I nod at the stack of stone and stucco fronts, their pastel colours fading to monochrome in the greyness. 'The calm swishing gets wrecked every time we almost get pitched into the effing sea.' Aunty Jo's cottage is nudging the skyline, and I'm trying not to notice how wildly it's swaying up and down as the boat rocks. 'My escape to solitude ends firmly at the beach, any further is too much like *Desert Island Discs*.'

There's a choking noise from behind the sail. 'You've picked the wrong place if you're looking for peace.'

Someone else said that, but I'm not picking him up on it. I give him my serious stare. 'And how can anyone relax when it sounds like the damn boat is about to split in two at any second?'

Somehow he looks totally at one with the thunder-grey clouds billowing behind him. 'The creaking is the beauty of a timber hull. With a whole world of ocean stretched out beyond us, there's such a wonderful feeling of freedom, that's all.'

'Probably more a feeling of totally bricking it.'

His teeth are closing on his lip. 'Don't worry, we're on our way back in now. We're going to drop the boat around the other side of the harbour. It's your first time out, I'm sure you'll enjoy it more next time.'

'I *seriously* doubt it.' It's not like there will be another, I won't fall for this twice. A thought flashes into my head. 'You don't make poor Cam do this, do you?'

He's shaking his head. 'For now Cam doesn't do boats. Mostly I come out in the afternoons, which is why I thought you might be up for the occasional blast around?'

'Not being rude—'

'But you're going to be anyway?'

'I'd rather have my teeth pulled.' All things considered. The heaving. My soaking feet and my soggy bum. The BOOMS! And that's before we get to the company, and feeling seasick. 'To express how much I enjoy that, you should know I once had a tooth out when I was eleven and I had to go all the way to Bristol to a special centre for nervous patients and be knocked out with Valium.'

He throws me a 'what the eff?' look then turns to the pontoon that's racing towards us. 'Well, that went well.'

As he stands up and unzips his life jacket I ignore the view up his sweatshirt. We're bumping up against some other jetty now and he's winding down the sail and bundling it into the bottom of the boat. And, just before he launches into his Superman routine again, he bends down and picks up this giant-size spanner. 'Here, hang onto this for a second while I tie up.'

My arms sag under the weight, and there's a lurch as he springs off the edge of the boat. I watch as he thuds onto the jetty and secures the boat with one deft twist of the rope.

He's holding out his hand. 'Okay, Edie, let's get you back on dry land.'

I shuffle as far as I can on my bum, then, as I stagger to my feet, the huge spanner slides through my fingers and plummets downwards. There's a second when I almost catch it somewhere around my knees, but it's like a slippery fish sliding down the Dayglo fabric. A moment later it plunges through the narrow gap between the boat side and the jetty's edge, and on into the soupy depths of the harbour.

'Crap!' My stomach is plunging faster than the spanner. *And SHIT, ARSE and BOLLOCKS for not being able to rely on my grip any more.*

'Last time you were throwing knives at me, now it's a wrench?'

I could kick seven bells out of the jetty side, but I'd rather jump into the harbour than have him know the truth. I grind my teeth, push my growl deep inside me. 'I'm *SO* sorry.'

'Don't worry, these oversized tools make bids for freedom all the time. This is nothing – last week someone dropped a twelve grand outboard engine out in the bay. We're in a fishing port, we'll send in the deep-sea divers.'

'Really?' That sounds major.

'Only joking – of course we won't, we'll hook it out at low tide.' He glances at his watch. 'Not that I want to rush you, but the class is almost over.'

As I clamber back onto the landing stage, I know I'm never going to live this down. As for where the time went, it definitely didn't fly because I was enjoying myself.

And that was my afternoon at Patchwork.

Chapter 10

Day 142: Friday, 23rd March
The day room at Periwinkle Cottage

Epic Achievement: Making a start.

'Remind me why we have to do this now?' Aunty Jo is tapping the toe of her least favourite rose gold pumps on the dust sheet we've thrown down on the flowery carpet.

This last week I've worked out the easiest way to deal with Aunty Jo is to ambush her. It's our first day in ages without social events, so me leaping out of bed this morning, pulling on my boyfriend jeans and my weekend Hush *C'est si bon* sweatshirt, then starting to rip the wallpaper off the walls in the day room straight after breakfast is my way of leapfrogging any resistance.

It's fine to roll out the reasons now it's too late for her to stop me. 'A decorator could take ages to come, and that's when we find one, so I made a start.' As boss of the job, *I've* decided – *without* consultation – it's best to begin with the room where we spend most time, then work backwards through the house.

She's still not convinced. 'But I've never decorated before, not *personally.*'

The part where I pull her along on a wave of enthusiasm isn't working. 'We'll do the easy bits, and call in the pro's when we get stuck.' Apart from anything else, it's good for me to get back to practical tasks. Aunty Jo's day room is only small and the ceilings are low so decorating it should be a great way to ease myself in and progress with 'the quest' at the same time.

When we were kids Tash and I used to scrap over helping Dad with the decorating. I was chief wallpaper paster, and a dab hand with a paint pot, so even if I didn't run interior jobs I'd know what I'm doing. I slide my fish slice under a join in the design near the floor. As I ease the edge away there's a wonderful ripping sound, and an entire panel of paper tears free from the wall. I bundle it up and grin.

Aunty Jo coughs and frowns down at a flake of paint on the floor. 'It's looking awfully messy, shall I get the vacuum?'

'For now, why not rip off?' However much she looks on the verge of a breakdown, this is my kind of fun and I can't let her miss out. So I pass her a slice and a bin bag. As I dip a sponge in my bucket of suds and slosh soapy water onto the bits of paper still clinging to the wall I take pity on her.

'Don't worry, we'll tidy later.'

She's still hesitating, but now she's staring at my legs. 'Why not borrow some of Harry's pyjamas? I've got lots of second-best ones.'

'I'm probably okay, thanks all the same.' Her wearing them is bad enough, but I can't tell her that so I take a different tack. 'How about some music?' I always work better with some trashy pop to help me along. I'd sort it myself but my speaker is upstairs, and, even if I'm ripping her living room to pieces, I'm still very much a visitor when it comes to choosing music and TV.

She hugs her chest. 'Would you like some Tchaikovsky? Or Vivaldi's *Four Seasons*?'

'Not if there's anything else.' We already had *The Nutcracker* right through our porridge and chia seeds. 'How about music for cleaning?'

'You mean *Housework Songs*?' Aunty Jo's brow furrows. 'It's not something I ever needed. In Harpenden I always had help.'

Of course she did – how did I not remember? 'Loaded and spoiled with it' was how my more robust mum put it, in her meaner, more frustrated moments. She taught French full-time and looked after a family of four, while Aunty Jo, who didn't work and only had her and Harry at home, had at least two cleaning ladies, window cleaners, personal shoppers and an army of outdoor helpers at any one time.

'Something similar, then?' My fingers are tightly crossed under my slice. 'A 'hills are alive' nun-in-the-mountains singalong would be good. Or *Mamma Mia?*'

'Will this do?' She fumbles in the sofa footstool and comes out with a CD case that she holds out to me.

And this is why I'm here and not at work. A few simple words for me to read, and any pretence of me being a normal, functioning human adult comes crashing down.

'Sorry, that might as well be written in Chinese.' I know a few of the letters on their own, but when they're strung together in a line I have no chance. I take a deep breath. 'Read me what it says, then I'll tell you.'

'I can't bear anything too jolly.'

I take it that's an excuse for what's coming next, not the title. 'So?'

'*The One Hundred Best Tearjerkers of All Time.*'

I give way to a silent WTF? moment. 'You're sure?'

'It flashed up on my laptop after I lost Harry, it seemed like a sign, so I bought it.'

That's modern technology for you. I'm not even going to ask what the tracks are, with my wonky emotions I'm practically crying buckets already.

'They're miserable, but in a good way.' She's already holding the disc up to the light and blowing the dust off.

'Watch out!' I leap across the dust sheet to grab my shades from the coffee table before the flash hits my eyes. For the first time since I arrived there's a break in the grey outside. Sun bouncing off things that shine is a whole other issue for me. Who knew one CD could throw up so many problems?

'There you go, *Everybody Hurts*.' She presses play then stands back to listen. 'Aren't those lyrics lovely? Then it's *Candle in the Wind* and *All by Myself*.' She's not even reading, so she must know it off by heart. As for *All by Myself*, even Tash weeps at that one and she's got a husband, a job, a house and two kids more than I have, so there's no chance for me.

As if that wasn't enough to make my heart sink to my elasticated ankle boots – which neatly sidestep all that tricky bow-tying that takes so long, in case you're wondering why I'm not in Converse like everyone else my age – the stare she's giving me is about as penetrating as a CT scan.

'Which reminds me, I haven't seen you practising your calligraphy.'

Why she's jumped to that I don't know, but I can't say the same for her. 'You've been doing enough for both of us.' Her pile of sheets practically reaches the ceiling.

'And your mum was asking about your reading too.' Her stare powers up a notch.

Crap. I hadn't expected she'd be on my case like this. To be honest, I've made so little progress so far, I'd decided to give it a rest for a while. I was hoping if I stopped worrying, when I came back to it in a few weeks' time I might have made one of those huge accidental leaps of progress. I'm opening and closing my mouth to say that, but nothing's coming out.

'You're going to have to put the time in.' Three more power

notches, and her eyes are like saucers. 'I mean, it's not going to happen by itself, is it?' How did I ever have her down as a lightweight?

'Well . . .' I'm wondering how to explain that's *exactly* what I'm planning, but I'm saved by a knock on the French window.

'Barney! Again! So soon!' My jump of surprise as I open the door and stand back to let him in sends my slice skittering across the floor, but I still get in first to stop Aunty Jo over-gushing. However much I wish he was anyone else, saying 'hi' to him is a damn sight easier than dodging awkward questions from Aunty Jo. I know I don't have wet patches on my bum today, I'm not crawling through any upstairs windows, and I escaped the embarrassment of getting caught wearing Harry's cast-offs, but I'm still kicking myself for rushing my eyeliner and skimping on the highlighter. 'If you're planning a two-minute trip round the bay that lasts all day, I'm probably too busy.'

'Great to see you too, Edie.' He picks the fish slice up and passes it back then he turns to Aunty Jo. 'Sorry – am I missing something here? Are those *Christmas* reindeer on your pyjama jacket?'

Some of us would have shrunk in the spotlight, but Aunty Jo stands her ground. 'They're Harry's, he had so many pairs I'm using up the festive ones for decorating.'

'Go, Josie!' There's suddenly a sheepish hint to his expression. 'You wouldn't like an extra elf for ten minutes, would you? It's years since I stripped paper, there's nothing quite like the feeling of ripping it off the wall, is there?'

'Absolutely right, Barney.' She's talking out of her Christmas tree-clad bottom here; she's barely touched a piece of wallpaper yet. 'Would you like a cup of tea while you're here?'

I don't believe what I'm hearing. As if things weren't bad enough, Barney's at my elbow and, without even picking up the spare cake slice, he's already ripped off three huge lengths.

'There we go.' He isn't even giving me the satisfaction of throwing his paper on the floor, he's bundling it straight into the bin bag, dammit. 'I'll pass on the tea though, Josie. I can't stay long.'

That's the best news I've heard all morning.

He rips off two more strips whole, then he stoops to do the next one and ends up holding up a piece the size of a postage stamp. 'Oops, my beginner's luck ran out.'

I put my hands on my hips. 'Too bad – looks like you've hit a superglued bit there, Barney. They're way less fun.'

'In that case I'd better leave it to you professionals.' He gives a shrug and dips into the back pocket of his jeans 'Before I forget, I came to give you your scarf. You left it in my sailing jacket.'

He's pressed it into my hand and he's reached the door before it sinks in. First, it's been washed and beautifully ironed and folded. Second, and *way* more disturbing, the warmth currently seeping into my palm originated from his tush. As heat transfers go, that one's too much.

'Happy stripping, then.' He pauses in the doorway. 'And have a wonderful Christmas, Josie.' Then he breaks into a run and, as he crosses the courtyard, for some inexplicable reason he's punching the air.

I can't decide whether to be annoyed he gave up so easily or ecstatic he's left us to strip in peace. If I'm honest, I'm also struggling slightly with what happened when he whisked me away from Loella's class. It's not like I'm a pushover, I wouldn't last two minutes in my job if I was. And I take a pride in taking responsibility for my own actions, and owning my decisions. More importantly, I'm definitely not a 'Jane gets dragged through the jungle by Tarzan' type of woman. Not even in my fantasies. Even in my wildest dreams I never imagined Marcus making me do something I didn't want to, although I did occasionally fantasise about him helping around the house more. Or him not wanting clockwork sex *every single* morning. But, coming back to Barney – and even I have to concede the 'but' is a huge one – somehow, however it happened, whatever went wrong, I ended up bobbing around in the bay, even though it was not something I'd ever have signed up for, or willingly done.

However many circles I go around in, I haven't quite resolved this satisfactorily in my head yet. At best, this was Barney asking for help he didn't actually need at all, and taking advantage of my better nature, which I was completely aware of by the time I got down to the harbour. In which case, that still leaves me puzzling – why the hell did I get into that boat? I mean, at my age, I assumed I'd be past surprising myself, that's all.

Except by the time I've peeled the next strip of paper, I've remembered. I never actually expected my new job, because I've always been a chancer not an achiever, so that was a surprise. Then I shocked myself when I stood my ground and broke up with Marcus. And shocked myself all over again when I walked away from that perfect life we had.

One thing's for sure – when you're picking bits of sticky paper off the wall there's plenty of time to ponder. As we work our way around the walls we get claggier and claggier, but I'm still no nearer an answer. We're onto the last wall when Aunty Jo pipes up from nowhere, 'That's the other good thing about the classes, you can get a lot of information from them.'

'Really?' I'm bracing myself for another very long monologue about quilting. After Fun with Fabric she talked about wadding for two hours straight, but that was a relief because it meant I could skip the details about my afternoon.

The breath she takes is worryingly deep. 'Yesterday I found out Barney's not a window cleaner at all – he actually makes shepherd's huts along the road. That's impressive, isn't it?'

That's definitely not what I was expecting. I look up at the ceiling, count to ten and get to seven. 'Maybe it's significant if you keep sheep, otherwise not so much.' Given a choice, I'd have preferred sewing tips.

'According to Loella, people your age buy the huts and do Airbnb in their back gardens.'

'Good for them.' Not even having a teensy terrace to my name, I wouldn't know. I was a week away from signing for a lease on my own tiny flat when my stroke happened and I pulled out. At least this way I might be homeless on paper but I'm not worrying about covering rental payments when my salary's all but disappeared.

'Unlikely as it seems, if I ever did have a lawn, a shepherd's hut would be the last thing I'd buy.' I might as well get it out there. 'As garden ornaments go, I suspect they're a bit like designer tree houses – mega hyped, overpriced and underused.' Even when I lived with Marcus I never had that much cash to spare because we mostly spent it on his place, on eating out at weekends and on far-flung holidays in obscure places. If I struggled to run to a Hush pineapple sweatshirt – which was reversible, so you actually got two for the price of one – I'm damn sure a caravan you can't actually tow would never have made it to the top of my shopping list.

She's still going. 'Every hut is unique, handmade by Barney to individual measurements.'

'Good luck to his customers.' I'm scraping so hard I'm making dents in the plaster. We're going to have to agree to differ on the sun shining out of that particular bottom, because I couldn't give a flying fuck. He could be making caravans for that 'rags to riches' woman's fairy godmother, but it doesn't change the fact that he has no idea about social norms. I mean, who hangs around for a conversation up a ladder when they're crushed against you to stop you falling off, then takes you off for a boat trip you don't want, or invites themselves in and starts pulling your wallpaper off? I can only hope he's more appropriate with his boundaries with his clients than he is with us.

Aunty Jo has stopped again. 'Oh dear, visitor alert. With all this rubbish on the floor too.' Even though the patch of wall she's stripped is tiny, Aunty Jo and the dust sheet where she's standing are both plastered in pieces of gluey paper.

'Bloody Barney.' Not again. As I brush the claggiest lump off her cheek I'm suddenly baking in my sweatshirt. I'm picking the biggest pieces of rainforest out of my hair, but not because I give any kind of a damn. Tugging up my jeans because, *whoever's* here, I don't want to be caught out with a muffin top twice in one day.

'Who said anything about Barney?' There are wrinkles in Aunty Jo's forehead.

'What?' As I follow her gaze and see Loella hurrying across the courtyard I'm ignoring the fact my insides just deflated faster than one of those things that go 'pop'. She's got so many kids with her she looks like a school outing.

As I pull open the door Loella's smiling over the crowd of tousled heads. 'Wowsers, are you culling the zebras? Tigers by the sea were never going to work, were they?' At least she's overlooked the festive pyjamas. 'We were dropping Cam off, so I thought I'd pop in. We forgot to say – there's a book group you might like to join. And the Wild and Blooming Cottage Garden group are having a talk tonight. I could give you a lift down if you'd like to come?'

There's that familiar feeling of steel hands closing around my stomach. How the hell am I going to explain my way out of this? Book group was one thing I always loved and really miss. Bella, Tash and I have belonged to the same one for years. Obviously I'm not going again until I progress far enough to avoid a pity party when I turn up. Let's face it, if I was up to going I wouldn't be here. *Reasons not to go . . . Words . . .* I'm flailing to get to grips with either, when Aunty Jo jumps in.

'I'm so sorry, my concentration's shot to pieces, so novels and book group are no-no. Just for now.'

I'm trying not to gasp at how easily she's covering for me. Reading is the one thing she still does, her to-be-read pile is under the dust sheet and as high as the sofa and, even if she's driven me to distraction all day wittering about mess, I want to hug her for this.

Loella's reaching out and patting her arm. 'Of course. I'm *so* sorry, Josie, I should have thought.' Her smile is full of warmth. 'But you will think about this evening? It won't be late.'

If Loella bothered to take half a glance at the wreck of the lawn she'd get the picture. Outdoors equals mud, and dirt gives Aunty Jo a hissy fit, so I'm expecting to get a firm 'no', but I might as well give it a try. I turn to Aunty Jo. 'Well, you've got a cottage and you've got a garden, so shall we try it?'

I know grow-your-own salad is huge now, but Marcus is the trend-freak, not me. I'd be totally out of my comfort zone here, yet again. But Aunty Jo is definitely brighter for getting out, so I'm up for persuading her.

She's pulling a face. 'I don't know.'

Loella catches my eye, then leans in closer. 'You've got quite a kingdom here, with your outbuildings too, Josie-pie.'

'They're next on the list . . .' I peel a piece of wallpaper off my jeans '. . . after this.' That's on the list in my head, obviously. We haven't got any further with the one on the clipboard. Realistically, seeing how far we've got after a whole day working here, and knowing how far the cottage rambles, and the size of the barns, I'm going to have to pull in some help fast. But with my 'professional' head on, I know it'll be better to wait until we make more contacts. Which is another good reason to get out and mingle with the gardeners.

Loella's straight back at me. 'Great then, I'll take that as a "yes". I'll pick you both up at seven sharp?' She doesn't wait for an answer. A moment later she's marching off across the courtyard, followed by her band of children.

And I'm wondering what the hell I've let us both in for.

Chapter 11

Epic Achievement: Pretending to be a gardener, and not being found out.

If I didn't know stripping walls was good for you before, I do now – my arms feel like they've had a full-body workout, and then some. Not that I've actually managed that many of those in my life. If I'm honest, I'm one of those classic fails who signs up for the gym in January then never goes. As I say to Bella, if it wasn't for people like us, the cross trainers would be horribly overcrowded. But the good news from St Aidan is, we finally wave goodbye to the rainforest in the day room. I'm not the only one around here planning ambushes either. After a meticulous round of tidying up, Aunty Jo literally comes at me out of nowhere me with a pen and paper and an order to do some calligraphy practice. Luckily I get over my horror fast enough to persuade her there isn't time to do that *and* get into my Audrey H slim tailored slacks and my little Gap cashmere polo neck. Obviously I will need to work on my writing. It's just more auspicious when there's less compulsion and, truly, my biceps have had enough exercise for one day.

For dinner we have grilled chicken and carrots, which suddenly come back on-limits when I explain that's what Cheryl (formerly Cole) eats when she's getting in shape for a tour. And I know this because Sadie the 'do everything in the office' person at Zinc Inc used to lend me her *Closer* magazine every Friday afternoon, then ask questions to check I'd read it from end to end. I just never imagined it was knowledge I'd ever get to use.

It was dusk when Loella pulled up in the lane, totally blocking it with her battered red off-roader. I can only assume she has some local artistic licence which allows that, or else shepherd's hut man has seen the size of the thing and the scrapes down the sides, and on balance decided to shut the fuck up. I was worried Barney might hitch a lift too, in the hope of bagging more gullible Airbnb cottage garden owners, but luckily he didn't. In any case, it was literally a couple of bounces around bends and then we were down at The Deck, blocking the mews there.

While Loella goes off to find somewhere to double park, I send Aunty Jo ahead of me through the door with a shove that's considerably bigger than she is. 'No need to get all fidgety, Aunty Jo, there are lots of people we know.'

As we make our way towards the chairs arranged in rows in front of a white pull-up screen and Beth dances over, I'm waving back at so many people I feel like I've been here way longer than a week.

'Josie, you must meet my dad, Malcolm. I saved you seats next to him.' As Beth turns to me she drops her voice. 'We lost Mum five years ago, but it's been *so* much tougher since he retired in the autumn.'

By the time I wriggle out of my jacket and into the chair beside them, they're already deep in some discussion about perennial geraniums, whatever they are. When they finally pause I hiss into Aunty Jo's ear, 'How do you know so much about gardening?'

She gives a sniff. 'I've heard about it from Harry over the years. I can definitely hold my own on alliums.' She glances behind us to where there's a guy arranging boxes of slides. 'And you can't beat a good magic lantern show.'

As Loella claps her hands at the front I have a brief moment of polka-dot dress envy, then everyone goes quiet. 'So welcome everybody. Jeremy's standing by at the projector with an hour's worth of slides showing his take on last year's Wild and Blooming Festival in St Aidan. Then afterwards we'll move on to coffee, cake and chat.' As everyone claps she slips to the back, switches off the lights and sits down.

As I settle into my seat my main worry is about what's going to happen if I snore. With the promise of so many flower pictures, probably all the same, I'm already biting back a yawn. Realistically, my concentration isn't great at the best of times. In the dark, after a hard day of paper stripping, I'm likely to stay awake approximately a nanosecond. Then Jeremy starts clicking his handset, there's a flash of lights on the screen as he flips through his first few slides to find where to begin.

My stomach clenches and I clamp my eyes closed. Why the heck did I not think? I prod Aunty Jo as I get up and whisper, 'The flashing isn't good, I'd better go.'

'Shall I come with you?' She's wrenching her gaze away from daisies blowing in a summer breeze.

'You stay – I'll see you at the end.' I ease into the aisle and dip to avoid the light beam from the projector. The last thing I want to do is disturb everyone by causing a big on-screen shadow as I go, so I drop down and crawl between the chairs, returning all the perturbed looks with smiles and little waves, trying to look like I planned this all along.

On my hands and knees, trailing my jacket along the rough-hewn boards might not be the most dignified way to leave, and it makes a mockery of how long I spent getting my eyeliner perfect. But it's better than staying and ending up like I did a couple of weeks after my stroke – coming round on my parents' living room floor, looking up at my mum and dad's terrified faces with my words extra blurry and wet pants. And all because the strobe lights on the *Top of the Pops* revisit to 1977 gave me a seizure.

Afterwards my mum was furious with my dad for making us watch it, but those two love their nostalgia. That was the year of Queen's *Good Old Fashioned Lover Boy* and they always go all moony when that comes on. My mum once confessed to Tash and I about having Freddy Mercury posters on her bedroom wall, but obviously Dad thinks it's all about him. Usually Tash and I end up fake vomming over the chair arm, which they hate, so at least me sliding off the cushions and hitting the floor jerking saved them from that.

Even though the fit only lasted seconds it was lucky Tash was there to take control. Luckier still that Dad hadn't given in and let Mum take up the old laminate floor and put down carpet instead. She'd actually got as far as choosing one, but it's a point of honour in their relationship that Dad resists every one of her forward pushes. Imagine if I'd made a massive wet patch in front of the sofa on her brand new Nordic loop. She'd have been beside herself.

As it was, the puddle ran all the way under the coffee table and out the other side, where it hit Tiddlywink's foot. Apparently Tiddlywink didn't move a muscle, she just stood rigid and watched it soaking into the blue velvet of her Little Mermaid slipper. That child is one cool cookie, nothing fazes her. By the time I came round and got back downstairs in some dry clothes, it was all mopped up, and we got in before the Friday night rush at A&E. But, needless to say, I don't want to relive that. Especially not in front of the happy gardeners.

Plum is waiting for me by the door, her paint-spattered overalls looking a lot like her sea pictures. 'Everything okay?'

I nod. 'I don't do flashing lights, I'll go for a walk instead.' I'd rather they didn't know the details.

'Right.' Her eyes are full of concern, but she skips the awkward questions and sticks with the practical stuff. 'You're welcome to come and wait upstairs, I promise to find you a paint-free corner.'

'Thanks, but I'll grab some alone time.' I make my smile extra bright.

Her whisper turns to a chortle. 'Good luck with that – no one's ever on their own for long in St Aidan.'

I step outside, still doing up my coat. As I pull my scarf tighter against a flurry of wind, the cobbles are washed with pale light from the shop windows. I stop by Crusty Cobs to count the strawberry tarts – four – and custard slices – three – and only hurry on when I start to shiver. When I get to the harbour the water is shiny black, and the rigging is clinking against the dark lines of masts as they bob against the sky. As I stride past the rows of tiny pastel-painted cottages fronting onto the quayside Aunty Jo's tunes are on slow-mo in my head.

Whatever I'm doing, I always have a mental backing track playing. The day of the jump I had *Titanium* on repeat, when I was out on my building sites it was always something fast and bouncy. Blasting around the country with Marcus in his ever changing convertibles, Cold Play was where our musical tastes collided. For me that *When I Ruled the World* song was like Marcus's signature tune and the backing track to our life together. Since I've been ill I can't believe how much lippy I get though making damn sure my happy, super smiley outside shell hasn't changed any. But, however hard I try on the inside, all I can get in my head are slow chords and heart-wrenching, minor keys. At times, even Aunty Jo's 'wring out your hanky' songs feel too upbeat.

That's another strange thing. Just as reading and writing and speaking are all powered by different parts of the brain, singing stems from yet another area. I might struggle to put two words together, but entire lines of lyrics pop up in my mind without me wanting them to be there at all. It's happening as I slip along the dune path down to the beach. There's a crescent moon in the sky, and the music playing in my ears slows to a Johnny Cash plod . . . *full of broken thoughts . . . I cannot repair . . . I will let you down . . . I will make you hurt . . .* It's as if the working part of my brain automatically knows those are exactly the right lines. However much I put on a happy face to the outside world, really, really mournful music is the true expression of who I am and where my life is right now.

As I thread my way down to where the breakers are rushing up the beach in pale wavy lines my eyes are getting more used to the darkness. Around the bay the arc of pinprick lights follows the line of the coast, but their gentle twinkle against the mottled black of the sky isn't a threat. When I slide my phone out of my pocket, it lights up and tells me what I already know – the little line of dots in the screen corner has gone. The signal and internet give out somewhere higher up the hill which means my phone genie, Siri, has gone all silent on me, not that she's ever *that* cooperative. Not only that, but even if I needed to, I couldn't ring Mum or Bella.

The realisation slides into focus as slowly as the music – for the first time in months I'm totally on my own. Out of reach. Away from the protection of the people who love me and who have been keeping me safe by never letting me out of their sight. It's like I've accidentally wandered into a no man's land away from where I should be. There's a sensible voice in my head telling me I should go back to where I'm safe, where there are people at least. But at the same time I don't want to rush.

As my foot catches on a stick of driftwood I stoop and pick it up. It's straight and smooth like a bone and, without thinking, I head to where the beach is firmer and begin to scratch marks in the sand with the wooden point. It's easier when there's no one watching. When there's no one there to see how badly I'm doing, my hand is somehow more free to move. I try one small line, then another crossing it. Then do the same again. And again. Then I try a row of those 's's that always catch me out on paper because the pen won't curl fast enough so, however hard I try, they end up twice the size of all the other letters.

Scratching with the end of a stick with the wind snatching at my hair, knowing that soon the crash and fall of the tide will thunder over the marks and suck away the traces of where I've been, it's easier. My lips twist into a smile as I look along my wandering line of 's's and 'x's and see a whole empty beach stretching into the distance, all waiting to be written on.

A cry in the darkness behind me makes me turn. There's a big figure and a smaller one, their jackets flapping in the shadows, and another shout as the smaller one springs towards me.

'Edie Browne! What are you writing?' Only one person calls me that.

'Nothing much.' The wind snatches my words away.

He lets out a wail. 'That's way more than when you were writing on paper.'

'It's easier here.' Anyone else, I'd be fed up at them finding me. Cam I don't mind, although I can't say the same for Barney.

'What? On the *beach*, in the *dark*?' He's very judgmental for six. 'We're going for ice cream.'

'Brill.' Shouldn't he be asleep by now?

'At the Surf Shack.' He points to a wooden building with swinging lights on its deck, further along the sand. 'You could come too.'

That's a bad idea, for a hundred reasons I can't immediately put my stick on. I'm hesitating when Barney arrives.

'Best coffee along the bay. They do a mean hot chocolate too.'

'I'm not . . .' Not getting my excuses together fast enough for starters.

'Cam wouldn't ask if it wasn't important to him.'

Even in the dark, with only the smallest shimmer of moonlight reflecting off the blackness of the sea, I can sense his disapproval. If he's trying to make me feel hugely that I have to, it's working. If I hadn't been caught out before, I might have given in already. I slide out my phone, then slide it back in my pocket because it's not telling me anything. Realistically, I reckon they've barely started their flower slides yet.

Barney's insistent. 'Five minutes. Then you can go back to what-ever's so pressing.'

He's overstepping again. Totally ignoring that I'm on a private walk. If it wasn't for Cam, I wouldn't be considering this. But, to be fair, without Cam he wouldn't be asking.

As we kick our way along the beach and up the broad wooden steps of the Surf Shack I'm hoping this won't be another 'boat in the bay' fiasco. But I have to admit there's something about Cam's small scrap of a figure beside me, kicking sand in the half light, that makes my heart turn over. That's what's tugging me.

As we push through the door into what looks like a hut made from thousands of mismatched planks hammered together, we're hit by a wall of warmth, and a broad smile from the guy behind the counter. Apart from a few salt-streaked surfers, we're the only customers. Cam heads for a rough-hewn table, slides onto a metal chair, swings his feet and looks up expectantly.

I grab the chair that's close to Cam and as far away from Barney as possible. It's only when he slides into his seat and I get the full benefit of taut denim stretched across muscly thighs that it hits me. I'm so used to thinking of myself as out of the dating scene I forgot to worry that people could think I was here for entirely the wrong reason.

There's not even time for me to have a good look at the piles of goodies under glass domes on the counter because the guy from behind the counter is already at the table. The glass he puts down in front of Cam is filled with scoops of colourful ice cream, and topped with wafers and a long spoon.

'Wow, quick work.' It's one of my blurts.

'Thanks.' Cam's eyes are huge, but as he picks up the long spoon, he still hasn't smiled.

The waiter laughs. 'Same order, same time every week. We like to be ready for our regulars.' He turns to me. 'So what can I get for you?'

'A small coffee, please.' Despite the cake stacks, sometimes it's best to be minimal.

Barney turns to me. 'Way too boring – this is chocolate central. Look at the chalkboard – you have to be wilder.'

As far as I'm concerned, the board he's waving at might be taller than the waiter but it's still just a load of squiggles. At least I remember enough about cafés to wing it. 'A small coffee with chocolate then.' There's definitely a name for it, I just can't nail what it is.

'A mocha?' The waiter beams. 'One mochaccino, coming up.' He turns to Barney.

'Great choice – same here, but I'll go large.'

It's not just never being allowed to be on your own that's off kilter here, it's also coffee sizing. When the waiter comes back it turns out 'small' means enormous and 'large' is more like one of those boat things that crosses the channel with cars on. They've both got lumps of floating cream approximately the size of the Isle of Wight. Around the island the liquid is so thick and chocolatey I wish I was getting the full benefit. But at least it warms me, and the cream is fabulously thick and sticky as I suck it off my spoon.

Cam takes a bite of his wafer then gives me a hard stare. 'But why didn't you have ice cream?'

It's easier being put on the spot by someone Cam's size. 'I was too icy already.'

'*Next time* you *have* to have ice cream.'

If I was shivering before, that thought makes my insides go glacial. 'We'll see.' By next Friday I hope to have come up with a plan that doesn't involve crawling or gardeners or freezing my shit off on the beach. Or not being able to read the menu at whatever this place is called.

Barney watches Cam working his way down his ice cream, then turns to me. 'Cam's ice creams at the Surf Shack are a long-standing Friday night tradition.'

As if that explains anything. And then suddenly it all falls into place. Sadie from Zinc Inc had kids and an ex, and didn't spare us the details. Single dads and mahoosive 'daddy loves you more' sweeteners? Compensatory ice creams don't come any larger than the one Cam's wading through now. The warning bells couldn't be clanging any louder.

Knowing the tussles Sadie and her husband had, if this is a divorce, I need to keep my distance. Run for the hills, and now wouldn't be a moment too soon. As if Sadie hadn't drilled it into us single women, going within a country mile of a single dad is too near, especially if they're using the kids to draw you in.

'That's great.' In my head I'm already taking giant strides towards the door. 'But you have to be careful with . . .' I rack my brain, and for once it comes up trumps '. . . inducements . . . especially with children.'

'What's that supposed to mean?' Barney's rubbing his lip with his thumb, but by the way his eyes clash with mine he's being deliberately bloody-minded.

'Bribery's never good. And it's late too.' Simply by being here, I'm condoning all of it.

Barney's voice rises. 'And it's *so* wrong to have a blast on the beach and an ice cream to make ourselves feel better?'

I squeeze Cam's shoulder as I get up and focus on the freckles on his nose, not how sad his eyes are. 'Sorry Cam, I have to go now. I promised Aunty Jo.' I hope he'll understand. And it is the truth. If I'm not back at the gallery when the lights go on again, Aunty Jo will worry. Ring my mother. Send out the lifeboats. I dip in my pocket, pull out some cash and wedge it under the bottle full of fairy lights in the middle of the table.

Then I back towards the door and give them a wave. 'Okay, see you soon. Love you, bye.' This time I don't mind I've blurted it, so long as it was for Cam. It's only as I'm speeding down the steps outside that I remember I should have looked at the numbers on the note.

Chapter 12

Day 145: Monday, 26th March
At Periwinkle Cottage

Epic Achievement: Finding Unicorn slices really exist.

If I thought a gardeners' slideshow was bad there was worse to come. That's the trouble with a deserted seaside town in winter; now people know we're here they expect us to come to every event. Somehow we manage to dodge Saturday's picnic and daffodil walk near St Austell with the gardeners' club, because they're all going in cars and, until one of us gets back behind the wheel, Aunty Jo and I don't have our own transport. It's one thing getting a lift into St Aidan, quite another committing to all day in someone else's car. As if that wasn't bad enough, Beth was pressing us to go to a *Dance Till Your Feet Drop Off* eighties disco. I couldn't even fall back on the flashing lights excuse, because she said they don't run to those. Much as I love retro tunes, dancing in the dark is what you do with besties, not strangers, but some lucky star must have been passing over because Aunty Jo did another of her surprise interventions and insisted our Saturday evening was already spoken for.

So instead we have a riveting night in, watching some ballerina version of *You've Got Talent* – according to Aunty Jo they hadn't.

And between times we carry on de-flowering the kitchen, and try out some paint samples that arrived in mini pots. I head her away from the fuchsia and daffodil palettes she's hankering after, and insist we start with broken white.

Whenever Aunty Jo's steered me towards writing practice – which is even more often than she mentions the good times back in happy Harpenden – I've headed her off. When I came down to porridge yesterday to find the fridge covered in Dayglo magnetic letters and numbers, she replied to my appalled, 'What the eff have you clicked on now?' with a sniffy, 'I'm sure Cam might enjoy them, even if you don't.'

She certainly doesn't hold back with her buying finger. We've just had yet another mega delivery now, so I'm sitting next to a pile of paint buckets, rollers and brushes, and she's unwrapping some oversized sticky labels.

'So what are *they* for?'

'Don't you love it when things have two uses?' She picks up a felt tip and starts to write, then leans across and slaps a beautifully written label on the back of the settee. 'See, *s-o-f-a* – isn't that great? I get to do my calligraphy, and you get to take in the words by osmosis.'

'Osmosis – isn't that what amoebas do?' Wherever I dug that up from, I'm damn sure it's not a flattering comparison.

Her beautifully pencilled eyebrows close together as she concentrates. 'I have no idea, Edie, I'm just doing what your mum tells me.'

No surprise there then, even though that has to be a first. 'What are you writing?' It's not as though I can read it.

'Cushion, door, paint pot, microwave, kettle . . . ' She sniffs and slaps a label on the table. 'I'm going to need to order more of these if I'm going to put names on *everything*.' Once she begins a task, she's alarmingly thorough.

'You do know I'm on a break?' Emptying my head so it'll fill up better when I begin again.

She pushes a label onto the cushion. 'I wanted to train to be a teacher like your mum after I gave up dancing.' She's pursing her lips and ignoring my question. 'Harry wasn't keen, he always told me not to worry my pretty head about work.'

'That's a shame.' Attitudes like that drive me wild on a regular basis, but that was Uncle Harry. Building sites aren't the most forward-thinking places, but most men on them now acknowledge women aren't purely for decoration. And if they don't, they do after I've finished with them.

She shuffles. 'It's coming back to bite me now. Things would be *so* much easier if I'd taken more of an interest in the finances. Lovely George from the solicitors has been struggling with them for over a year now, I'm seeing him again this week.'

It's the first I've heard about it not being straightforward. 'You have got enough cash, though?' She has to have, they always had pots of the stuff. Uncle Harry drove the kind of flash limos that wouldn't even begin to fit on our drive. One time he blocked the entire close. But the work in the stable yard won't come cheap if we want a decent finish.

Aunty Jo shakes herself back into the room. 'We were really well off, I can't *not* be fine, can I?'

The question's so complicated I've got no idea if the right answer is 'yes' or 'no', so I force myself and take the label she's holding out. 'Can I help with that?'

'*d-o-o-r* . . . so where does that go?'

'On the French window?' I'm grinning at her, deciding where on the glass to stick it, when I see a blue blur running across the courtyard. 'Looks like we've got a visitor. It's a good thing we bought those Unicorn slices.' Once Aunty Jo accidentally pointed out that cute name, I was hardly going to leave them in the shop.

As I push open the door Cam runs in and throws down his school bag on the floor.

'Hi Cam, have you had a good day? How about a drink?'

'I hate school, but I'd like juice.' He popped in a couple of times over the weekend, but he's heading for the kitchen now as though he's been here all his life.

'Tea, Aunty Jo?'

'Mango and passion fruit please – it's the orange one, and you can take the label for the kettle when you go. You choose – it starts with a "k".'

Just when it was all going so well. 'Hmm . . .' When it comes to letters I'm okay on a, b, c and x, y, z – it's the ones in the middle that are troublesome.

Before I can even think 'brain freeze' Cam's into the kitchen swiping a letter off the fridge and he's back holding it up for me. 'See, Edie, "kicking k" is easy because its legs are kicking.'

'Thanks for the tip.' I grin at Cam, and look for the best match on the labels. 'This one?'

Aunty Jo nods. 'That's it, Edie, there's more in your head than you think. Now go and stick it on.'

Cam turns to me. 'So it's not just writing. You can't do reading either?'

There's no wriggling out of it. 'Pretty much not, no.'

Aunty Jo steps in. 'Edie used to be able to read but she hurt the bit inside her head, and now she's got to learn all over again.'

He rubs his forehead. 'Actually, your brain's in your head.'

'It is – that's what I broke. Only a little bit of it, though.'

There are wrinkles in his forehead. 'But *how*?'

'I jumped out of a plane then fell over a bucket.' As his eyes go even wider I realise I'm not making this clear enough. 'Definitely *PLEASE DON'T* try that at home.'

'She had a parachute.' Aunty Jo's jumping in to fill in the gaps.

'And she'd been drinking champagne, that's like wine with lots of bubbles.'

'Weren't you scared?'

'Only at first, then it was brill.'

'I'm not brave.' Cam pulls a face at me, then dips into his bag. 'I've got my reading book from school, it's *Biff, Chip and Kipper*.'

'Hey, I know them.'

His lower lip comes out. 'Everyone else is on harder books than me, but I can't do my words.'

'I'm not on *any* book.' However bad he is, he'll still be beating me.

Aunty Jo turns to me. 'Don't worry, Edie, you'll get there once you decide to try.' As she keeps reminding me. 'You did a free fall, this should be easy.'

I'm shaking my head as I go to the kitchen, not only for that but because *Biff, Chip and Kipper* are waving at me sharp and clear from the past when so many more important things have faded. At school we learned without thinking, I just never imagined I'd have to do it all over again, or find it so hard the second time around.

I make the tea, pour Cam and I some apple juice and trace my finger over the 'U' as I open the pack of Unicorn slices. As I put out the cakes with their rose-coloured sponge and the pink and yellow zigzag icing I thank my lucky stars that I still know my colours.

I carry the tray through and grin at Cam. 'Are you going to give me a peep at your book then?'

He shrugs. 'I s'pose we *could* look at the pictures.'

'That's fine by me.' I put the drinks on the table, then flop onto the sofa and pat the space between me and Aunty Jo. 'Sit here so we can all see and you can tell me the story if you want.'

I'm not expecting him to do it but he begins, halting over every word. I pore over from one side and Aunty Jo gently nudges him along from the other. By the time he gets to the end of a page there's a tourniquet closing around my neck. He's finding it *so* hard, and yet he's *so* far ahead of me.

I make myself sound bright as he hands me the book and I flick through the pages. 'Yay, go Cam! That was lovely . . . ready for cake?' As I offer him the plate I'm *not* going to stress over how much I don't know. 'Not too girlie for you? I actually bought them for me.'

'Strawberry ice cream's pink, and that's my best one.'

He's on his third slice when there's a knock on the French windows and Barney pushes his way through, pointing at the dog – calling him Robert and telling him to stay outside. You know when a guy comes in, and somehow he's just too big for the room? Before I can think further on it, somehow Cam's book springs out of my hand, and lands in a heap at his feet. He picks it up and rearranges the crumpled pages without comment, but I can tell by the shake of his head that he's judging me. As he passes it across he's holding something up between his fingers.

'We pay St Aidan prices here, Edie, not Bath ones. However good the Surf Shack mochaccino, twenty's too much to leave for a tip. So have this back.'

As he slides the note under my coaster I'm kicking myself for my blunder. I'll have to be more careful. Or I would if there were going to be a next time. Which there definitely won't be.

Cam's frowning at me. 'Can't you do counting either? Or sums?'

'Er . . .' My mouth's open, but nothing more comes out.

Cam's on a roll here. 'I had to show her a "kicking k" – she can't read 'cos she's broken her brain.'

'Really?' Barney's eyes are narrowed.

'She drank too much fizzy pop then fell out of an aeroplane. And she's even slower at writing than me.' He sounds delighted.

'Something like that.' I hadn't planned on sharing, but it is only temporary. I've got all the summer to turn this around. For now I might as well own it, so I sit up straight and flash Barney my widest smile. This is why it pays to have your lippy in tip-top shape, regardless. At least this way I'm the one feeling a-okay, and he's the one who's shuffling around looking like he wants the floor to open up and swallow him.

Aunty Jo is holding up the school book. 'Cam's been reading to us, it was lovely.'

Cam's pointing at the plate. 'And we had pink cake and it tastes like strawberries.'

I stare at him. 'Strawberries? Really?' I can't believe what I'm missing there.

He's being very direct, and very serious. 'You know it did, Edie Browne – you had four pieces.'

Barney rolls his eyes. 'It's not always helpful to count, Cam, but I'm glad to hear you were reading.' He turns from Aunty Jo to me. 'He refuses to get his book out for me, *whatever* I bribe him with.'

As Barney lingers over the word *bribe*, I sense that thrust of his jaw is all for my benefit. If there's one time I'm happy to have lost my sense of smell it's now, because not being able to smell him makes him so much easier to ignore. When Marcus swapped from Armani to the stuff made by the French guy off the Eurotrash programme, he joked it was for bad boys who wanted to get laid and stand out from the crowd. Who knew he saw himself that way? Or that, despite us having *all* the sex, it still left him thinking he'd like more. Bella weighed in and told me it was 'men's bollock talk', but at the time I still worried. Not that I'm saying there's any reason to bring Marcus into this, other than them both being guys.

If I'm trying to think of my favourite scents, it's purely a memory exercise I'm probably failing at. As for matching Barney to one . . . well, hell, no. Given how rough his edges are, I'd put him down as a basic wash and go guy. Realistically, he's hardly going to splash on Christian what's-his-name to hang out in a barn. Despite how fabulous I remember the scent to be, I'm damn sure the body spray that sounded like it was for savages wasn't actually meant for shepherds. Or anyone else in that hut industry.

Aunty Jo's cheeks are rosy under her foundation. 'Any time you'd like to read again, Cam, you know where we are.' She flashes a glance at me. 'It would really help Edie too, she won't try at all when you're not here.'

Barney ruffles Cam's hair. 'If the big guy here is happy to, that would be great.' He's reaching for the handle to let himself out, then at the last moment he stops and fixes his gaze on the decorating pile, then runs his eyes around the stripped walls. 'I see the stripping went well after I left. You've certainly taken a lot on here.'

'This is just the beginning.' Aunty Jo's sigh is a bit over-dramatic, considering how unbothered she's been for the last year.

He rubs his chin. 'I could always do some painting, as payback for help with the reading.'

Just like that. As if we'd want him anywhere near. It was super uncomfortable when he muscled in the other day, and he was only here a few moments. And Aunty Jo just lost Harry. This is a very private time. I mean, look how reluctant she was for me to strip her walls, and I'm a relation. As she opens her mouth to reply, I'm confident she'll give him the knockback. Quite apart from anything else, we can't have him close by when we're painting because he uses up all the oxygen. I can't reach up to paint the ceiling if my head is even more light and woozy than it usually is. And he makes me drop things even worse than normal.

'Well, actually, that would be . . .'

It's only when I see a slight curl to her lips that it hits me. She isn't going to refuse at all.

I'm straight in there, only because I'm desperate. 'No, definitely not, no, totally, totally, NO!' I think he'll get that. And, with any luck, so will she. 'Thanks, all the same.'

Aunty Jo wades in. 'I know you're the decorating expert, Edie, but there's a lot to paint for one person, and we don't want you getting over-tired.' She's obviously forgetting she offered to help too.

From somewhere I finally find some other suitable words to put a stop to this. 'We'll see.'

Barney shrugs. 'Okay, well, the offer's there.' There are lines of concern around his eyes as he looks at me. 'We can't have you going up ladders painting if you're . . .' it's funny to see someone else searching for a suitable word '. . . unwell.'

Holy crap. How many times? 'I'm n-not "unwell". My issues are in other areas, not climbing up steps.' It's coming out through gritted teeth, so maybe I should try that again.

'Great, sorry, revise that. Not a hundred per cent then.' He blows out his cheeks. 'Jeez, you could so easily have hit your head on the boom the other day too.'

'BOOM!' Somehow it's out before I can stop it.

His lips are twisting. 'Good to see you picked that up so fast – any time you'd like another go—'

'Totally not.'

Aunty Jo lifts her finger. 'I think you'll find Edie's a hundred per cent in every area that matters, Barney. She works in interior design, and she's the one who's here to help *me*. As you said before, we've got our hands full fixing this place up. Edie wouldn't be here if she wasn't up to managing every aspect of the project.'

Thanks for the intervention, Aunty Jo, I couldn't have put it better myself. If the space between us wasn't full of hut builder, and she was slightly less rigid, I'd throw my arms around her for that. 'Exactly right, we're here to nail this p- p- p—' *Oh, fuck.*

As Aunty Jo sees the whites of my eyes she's in there saving me again. 'Yes, this, er, project, yes, will be fully nailed everywhere that needs it, and it's going to be, er, totally fabulous.'

There's the hint of a crinkle at the corner of Barney's eyes, but his expression and tone are deadpan serious. 'Brilliant, I'm pleased we've got that one sorted. And thanks for today.' As he finally turns to leave, and he stops and taps Aunty Jo's label, there's finally a tiny lilt to his lips. 'It says "door", but isn't this more of a window?'

Aunty Jo comes to wave them off. 'You're the second person to say that in half an hour. It's no problem, I'll make another sign.'

And as they stride off across the courtyard, with Robert the dog scuttling alongside them, I could have sworn I heard Cam say, 'Love you, bye.'

Chapter 13

Day 146: Tuesday, 27th March
More calligraphy at The Deck Gallery

Epic Achievement: (More awful than epic, but too significant not to record.) Discovering the extent of Aunty Jo's financial difficulties – managing to stop her going ballistic and leaving town. (Although, realistically, where would she go?)

I know we've been busier lately, but you'd hardly think double-booking would be an issue. But, sure enough, Aunty Jo's next appointment with George the solicitor turns out to clash with calligraphy. Whatever she says, I'm confident Aunty Jo has no need to worry about finances because, compared to our family, they splashed the cash like there was no tomorrow, but there's no point George making an expensive home visit when we're practically passing his harbourfront office anyway. Even though there's hazy sunlight filtering through the cloud cover as we make our way down into the village, the wind is blustery enough to dapple the pale grey sea and streak the bay with white dashes.

I take Aunty Jo as far as the main waiting room and have a fleeting moment of dress envy when I see the orange starry print that the receptionist is wearing, which is a bit silly considering

I'm always in my office capris. Then I give Aunty Jo's elbow a last squeeze, and run.

I arrive at The Deck Gallery just as everyone else is taking their seats around the big table. We've seen most people around since last time, so I grab myself a coffee and join them.

'Just me for now.' Aunty Jo emailed Loella earlier with her apologies, to save me having to explain why she wasn't here in front of everyone. As I smile around at the familiar faces there's a twinge of guilt in my chest that if I could stay at home on my own there's no way I'd be here. Aunty Jo's been poring over her calligraphy sheets night and day, but I've done approximately zilch since the last time I came.

As I pull out a chair Loella comes across. 'So, I expect you're ready for your first project?'

'*What?*' I did not see that one coming and my lurch of shock leaves my coffee wobbling wildly. I can't tell her I'm mostly here for tips on hot decorators, and I was counting on at least another week writing lines of letters – or, in my case, not – because anything more will mean spelling. I know I can still officially write, but it usually comes out as a jumble all over the paper. I have no clue how many mistakes are in there, but I can tell from Mum's zigzaggy eyebrows it's not brilliant. And, at a guess, for calligraphy the spelling has to be spot on.

I swallow hard and try to forget my mouth's gone dry with nerves. 'A p-p-p-project?' At least I've got that out for once.

'There's no need to look so terrified.' Loella's laughing.

'Maybe next week?' When Aunty Jo's here to help me.

'We're here for fun, not perfection. Our plan is, if you get a taste for creating, you won't be able to stay away.' Loella's got a little piece of blue paper in her hand. 'If you write the word "beach" you'll be using all the letters you practised last week, and you can add in a little arrow and some decoration and make it look like a sign.'

She seems to be overlooking how shit the few letters I wrote last week were.

'Beach?' I'm staring out through the gallery windows, across the deck to the grey swirls of the sea in the distance and the clouds whipping across the sky above as I try to think how the hell to spell that. Inside my polo neck jumper, there's sweat running down my back.

'Don't worry, I'll write it down first so you have something to copy from.' As she rules some faint pencil guidelines on the paper there's something about the kindness in her smile that's not pity, more understanding. Whatever, it's a huge giveaway.

'Did someone tell you about my writing? About my head?'

'Actually Cam mentioned it on the school run this morning.'

Damn. 'To *everyone?*' I'm guessing the car was rammed, it usually is.

'Yes, I'm sorry, it was most of the kids, and Beth was there too. Are you okay with that?' Her eyes are anxious as she waits for my reply.

I shrug, try to ignore that my stomach just hit the floor and tell myself to breathe. 'It's . . .' really not that big a problem. When you're passing through, things matter less. It's no big deal, it's actually completely '. . . fine.' So another six people know, and the sky hasn't fallen in yet. In any case, it's only for now. In a few weeks it's all going to come together again. I mean, realistically, I'm looking at getting back to my job so I'll *have* to reconnect with those old skills soon. I was never the world's best speller, in any case.

Loella's frown is apologetic. 'It's hard to keep a secret around here.'

I'm not even sure why I wanted to keep it secret. Maybe because I didn't want people to pity me, I didn't want people to be watching out for all the things I still can't do. Maybe even because not being able to read and write and talk and use my hand properly makes me feel inadequate. I want to hide the things I can't do so people don't find out and start to treat me like I'm stupid. Maybe because so long as I can hide my problems from people, I can almost pretend they're not there.

Beth slides onto the chair next to mine. 'Although, I have to say, secret-keeping in St Aidan improved a lot when the doctors' surgery stopped phoning out the pregnancy test and STI results from the reception desk in full earshot of the entire waiting room.'

Loella rolls her eyes. 'Unbelievable, but it did used to happen. When my mum had me, my dad was literally the last person in St Aidan to find out I was on the way.' She pauses to laugh then her tone changes. 'We were actually thrilled, because it's the first time Cam's ever told us anything without us prising it out of him. Cam's had a rough time the last couple of years, but he's really taken to you and Jo.' She's writing words on a piece of scrap paper. 'There you go – "Beach" and "At the beach . . . Back when summer's over", in case you feel like a real challenge. Unless there's something else you'd rather have?' She cocks her head.

With patches of my memories wiped out, my head feels less full and more floaty than it used to at the best of times, but when I try to think of something – anything – witty or sassy to write, there's spectacular nothing there.

'No, that's good.' I'm smiling at how well the 'I'll be back when summer's done' one would fit as an ironic sign on my empty desk at work. At least that way they'd know I hadn't lost my sense of you know what. I'd send them it, but by the time I get it written the better weather will be here and it might piss everyone off. It's fine to be having some leave-by-the-sea when there's sleet lashing against the office window. Being away to play when the pavements are baking and Bath's honey-coloured sandstone crescents are all wiggly with the heat haze, not so much.

Loella's missed that I'm daydreaming. 'Once you start, you'll find the letters link themselves. Rough it out on a practice sheet a few times first, then, once you're happy with how it's looking, go for the real thing.' She sends me a wink. 'And remember, it's the same for calligraphy as hair, "messy" is well on trend, everyone's trying for that "less than perfect" look.'

In which case, I should be well ahead.

Beth comes in closer. 'It's not like the city – we *do* like to know things in St Aidan, but only because we care.'

Loella joins in again. 'A lot of people like it here because it's an easy place to be different. We're laid-back and accepting, we don't judge.' Her eyes widen. 'Not that we're saying . . .'

Beth's touch is light on my arm. 'What she means is, no one here is going to mind what you were before *or* how you are now.' She laughs. 'You just carry on being your amazing self, and we'll all be happy you're here.'

'Thanks, it's sweet of you to say.' I'm finding it hard to swallow and my chest has clamped up just because they're being so kind. That's the thing though, right now I'm not entirely sure who I am, or what that self is. I'm a lot like the calligraphy – a work in progress that should get a lot better soon, once I start putting the time in.

Loella rolls her eyes again. 'You'll soon get the picture. Everyone's cool that Beth's other half, Morgan, is a wife not a husband, and that three of my four are my partner Jack's, not mine. And no one minds that we never have any cash because our online shops are in crisis, or that we're always running late and get confused about where our kids are. We all live in hope that one day our art and craftwork might accidentally become saleable and our lives will work like clockwork.'

Beth nods. 'But, until that happens, we're all just muddling through.'

'We probably always will be.' Loella laughs.

'So welcome to the chaos club.' Beth's eyes are shining as she looks into mine. 'We've got some little boxes of watercolours here if you feel like adding some extra colour when you've finished your word.' She's acting like she's already forgotten what she knew. And, realistically, I can tell from the rundown they just gave me – people are busy, they have complicated lives. If anyone else finds out, they'll have a few seconds of surprise then get back to their own stuff. For the time being I'm going to have to get over myself.

'Fab.' I always loved messing with my paint box, so for once my enthusiasm is genuine. When I was a teenager, art homework was what I spent most of my time on, so long as there wasn't a party. As I beam back at her I'm waiting for Loella to say more about Cam. But then someone else waves her over, and Beth goes off too, and I'm back to my piece of empty blue paper.

It's exactly as Loella promised. I might be writing different letters, but so long as I keep a close eye on which one I'm supposed to be doing, they're joining up on their own. Even when I've done a big pile of practices and finally written the word 'beach' in my best writing, I've definitely hit the messy target, but the blue paper still looks very empty. So I add in the arrow that Loella suggested, then get a twisty shell out of my bag, and load up a brush with cream paint. Strokes of the brush are way easier than working with the pen, a couple of splodges and I've got what looks like a cockle shell, a few more and I've done a row. It's higgledy, but it doesn't look bad. And while I leave them to dry I go to the pile of papers in the centre of the table and choose another bigger one, and a whole load more scrap pieces, and set to work on the longer sign.

I'm working so hard putting blue blots all around the edge of the paper, before I realise Aunty Jo is tapping me on the back and looking over my shoulder.

'"At the beach . . . " That's nice, Edie. I like the dove sitting on the fence.'

Don't they have birds in Harpenden? She has no idea about wildlife. 'It's actually a seagull.'

Loella wanders over. 'Whatever it is, it's easy to tell you're creative.'

'Has Cam been filling you in again?'

'Sorry, no, the interior designer bit came from Barney, he knows we want to hear when any artistic talent arrives.'

'I wouldn't go that far, I do site work, not design.' It's funny how we make our choices. I've lost count of the times I've passed the designers in the office and kicked myself for missing out. As a minimalist eighteen-year-old I opted for the management course, not the design one, because it looked easier. I laugh. 'I'm open for orders any time.' It's funny how the words come out without thinking when I'm all softened up from the painting. I turn to Aunty Jo. 'Why not try a p-p-p . . .?' Damn, I spoke too soon there – the 'p' word's gone again.

'It's much too late to start a project, the children will be back any minute.' Her voice is even more clipped than usual and as she checks her watch her mouth is puckered with tension.

'So how was it?'

An inch closer, she'd have bitten my head off. 'George was fine, but the pension pot and nest egg are up the creek. Out the window. Christmas crackered, or whatever it is those bloody men say. As a stuff-up, it couldn't be any more hideous or disastrous. Truly, Edie, there are no words.' As she leans across to look at the paint box, despite the Hollywood Highlights, her cheeks are grey and she's still snapping. 'If those are Windsor and Newton watercolours, we must put in an order the minute we get home.'

If she's a 'bad news' compulsive buyer, all I can say is heaven help her bank balance. And if she was in any way hoping to keep this quiet, well, if she's announced it to the table of St Aidan grapevine central, she just blew that one too.

Chapter 14

Day 146: Tuesday, 27th March
At Periwinkle Cottage

Epic Achievement: Holding it together for Aunty Jo.

I get the full story of Aunty Jo's financial crash on the way home. And, because it's so devastating, we make a detour via that place made from planks where I persuade her that a salted caramel sundae is savoury enough for a weekday, while still offering the amount of emotional rescue she needs. Which is a lot. Then, while we look out at the empty beach and watch the frill of the water sliding in and out up the beach, between spoonfuls of ice cream she tells me what's been going on. For the past year George has been trying to track down Harry's missing pensions. However clueless Aunty Jo is with money, she knew there should be more than she had. But it now turns out the reason they couldn't find them was because Harry had cashed them all in to buy the barns and the cottage.

George went out of his way to say that Harry's over-stretching was temporary, that he'd have been fine as soon as he'd got the holiday lets up and running. The only flaw in the plan was him dying when he did, and no one could have foreseen that.

Considering what she'd been told, Aunty Jo did very well to hold her shit together and turn up at Calligraphy acting like it was just another Tuesday afternoon. Had it been me in her position, I'd probably have run around the quayside screaming. I can only think she was too stunned by what she'd heard to react.

Realistically, even if it's delicious – and she assured me it was – it's going to take a lot more than all the toppings and one tall glass of fancy ice cream to get Aunty Jo over the shock that the income she was relying on for the rest of her life isn't actually there at all. For me it means it's more important than ever to get the cottage sorted out, on the market and sold, before she goes broke. No pressure there then. We ring Jake from Zinc Inc, who's happy to help out, and Aunty Jo emails him some plans of the stables so he can do some rough costings.

I was right about her spending spree too. With every penny counting, I tried to direct her towards the items we'd be buying anyway, like decorating supplies. Sadly, we didn't order paint, because our visions on that were so far apart. Realistically, if she's going to insist on bilious apricot, or the sky-blue with sponged pink clouds that Harry once denied her back in nineteen eighty, we might as well save ourselves the trouble and stick with the monkeys. Then, to make up for losing out on the paint argument, despite already having enough hardly-worn Christmas painting pyjamas to clothe a small army of Santa's helpers, she went on to buy an entire box of disposable overalls.

'We might be paupers, Edie, but at least we'll be appropriately dressed for decorating.' That's if we ever agree on colours, which seems unlikely. Then she gives a little cough. 'I think we might need to give the classes a miss, just until the fuss dies down.'

I give her arm a pat. 'We'll see.' We definitely can't stay at home until we've found some decent workmen with reasonable rates. Suddenly this isn't just about throwing cash at the job and making everything okay. The areas are vast; if we're on a tight budget heaven knows how we'll ever afford to fit out all those flats.

There's a knock and I open the French window to Loella, who presses a DVD into my hand.

'I'm not coming in, but this is Mia's *Swan Lake* for Josie.' She comes close enough to hiss in my ear, 'Same music, a few extra characters, I thought you could use a happy ending today.'

I'm opening and closing my mouth for all kinds of reasons. 'It's her favourite, but how *on earth* did you know?'

She's staring at me like I'm the silly one. 'We only hear it every morning, wafting on the breeze when we pick Cam up.' Her grin spreads. 'I reckon Jo must be even more obsessed than Mia, and she's worn out two DVDs already.'

Shit. 'Thanks, but I promise we'll keep it down in future.'

'One more thing – those little pictures of yours?' Her hand's on my wrist. 'From one struggling artist to another, pop them in little frames at Plum's and they'll sell like hot cakes once the season gets going.'

I can't believe what I'm hearing. 'For money?'

'That's what we're all short of.' Her laugh is husky and her tartan coat tails are flapping round her head in the gale. 'The trick is to build up your stock in winter then it's like cash in the bank. Seriously, you should think about it.'

If I didn't know better I'd swear that was a travelling rug she was wearing. I'm thinking so hard I miss that she's turned and is back on the lane. Mostly that she's very thoughtful, but if she thinks there's a market for some scraps of paper with scribble on, she's super deluded.

So tonight as we watch Mia's DVD, even though I'm certain Loella was only being kind because we'd had such a shit day, I trawl my brain for beachy or inspiring words to put on pictures and Aunty Jo jots them down for me. Nothing too twee – they have to make me smile, not reach for the vomit bucket and, most important, they have to be short.

'Beach ready' – 'sparkle' – 'make waves' – 'sun, sand, salt' – etc etc.

We all know a wedding isn't the only route for women to get a happy ending, and having a husband isn't always a walk in the park. But for one evening only I'm happy to overlook that with Mia's version. By the time Odette gets married to a prince called Derek (yes, really, and it still has us dabbing our eyes as the final curtain comes down), I have a lovely sea of daisies waiting for the words *'Be Awesome'*, which I'll obviously add later.

If Aunty Jo hadn't dropped off I might have got her to add *I heart art* to the list too. But she can't have been *that* tired because I heard her along the corridor upstairs, Skyping my mum late into the night.

Chapter 15

Epic Achievement: Being epic – at football.

Despite forcing Aunty Jo along to Loella's fabric fest on Wednesday, we don't come across any friendly builders on the way down. If a tiny part of me was secretly hoping for someone – okay, Barney – to come along again and give me an 'out' from the class, it was only because it's *indescribably* tedious watching people chop up material and stitch it back together again when I'm so bad at it myself. I'm starting to feel silly for putting so much effort into polishing my get-out clause too. But at least this time I've come with my own alternative activity, so I spend the afternoon with the paint box that arrived this morning. I'm planning to write *love flamingoes* at some point down the line, but for now I'm filling the paper with exactly what it says on the tin, even though their legs and necks end up a bit wobbly. When Loella comes over to ask what I'm up to, I say, 'Being awesome, doing my project,' which makes us both laugh. And she doesn't have to know that I won't actually be finishing the projects and getting around to all the writing until much later.

By the time everyone's clearing away I've given up glancing around every time the tall glass door by the entrance swings open. So when a shadow falls across the pink birds I'm wafting around to help them dry, and I peer down at the floor and spot a pair of scuffed Timberlands, I'm muttering silent curses, not what I've been practising.

'Edie, just the woman I'm looking for.'

I blow out, screw my eyes tightly closed and focus my mind. 'If you want me to circumnavigate the world, you missed your window.' And 'yay' to getting that mouthful out.

'Much better than that. The infants' end-of-season penalty shoot-outs are after school, Cam was hoping you'd cheer him on.' All my effort's gone straight over his head.

'Football?' I know everything there is to know about that from Marcus and have no wish to learn any more. Enough said.

'Everyone's going.' Across the table Loella and Beth are both nodding, backing him up. He's rubbing his hands. 'If we hurry we'll get a good place.'

'Great,' I say, and smile, even though it's my idea of hell. And before I can say 'own goal' we've been whisked across town, and we're walking across a field behind the school which is teeming with parents and dizzyingly close to the cliff edge. It's so exposed, me hanging onto Aunty Jo's anorak is all that's stopping her getting blown out to sea. Although I have to admit in passing, the view from here is amazing, and watching the sea tumbling in and crashing onto piles of inky rocks is so mesmerising I could happily watch it all day. Which I'd definitely never say about football. Calling it a field is a stretch too because, to be fair, we've walked the length of the pitch, which is thankfully shortened for kids and unfit people like me, and I still haven't seen a blade of grass.

Beth comes up behind us. 'Don't worry, some of the school

tournaments go on all afternoon, but this is an abridged version for the small ones. The kids take penalties, Mr Wagstaff goes in goal and lets them all in, we roar until we're hoarse and it's over in seconds.'

I beam at her. 'What's not to like?'

When Cam comes belting across, his hair sticking out at even more angles than usual, his body's almost non-existent under his baggy shorts and red shirt.

'Hey, Edie Browne, you came.'

'I reckon I deserve a high five for that.' As his fist hits my palm I can feel Aunty Jo's full body shudder as she takes in the state of his knees.

'If there's dirt, boys will find it.'

I need to tell her that's sexist, but Beth gets in first. 'If anything, the girls are worse, Jo.'

Cam's hitting my hip. 'I was worried you didn't play football.'

I shrug. 'I don't. Not since junior school anyway and I've no plans to play again.'

'Barney didn't tell you?' Beth's head's tilted and she's holding back a grin. 'Kids go first, then all the grown-ups have a turn too.'

'Nice try.' I grin at her. 'Me and Aunty Jo are exempt, count us out.'

'But I need you on my team.' Cam's at my elbow. 'You have to, Edie – everyone else has got teams and I haven't.'

'Fine.' If this was Barney the answer would be a big fat 'no' for sure, but with Cam it's harder to refuse. It could be worse; in year four Bella and I had a crack women's five-a-side team, we beat the boys hollow and left them for dead. It was so long ago, for once I'm glad I can't do the sums, but it can't be beyond me to boot a ball. 'Give us a shout when you want us, Cam, we'll smash this.' Aunty Jo's gold pumps are welded in first position, so I give her a nudge. 'Won't we, Aunty Jo?'

Before she can reply, Mr Wagstaff blasts on his whistle and all the kids belt across to him and line up in a disorderly queue a few yards out from the goalposts, where a woman with a ponytail in full footie kit is standing with a net of balls and a whistle of her own.

I turn to Beth, who's got children hanging off both hands. 'So *what* do we do?'

'No need to look so worried, this isn't Man United. If you yell like mad every time one of them kicks the ball you won't go far wrong. If in doubt, yell anyway.'

'If we shout "Boom!" here too, I'll be right on point.'

'Boom?' Beth looks like she hasn't got the first clue what I'm talking about.

'Isn't it a Cornish thing?' I must be less on point that I thought, but there's no time to ask more because Mr Wagstaff's backed between the goalposts, the woman blows a whistle and a small girl taps a ball that's almost as big as her. As it rolls slowly towards the line Mr Wagstaff falls in entirely the wrong direction and the whole crowd erupts and yells, 'GOAL!!!'

It happens so many more times I start staring at the sky, watching the seagulls getting blown in the wind, then Beth shakes her hand free for long enough to prod me. 'Okay, Cam's turn next.'

Barney's muttering behind me, 'Get ready, anything could happen here.'

Beth puts a hand on his arm. 'He's been much better lately.'

I give Aunty Jo a shove. 'Here we go. This is us, as loud as you like.'

I'm holding my breath, then as Cam steps back we start waving and screaming and jumping up and down. He misses the ball completely with the first kick and the crowd dissolves with a collective 'ahhh'.

As Cam's face crumples Barney groans. 'Just what we don't need.'

Beth's watching anxiously. 'No, he's holding it together.'

I have to ask. 'Doesn't he always?'

Loella raises her eyebrows. 'He has been known to go into total meltdown.'

Cam turns towards us, and Loella, who's standing beyond Beth, leans forward and gives me a shove. 'It's you he's looking at, Edie – you've got tissues, see what you can do.'

I'm dabbing my eyes because they're streaming in the wind, but Beth's nodding at me too, so I forget the mud sucking at my shoes and dash out to the middle of the pitch. I bob down, pull Cam towards me, stare straight into his eyes and try to ignore the mayhem around us.

'Okay?' It's a stupid thing to say, because he obviously isn't.

His sniff gives way to a wail. 'I can't do it, and now everybody's laughing.'

'Don't listen to them, just look at me.' What the hell is there to say about penalties? And then it hits me. 'The best pro footballers always miss first time, then it fools the keeper. That's all you did there, you didn't touch the ball.'

He scrapes his sleeve across his face. 'Really?'

I decide to spare him the embarrassment of going in with my hanky. 'Get in there for a second kick and you'll catch the keeper napping. Look at the ball then whack it, you'll have to be quick.'

'Now?' He sounds very doubtful.

'High five me first, then go for it.' I hold up my hand and as he barely taps it I turn him back onto the ball. 'Come on, Cam, we've got this.'

I'm willing him on so hard I'm barely breathing. For a second I think he's going to crumple, but I send him a manic grin and wiggle my eyebrows, and then he pulls his leg back, kicks, and this time his foot touches the ball. As it wobbles towards the goal Mr Wagstaff does a huge dive and hits the ground as the ball rolls over the line.

I can hear Aunty Jo screeching like a banshee from the sideline, I accidentally let out a couple of 'booms', and by the time she launches into a series of grand jeté leaps across the pitch to join us the roar around is so loud I'm holding my hands over my ears as I yell.

Cam's back at my side, pummelling me with his fists. 'I got my goal and I got the loudest shout.'

'Brilliant!' The wind's whipping my words away, but beyond Barney sticking his thumbs up at me I'm staring at the seagulls lined up along the fence, feathers parted to the skin by the wind, the iron grey of the sea beyond streaked with foam where the breakers are rolling towards the shore. So much for sun, sand and summer. Right now this has to be a contender for the least hospitable place in England, if not the world.

'C'mon Edie, it's your turn now.'

I punch the air. 'Wooo-hooo, bring it on.' I want to boot in my goal and get the hell off this clifftop. It's only as I turn around that I realise. Those few moments staring out to sea, I've missed the damned boat and I'm literally last in the queue. Somehow Aunty Jo's at the front, and as she waves her arms and glides forward towards the ball she could be dancing the lead in *Giselle*. No one cares that all that's missing are her point shoes and tutu because she scores. Then what looks like the whole of St Aidan follow her, balls flying in all directions, every kind of parent from yummy mummies in pink fur fabric to dads in oily overalls. And then suddenly it's my turn.

I've seen it a thousand times before, on PlayStation and *Match of the Day*, so I know what I'm doing here. So long as I ignore the distraction of Barney's cheekbones and windblown hair looking more like they belong on a Hollywood film set than an infants' footie pitch, I've got this. Or I would have, if Mr Wagstaff hadn't started showing off his keeper talents. I can't mess about if I want to score here.

My best chance is to go for power and speed and a long run up. By the time I put my ball on the spot, the ground is more slippery than an ice slide. I back half way down the pitch, sprint forward like a mad thing, then hurl myself at the ball. There's a satisfying thud as my foot hits it and as it hurtles through the air like a missile I'm still running, because my feet won't stop. Then my boots hit a huge puddle and as my feet slide out from under me I see the ball make contact, slapping Mr Wagstaff square in the face. My back thumps onto the ground and I skid feet first into the goal mouth. Then Mr Wagstaff lands on top of me, clutching his nose, which is now bleeding.

All I can think as I lie there, pressed down in the mud, staring at a hairy calf, watching drips of blood landing on my capri pants is, if I stay here a lifetime, I'll never live this down. Being accidentally sat on by some hunk is definitely more Bella's thing than mine. Where she'd lose no time jumping him, I'm too mortified by injuring him to think of anything more than groaning my apologies.

Then someone comes over and disentangles Mr Wagstaff, and as someone else comes in to mop his face Barney's pulling me up. 'Shit, Edie, I'm so sorry – tell me you didn't bang your head?'

'I'm fine. Or I am now I haven't got a hot muscly teacher pinning me down.' It was worth saying if only to see Barney's eyes almost pop. As for the mud I'm plastered in, if Aunty Jo hasn't had a dirt-induced nervous breakdown yet, she will now.

'Mr Wagstaff's the headmaster.' Cam sounds awestruck. 'You *knobbled* the headmaster, Edie.'

More importantly, I made an even bigger spectacle of *myself*.

This makes me crawling out of the garden club look like a Prosecco picnic. Thank Christmas we're not staying.

I'm picking clumps of mud off my pink and black checked jacket when I spot a guy in paint-spattered overalls disappearing over the horizon towards the playground. There was a decorator here and I missed him. This goes down as a fail in every area.

Chapter 16

Day 149: Friday, 30th March
At Periwinkle Cottage

Epic Achievement: Facing the critics.

The last couple of days, people have been calling round with random gifts. The milkman dropped off some pots of luxury apricot and mango yogurt, knocked at the door and made clear he had definitely meant to deliver them, and they weren't going to be added to the bill. Then Helen from the gardeners' came round with a jar of homemade shortbread biscuits with a pretty tartan ribbon tied around the top, and Beth called by with a bottle of five-flower pick-you-up essence and recommended we should both take double doses. When Loella dropped in on Thursday and brought some yellow fabric Aunty Jo had been admiring at the class, I had to mention it.

'We've had a lot of presents this week.'

She laughs. 'Like Beth said, there's a good side to the whole of St Aidan knowing your business.' She stops and puts her hand on my wrist as she does. 'You're a bit of a legend, ending up in the mud and all – I'll have your jacket back tomorrow.' And then, before I can say any more, she's off across the courtyard with a flap of her coat made out of coffee sacks and a cheery wave.

She's as good as her word. When she turns up with my jacket after school on Friday Cam's tagging along. He settles in what's now his usual place at the centre of the sofa, with his reading book open, waiting for Aunty Jo, and I get my spotless jacket in a zip-up Iron Maidens Cleaners cover.

She hands it across to me. 'For the record, Barney wanted to pay, but two of the assistants were at the football and they wouldn't charge.'

'Thanks, that's brill.' I'm not sure I'm comfortable with my legend status, but after the news we've just had from George that's the least of my worries.

'You're going to have to pull a whole lot out of the bag at next year's penalty shoot-out to top this.'

Aunty Jo's coming through behind Cam, carrying his juice. 'We definitely won't be around for that. After the call we've just had, it looks like we'll be selling straight away.'

Loella looks at me. 'Surely not?'

'Seeing there's no secrets in St Aidan, you might as well know. We've had some figures and there's no way we can afford to finish eight apartments in the stable yard. Aunty Jo's best bet is to sell right away at a knockdown price.' Basically, to grab her cash and get the hell out of here.

'And lose money?' Loella takes in my nod, then her frown deepens. 'I can't believe you're giving up like that, Edie.'

And I can't believe she just said that. 'Excuse me?'

'We don't walk away at the first hint of trouble in St Aidan. Weren't you in charge of the whole south-west?'

'Who said that?'

Aunty Jo winces. 'I might have . . . at the football.'

Loella's carrying on. 'Whatever the fancy title, you're a designer, you're sassy, so get on and sort it.'

'How many times do I have to explain? I'm not a designer.' I let out a groan. 'This is more than a hint of trouble, Loella, this is *no money for the job*.' In project terms, that's full scale disaster.

But in my heart I know she's partly right, I am giving up without a fight. As I was before, I'd have come up with a solution, Jeez knows what, but I would have. I used to think I was creative too; coming at things from a different angle from everyone else on a site was easily as useful as my smile. But, as I am now, I have zero ideas, even less inspiration, no contacts and hardly any energy at all. And that's on top of not being able to read and write. I'm no use to anyone and, worse, I let Aunty Jo think I could help when I couldn't at all.

'Then do a *different* job!' Loella's straight back at me, and feisty with it. 'Get around the back, look at the problem from every side. And if you still come up with nothing, *then* give up. But don't walk away now.'

Aunty Jo's joining in. 'Loella's right. I would lose money.'

Loella's eyes narrow and her voice drops. 'It's not only about the cash. Think of the good you're doing here.' She gives an imperceptible nod in Cam's direction. 'You wouldn't believe the difference you being here has made in two short weeks.' She turns back to me. 'In any case, I thought you came here to recover? Surely you can't cut that short?'

I'm shuddering at how blunt she's being. 'The sea air isn't doing me any good. I'm not exactly improving.' Which is another good reason to leave.

Loella's eyes are almost closed now. 'Hang on. If anything doesn't come easy, you duck out. You'll never make progress doing that.'

My jaw's sagging.

Aunty Jo butts in. 'She's right, Sweetpea. You haven't worked your hardest, not yet.'

Loella's hugging herself. 'We're not ganging up.' They totally are. 'But it would be a shame for all of us if you rushed off when summer's so close.'

'Well, thanks for that.' As for these legendary blue skies, I'm not holding my breath.

'You're a problem-solver. If anyone can do this, you can, I just know it.' Her eyes are shining under the dark curls of her fringe. 'Think how amazing you'll feel when you smash it.'

I wish I had a tiny bit of her optimism and confidence. But, realistically, if I did I wouldn't be hiding away here, I'd be toughing it out back in Bath.

Cam's flicking through the papers on the coffee table. 'Edie already smashed it with her pictures.' He's pointing to a seagull I'd drawn, and I'd like to hug him for sticking up for me. 'See, I told you drawing by yourself was better than colouring in.'

Loella nods. 'If you ask nicely she might make one for you too, Cam.' The 'look' she sends me over his head tells me I'm not getting a choice in this. 'What would you like yours to say?'

Aunty Jo jumps in. 'You could write *What a lovely springtime day on the hilltop barn*, and have pictures of cows and pigs and hens and llamas and buttercups.'

Cam rubs his nose as he thinks. 'Can you draw a tractor towing a grass cutter, or a baling machine?'

This is getting out of hand from every side. 'I'm better at birds. Or doughnuts.' There's one sure way of getting back control. 'How about I surprise you?'

'Good plan.' Aunty Jo nods at me then turns to Cam. 'If you're ready to read to us, maybe Edie can try a little bit too today.'

I know when I'm beaten. If my holiday's over I'm going to have to look out for myself here. 'Do we get cake after?'

'For definite.' Cam's so serious yet so cute. 'Then it's like a prize.'

I'm nodding furiously to cover up how much the shine in Cam's eyes is making my heart melt when there's a knock at the French window. I'll never be pleased to see Barney, but at least this time he saves me from getting all teary.

Aunty Jo waves for him to come in as Loella slips out. 'Barney, lovely to see you – we haven't started yet.'

Cam is clamouring at Barney's elbow as he steps inside. 'Edie Browne's making me a special drawing, only for me, but not with tractors.'

'Great.' Barney manages to get his bemused stare under control and gives Cam's shoulder a squeeze. 'You're one lucky guy, then.'

'She might make you one too – what would yours be?' Cam's hitting Barney's arm.

The beam I send him is to say 'dream on'. Anyone who calls me a burglar and takes me out to sea on false pretences doesn't deserve any favours. I may not remember a lot of things, but I'll never forget that.

Aunty Jo's chipping in. 'Something about sheep? Or caravans? Or both?'

As he gives a cough he's holding out a trug of leaves and earth. 'I'm probably okay. Actually, I brought you some periwinkles.' There's a gleam in his eye. 'That's if you can stand to see mud after the other day?'

I'm smiling at the absurd change of subject, not his attempt at a joke.

'Seashells? How very nice – what are they for then?' Aunty Jo is the one looking bemused now.

Barney shakes his head. 'Not shells – these are plants, cuttings from further along the lane. If you have other plans for the border by the house, it's fine.' Barney's shifting from foot to foot as if he doesn't quite know where to begin.

'No, definitely no plans.' I jumped in there when I didn't even mean to.

He seems happier to hear that. 'Until the previous owners got their Roundup out, the lane was always lined with blue periwinkle flowers in late spring – it's where the cottage got its name.' He stops to rub his jaw, then goes on. 'They do very well here, it would be nice to see them growing again, and March is the right time for planting.'

'Cool.' Anything that helps the sale appeal is fine by me, so I maybe need to up that. 'Great in fact.'

'I could put them in for you, it wouldn't take me long to turn the soil over.' Barney's looking less tense now he realises he's not overstepping.

'You don't mind?' He'd be on the lane, we wouldn't have to see him.

'No problem at all, I'll do that over the weekend.' He nods at the wall. 'I see you've managed the painting without me. It's quite a change – for the better.'

For once I have to agree with him. It's amazing how fear makes you get down to the job. Aunty Jo's bad news was just the push I needed to get the paint rollers out and finally overrule her on the colour. With creamy white walls the room looks much bigger, and they show off the lovely old stone fireplace and the plank cupboard doors at the side.

Aunty Jo reaches across and pats me. 'Edie's worked wonders.'

Barney looks down at Cam, who's tugging on the cuff of his denim jacket, then back at Aunty Jo. 'I take it you'll be going to the gardening club slide show this evening?'

Auntie Jo sounds hesitant. 'I'm not sure about that . . .'

'It's just Cam was wondering if Edie would be around for ice cream at the Surf Shack. As a thank you for helping out at the football.'

Aunty Jo frowns at me. 'Edie's had such a busy week.' As I open my mouth to protest she's talking over me. 'I'm under strict instructions here. If I let you get overtired, I'll have your mum to answer to, and we know how scary she can be. With all these outings and decorating too, let's see if an early night will get rid of those dark circles under your eyes.'

Thanks a bunch for that. Talking to me like a child, letting out the truth that I've got a Rottweiler for a mum *and* bringing up that my concealer's failing me. Although, when I stop to think about it, I feel shattered. And damn that I'm feeling like I'm disappointed to be missing out. It's not as if last week at the Plank Place went well. If I'm remembering rightly, it was awful.

'It's true, you mustn't overdo things, Edie.' Barney's giving Cam's hair a ruffle. 'We'll ask again another week.' And when exactly did he become the expert?

Aunty Jo's winding up. 'Well, thank you for the periwinkles, and for planting them.'

'Actually, there is something else.' Barney's looking even more uncomfortable than before.

I'm mentally rolling my eyes that he's still here, but Aunty Jo is still being lovely. 'So, is it anything we can help with?'

'Two things.' He's suddenly very direct. 'We having an Easter egg hunt on Sunday, and Cam would like you both to come. So long as you're not too tired, it starts at twelve.'

'We'll make sure we're there.' If Aunty Jo hadn't lost the use of her smiling muscles at the same time she lost Harry, I'm sure she would be beaming. 'Where is it, and how many people are coming?'

Barney takes a deep breath. 'Well, it's a long story, but before the jungle people moved into your house, Pearl lived here and she'd run the egg hunt every year since forever. After she sold, everyone wanted to carry it on, so we used the orchard at mine.'

Aunty Jo's looking thoughtful. 'You're very welcome to use the barn yard if you'd like to, and the field. Why not use the garden too?'

What just happened there? My eyes are open so wide they feel like they might pop. There are times when I'm desperate to shout out *all the words* in my head, and this is one of them. I mean, wasn't what Barney did basically someone inviting you to a party, then when you accept saying, 'Oh, by the way, it's at yours'?

Barney's straight back. 'That's really kind, but only if you're sure?'

She's nodding so hard her hair's shaking. 'It's so important to keep these village traditions alive.' She's completely overlooking that this one technically already died, and that it'll die all over again next year because Aunty Jo will be gone. She's turning to me now. 'We'll get straight onto this, won't we, Edie? We need to order some chocolate.'

Barney cuts in. 'Don't worry about eggs, everyone brings some.'

It's hard to hold Aunty Jo back. 'We can't have it without fluffy chicks, and it'll be way more fun with bunnies.' There's a gleam of excitement in her eyes. 'And bunting. We'll need lots of bunting.'

I can't hold in my groan. 'It's a few minutes in St Aidan, Aunty Jo, not Mardi Gras in Rio.' I was always surprised that one wasn't on Marcus's 'must do' list, but thinking about it, he didn't do mass enjoyment, he much preferred to go for things other people hadn't done yet.

As for Barney's part in this, what *is* he thinking, taking advantage of a sad, vulnerable person like Aunty Jo? As for me, I've got to pull a lot more than an Easter bunny out of my magician's hat if I'm going to save Aunty Jo.

Chapter 17

Day 151: Sunday, 1st April
The Easter Egg Hunt at Periwinkle Cottage

Epic Achievement: An epic idea.

I must still have some of my persuasive super powers left, because I manage to talk Aunty Jo out of her plans to buy enough bunting to decorate most of St Aidan. Instead we settle on one Happy Easter banner, and Barney gets out his ladders and hangs it across the entrance to what we now call 'the barn yard'. When we spot the first children wandering along the lane to the Easter egg hunt late on Sunday morning and go out to join them, the fluttery yellow flags of the banner are blowing against a sky the colour of cornflowers and the white fluffy clouds racing across it are like something out of a picture book.

I nudge Aunty Jo. 'And finally . . .'

'What is it now, Chickpea?' She's in a bit of a flap, due to hosting. She's also reverted to the pet names she used when I was six, and I'll be talking to her about that later. We've been up since the crack of dawn, sorting out eggs and mini cakes and paper egg collecting bags, and clearing back the chairs to make more room in the garden room.

I lift up my sunnies and grin at her. 'Only that the sea is blue.' Since I arrived it's been heavy and brooding and angry, but today it's the colour of duck eggs, and the shimmer of sun on water is taking my breath away.

'Right.' For someone who's retired to the coast, she shows very little interest in the ocean.

Loella's striding towards us, surrounded by a crowd of children, all bobbing around. 'Hey, you two look spectacular. Well done for getting into character – you might want to put your hoods and ears up now everyone's arriving.'

She's talking about what I thought was Aunty Jo's April Fool's joke, because that's what they were talking about on Breakfast TV when she walked in with the parcel. It took a while to sink in that she was seriously expecting *me* to get into the rabbit onesie she pulled out, and the only thing she'd back down on was letting me have the grey one instead of the pink. If she'd only let me into the secret earlier, we could have saved her cash and used our new decorating suits instead and got some bunny-ear headbands. I can't remember if I ever knew what colour Easter bunnies should be, but I'm certain white ones would have worked just as well. From now on, we have to seek out the cheapest option every time.

Beth's collecting the children as they arrive, and sending them towards the garden. 'Okay, you're all going into Aunty Jo's conservatory to begin with, for your first surprise.' She turns to look at me over their heads. 'We've been coming to Pearl's egg hunts since we were kids, it's lovely it's happening again.'

The plan is that while Beth and Aunty Jo give all the kids their own fluffy chicken, complete with a blue periwinkle-coloured bow around its tiny neck – that came from me, I might have lost it in a lot of areas but I'm totally on it on this – the adults will hide the eggs they've brought. Much as I love Tiddlywink and Wilf, I kept well away from Marcus's friends' babies so, apart from Cam,

I haven't had much to do with kids at all. Obviously I chickened out of ten minutes in a room full of excited ones and got myself on the egg-hiding team instead so I'm currently lugging around my weight in chocolate in a couple of smart black and white checked M&S carrier bags.

If the down side of dressing up is that I look like a rabbit, the advantage is that once I pull my hood up, as I dash around poking eggs into holes in the stone walls and behind the plant pots and buckets in the garden, I'm getting a few cheery waves but it's obvious that without my check coat the people I know by sight don't have a clue I'm me. It's worth the indignity of looking like I escaped from a Beatrix Potter film set to avoid any wisecracks about my mud bath at the football. When I've got rid of the first bag of eggs I move on from the garden to the barn yard and my second bag is soon empty too.

As Loella hurries towards me with the crowd of mums and dads, she's flapping an empty egg bag too. 'Okay, brace yourself, I can hear the squeals, they're on their way.'

What happens next is like a stampede as children of all ages and sizes come careering into the courtyard, bobbing down, scouring the ground, peering into all the nooks and cracks, whooping every time they find chocolate.

Loella sidesteps to avoid a group of little figures who almost look too young to walk, but hare past us anyway with one worried-looking dad in pursuit. She steers me towards the tree at the end of the courtyard. 'If we all stand back here we're less likely to get trampled and I can tell you who the parents are as they come in.'

'Any decorators who work for free, introduce me right away.'

'Nice try.' She laughs. 'With all St Aidan's holiday lets, decent painters are rare as rocking horse shit. It's the same with all the building trades. Beth's Morgan's booked up for the next two years.'

'Right.' I'm so stunned my knees feel like they're going to give way, but why haven't I thought of that? Obviously it matters less if there's no money to pay them, but if the quest wasn't stuffed before, it is now.

Loella's oblivious to my silent nervous breakdown. 'On the other hand, if you're looking for smelly bath stuff that's better than Lush so you can relax and forget your decorating worries, see Maggie in the gold trainers. Charlie in the denim micro mini teaches part-time and makes waistcoats and sells them around the festivals. Nance with the double buggy works with concrete and makes table lamps and planters, Penny in the blue Doc Martens does vegan cakes, and the one who looks like she walked off a Nordic drama is Ebba.'

I'm keeping the conversation going even though my world just caved in. 'She's into Danish style?'

Loella gives me a nudge. 'The huge cashmere shrug and those knitted slipper boots give it away, don't they? She's the queen of homemade Hygge, she sells it from her Facebook page.'

'Thanks for the lowdown. At least now I'll know where to go if we need chunky cushions and driftwood mirrors.' Luckily for me, I don't have to worry about keeping out of Barney's way because Aunty Jo nabbed him to be on duty with her in the garden, along with Beth's dad, Malcolm, who apparently wouldn't stay away. 'So are all your friends into handmade products then?'

She shakes her head. 'No, that was just a craft cluster. In the next group there's a conveyancing clerk, Jill from the checkout at B&Q, the waitress from the Cupcake Café, and the ladies from Iron Maidens.'

Beth's making her way across to us. 'Have you noticed, it's very strategic? Some of the kids go slowly and cover every inch of the garden before they leave, then others go as fast as they can to where no one else has been yet.' She steps out to stop a girl with a glittery flamingo on the back of her denim jacket. 'No, it isn't kind to take them from the little ones, Mia.'

The girl pushes back her braids and smiles at her. 'Actually, I'm helping Tallulah to carry them, they were very heavy for her.'

Beth growls under her breath. 'Unlikely.' Then she carries on, 'I'm sure Tally can manage fine on her own, Mia.'

'Nice jacket.' My last Paper Moon site notebook had flamingoes all across the cover. It's probably in Dad's garage, still where I left it in the passenger footwell of my car, along with my hard hat and my pink high-vis Zinc Inc body warmer.

Loella gives a grimace. 'Mia's mine, she's got an answer for everything. And the flamingo's also one of mine.'

Beth laughs. 'If you want one, just look on Etsy – she does them in adult sizes as well, or for slightly less she'll embroider on the jacket of your choice.'

'So where do all you craft people work then?' It's another automatic pilot question. There were lots of crafters in the converted warehouse where Marcus had his office; it went with the 'on trend' territory.

Loella's voice rises in surprise. 'At home – why, where else would we do it?'

'That can't be very practical.'

'It isn't, but none of us are exactly earning enough to sign up for a long-term lease.'

I'm puzzling, trying to remember. 'In Bristol they have flexible work spaces. You can rent a desk for half an hour, or an office for a day.'

Beth gives a chortle. 'Bliss – in twenty years' time when St Aidan catches up we'll be first in the queue.'

I'm staring at the new plank doors around the barn yard, and my heart is starting to thump against my ribs. If we're aiming for holiday lets they need massive amounts of cash and builders' time to finish them, but if we use them as basic work spaces they're almost complete as they are.

'I can't believe I didn't see it before.' I'm croaking again, this time because my throat is dry with nerves. 'Why wait twenty years? The stables here would make perfect spaces for crafters.'

Beth turns and peers through a window. 'Now you're talking – what's inside?'

'They've all got wood-burners, bare walls, wet rooms with loos and basins but no tiles, and kitchen spaces with a sink but nothing else yet.'

A smile spreads across Loella's face. 'This is why I didn't want you to give up before – I knew you'd come up with a solution. Obviously you'd have to sort it with the planners, but the spaces here would suit small businesses down to the ground.'

It's a total accident that I've hit on this. 'So, with minimal work, when Aunty Jo comes to sell we could market them as craft units with the potential to be holiday lets if the next owner wanted that.' I'm mentally punching the air. Something finished and ready to go has so much more value. But it would be even better if they're proven. 'Would you be willing to try them out?'

Loella's hugging herself. 'There's a buyer in London who'd like ten of my bed quilts, but if I tried making those at home, with six of us in the house I'd end up smothering someone.'

Beth's eyes are gleaming. 'But if you had a stable to work in for a few weeks you'd knock them out no problem and have enough to pay for rent too.'

Loella's almost talking to herself. 'It's a no-brainer, I'm in. How soon can I start?' As Beth scowls at her, her eyes flash open. 'Oh, shit, Edie, I didn't mean . . . if that's offensive, I'm *so, so* sorry.'

'No, some days I do actually feel like I have no brain.'

Beth's shaking her head. 'Take no notice, Edie. With a brainwave like you just came up with, I'd say you're not doing so badly. Taking it a step further, we all know Josie could do with the money, and this would give a temporary cash flow without tying her in.'

Somehow it's great to find someone who will come straight out and joke around about my problems instead of tiptoeing. In my head I'm doing cartwheels and high fiving myself for hitting gold, when it suddenly hits me. 'Except . . .' I'm remembering the rubble piles and the bare walls. 'If you're going to sew in there I'll have to get them cleared and whitewashed first. So we're back to those elusive decorators.'

Beth's beside me in a second. 'If that's all, there isn't a problem. Get us the paint, we'll soon have that sorted.'

'We'll have to run all this past George, but if you clear and paint them you could have them rent-free for a while at least.' I might be getting ahead of myself here, but I'm seeing crafters spilling out onto the barn yard from every door. It could be a complete crafting community.

Loella's got her nose on the glass. 'That sounds good to me. You get a stable sorted, I get my quilts made, we're all happy. And Beth can do the same.' She closes her hand over something on the stone sill. 'Better still, I just found chocolate.' She drops a foil-covered egg into each of our hands.

'Aren't they for the kids?'

Beth laughs. 'They had their chance, these are ours now. What better way to seal the deal than with chocolate eggs?'

Loella's peeling off the shiny green paper. 'We won't tell if you don't. They're melting in the sun, careful you don't mess up your bunny outfit, Edie.'

Beth's giggling. 'You'll have to excuse Lo, she has this horrible habit of talking to us all like we're her three-year-olds.'

Somehow I don't mind at all. Being included in the 'us' gives me a warm glow in my middle. It's so long since I did something as simple as standing with people, laughing in a patch of sunlight. Aunty Jo is lovely. But when I don't go to work and don't see my friends any more, even though I'm never actually on my own, there are times I do get very lonely. Having people around the barn yard will be great for that too.

Loella jumps. 'Watch out – Josie's coming now.' She's looking at me expectantly.

'I'll tell her later when we're back at the cottage so I can explain it properly.' When she's less uptight about having hordes of children careering around her barn yard. When she's relaxing over her chicken with apricots, done in the slow cooker, looking forward to *The Nutcracker* or *Dancers With No Talent*.

'Good plan.' Beth gives my arm a little punch, then starts to smile again.

Aunty Jo is coming towards us, taking tiny steps over the gravel in her coral pumps, still with her ears up. There are children running beside her, all tapping her legs, holding out their bags to get her attention. It's only as she spins around we get the full benefit of the damage.

'Look at that chocolate hand-print on her bottom. I'll save that for later too.' I wrinkle my nose.

Beth's smiling at Aunty Jo. 'They've all had a wonderful time, Josie. Thank you so much, it's been just like old times – only better.'

Even though she's not exactly smiling, Aunty Jo's cheeks are as rosy as her velvet suit, and that has to be down to pleasure as much as her onesie overheating.

I smile at her too. 'Time to go home?' There's a catch in my voice as I say it, because I'm so happy to see her enjoying herself.

She suddenly frowns and points at one tiny smear on my leg. 'Oh my, you should have had a tan suit, Honeybunny, how *did* you get so much chocolate on you?'

I have to bite my tongue to stop myself saying, *You too*. 'I'm good with grey.'

'Well, bear that in mind for next year.'

I absolutely won't and neither will she, for that matter, but I don't say that either.

Her tone is bright. 'Anyway, we're all going to Barney's yard for more juice. And then . . .' she stops for dramatic effect '. . . and then he's going to show us his caravans. I can't believe I've been here all this time and have never seen them.'

Now I've heard it all.

Chapter 18

Day 151: Sunday, 1st April
At Barney's barns

Epic Achievement: Not being rude about shepherd's huts (eye roll).

It might sound harsh, but if Aunty Jo wasn't interested in shepherd's huts the first day, I'm not sure why she suddenly wants to see them all this time later. It's highly unlikely anyone would *suddenly* develop a burning interest in anything on wheels, let alone huts. I'd think it's one of those things a bit like short sight or a heart murmur; you either have it, or you don't. It doesn't just arrive late one morning, no matter how sunny the day is. It's like the Easter eggs had fairy dust sprinkled on them.

After all the excitement of the egg hunt and my brainwave for the barn yard, I'm past ready for some time out. I take in a breath and try to plunder my memory for the right persuasive words that will speed us back to the day room, two frothy hot chocolates, some real-life clothes and a lippy rescue. It's funny, when you don't give a damn the phrases come tumbling out. The minute you care, it's like there's chicken soup in your head and dry grass in your throat. I'm still racking my brain when there's a tug on my sleeve.

'Cam!' I can see his hair is even spikier than usual. 'Having a good time?'

There are chocolate smears on his cheeks and Robert the dog is running alongside his ankles. 'We're going to *our* house now.' He's squinting in the bright light. 'I've been doing pictures, I'll show you if you like.'

'Brill!'

Loella winks at me as he runs off. 'Looks like you can't escape, but don't worry, you'll love Barney's barns.'

If they belonged to anyone else, I'm sure I would. At least with the crowds it'll be easy to keep out of his way. Every time I see him I stuff up in some spectacular way. Throw in a onesie too, and it's like I'm fighting him with my ankles tied together then adding in a blindfold.

Loella puts Tally down, takes her hand and slides her other arm through mine. 'This way, come on.' As we watch Cam dodging ahead, she's guiding me further along the lane, past the field behind Aunty Jo's biggest barn and around the side of a bulky stone building with a high slate roof that's shining in the sun. As we round the corner she slows down and grins at me. 'There, so tell me what you think.'

There are long tall buildings on two sides, with lots of glass and grey paint and wriggly metal, and beyond the central flagged area there's a broad field with trees, their branches dark against the pearly blue of the sky, and neat wriggly tin shepherd's huts with criss-cross windows and wooden steps up to their plank doors, dotted in the spaces between the boughs. And, as if that wasn't already enough, there are drifts of daffodils nodding in the wind.

'It's nice . . .' Okay, I give in. 'Amazing, even.' And so much slicker and tidier than Aunty Jo's barn yard with its rubbish piles and wood stacks.

Loella's nodding. 'I told you it was worth a visit. We used to come scrumping for apples in the orchard here when we were kids. It'll be even nicer in a few weeks when the blossom comes out. Barney's split the buildings into live-work units, and what about those shepherd's huts?'

'They look very rustic among the trees.' Okay, I admit, they do look as if they belong there, but it'll take more than a scene of rural idyll to convert me. If you were being mean you'd say they look a lot like the love child of Thomas Hardy and a Hoseasons holiday park. But as I can't even say 'excuse me, but let's go home instead' I probably haven't got a hope in hell of unleashing a thought that complicated into the world today.

And if I was expecting colours, I'm disappointed again. 'They're very, er . . . grey.'

'That's the undercoat – come and have a quick peep inside.'

There's no point declining because she's already steered me across the grass and is climbing the plank steps to an open door. As I gaze in at the sea of ply and boarding, I'm struggling for something positive to say. 'It's . . . er . . . woody. I'm sure pretty curtains will transform it.'

'He sells them unfinished, then people paint them once they take them home.' She's smiling at me. 'I can tell you're not convinced.'

'It's that obvious?'

'It's taken a lot of work for Barney to get this up and running, it's nice to acknowledge how well it's turning out.' If we're talking fan girls, she's up there with Aunty Jo. We veer back towards the crowd and she points us towards a broad trestle table where all the dads are clustered. 'Let's get a drink, and then you can admire Cam's artwork and make a run for it.'

As I pick a cucumber slice out of my glass of fruit cup, with my rabbit hood still firmly up I'm feeling fabulously anonymous and standing slightly apart from the crowd. Whatever Loella says about rocking horses, I'm still listening out.

There's a nudge on my hip and I look down to see Cam, clutching a handful of paper.

'I've been doing tractors with writing.'

I smile and take the sheets he's holding out, then sit down on a step to leaf through them. 'Brill, that's a great tractor, I love the wheels.'

He laughs. 'That's not a tractor! Can't you see, it's Loella's truck?' He's reading for me as I pore over each picture. 'Driving my tractor . . . on Cam's farm . . . hurry hurry hurry . . . all the mud . . .'

There's a cough above our heads. 'That one was my idea.'

Attention-seeking, and trying to take the credit? 'Barney, hi . . . Thanks for the . . . er . . . drink.' I hold up my glass and stare at it as I flounder to find the right name.

Cam cuts in and saves me. 'It's punch – we made it from apple juice and lemonade and it's got cucumber and strawberries.'

'It's great.' I beam and hope there's at least *some* lippy left. Even if he's smoking hot, and smart enough to make these super-stylish barns, there's no need for me to feel completely inadequate. At least I can smile when he can't. 'I never had it with strawberries before.'

Barney's leaning one denim-clad shoulder against the wall of his barn. 'Well, it's firsts all round then. I never saw an Easter rabbit in sunglasses either.'

Oh my. Not funny, and not that clever either. I have a feeling my face is flushing as red as Aunty Jo's.

'All these people – shouldn't you be off working the crowd? There must be someone here in the market for a shepherd's hut.' It's not brilliant, but it's the best I can come up with at short notice. I make a mental note to gather more Barney comebacks.

If I make them in advance, I'm more likely to get them out in an emergency.

'Good thinking, thanks for refocusing me, Edie Browne . . .' there's the hint of a twist to his mouth '. . . or should that be "Honeybunny"? I'm sure I heard Aunty Jo calling you that before?'

There are moments when you want to disappear into the air in a puff, like that pantomime with the person with the coach and horses, and the pumpkin and the missing shoe. And this is one of them.

Now would be the perfect moment to say 'love you, bye' and dash, but for some reason my legs won't push me up to standing.

Chapter 19

Day 154: Wednesday, 4th April
In the barn yard

Epic Achievement: Avoiding an emergency call-out.

The daytime classes at The Deck have stopped while the children are on Easter holiday. But Aunty Jo loves the idea of Loella and Beth finishing a stable unit each in return for using them for a while, so on Tuesday we head off to the builders' merchant to get paint. Then, on Wednesday, Beth, Loella and so many people they could easily pass for rent-a-crowd all appear on the lane, armed with brushes and picnic baskets. From the amount of food in them it looks like they're thinking this will be a long job. The plan is – and yes, we finally have one – that if Beth and Loella try them out and find the spaces are good, we'll spread the word to more crafters.

When I go down to the stables early on Wednesday afternoon, I pick my way through the crowd of paint-spattered children running across the yard, then wander through the first open door and see that most of the rubbish has already been cleared and there's already whitewash on the walls.

'My, Loella, if this was a Zinc Inc site I'd be questioning the ethics of child exploitation.'

Loella steps back, paintbrush in hand. 'It's the best fun they've had in ages, but they were on a promise, weren't they, Barney?'

As she looks past me I turn and see him finding a comfortable place to lean his shoulder on the door frame.

He looks across at me. 'That's if you're up for taking them out, Edie?'

'Me?'

'No water or competitive sport, dressing as a rabbit is optional, and we'll only take in a mud run if you insist.' He seems to pick up that I'm about to tell him to eff off because he stops and begins again. 'It has to be you. Everyone else is busy . . .'

Busy helping me with my quest. That's the subtext. I'm not exactly happy, but I can't argue. Which is why, not long later, I'm bouncing along in the front seat of Loella's truck, looking across at Barney tapping those beautiful fingers of his on the very big steering wheel.

'Shania Twain, *very* loud – is that the best you can do?'

Barney shrugs. 'The cassette's jammed in the player. It's a choice between "silent" and "burst your eardrums", and Loella's the only one who knows how to switch it on and off.'

'So we're stuck with it?'

'Right answer.'

At a rough estimate, half the school are in the back with us. They're word perfect on every track, and all yelling at the top of their voices.

I'm shaking my head. '*Man! I Feel Like a Woman*? Is that even suitable for seven-year-olds?'

Barney shoots me a glance across the dash. 'Who knows, but it's indirectly your fault.' He pulls down the corners of his mouth. 'Loella only turns it on when she's super happy, and that's down to you.'

'So it's the opposite of a silver lining. What the hell is that called?'

'Don't ask me, I'm just the driver. Luckily we're not going far.' And with that he pulls off into a gravelled parking area. 'Is this okay for you?'

It's only when I hear a cheer from the back I realise he's not just talking to me. As the kids spill out of the truck I'm staring out across a very stony beach to a silver-streaked expanse of sea beyond and a sky that's the kind of blue with fluffy clouds that you might find in a picture book. 'I thought you said we weren't going to the sea?'

'We're not, we're going rock scrambling.' He holds up his hand, and all the kids come running. 'Okay, watch out for each other, stay close together and we'll work our way along.'

Mia's holding Cam's hand and jumping up and down. 'Can we go all the way to the creek?'

Barney locks the car and slings a rucksack on his back. 'Sure, wait for us if you get there first.'

Cam's still serious. 'What about the tree?'

'We can do that too.'

Mia's smiling down at him. 'But only if you're feeling really brave.'

Cam stands up straighter. 'This time I will be.'

And then they're gone, hurling themselves down onto the path and along to the rocks.

Where the bay at St Aidan is broad and soft and sandy, here the shore is gritty sand, dotted with black rocks and stones. Where the cliffs rise and run in and out along the beach edge the scattered rocks become boulder piles.

'So what are we doing here?' I'm picking my way across a shiny black rock shelf, slithering between the salt puddles, the wind battering my ears as I shout across to Barney.

'Just making our way along, taking whichever route we fancy. The older ones go clambering over the bigger rocks, but if you're not up for adventure we'll stay down here where it's flatter.'

'On balance, I feel more secure on pavements.' I catch the tail-end of an eye roll as he turns around.

'You're such a townie.'

I've come a few steps and my legs are already aching. 'Is Cam okay?'

'We'll soon hear about it if he's not.' Barney closes his eyes momentarily. 'He's usually the first one moaning, it's nice for him there's someone slower.'

If that's a jibe, I ignore it. 'Does he get upset a lot?'

Barney's bouncing from stone to stone with long, easy strides. 'He's better than he was, but he loses it at school over the smallest things.'

I know where he's coming from on that. When I first found I couldn't tie laces I felt like banging my head on the wall. 'They probably seem big to him.'

He lets out a sigh. 'Yet at home we were living in a building site and it didn't bother him at all.'

I let out a groan. 'The joys of going up ladders instead of stairs and crawling over rubble piles to get into bed.'

'You've done it then?'

Damn for letting that out. 'A while ago, in Bristol, the house belonged to my partner.'

'And?'

'It's a long story.' However much I'm accidentally spilling, I'm not up for telling him how I met Marcus. Zinc Inc had a project in Clifton where we were gutting and extending a terrace house. Marcus was living in an identical house further down the street, also ripe for restoration, and, needless to say, he talked/charmed/blagged his way in to see what we were doing. It was always my last call of the afternoon, and after lying in wait so he could 'accidentally' bump into me so many times we started to laugh about it. He suggested supper at the bistro round the corner, and we went from there.

'It's a long beach.' Barney gives a shrug.

'You know what it's like . . . You spend every free hour for years knocking down walls, trawling reclamation yards . . .' If I wasn't leaping from rock to rock there's no way I'd share, but somehow with every spring another secret's spilling. 'You pour in your whole heart . . . make the place fabulous . . . all on a shoestring . . . then you split up.' Probably because I'd done so much of the physical work, when I moved out it felt like I left a big part of me there too.

'That must have been tough.' He's tilting his head as he looks back at me. 'So there *was* a Mr Browne then?'

How did we get to this? 'Only in that I did once live with my boyfriend, who's now my ex.' I need to turn this around. 'So what about you?'

'I had my share of rolls in the hay, then things got complicated.'

As Cam's waving at us from the top of a distant boulder, he could spare us that particular detail. 'I was thinking more about your barn conversion.'

He pulls a face. 'We're going to the creek, not all the way around Britain, so I'll give you the short version.'

I never knew slithering across rocks would be so tiring. Maybe it's because I've got to keep up with a load of hyperactive kids and Superman's giant strides, but by the time we get to where the kids have come to a halt in a cluster I've barely replied to Barney and I'm panting to get my breath back. I know Barney told them to stop at the creek, but they don't have a choice because the river gushing across in front of us flows all the way across the shingle and down to the sea.

Barney looks at a huge mound of rocks on the shore side. 'Okay, let's go up. Remember, little steps let you balance better, and don't kick stones on the people behind you.'

I let out a squeak. 'We're going all the way up *there?*'

'It's not far.' There's another barely concealed eye roll. 'Relax, Edie, you might even enjoy it.'

'I'm not sure.'

There's a line between Barney's eyebrows. 'How are you such a wuss, I thought you jumped out of a plane?'

Another story that's too long to tell. 'That was different, back then I had a lot to prove.'

Barney's voice goes up. 'Like *what*?'

'I was proving life was wonderful.' At the time it actually was.

Barney's muttering. 'Let me guess, for your ex's benefit?'

Cam's got his hands on his hips and his cheeks are pink. 'It's easy-peasy, Edie, there's lots of handholds, me and Mia will show you.'

If it's a choice between justifying myself to Barney, or following Cam up a cliff-face, give me the scramble every time. It turns out to be a lot less steep than it looks, and a few minutes later, with most of my nails still intact, I'm rolling onto the level ground at the top, with a sea of faces to cheer me to my feet.

Then a cry goes up. 'Now for the tree!'

Not that I'm intending to climb any higher than I am, but as I get up I scour the skyline for branches to be sure, and the highest thing I spot are a clump of bushes.

'So what tree is this?'

Mia's waiting as the others dash upstream. 'It's further along – it's a huge one that's fallen across the creek.'

She skips ahead, grabs the rucksack from Barney, then clambers onto a massive fallen trunk that spans the stream rushing below. She's so sure-footed, she doesn't even hold on or look down at the torrent of water in the gorge underneath; she just springs across the bough, and jumps down on the opposite bank.

She's laughing at us from the other side. 'Anyone who wants chocolate has to come over here.'

As I watch them all make their way across, for the first time in my life I can see the advantage that I can't be bribed by cocoa any more.

Cam and I are the last ones standing by the tree roots and I look down at him. 'Shall I help you up?'

Mia's calling again. 'Come on, Cam, you can do it, you're big now.'

'I'm scared.' As he looks at me the sadness in his eyes makes me want to hug him. 'But if I don't go they'll think I'm a jellyfish.'

I don't blame him, that's the last place I'd want to go. 'How about we both shuffle over together?' I really didn't mean to say that, but I doubt he'll take me up on it.

Barney's calling across. 'Great idea, let Edie go behind you, and I'll come and help you from this side.'

Mia's calling again. 'You're big and brave now, Cam, of course you can do it.'

As Cam looks up at me his eyes are wide. 'Okay.'

It's the wrong answer, but as I heave him up I'm talking myself through this as much as him. 'See, the bark's nice and rough and not slippery at all, we can lie on our tummies and wiggle across. Take as long as we like. The tree's huge, it's completely safe.'

Cam's horizontal, arms clamped around the trunk, inching forwards.

As I scramble up behind him, the green streaks I'm picking up on my washed jeans from the mossy bark are the least of my worries. 'Great, Cam, keep going, we've got this.' We haven't, it's bullshit, but somehow I'm following him because his little moans won't let me do anything else. 'Hold on tight.'

It feels more like eternity than the length of a tree, and I can hear Barney coaxing him all the way.

'Half way, Cam, that's brilliant. You can come a bit faster now, come to me, a little bit more, and you'll be touching my hand.'

And then there's a roar and a whoop, and Cam's made it to the other side.

'Edie?'

It's Barney. I'm not sure if the roaring is coming from the water below or the blood rushing through my ears. All I know is, my eyes are screwed shut and my arms are clamped tight around the tree trunk and my legs feel like they've frozen. And I can't stop shaking.

'Move, Edie.'

My jaw is juddering, but somehow I force the words out. 'I'm t-t-too scared.' Out in the middle over the water, and I can't go forward, and I can't go back. I let out a wail. 'It's like my life in a microcosm, I'm shit at everything now.'

'That's not true, Edie. You're absolutely fine, we've totally got this.'

My mind's whipping through the possibilities and it's stopped at a rope and a winch. 'It might be best to call the air-sea h-h-helicopter?'

There's something that sounds like a low laugh, then a creak, and a thud, and when I open my eyes a tiny crack I'm staring at denim. As the view slides into focus, I'm beyond appalled to find what I'm looking at is Barney's crotch a hand width from my eyes.

'Waaaahhhhh.'

I couldn't have woken up faster if I'd had a whiff of smelling salts. Then I'm feeling those broad thumbs wrapping around my forearms and easing up to my shoulders.

'Right, Edie, I've got you, you're not going anywhere, we're going to take this one tiny push at a time.' There's something so re-assuring in the low resonance of his voice, it makes five-flower calming essence seem like nothing.

It's a shame Bella's not here, she'd max out on a view like this without her insides curling up with guilt.

'Thanks, panic over.' As I start to ease my chin across the bark, and my limbs begin to unfreeze, I'm hoping no one thinks this was an attention-seeking stunt. However much we laughed over naked fireman calendars back in the day, being rescued isn't my thing.

By the time I've reached the safety of the far bank, it's an embarrassing amount of time later and the kids have eaten all the chocolate. But they give me a huge cheer, I get high fives from everyone, and at least I've impressed Cam. Even more embarrassing than what went before is when everyone insists on coming back with me over a footbridge which is no distance at all up the creek. I can't believe I'm proving to be more of a liability than the children I'm supposed to be taking care of. On the up side, I doubt Barney will be dragging me out of my comfort zone again any time soon.

*

I'm not the only one to have had an exciting time. When I finally make it back to Aunty Jo's garden room it looks like there's been some kind of fabric eruption, and all the kids who weren't out on the rock scramble are pulling on their jackets, about to leave. As they rush for the door I join in the tidying, picking up the last of Aunty Jo's pins.

'So many people – and then it's just the two of us.' She gives me a hard stare. 'Look at you with those roses in your cheeks, Loella said you'd had a noisy afternoon too?'

'Pretty much.' As I smooth my fingers across the throb in my temples I'm kicking myself for being wet and weedy as well as a jellyfish, but I'm also pleased that's the only part of the afternoon Aunty Jo's found out about.

Her eyes narrow. 'We should try you with meditation, you'd find it very soothing to let the tension go, and empty your mind.'

'Maybe.' By which I mean, *Totally not*. She seems to be

overlooking that I'm actually trying to fill my mind up again, not throw stuff out of it.

As she takes the pin cushion from me and puts it in her work basket, her voice is all warm. 'Well, that afternoon sewing with the small ones made me feel marvellously artistic and very wanted. It's a long time since I felt that.'

'That's nice.' I smile and give her hand a squeeze. '*I* need you every day, you know that?' I know she can be sharp, and we both try to pretend it's the other way around, but I lose count of the times she quietly has my back.

'Thank you, Sweetpea, we make a good team.' She's folding the last of her fabric pieces. 'Did you and Marcus ever think of children, then?'

'Us?' Her question makes me gulp so hard I almost choke. 'Not. No. Definitely not.' Even if she hadn't caught me off guard, it's definitely in the 'too difficult' box for now, but I throw out a last thought. 'I'm not keen.'

She looks thoughtful. 'Children have a wonderful way of challenging you. They shake up your thinking and keep you young, when you get to my age, that's no bad thing.'

I shrug. 'I like the ones I know, like Tiddlywink and Wilf, and Cam. And Mia. But if I think of having any of my own it scares the bejesus out of me.'

She's patting my hand now. 'You shouldn't write them off, that's all I'm saying.'

'Great. I'll keep an open mind on that then.' I'm looking at her. 'If I ever find another partner.'

'I'm so sorry, Edie, I didn't mean to bring that up.' Aunty Jo clasps her hands together. 'Let's talk about something nicer.'

'Like what?'

She takes a deep breath. 'Like how much I'm looking forward to life drawing tomorrow.'

It comes out as a shriek. 'Where did *that* come from?'

'Sorry, I thought you heard. Loella can't always find a model, but her best one's unexpectedly available tomorrow, so we have to get easels and sketchpads at the ready.'

It's a faint hope, but it's worth clinging on to. 'But we don't *have* easels.' I'm not sure they're essential, but I'm not sure Aunty Jo knows that.

'Don't worry, Chickpea, I'm sure by tomorrow evening they'll be here.'

Chapter 20

Day 155: Thursday, 5th April
At The Deck Gallery

Epic Achievement: Remembering forsythia is a flower that's yellow.

So this is how the conversation went between Aunty Jo and me, as we unpacked the easels . . .

Aunty Jo: 'You don't look very happy about coming to life drawing, Sweetpea?'

Me: 'That's because I'm not.'

Aunty Jo: 'When we lived in Harpenden, Harry wasn't ever keen on me going. It's a bit like being a suffragette – when you've had to fight for the vote it feels wrong when someone who can take advantage doesn't seize the opportunity.'

Me: 'Sorry?' I got as far as Harpenden, or maybe Harry.

Aunty Jo: 'You need to come, Edie. Simply because you can.'

Me: 'Huh?'

Aunty Jo: 'If you don't like it, then next time we go . . .'

Me, shuddering: 'There's going to be a *next time?*'

Aunty Jo: 'Of course there is, we've got the easels now. But if you really don't want to, then you could always pop along to that Plank Place with Cam and Barney for some of that nice ice cream instead.'

So this is what I'm dealing with. Sometimes Aunty Jo is a complete treasure, then others she entirely loses her grip on the reality of what I'm thinking. The good thing about this evening is that Barney himself won't be anywhere near The Deck tonight, because he'll be safely at home with Cam.

The trouble for me is that tonight brings up another one of those awful choices. The kind it's impossible to make, because *neither* outcome is ideal. Would I rather be home alone . . . or go along and risk expiring with embarrassment or suffocating with boredom? It's one thing complaining loudly in my head and kicking up a fuss about not wanting to join in. And another completely when I'm faced with the shudderingly horrible thought of being in the house on my own. Worrying what actually might happen if I start to fit and there's no one here to help. It's way worse at the cottage than down in St Aidan, because at least down there it's never too long before a dog walker comes along.

But if you take a whole life drawing class, add in chatting at the end, the journey there and back, pausing to gaze at how the moon is half hidden behind a cloud on the way across the harbourside and stopping to look up at how brightly the scattering of stars are shining against a velvet sky above the lane . . . Well, it all adds up. To way too long for me. There's actually no contest. I'm going to have to put up and shut up. And go drawing.

When Loella picks us up on the lane, at least she's turned off Shania for now. Aunty Jo clambers up into the front seat of the car and I scramble into the back, along with enough gear for a trekking expedition. Loella waits until I've pulled on my seat belt, then hands me a bunch of yellow flowers.

As she sets off down the lane she grins at me. 'I heard you're not best pleased about christening your easel drawing naked people, so I bought you daffodils and forsythia to paint instead.'

'Thanks for that.' There she goes, full of thoughts again. I've got my phrase list in my pocket too. If all else fails I'm planning to use my superior artist's charcoal – as if Aunty Jo would order anything less – to do some writing practice.

Her laugh is throaty. 'Don't worry, we don't endorse wobbly willies at the St Aidan sessions, our models always keep their boxers on.'

'You draw GUYS?' I'm embarrassed as much by my unplanned squawk as by sounding like I came out of the ark and have a world view that's tiny.

She's nodding as she wrestles the steering wheel to turn out onto the road. 'Uh-huh. We mix and match, but most of the artists are women so there is a certain appreciation for the muscular male form, although, obviously, we never objectify.' Loella nods as she wrestles with the steering wheel. 'It would be a shame not to use our lovely local collection of firemen and lifeboatmen when so many of them are happy to share their assets.'

Aunty Jo doesn't reply to that, but I hear her swallow and can sense her quietly melting into the upholstery.

When we get down to the gallery, first Loella has to find a road to block with her big red truck and then we've got to haul our giraffe-leg easels along the street, so by the time we get to The Deck a lot of the chairs are already taken. There's a screen for the model to undress behind, but the model is already stripped off, out in the open and sprawled on the floor, while Plum, in her usual paint-splashed boiler suit, directs him into his pose. The way he's sitting with one leg bent under him, the other stretched out sideways, with his back bent forwards and head bowed to the floor, I can only hope we're paying him a big supplement for discomfort in the workplace. If anyone's here looking for a muscle fix, they've certainly got them. And then some.

We wave at a couple of people we recognise, and as Aunty Jo takes off her coat she's talking in a low voice. 'Next time we might fit in better if we put some rips in your jeans.'

It's only after we've sidled into a couple of spare seats in the circle that I remember I had meant to sit as far away from Aunty Jo as possible, but it's too late to change now. Somehow, we wing it, and manage to erect our easels without looking like we haven't got the first idea what we're doing. Then Loella slips past and quietly adjusts all the bits we've accidentally put on upside down. The way she carries on a conversation with Plum and Beth over her shoulder all the time she's fiddling with the wing nuts makes me think she's the kind of supportive friend who'd adjust your princess crown to the right position without letting the world know it was crooked.

'Masking tape, Edie?' Aunty Jo dips into the bag she's brought, which is at least as big as Marcus's sports bag – in other words, humungous. Then she hands me a ring.

'Why do I want this?'

'You use it to fix your cartridge paper to your back board.' Her voice drops as she leans closer. 'I've spent the whole afternoon checking it out on YouTube. Do you know, they even have models posing on there? I've done so many practice sheets, my portfolio is bulging already.'

Which kind of begs the question, why are we actually bothering to be here? But whatever. I suppose it's similar to the difference between clicking on Street View and actually visiting a place; real life is just more, well, real. With more of those dimension things I've totally lost track of. I try not to dwell on the fact that my aunty has an expansive yet secret internet life that I am blissfully unaware of. If she were a child, I'd be reaching for the buttons that mums and dads use when they've totally got their pants in a twist about what sites their kids have been clicking onto while they've been entirely oblivious cooking fish fingers, or fairy cakes, or whatever it is parents do.

I watch her stick her paper on the propped-up board, do the same with mine, then, as I look around, Plum comes up. 'I see you're well equipped, if there's anything else you need, just shout.'

I'm about to ask for my flowers but Aunty Jo gets in first. 'So how long do you hold each pose for?'

As I take a moment to get over my surprise, Plum pushes back her dark ponytail.

'This first pose will probably be for about an hour, then we'll do a few minutes of action sequences, take a rest break, then go back for another couple of shorter ones.'

Loella checks around the other people, who are getting down to work with biros and pencils and even ink and brushes. Finally she comes over to where we're still frozen, not knowing where to begin.

She gives us an encouraging smile. 'So grab a piece of charcoal and let it make its own way around the paper. Forget about rubbing out, you have an instinctive link between your hand and your eyes, as soon as you start to draw you'll feel this getting stronger. Don't worry, just enjoy.'

I turn to Plum with what I hope is a pleading smile and whisper, 'Could you possibly pass my flowers over? On top of the bracelet display cabinet would be fine.'

Plum bobs down at my elbow. 'Just try this with me first. Look at the wonderful lines of those muscles, the play of light and shade where the ribs sweep down from the spine, the fabulous strength in that back.' She turns a lump of charcoal on one side and puts it in my hand. Then she closes hers over it, makes a couple of sweeps, then stands back.

'Wow.' There's something about the marks on the paper that exactly express what we're staring at.

'See, you've only drawn two lines, but you've already captured the feel of the figure.'

'You're right.' Except there's one unexpected problem; in my head it's not a figure, it's very definitely a man. For a moment I focus on the soft cotton stripe of the boxers. How they're looser, yet so much sexier than the tight pants that Marcus used to wear. They had different names on the elastic waist bands as the designers slid in and out of fashion. For the teensiest second I'm imagining pulling that hot stripy cotton out of the tumble dryer, my thongs clinging to the inside. The crackle of the static as I peel them free and put them on my own knicker pile. Then I give myself a good mental telling off because if objectification's banned, who knows what the punishment for personification is? If they had so much as a fabric conditioner whiff of my washday fantasy they'd probably push me off the end of The Deck balcony, into the oblivion they save for artists with inappropriate thoughts and dirty minds.

I go back to the charcoal. Concentrate really, really, really hard on the knobbles of the backbone, the way I can see the ribs moving ever so slightly up and down as he breathes, the ragged curls of hair at the nape of the neck, and make a sweep of my own. If there's another shiver down my own spine as I notice the tautness of the fabric over the buttocks, I promise to give myself a slap on the wrist later for that.

'Nice work.' Plum's so close I can hear her breathing too but there's no tingle from that. 'If you concentrate and let yourself go at the same time, you get to a kind of dream state, and that can be really beneficial for freeing up the brain's pathways. A good life drawing session can actually be as replenishing as meditation.'

I'm hoping Aunty Jo took note of that. If it's a choice between drawing my own foot or emptying my mind muttering mantras, I know which I'd rather do. Even better, I might be able to draw them with my shoes on.

This actually isn't the first time I heard this. Bella and Tash were both on FaceTime last night, telling me about the benefits, and how life drawing can improve your critical thinking skills and your emotional well-being too. And I can't turn down anything that helps my head. Although, thinking about it, that was Tash. Bella was more into the immediate delights of drawing hot people in general.

Loella's beside me. 'So, you'll stay with the model for now?'

My reluctant squirm is just for show, because I'm already hooked. I'm not sure where the time goes after that. All I know is, I fill a lot of sheets. I'm concentrating so hard turning this real live body into light and shade on the paper without realising its beauty and its strength reach right out to me. The pent-up vitality. The way the wrists tense, and the knuckles are wide and a little bit roughed up. Those broad thumbs, stretching out beyond the head I can hardly see. The curve of the calf, the stretch of the thigh bone, the knot of the ankle. The tiny criss-cross of a white scar on the foot. Staring at him for so long the essence of this person doesn't just seep onto my paper, it forces its way into my soul too. Just a little. If every woman in the room had fallen the smallest bit in love deep inside their secret hearts tonight, no one could blame them.

All too soon, Plum is standing up, smiling at the front, saying, 'In a minute we'll break for a few seconds, then move straight into the motion poses.'

I'm bracing myself. Although why I'm holding my breath, hoping the face behind the body isn't a disappointment is a mystery, and ridiculous on every level. Any fireman this hunky will be sure to have a partner and, in any case, I'm definitely not on the lookout. In my current halfway-back-to-myself state, I couldn't be less available. Being removed is not a bad feeling. Looking in from behind a fence in no-man's land is a safe place to be. Even so, as we put down our charcoal, I take the precaution of dropping the sunnies down from the top of my head. If I accidentally make eye contact with this guy, the last thing I want is everyone in the class being forced to eavesdrop on my thundering heart.

As Aunty Jo takes down her latest sketch, I'm making sure I keep my smile small enough to be distant. And dammit if I'm even caring that I'd like it to look in any way attractive.

Plum gives a little cough. 'Okay, we'll move on with some action, if you'd like to get up now please, Barney.'

'Barney?!' Just when I could do with my mouth not working, not only does it leap into action, it also lets out a shout loud enough to echo so hard around the gallery, the lights above our heads start to spin. The sudden sound of my own shout makes me jump, and my lurch is so huge that my arm catches the edge of my drawing board. For a few seconds my easel wobbles in the balance, then there's a huge splintering crash as the giraffe legs clatter across the floorboards and come to a halt, resting on Barney's naked, rippling thigh. Wishing the floor would swallow me up doesn't begin to cover it. If I wasn't totally rigid, actually I'd run. As it is, as I watch Barney's head and face rise up from the pose, my feet are literally welded to the floor with embarrass-ment superglue.

Aunty Jo's hand lands on my leg. 'Okay, Sweetpea? You're not going to . . .?' From her iron grip, she's fearing the worst.

I let out a sigh. 'Don't worry, it's not a seizure, Aunty Jo, it's just my easel falling over.' I turn to the sea of faces around, and let out a moan. 'Shit, I'm *so* sorry.' For overreacting. For wrecking their class. For showing myself up. And that's just for starters. And yes, they are all looking, and they're laughing and smiling, not *at* me, but in a sympathetic way.

A woman from the patchwork class peeps over the top of her drawing pad. 'Don't worry, Edie, we've all done it. Rogue easels galloping off down the gallery are why I stick to a sketchpad now.'

Loella's out of her chair, picking up the wreckage. 'That sounds like one of your calligraphy quotes, Edie, you should put that one down on her list, Josie.' As she hands me my board, she's laughing.

As Barney gets to his feet and picks up the rest, I'm pleased to see he's having as much difficulty as me gathering the legs together. He hands the bundle of wayward bits of stick to me with a rueful grin. 'I'll have to leave this animal to you, who designed these things?'

'Come here.' Loella's back and, with a couple of expert twists, she's not only tamed it to submission, she's also taped some more paper into place on my board. Which I take as a message that, however much I'm dying here, I'm not going to be allowed to escape.

Barney's hitching up his boxers and rubbing the life back into those disgustingly honed forearms. 'What's this, Edie, still wearing those sunnies of yours? Have I accidentally dazzled you with my biceps?'

I ignore how close to the truth that is, focus on how grateful I am to have them to hide behind, and move this on to a more important question. 'But where's Cam?' And, more to the point, why couldn't I rely on him to keep Barney out of the way? Even if it's the holidays, it's so long since teatime he should surely be in bed by now after his busy day. Fast asleep and all the rest of it.

Loella's eyebrows lift. 'Cam's off adventuring with the rest of the kids. Beth's dad has taken them off around the bay to make a driftwood fire on the beach and toast marshmallows.'

Beth's joining in too. 'That's why we jumped at our chance to get Barney, he's not often free. He's one of our favourite models because he's so good at staying still.' Obviously nothing to do with his physique then.

Plum's handing Barney a top. 'So, for the next bit, we're doing ten minutes speed sketching, trying to capture the movement as Barney gets the feeling back in his legs and pulls the sweatshirt on and off.'

As Barney tugs the fabric over his head Aunty Jo's murmuring beside me. 'Now this *is* a first. They never talked about action sequences in Harpenden.'

As if it wasn't bad enough drawing his back when I didn't know it was him, watching it appearing and disappearing as the sweat-shirt slides on and off, when I do know it's him, is . . . agony? awful? excruciating? All of the above. I give a mental scream to block out the tiny voice in my head that pipes up and says 'deli-cious'. Who knows where the hell that came from but, take it from me, it's totally not what any part of me thinks or feels. Even worse, watching him put his clothes on is like mentally undressing him the wrong way around. When I get home and tell Bella about this, she'll be on the next train. Although that's not quite true, because she drives. So she'll actually be jumping in her car.

I look longingly down the gallery at the vase of daffodils, then catch Plum's eye. 'I don't suppose . . .?' With my record on toppling easels, I'm not going to risk getting up to get them myself and disrupting the class all over again.

Plum smiles at me and gets up. 'Would you rather have the forsythia?'

I'm nodding and letting out a sigh of relief.

Then Barney's face appears from the sweatshirt and his eyes are boring into me. 'Edie Browne, I don't believe you. I'm going to *all* this trouble and you're asking to draw *flowers*?'

If he didn't sound so wounded, I'd be laughing less. 'Since when do models answer back?' Him cheeking me wrecks any tiny bit of artist-model divide we had left.

Loella's laughing too. 'We break all the rules in St Aidan. I'll get you the daffodils.'

From the crinkles at the corners of Barney's eyes, he's seeing the funny side. 'Totally not, if I'm suffering for art, Edie can too.'

The only answer to that is an eye roll. But somehow, after that, even though I limit myself to drawing from the knee downwards, any concentration I have goes out the window. And when I look through my drawings later at home, I'm shaking my head at a guy who even has ankles that are beautiful.

Chapter 21

Day 163: Friday, 13th April
The barn yard at Periwinkle Cottage

Epic Achievement: Discovering the old Edie Browne maybe wasn't completely perfect after all.

In a way I should be thankful for finding out that the sensual part of my head didn't get killed off along with my reading brain cells. That it's still there ready, for if I want it in the future. When I've closed my circle, that is. Gone all the way back to the start again. It's much the same as when Bella brought her bike round a while after I had my stroke and I got on and found I could still ride it. Even if I was a bit wobbly and got straight off again, everyone, including me, was over the moon. But it was just good to know as a random fact; it didn't mean I was going to start road racing or even leisure riding. I haven't been on a bike since I left junior school, and I have no intention of starting now.

It's the same with my appreciation of the artists' model. It's good to know I still can, but it doesn't mean I'd consider opening up that box any time soon. I know from being with Marcus how much time a relationship can consume. For now I want to put all my energy into getting well. Then when I'm back to being that whole, proper person – well, then we'll see.

With the school holidays still going on, Aunty Jo and I go back to painting and wall-stripping in the downstairs areas, but even after another solid week of work, we've only done a small amount of what there is to do. Meanwhile, Loella and Beth are busy in the barn yard, with their crowd of children floating between there and the cottage.

They're amazingly good at amusing themselves. The bigger ones look after the smaller ones and they spend a lot of time hunkering down in the little space that was once a piggery at the end of the barn yard. They also spend an unexpected amount of hours chopping up and wearing Aunty Jo's outfits left over from golf club dinner dances. Let's face it, she won't be needing those again. I have no idea how she came to actually bring them all the way to Cornwall, because mostly they're so over-the-top they should have hit the charity shop years ago, but as they aren't short on glitz or shimmer they're perfect for dressing up. And if the kids ever get bored, Aunty Jo's always happy to leave off supervising me and my paint roller to step in with a story or a film or a craft activity.

Cam comes around at some time each day, and we read together. When I give him the mini *Eat more strawberry ice cream* poster with a picture of a giant ice cream cone that I've put in a little frame his face lights up into the closest I've yet seen to a smile. As for Barney, since what I'm now thinking of as *the* most embarrassing moment of my life at the life drawing class, I'm happy to say I've somehow managed to avoid coming face to face with him. Okay, I know some things get worse, the longer you put them off, but my fantasy slash master plan is to avoid him – *forever*. Aunty Jo pointed out I've already been here a month, so it's not that unrealistic to think if I make a big effort and have a sensible strategy, staying out of his way for a few more should be completely do-able.

One other significant thing has hit me as I've replayed that awful scene over and over in my head until my insides curl up so tight I can't open my eyes. The biggie is, I can't blame tipping up my easel on top of Barney on anything to do with being ill, because it wasn't. Not that I'd ever make excuses because of what I can't do any more. But the important thing for me was, the biggest blunder of my life to date wasn't to do with the lesser, more recent, lower-functioning version of myself. It's the fully operational, properly working part of Edie Browne who has to take full responsibility for this stuff-up.

So long as you overlook that if it hadn't been for being ill, I would never have been here in Cornwall, this one would have happened, regardless. Not only is it a bit of a shock, it also takes time to get my head around the realisation that the person I'm striving to get back to being wouldn't actually have handled it any better than I did. In fact, in that incarnation it might have been worse, because at least as my current self no one expected me to make any fancy apologies or explanations. They accepted that my 'Shit, I'm so sorry' came straight from the heart of a person who makes mistakes all over the place. Then they left it at that, and all moved on.

We all agreed that when Friday morning came Aunty Jo and I would make our way around to the barn yard to see the full effect of the Easter holiday transformations.

Aunty Jo's leaning towards me, whispering as we go under a new string of colourful bunting at the entrance. 'Oh my, it's all looking very spick and span.' From Aunty Jo, nice words do not come any better.

A lot of the rubble has been taken away by Beth's partner Morgan in her builder's trailer. Now it's empty, even if it's a long way off Barney's neat and tidy next door, the courtyard is looking so much more spacious and the lovely stonework of the stable walls is much clearer to see.

The whispering is catching. 'Look at those pretty trees.'

Aunty Jo's hand tenses on my arm. 'Yes, bay trees either side of the doors, and look, Loella's painted her stable door pink, and Beth's painted hers blue.' She stops to take it all in. 'And they must be the lanterns Beth makes. Malcolm told me all about those that night at the gardeners' club.'

Just as we get there, the blue door bursts open and all the children rush out in a cloud of purple and green and orange chiffon and sequins, which I'm sure Aunty Jo recognises. Since yesterday they've obviously plundered her hat boxes too because, looking at their heads, they could be on their way to a royal wedding.

Beth is beaming as she shows us in. 'Come and see what we've been up to.'

'So many shelves.' For a moment all I can do is gasp. Not only have the walls been whitewashed, there are lanterns and other stock and materials neatly arranged on one side, and then a more arty cluster near the front, with a workbench towards the back and a welder's helmet. 'Truly, it's . . .' I can't actually think of a word that's wide enough. '. . . amazing.'

Loella springs in front of us. 'You haven't seen mine yet.'

The kids are leading the way, and they've already flung back the door to show the same painted walls and shelves, but this time they're bursting with vibrant, coloured fabrics.

Aunty Jo's running her hand over a velvet chaise longue covered in folded quilts. 'This one looks comfy.' Then her eyes light up all over again when she sees the tables at the back, covered in cut pieces of fabric waiting to be sewn, with the sewing machines beside it.

I pull Loella into a hug. 'You've done so much work.'

Beth's laughing. 'We thought if we made it *really, really, really* nice you might want us to stay a bit longer.'

'It is going to work, isn't it?' I'm pursing my lips, then waving my arm along the yard towards the rows of doors. 'Is it too soon to ask if anyone else would be interested in doing the same in the other stables? More to the point, do any of your friends make chocolates?'

'I wish they did.' Loella's laughing. 'Leave it with us, we'll ask around our inner circle and see what we come up with.'

Aunty Jo's rustling in her bag. 'There are just a couple of things here for you two.' As she pulls out the first cushion, I'm holding my breath.

Loella's smile widens. '*Hold on tight to your dreams* . . . Thank you, I couldn't put it any better.'

'And this one's for Beth.'

Beth smiles too. '*Shine a light* . . . That's brilliant, those little candle flames over the "i"s are perfect!' She plants an air kiss on each of our cheeks, then goes back to examining her cushion.

'So what's the verdict?' I'm watching her face. 'Do you think anyone would buy them?' This is my plan to get Aunty Jo earning. I painted the words with fabric paint, and she made them.

Loella pulls in a breath. 'Josie's sewing is impeccable, and the idea is quirky and fun.'

Beth turns to Aunty Jo. 'There's one sure way to find out. Make me a couple more, I'll pop them in our online Etsy shop, we'll see how they go.'

'I can't say I've ever sold anything before.' There's a curl to Aunty Jo's lips, and she's fanning her fingers in front of her face.

Loella pats her cushion. 'At the risk of sounding like a pillow quote, there's a first time for everything, Josie. Beth's right, they're witty, and the stitching details are top notch. I reckon they'll fly off the shelves.' She grins at me. 'Well done you two, that's a great place to begin.'

Beth's looking at her phone. 'I don't want to rush you, but we've promised the kids a picnic and a day out.'

'You're off to Lanhydrock?' Aunty Jo raises her eyebrows.

'It's a shame you won't drive and come too.' Beth stares over at Aunty Jo's car, tucked under the open section of the stables. 'It's not like the Home Counties, the roads here are very quiet out of season.'

Aunty Jo shrinks. 'It's been a very long time. When I tried to start the car after Christmas the Amazon man said the battery was flat.'

I'm pushing my neck out here. 'Have you got any jump leads we could use to start it? Then we could both have a little practice here in the barn yard while the kids are out of the way.' I smile at Aunty Jo. 'I'm sure you'd soon get your eye in again.' Okay, I'm being completely selfish here, thinking of the fish and chip suppers as much as Aunty Jo's progress. How blissful it would be to be able to whizz down to town whenever we felt like a takeaway. So, most nights, then.

Loella's taking it in. 'Give me a minute, I'll bring my big red truck and start up the Mini. Then you can both have a go.'

Aunty Jo's voice is breathy. 'I'd better go and put my driving shoes on.'

'Great, give me five, I'll be back with the Lo-mobile.' Loella's pointing at me again. 'Cam's coming with us but, any problems, Barney's here. Give him a shout, he'll sort you out.' The dimples in her cheeks get bigger. 'If he doesn't come fast enough you can always throw your easel at him.'

I pretend I didn't hear that. If there was any chance this wasn't going to be full speed ahead, we wouldn't be doing it. I'd rather eat my own head than go to Barney for help. Just saying.

Chapter 22

Day 163: Friday, 13th April
In the car at Periwinkle Cottage

Epic Achievement: Getting back behind the wheel.

'A re you okay in there, Edie?'

As Loella's face appears around the side of the up-tilted bonnet of Aunty Jo's car, I pop up from finding the keyhole to give her a thumbs-up sign. In spite of the salt smears dulling the blue metallic paintwork on the outside, the stripy seat under my thighs feels almost un-sat on. As I push the key into place, even though I can't smell a thing I instinctively know I'm breathing in that new-car scented air. My Audi had that too. Probably still has. As Jake says, it's pointless him sending it back when I'll be needing it again so soon. In a way that car being there is like a symbol; Jake having confidence I'm going to get better makes it a lot easier to believe it myself.

As my feet find the pedals in Aunty Jo's car and I let off the handbrake and wiggle the gear stick, it's strange to be flexing my fingers around a steering wheel again after so long. I reach up and adjust the rearview mirror, then, out of sheer habit, dip in closer for a lippy check. It's still just as orange as when I put it on as we left the cottage.

'Okay, leave it in neutral, and as soon as you hear me revving,' turn the key, put your foot on the throttle and we'll get her fired up.' Loella's shouting over the noise of the truck engine as she bobs back outside.

I wait for the roar of the truck, then I do as she said and on the third turn of the key the Mini engine springs into life and as I feel the thrum through the accelerator my spirits soar. As a teenager I couldn't wait to pass my test because being a confident driver means you can literally take yourself anywhere. Better still, as a skill, driving has no link to how clever you are. There weren't many areas where I could beat Tash, but parallel parking was one of them. Even now I pride myself on being able to squeeze into the tiniest spaces ever. I'm sure me being able to zip from site to site with no worries and only the occasional speeding ticket was one reason why Jake came to rely on me so much.

'And we're cooking on gas!' Loella slams down the bonnet, then she's back by my window again, winding in the jump leads. 'Give me a minute to get clear of you, then back her out into the yard.'

'Cool.' As I push the button and let down the window I have zero idea what she means about the cooker, but who gives a damn when I'm driving again.

The gears clunk as I hit reverse, then I turn round to see where I'm heading and gently let my foot off the clutch. As the car starts to inch backwards, I know I need the back end to swing around up the barn yard, but I can't for the life of me work out which way I need to pull on the wheel to make that happen.

I put my foot on the brake, stop and take a breath. *Okay. I've got this.* I set off again, pull the wheel the other way. Stop again. *Totally wrong. What the hell's going on?* The back of the car isn't going remotely where I expect. So I start again and spin the wheel back the other way, but that's still not right. So I yank it back again. *Fuck.* As I see the stable wall and Loella's pink stable door careering towards me through the back window, I ram my foot on the brake and as I skid to a halt I hear a minor crashing noise.

As I jump out, I'm flapping my jumper to get rid of the sweat. I try to smooth the marks in the gravel with my boot where I've been wrenching the wheels from side to side. At least the car is out of the shelter, I haven't stalled it and the engine is still running. If I was a bit confused back there, I think I got away with it. No one seems to have noticed.

'Over to you, Aunty Jo, you can take it from here.' Nice recovery, even though I say it myself.

'Just a moment, Sweetpea.'

Aunty Jo is picking up one of Loella's bay trees from the gravel next to the car boot. I'm about to tell her she can't put this off by messing about, then I see the soil on the ground and my heart does a nosedive. Do hearts even *do* nosedives?

'Did someone hit that?'

'Nice try, Edie.' Loella's laughing from the open window of the truck. 'For once it *wasn't* me.'

Aunty Jo's hugging the tree and tilting it back into position. 'No harm done, it was probably in your blind spot. You get in the passenger seat, I'll just have my five-flower essence drops and I'll be with you.'

Maybe that's what I was missing. If I'd have been less stressed out, I'd have managed fine. As soon as Aunty Jo's doing the steering, I'll know which way to tell her to go.

'Okay, ladies, don't go burning too much rubber, I'll see you later.' Loella's drumming her fingers on the truck side as she shouts at us from the open window.

I'm waving wildly, dodging the gravel spray as she turns out onto the lane. 'Thanks, have a great day.' It's a shame I couldn't add in something about cooking.

As we both get into the car, I'm looking at Aunty Jo's feet. 'Nice pumps.' They're blush *and* covered with so much glitter they're almost crusty.

She pushes a stray wave off her forehead. 'They make me think of Fairy Godmothers, whenever I take the car out I like to feel mine's looking after me.'

'Great.' It's not at all. I'd actually rather not know.

Her knuckles are white where she's gripping the steering wheel. 'Engine on, in gear and . . . off we go.' She turns the wheel to straighten up, then we teeter forward all the way down the barn yard to the lane. Then come to a halt and go backwards all the way, at the same speed.

'Brill.' I flash her a smile. I have to give it to her – she's cracked the crawling in a straight line. In both directions.

'Do you know, this isn't anything like as bad as I remember. Maybe I could try it a bit faster?' Her eyes are still wide, but she's sounding bright.

I wiggle my eyebrows. 'Go for it.' As she does it four times more at the same speed, I'm wondering how my dad does this all day long. 'Okay, now press harder.'

Aunty Jo's eyebrows close up. 'On what?'

'With your foot – the pedal near the door, NOW!'

There's a sudden lurch and we swerve across the barn yard, shoot straight across the lane.

'St-o-p!' I manage to yell then make a grab for the handbrake.

The car slews round and if we'd hit a wall we couldn't have stopped any faster. It's a shame no one was filming because it's the kind of clip that would have gone viral. Then Aunty Jo lifts all her feet off the pedals, and there's another huge jump forwards as the engine stalls.

'Fuck!' That's my shout, not hers.

'I thought I wrote on your calligraphy list that you didn't say fuck any more?' She gives me a wounded stare.

'No, I wanted to stop giving a fuck, not saying it.' I let out a groan, and put it in the too difficult pile.

'So what now?' She's sounding remarkably unconcerned, considering her bumper's wedged against her house wall. Which she well might. After all, none of this was her idea. Which is probably why she's expecting me to sort it.

'What do *you* think?' For once I'm going to pass this back to her.

'Well, the battery's buggered, so it's not as though we're going anywhere. And you know what Barney says about not parking on the lane.' There's definitely a pucker to her lips. 'There's only one thing to do, and that's what Loella suggested. If you pop along and get Barney to help, he'll feel involved. That might work?'

There's only one drawback – I wasn't planning on seeing him again. Not for months and months and months. In fact not ever. Seeing him today is my whole life too soon.

Aunty Jo's chiding me. 'Hurry along, Sweetpea, one of Barney's delivery lorries could arrive at any moment. They can't possibly get past when we're stuck like this.'

I let out a long sigh. There are times when it's easier not to argue. A few seconds later I'm standing on Barney's doorstep, wondering how he can possibly be taking up the entire grey-framed doorway.

'You remember what you said about when cars blocked the lane?'

His mouth is twitching. 'That I tow them?'

'That's the one.'

'Loella mentioned you might be knocking.' There's another twitch of his cheeks. 'Knocking on the door, that is, not knocking things over onto me.'

If I didn't know better, I'd think that low rumble was a laugh. But Barney never laughs. If he's bringing this out now, I might as well bat it straight back to him. 'So why do you do it?'

'Do what?' From his double-take, he's not expecting that.

'Take your clothes off for money.' It's a valid question. He brought the subject up.

'That's not quite how I'd put it.' He pulls a face. 'Like a lot of things around here, it's down to Beth and Loella.'

'You're *blaming them?*'

'Not entirely.' His shrug says he is. 'I'm on my own with a five-year-old. It's my best chance of getting out for some adult company.'

'Really?' I'm frowning, but my voice goes high because it's another of those times I can't tell the truth from the bollocks.

'Do I need the truck?' He's moving this on. 'And the jump leads?'

'Yes, two times.' He might not have noticed, but adding up and a snappy comeback all in the same sentence has to be a first. 'Anyway, isn't Cam six?' Me pulling *him* up on numbers too? I might have stuffed up mightily with my driving, but it's all going right in other areas this morning.

He's staring at me. 'Six . . . five . . . it's near enough.'

Except it isn't. What kind of dad doesn't know how old their child is? I'm shaking my head and opening and closing my mouth, but my fast retorts must be all used up because this time nothing's coming out.

He gives another 'nothing to do with me' shrug. 'Well, you might have all day to chat, but some of us are busy. Shall we get on with this?'

I'm not going to argue with that. By the time Barney comes up behind me on the lane in a truck very like Loella's, only black, Aunty Jo's made it out of the car and is resting her bottom on the bonnet of her Mini, a lot like those models Bella and I saw on that retro TV programme, *The Girl's Guide to When We Were Helpless*.

'What's all this? Stopping the traffic again?' Barney comes up beside her and gives her a nudge.

She's fanning herself with her scarf. 'I think I might have over-done the flower essence.'

'Were those Cinderella slippers a bit heavy on the accelerator?' As Barney looks at her, it's almost like he's teasing. 'Can you keep hold of Robert for me?'

She lets out a strangled hoot, then immediately goes back to looking sombre.

I'm staring at her. 'Aunty Jo, did you just laugh?'

'Me?' She stares at me like I'm the one who just shrieked. 'Edie, look at where we parked my car, there's absolutely nothing funny about that.'

Now she mentions it and I take a step back and see the car slewed sideways across the lane, its wheels up to their middle bits in periwinkle cuttings and freshly dug earth, I'm having to bite my lip to stop my sides splitting.

Barney catches my eye over the car roof as he eases into the driver's seat. 'Laughing is mean, Edie Browne.' Then he turns the key and the engine roars into life.

'Jeez, how did that happen?' What about his clips and his red and blue wires?

Aunty Jo leaps off the bonnet and lands among the daffodils further up the verge.

'The battery must have recharged while it's been running.' Barney's still half hanging out of the car. 'Shall I move it to a better position while I'm in here?' He's not even implying that we're wasting his time.

'That would be lovely, Barnaby.' Aunty Jo's answering from the ditch. 'So long as you don't mind?'

He's looking at her gravely. 'Barnaby's my surname, shortened to Barney because of the barns. If we're going for first names, Josie, you need to call me Guy.'

This is how laid-back he is – a couple of quick shunts back

and forth, the car's back on the lane and he's still got the door open.

'Will your Aunty Jo take it from here, or have you had enough adventures for one day?' He's tilting his head on one side, looking at me. 'Shall I run it back under cover in the barn yard?'

'That might be a good idea.' I think we'll revisit the driving if ever my dad comes to stay. For a year. Just in time I remember how grateful I am. 'Please, Guy.' I give myself a pat on the back for that instant recall, and hope he's not expecting it to happen again.

By the time I've helped Aunty Jo back onto solid ground, the car's away and he's walking towards us, throwing the keys up and catching them from the air.

For a moment I want to throw my arms around his neck and hug him for getting us out of this mess. Then I come to my senses and kick myself for thinking like someone from the olden days. All I need is a spangled bikini and a sports car to sprawl across and my degradation would be complete. Realistically, if he wasn't so territorial, us almost demolishing Aunty Jo's house would never have been a problem anyway.

'Thank you, Guy, thank you so much.' Aunty Jo takes the keys from him.

'Yes, totally.' What she says, but a bit less.

'Any time.' He's locking eyes at me over her head. 'You're welcome.'

Me thinking of blue striped boxers isn't helpful. 'Cake on Sunday! Come and have some!' It's another of those gushing Tourette's moments I have no control over. I'm thinking of what I can add to neutralise it. Not. One day. Some time. Next year.

But Aunty Jo's on it. 'What a lovely idea, Sweetpea, you can make us some of your lovely cupcakes.'

'I *can*?' I've only got myself to blame. Edie 'the original version' would not have stuffed up like this. Whatever I thought about toppling easels, I need to find her again, and fast.

'Great, see you Sunday.' He's walking off down the lane, his hand in the air. 'Until then, love you, bye.'

And just for a moment the tune in my head isn't dreary. It's not *Leave a Light On* from the TV advert. Or Harry Styles' *Sign of the Times*. Okay, it's not anything upbeat like *Viva La Vida* or Razorlight singing *America*, like my dad used to force us to sing along to. But for once I can't fault my brain for the song it's thrown up.

It's all over the front page, you give me road rage . . .

Chapter 23

Day 165: Sunday, 15th April
At Periwinkle Cottage

Epic Achievement: Cooking on . . . you know . . . that thing . . .

Fact for today: *Voice recognition gadgets are nothing like they look on the TV ads. So Siri, tell me a cake recipe was* never going to work. But it's actually fine to turn to Aunty Jo for help, because she blew the event into something huge by inviting Beth and Loella's crew along too.

I'm musing on exactly what to bake, and reaching for the ingredients I'm going to need as Aunty Jo shouts them out.

'Eggs . . . flour . . . sugar . . . butter . . . icing sugar . . . and there's brand-new pipes and a piping bag in the drawer by the sink.'

I used to do a mean chocolate tower cake for office birthdays, with squishy swirls of icing and slices of chocolate orange stuck in. Variations, with Oreos, and Maltesers. Sometimes with them all at once. Honey cupcakes with crunchy toffee drizzled over them and teensy golden sugar balls. And Marcus's mates went wild for anything with popping candy.

I'm flicking through the photos on my phone to remind myself,

174

and it all feels a lifetime away. Then I find what I'm looking for. 'How about I make champagne cupcakes with rosewater butter-cream swirls?' Finished with a strawberry, colourful sugar flowers and tiny pieces of candied lemon. Looking at who's there eating them, I made them to take for Tash's birthday. I flash Aunty Jo the picture on my phone.

'They look lovely, Sweetpea, but let's get the little steps right before we move onto the big ones. We don't want to put you under pressure, so Beth's picking up a cake or two from Clemmie's too.' She's staring at me in that way she has, to see how I'm taking this.

'And?'

'Why not try plain sponge cupcakes, with vanilla buttercream. Just this once.' She's completely taken over. Which I should be happy about. This definitely wasn't anything to do with showcasing my talents, because there's definitely no one here I'd want to impress. 'I've bought suitable sprinkles.'

'And what the hell are they?'

'Yellow and orange sugar stars for the boys, and pink and white hearts for the girls. And I ordered chocolate chips too because you liked to put those in the bottom of your cupcakes sometimes too.'

'I did? Really?' I'm past caring.

'It was one of your signature moves, Edie.'

I should be glad she's here to prompt me on that, when all I'm relying on are pictures. Now I she's mentioned it, I *did* used to sprinkle chocolate chips in the bottom of the cupcake cases as a cheeky surprise. Nothing impressed Marcus's mates more than a twist.

'I'll leave you and Bella to it, then. Shout if you need me.'

Much as I love Aunty Jo, neither of us can work out when she last baked, and, as Bella's a whizz in the kitchen, she's agreed to FaceTime me and talk me through every move. It's not long before my phone rings, and we're away.

'Okay, first put the oven on. Show me and I'll tell you which knob it is, then I'll hold up the number you need to turn it around to.'

I'm determined to nail this, which is why she's supervising so closely. It's amazing how much you take for granted when you throw a cake mix together in the normal adult way. When you're relying on instructions for every move, it takes forever to do. It's a bit like the building site documents. They run to pages and pages, because every last action has to be spelled out and described in detail. I don't even want to imagine wading my way through one of those – which is fine because I won't have to until much later. By the time I do, it won't feel hard at all.

The up side of it all taking so long is there's time to catch up on all the goss with Bella. I sense she's keen to have another look at my life drawing sketches, but for now I've hidden them under the sofa. In fact not much has happened since last night when she went through my Facebook page for me, like she does most days. Instagram is mainly pictures, so mostly I scroll through that myself, with Aunty Jo filling in the blanks. It's weird that when I was posting and tweeting non-stop, if I lost internet for a second I used to panic. But now I've stopped it feels like I've got off a train. It's gone on without me, and the world is still turning. The world does turn, doesn't it? I didn't dream that. So how does that work then?

Although right now that's the least of my problems. Right now I'm more concerned with how my cakes look now they're coming out of the oven.

'And? Show me?' Bella's sounding impatient as I accidentally burn myself and crash them down onto the work surface.

'The bakery muffins are way bigger.' I wave my phone over them, but if I'm honest these are a bit small and wrinkly.

'No worries – you got the chocolate chips in, they're not burned, the red stripy cases are cute and, so long as we get a humungous swirl of buttercream on every one, they'll be fine.' Bella likes to look on the sunny side. 'With cupcakes, it's mainly the buttercream people go for anyway. Load it with vanilla, you'll be cooking on gas.'

'What gas is that?' It's that cooker thing again. We have electricity here, she knows because we've been talking about the fan in the oven.

'"Cooking on gas" is just what people say when everything's hunky-dory.'

'Hunky-dory?'

'When things are going well. *Cooking on gas* might work for your phrase list?' Her eyebrows shoot up, but her voice is level. 'Get Aunty Jo to stick it on there, then you'll remember it.'

I blow out a breath. It's one of those everyday moments I get, well, every day. One minute everything's going fine, then it all spirals out of control and within seconds my head's pounding so hard it feels like it's going to burst.

'How's it going, is everything okay?'

It's Aunty Jo, she's back, and she's dressed in leggings and a flowery tunic very like one Loella wears, with a yellow jumper on top.

'Come on, Chickpea, remember how I showed you to breathe in deeply and empty your mind?'

Fuck empty brains, that's what got us here in the first place. But when she's standing with her face two inches from mine, eyes closed, her nostrils flaring, it's hard not to join in.

It's Bella who finally jerks me back into the room. 'Well, well, well, Edie, who'd have thought deep breaths could be so calming?'

It's hard to tell if she's being real or taking the piss. Seriously, I hope it's the piss one. I laugh, because somehow we've put the stressy moment behind us. 'Are you cooking with gas then, Bells?'

It's nice that she's laughing. 'Shall we move onto buttercream now, Edie? So long as you're not too exhausted.'

'Would it help for me to whizz the icing together, then you can do the piping?' Aunty Jo's at the sink, tying up an apron and rinsing out the bowl from the mixer. Before I have time to blink, she disappears in an icing sugar cloud, and faster still she's handing me a full piping bag of perfectly soft buttercream. 'There you go, Sugarplum, you take it from here.'

'Do you want to try a cake?' There's no point me tasting, and it is 'eat all you can' day today.

'They look lovely, Sweetpea, but I don't want to spoil my lunch. How about I save them for this afternoon?'

'We're having lunch so soon?' All that morning to make two trays of cupcakes. The good bit is I counted them. All the way to nine, all on my own, twice.

Bella's still laughing on my phone screen. 'Time flies when you're having a great time.'

The other good bit is, it might have taken me forever to work out the weighing and the mixing but it turns out I'm still an ace on the piping bag, and with a few prompts from Aunty Jo I count all the way to eighteen as I do them. And when we sprinkle the deccies on they look totally gorgeous, even though it's me saying it.

Cookers on full? They certainly damn well are.

Barney Guy, or Guy Barney – or whatever the hell he's called – prepare yourself to be wowed.

Chapter 24

Epic Achievement: Getting told I'm a bitching baker.
(Okay, crying over the cupcakes straight away after may negate that,
but no one can take it away from me, those buttercream swirls were
top class)
(One more okay, I put my hands up – technically the icing might
have been Aunty Jo's.)
(I'm sure no one even cared about that bit . . .)

It might be a party I never intended to have, but afternoon tea for twenty (I have to come clean, Aunty Jo did that counting) is pretty epic.

'So guess whose cushions have sold?' It's Beth, and she's coming into the garden room doing a little cha-cha wiggle, looking immensely pleased with herself. 'It's official, you two are totally commercial.'

Loella's right behind her, pulling me into a hug. 'Not only that, we also had a hen party enquiry. They'd like fifteen hand-sewn pillowcases, all with different "sleepyhead" slogans in hand-painted script.' She flashes her fingers up three times as she squeaks. 'Fifteen! How awesome is that?'

I grin at Aunty Jo. 'There you go, I told you we could do this. Welcome to the world of strong independent women, once you get a taste for earning you won't look back.'

Beth looks over to where Aunty Jo is surrounded by jumping kids. 'Are you up for this Josie?'

Aunty Jo's attempt at punching the air is so enthusiastic she spins right around and almost topples over.

Malcolm and Morgan are coming in, along with a couple of other friends they've brought to check out the stables, and they're all carrying containers.

'Time to put the kettle on, Edie?' That's my cue from Aunty Jo.

Loella puts up her hands. 'As we're celebrating, we brought bubbly, I hope that's okay?'

Beth carries on. 'Already chilled, there are plastic flutes for everyone, with fizzy grape for the small ones and drivers and paper plates for the cakes. Dad's just going out for a second load, aren't you?' She gives Malcolm a nudge away from where he's just sidled up to rest his bum just along the table edge from Aunty Jo. 'And Barney's bringing cold beer.'

'Brilliant.' I'm hoping Aunty Jo doesn't mind that afternoon tea has turned into a cork-popping fizz fest. From her pained expression, I'm guessing she's not entirely happy. 'Okay, Aunty Jo?'

She beckons me towards her, then whispers in my ear. 'I'm not sure about paper plates.'

Marcus used to object to them on ethical save-the-planet grounds, which is fair enough, and the kind of luxurious stand you can take when you aren't the one clearing up after barbies. But Aunty Jo is more about only eating from china.

'Let's give them a whirl, you might get to like them.' I grab a bag of flutes from Beth, then wave Mia to bring the piles of cake boxes she's collected from people through to the kitchen.

We put out blueberry muffins, bite-sized pieces of chocolate brownie, and slice up some nice sponge with jam and cream and an iced chocolate cake that Aunty Jo has got her hands on, probably on special request from the milk person. But my best moment comes when Aunty Jo disappears to the vegetable rack place and comes back carrying a special round glass plate on its own little glass tower. When I see my cupcakes arranged all over the top, for a second they look so beautiful I can't even swallow.

Aunty Jo's looking at me. 'Okay, Sweetpea?' She holds them up to Beth and Loella. 'It's a very proud moment, they're her very first cakes since . . .' She doesn't need to say more.

Beth comes in for a high five. 'Look at those amazing swirls, you didn't tell us you were a bitching baker.'

'Yay! for being back in the game.' Loella gives me a play punch on the arm and calls through to the garden room. 'Get those corks popping, this calls for fizz!' Then she digs in her pocket, hands me a tissue and gives me a wink. 'As soon as we've wiped your nose, Chickpea, let's go.'

Beth's rolling her eyes at me. 'She's thirty, Lo, not three, she doesn't need you bossing.' But, whatever Beth says, I'm very grateful for the hanky *and* the diversion.

As we parade through, Cam and Barney are arriving too but the best thing about having the garden room so full of guests is that once they're in those two hardly show up at all. I put down the tray of glasses then, while I give out the paper plates, Malcolm pours the drinks and Mia passes them around. As the others dish out cake, and the noise rises, I can't help thinking how dreary Sundays were when it was just Aunty Jo and me.

As soon as everyone's holding a drink, Loella takes a spoon and jangles it on a china plate and coughs loudly. 'Well, we'd like you to raise your glasses to say a big thank you to Josie, for letting us pop up in her stables for a week or two.' She beams at Aunty Jo. 'And we'd like you to raise your cupcakes to Edie

"Sweetpea" Browne with an "e", both for having that brilliant idea and for getting her baking apron on again.' She's beaming at me over the top of her stripy cupcake case. 'It's lovely to have you both on the lane, and we really appreciate you giving our businesses a leg up.'

There's the kind of manic cheer you only ever get from an infant school, and the dull click of plastic as the glasses crash into each other.

Cam's standing next to me, and I'm watching him scoop our vanilla buttercream into his mouth from his finger. 'How is it?'

'Sweet . . . and yummy.'

I let myself breathe again, knock back my grape juice to celebrate, then turn to Loella, who's peeling back her cupcake paper a tiny bit at a time. 'What are you doing?'

'Not everyone realises, but the way to squeeze the total maximum enjoyment from one of these is to eat absolutely *equal* amounts of sponge and buttercream with each mouthful.' She licks her lips. 'Watch and learn.'

At this point what I'm learning most is if you lick your lips that enthusiastically you'll demolish your lippy in the tiniest amount of time, whatever that is. I might need to let her into the secret of Laura Geller *Fifty Kisses*. It's not bollocks at all, the name is entirely right about how long it lasts for. Not that Marcus was enough of a snogger to ever put it to the test. If they'd brought out a lippy for women with boyfriends like Marcus, they'd have probably called it *One Peck*, and that was in the early days. If I was lucky. Sometimes we'd go for weeks without the briefest lip brush. The one time I mentioned it he went all, 'Well, Edes, you have *the* most designed kitchen in the street —' he seemed to be overlooking that the design came from my office, but whatever '— and *the* most "out there" holidays, and *the* best sex at least once every day. Asking for any more icing on that very perfect cake, you're coming across as a little bit needy.'

You see it's funny. Some bits of my past have been wiped, then there are other parts where I can remember every word, from every single second, even though I'd possibly rather not. But what I'm meaning to say here is, if you want colour that locks on your lips like superglue, *and* lets you stuff your face with builders' cake all day too, look no further. True, in my case they'd have been better to call it *Fifty Doughnuts* than *Fifty Snogs,* but whichever way you're wearing it off, it's well worth the cash.

As I mentally slide back into the sun room, Loella's eyes are closed and she's taking her bite in slow-mo. For me it's another of those 'hold your breath' moments.

Then suddenly her eyes flash open, really, really wide. As her jaw drops, she makes one short croak in her throat. It's only small, but it's enough for me to know I'm in big trouble.

As my stomach drops like a stone, I look over my shoulder and see Aunty Jo across the other side of the sun room. She does one huge leap over Tally and her friend, who are sitting on the floor, and arrives at my elbow.

'*What* is your problem, Loella?'

'No, no! No problem, Josie, the sponge is a tiny bit salty, that's all.' Loella's pulling at her tongue with her fingers.

'Even in this *deepest, darkest backwater* of Cornwall, you *must* have heard of salted caramel? Take it from me, sweet with a hint of saline is *very* fashionable.' Aunty Jo's cheeks are flaming through her all-day foundation.

Loella holds a piece out to her. 'See what *you* think then.'

'What I think is, you must be putting it on the wrong part of your mouth.' Aunty Jo's tongue is pink between her lips as she slides in a morsel of cake. There's a moment of silence then she lets out a gasp, 'Of all the fucks . . .' As she turns to me her gaze is so piercing it's like she's turned into that woman with red hair who used to be in charge of humiliation on tea time TV. 'Okay, Sweetpea, no need to panic.'

There's time for me to gulp. 'I'm not.'

'But . . . which sugar did you use?'

Sugar. I'm blinking.

She's prompting me. 'The flour was in the blue stripy bag, the eggs were in the green box, the sugar was in the white plastic container with the —'

'With the . . .' okay, I can do this one '. . . the yellow hat.'

Somehow she seems to get suddenly smaller. A *lot, lot* smaller. When she starts to talk even her voice is tiny. 'I'm sorry everybody, this is *all* my fault. That was salt, Sweetpea, the sugar was the one with the blue hat – I mean, lid.'

I'm kicking myself for not checking, but cursing for not being able to taste too. If I was baking with salt instead of sugar, there's no surprise the damn things weren't fluffy. I licked the bowl out, and slurped a lot of the mixture too, purely out of habit, so no wonder I feel like I could drink a river. But, truly, what the *hell* was I thinking? Not so much about the mix-up, more that if I was even imagining I was in any way capable of baking and impressing people I must have had a momentary brain lapse.

'It's an easy mistake to make.' Malcolm actually looks quite cheery. 'It's the kind I make most days, me and my kitchen don't get on. I'm exactly the same kind of walking disaster area in there as you are.'

Beth gives him a 'shut the eff up' look as she grabs a plate and leaps forward. 'Okay, there's been a bit of a mix-up at the bakery, kiddies, we've got a product recall for the cupcakes, eat your icing then give me back your sponge for now. We promise when we give you them back next Sunday they'll be sweet all the way to the bottom.'

I let out a groan. 'Don't make me do it again.' Throwing over my easel is suddenly looking like a very minor mishap compared to this.

Cam's looking up at me solemnly from where he's sitting on the floor, his back to the wall and legs outstretched. 'Mine's nice, it tastes of the sea, *and* it's got chocolate chips in the bottom.' Seriously, I want to squeeze him for that.

Loella's grinning at me. 'You've got to get back on the horse, Chickpea. And this way we get afternoon tea at Periwinkle all over again.' She's staring around the room. 'Will someone please bring this poor girl another drink?'

Mia comes over with her tray of grape juices and I grab one in each hand. I'm downing them both, hoping for a sugar hit, when guess-who sidles into view and blocks out every bit of daylight, even though it's cloudy outside. So much for not making eye contact, and kidding myself he wasn't here.

'Bad luck with the cupcakes, Edie Browne, at least they *looked* irresistible.' He' s frowning, so nothing new there then. 'Should you be drinking that?'

'Who are you? The juice police?' It's fast and slick, and as a comeback it's pretty much my best effort since my first trip to A&E.

'It's just . . .' The way he's staring it's like he's peering straight into my soul.

'Just *what*?' I'm on a roll here, and to show him I grab another glass in each hand and knock them back too.

'Never mind.' He lets out a sigh. 'Just take it steady, okay?'

Cam looks up at him. 'She's drunk five so far.'

Barney's eyebrows hit the ceiling. 'It's not always polite to count, Cam, but thanks all the same. Just this once, it's a good thing someone is.'

I make damn sure he sees my eye roll, and thank those lucky starfish things I'm not on anything as hardcore as Diet Coke.

'Anyway . . .' Malcolm's rubbing his hands together.

Beth cuts in. 'If you're going to bang on about the cooking crisis again, it might be best to give it a miss, Dad.'

'Nothing about kitchens, I was going to change the subject completely and ask if you'd like some hollyhocks to go by your door, Josie? Pearl always used to have them, they do well here. I could bring you some over?'

From the desperate glance Aunty Jo's sending me, she hasn't got the first clue he's talking about plants. Lucky for both of us, hollyhocks are on Dad's very short list of life obsessions. Along with climbing roses, the blonde girl from *Neighbours*, Bananarama and golf. I've heard so much about them for my whole life, I'm confident my memory bank could be wiped clean by aliens and I'd still know what they were.

'Yes, please, Beth's dad.' I'm so relieved to move this on from ocean-flavoured cupcakes. 'They're tall kind of wallflowers, Aunty Jo.' Hopefully she'll get the idea.

Loella joins in. 'They're very pretty, gorgeous in summer, Pearl's used to be pink and red.'

Aunty Jo's nodding. 'I'm very partial to pink.'

As I know to my cost every time we get out the paint charts.

Malcolm's looking pleased. 'And while I'm here planting them, that lawn of yours could do with a tidy before it starts growing again. I could get my strimmer on it, if you'd like?' He hesitates, and spins round to Barney. 'So long as I'm not treading on anyone else's toes here?'

Barney takes a swig from his beer. 'It's all yours, Malc, knock yourself out.'

I only hope he's drinking sensibly there. Just saying. Seeing as he's so concerned about everyone else's consumption.

'And any little jobs you need doing around the house, I'm your man.' Malcolm's obviously taking Aunty Jo's nodding to heart. 'I've plenty of time on my hands too since I retired from the ambulance station.'

Beth's shaking her head. 'He *is* very handy, and he *will* do you a good job. So long as you don't mind him arriving with a *Will work for cupcakes* sign around his neck.'

Loella's smiling. 'So long as they're not salty ones.' She looks at me. 'Sorry, but it's just *so* funny, *please* don't make me stay all politically correct and silent about it forever.'

From Aunty Jo's face she's not happy about that. 'Thank you, Malcolm, we can put you to straight to work, the minute the roller blind for Edie's room arrives.'

If me and Marcus managed to put in his designer-look kitchen ourselves, and all the blinds at his, if I can find a screwdriver, I'm pretty sure I'll be able to put up one roller blind in my room, so long as Aunty Jo checks the tape measure bit. I open my mouth to get in before Malcolm claims the job, but in the end Malcolm is left with his mouth gaping too, because Barney's jumped in.

'Okay, this one's mine.'

Oh my days, that's not good.

I'll need all my wits about me to fight this, so I beam at Mia and go in for more grape juice to help my parched throat. One, two. One, two. It's amazing how easily these little glasses slip down. I ignore Barney's wide-eyed judgement. And that he's looking a bit wobbly.

Aunty Jo's pushing back her hair. 'If you're sure you've got the right tools and skills, Barnaby?' It's funny, she's wobbling the same as Barney.

Cam's voice cuts in. 'That makes nine, Edie Browne. Even *I* know that's a lot.'

'Thank you, big man, maybe hold it there.'

Loella nudges Aunty Jo. 'He makes those lovely shepherd's huts, remember, Josie, I reckon he could fit a bedroom blind in his sleep. Hey, Barnaby?' She sounds like she's teasing him.

His expression is serious as he shrugs, but his eyes are dancing with amusement. 'Pretty much. It's the least I can do, with all the help you're giving Cam. It's not just his reading, he's acing his counting too.' His frown lines deepen as he turns to me. 'Are you okay there, Edie?'

I'm glad he's asked. Actually, I couldn't be any less okay. For a start I'm feeling woozy. My eyes aren't working properly, and it feels like my ears are turning on and off, and the sounds in them have gone all vibratey. And I'm horribly hot, even though I'm shivering.

It could be the salt so I grab another drink from Mia.

'You're not drinking *Prosecco* there, are you, Sweetpea?' Aunty Jo's frowning at me.

I've no idea why she's asking, because she knows I can't, so but I wave my glass at her anyway. 'Only the kiddie bubbles.'

But much more importantly, I can't bear to think of Barney in the same county as my bedroom, let alone in the room itself. Saying 'We'll see' doesn't feel any way strong enough to put the brakes on this. I'm mentally scanning through my phrase list for a firmer reply, but all I come up with are *Smell more roses, I'm doing this for me* and *Grow cactus*, and none of them come close to working. There's a random song line buzzing round my head too, and for once it's not one of the sad ones.

'*Robert De Niro's waiting, talking Italian . . .*' Dad used to make us sing along to this whenever we went out in the car. Which is probably why the lyrics are in permanent marker in my memory box.

'What, Edie?' It's Aunty Jo, and her voice is coming and going as the volume in my ears goes up and down.

Damn, I didn't mean to say it out loud.

'Robert De Niro . . . talking Italian . . .' There it goes again.

Aunty Jo's face comes in close to mine, she's all swirly. And as she reaches in for my glass she's got a rainbow halo around her.

I'm checking off the colours to see if they're real. 'Red, yellow, pink, green . . .'

As I lurch forward she makes a grab for my arm, but it's too late. The black slate floor tiles are already rushing towards me. And all I can think as I go down is how much it's going to hurt my head when it hits the slate, and how wetting myself in front of all these people will make salty cupcakes and falling easels feel like party time.

Chapter 25

Epic Achievement: Making a great recovery. (Do not ask from what.)
(Well, actually, several great recoveries. Yay to 1. carrying on like
nothing happened, and 2. looking like I give no shits.)

Not everything is what it seems. Picking up fizz, not fizzy juice, but not knowing because they both look similar and I can't taste either of them, then promptly firing down nine glasses – to be honest, the surprise is I didn't fall over sooner.

Then guess who came to the rescue? Don't ask me how that happened either, but Barney somehow caught me from behind under my arms as I fell, then lowered me gently to the floor. I came to rest flat out, my head wedged on his thighs as he knelt. If anyone else had done that, they'd have had immediate superhero status. I know I should be grateful he saved me, not squirming at the memory, but when you've had your face crushed against the soft denim of some guy's jeans for long enough to get seam marks in your cheek . . . Forget that I tried to give everyone salt poisoning, put aside that I managed to get accidentally drunk and fall over, the bit about the whole day which I'm most ashamed about is having my head cushioned on those legs. Having said that, Bella pointed out afterwards that at least I didn't have to look at them this time.

Beth's dad and Aunty Jo whisked me off to A&E to be checked over and eventually they decided I had had a seizure but was good to go home. The worst part is this might delay me getting my driving licence back again, although after the trouble I had with Aunty Jo's car last week I feel like I'm still a long way from getting behind the wheel.

After so much excitement Aunty Jo insisted we had a couple of days at home, doing what she calls 'taking it easy', although that didn't get me out of reading. There's nothing easy about joining in with her morning meditation, but it's less trouble to do what she suggests than to argue. I personally think getting up later would help my head much more than sitting on the floor in the day room, breathing in and out and telling myself I'm good enough. But whatever. Then for the rest of the day, while I caught up on my 'nap time' and played with some fabric paint and some little pictures for Loella, she got to watch ballet instead of watching me with my paint roller.

By Wednesday afternoon, when the delivery man knocks on the French window with my new roller blind, I'm ready to get back in the game. So while Aunty Jo goes upstairs to top up her blonde bits I help myself to Harry's FatMax tool bag. By the time she comes down again I've got as far as covering the floor with saws and hammers.

'But I thought Barney was doing that?' She's patting her hair with a towel and frowning at the blind package.

I ignore her and pick up the drill, squeeze the button, and jump as it whizzes round. 'Yay, it's working!' I'll take that as a sign. 'I've got this.' More importantly, when I put up all Bella's blinds at hers the weekend before the skydive, she went as far as calling me Mrs DIY. So long as I don't overthink this, it should be all good.

I slide off the plastic bag, unfurl the blind across the back of a chair and tip a load of plastic pieces out of another bag. 'So these bits fix to the window.'

'The muslin fabric's exactly what you need to shade the morning sun, careful, don't lose your instructions.'

'As if they'd be any help.' Now I'm staring at the bits, even though I keep laying them out across the coffee table, and re-arranging them, it isn't coming together as fast as I'd hoped.

Aunty Jo heads for the kitchen. 'Why don't we come back to this after a nice cup of tea?'

But even hoovering up every last piece of Sunday's chocolate brownie doesn't help any. When Cam and Barney come knocking at the door a whole lot later I'm still no closer to understanding where the bits go.

Barney's face softens as he sees the pieces. 'Oh, good, it's here, and you've made a start.'

Aunty Jo sniffs. 'Men never look happier than when there's a tool box around.'

That's not completely true. Dad's face is never as long as when my mum gets his tool box out. He much prefers buying the tools to actually using them, and he only likes doing DIY when it's his idea. But I'm not going to mention that now. If Barney had come in earlier, I'd have sent him away. As it is, seeing I've scored a complete fail here, I'm going to have to suck this up.

Barney's leaning over next to me. 'So if we turn the brackets the other way around, then they fit together.'

How have I sat here all afternoon and still not thought of that? 'Great.' I make my tone ironic. As I watch him scoop up the pieces, drop some tools into the FatMax bag and head for the hall I'm happy to leave this to him.

He's looking at me from the doorway. 'Why are you still sitting there, Edie Browne, you're supposed to be helping me.'

'I am?' However wonky my memory is, I'm damn sure we didn't agree anything of the sort.

'You need to bring the blind and the tape, please.' Barney's losing no time channelling his inner army commander. 'If you don't hurry up, it's highly likely I'll hang it at the wrong window.'

That might work as a joke if there was the smallest smile to go with it. As it is, it just adds to the list I was thinking about as I lay asleep on the sofa the other day. *Ten Things I Hate About You*, Barney Barn-person, or whatever it is he's called. With apologies to Heath Ledger, who we used to swoon over back in the day. Still do sometimes, when we're feeling all regretful that he's not here any more. But this 'Ten things' is the list that celebrates that I can count that far, and *'bossy'* is already added, in at number six. Straight after *being super disturbing – due to unleashing that naked modelling on the world*. And the faster we move on from that one, the better. Especially as we're heading off upstairs. Thinking about it, I could throw another in at number seven. *Makes people go all hot and wobbly*. And damn that Barney has the whole 'Heath Ledger moody bad boy' thing off to perfection. As well as the hollow cheeks, the pout and the unusually lovely pointy teeth. Not that I've seen any more than a glimpse of those when he keeps his lips in a straight line all the time.

'Don't forget this, Barnabus.'

Barney shrugs. 'You're all right, Josie-bus, those things are as good as useless, keep them for your afternoon reading.'

I grab them from her and have a good stare at them, because it's the only way to avoid her 'And who else threw those away before?' look.

As for what number comes after seven, that's where we'll put *arrogant and disgustingly over-confident*. Although we might have had that somewhere earlier too. Because, truly, he is. The way he marched around the first day I arrived, ordering me around, I wasn't getting the wrong impression, that's simply what he's like.

'Is Edie missing our reading?' Cam's frowning as he stands beside the sofa.

Aunty Jo smiles down at him. 'You and me will do some special games today instead. Then we can pick up the reading again with you both tomorrow, okay?'

Seeing I can't get out of this, there's only one thing for it. I grab the gear, speed past Barney, and take the stairs two at a time, making sure he's close enough to see where I'm going because I don't want to lose him and have to start again. There's no telling the energy you get in your legs when the alternative is having a guy trundle up the stairs after you, watching every wobble of your bum in your Audrey Hepburn slim-fits that are considerably tighter than they were when you were working 'all the hours' and some-times had to skip lunch. I reach the top in no time, make a dash along the landing and dive into my room to do a quick check for knickers and/or other embarrassments. I sweep a massive pile of bras off the chair and stuff them under the bed, then, as I look around for more blunders, it hits me that, because I was trying to get some cushion photos earlier, the bed is looking super pristine and styled. Which was exactly right for daydreams about me and Aunty Jo getting our own page in the *Not On The High Street* catalogue, but obviously the last thing I want Barney to think is that I smoothed my bed for him. If I do one huge leap I can mess up the quilt, total the pile of pillows by the bed head, and bounce back onto my feet again. Problem solved. As I hear the creak of his footsteps on the landing I launch myself.

Okay, I hold my hands up – I'm in a panic so I go at it with *way* too much force. First I feel the bed lurch across the floor as I hit it, then I follow it. I'd overlooked Aunty Jo's satin topper, spread out for the benefit of the Etsy customers. The moment I hurl myself, despite the springy mattress, I know there won't be any bouncing back. Instead it's like hitting a bobsleigh track. I whoosh straight across the bed, off the other side, and land with my nose on the wall, jammed against the rose garland paper and the skirting board, my legs still bent upwards onto the bed. And thanks to the weight of my body holding me down, I'm entirely wedged.

'Edie, what the frig?'

For a really short space of time I think about putting down swearing as Barney's number nine. Just to show I'm totally chilled with all this. But then I remember how much I personally love a good swear, so for the moment I leave number nine blank.

His tone deepens from surprise to concern. 'Shit, are you okay down there?'

'Fine.' It comes out muffled because when I try to talk my mouth's full of carpet. 'And don't you dare laugh.' It's only after I've put all the effort into growling the words I remember there's no danger of that. Barney never laughing would make a good gap filler for number nine.

There's a low rumble in his throat, and as I screw my head around his face appears over the edge of the quilt. 'I'd laugh more if my feet weren't caught up in, er, underwear.'

'In *what?*'

'There's this huge pile, it looks like it might have been jammed under the bed.' As he stoops down and pulls, my favourite nude and coffee bra twangs free and narrowly misses hitting him on the ear. 'Agent Provocateur 36C mean anything to you?' For a minute he sounds like he's choking. 'Okay, don't answer that. Stay right where you are.'

'Jeez, Barney.' I make my 'complete disbelief' face. 'It's not as if I have a choice, I'm not exactly going anywhere, put my clothes down and pull on my legs.'

The good thing is, Aunty Jo's satin is just as slippery coming the other way, except this time Barney is hauling me backwards by the ankles. On reflection, I might have been better to have left the bed as it was, and risked looking like I cared what he thought. He probably wouldn't have noticed anyway. It's not like he's that observant. As it is, as I lie there panting on the pale lilac silk, it's not me *or* the bed he's looking at because he's still busy disentangling his feet.

He tosses four bras onto the bed before he kicks his feet free. 'Jeez, it looks like a branch of Knickerbox, although, for underwear, there's a hell of a lot of straps to get caught up on.' For someone unobservant, that's too many observations.

'I was having a sort out.' I'm not about to explain that my lingerie drawer was my secret insurance against losing Marcus, or how keen he was on the 'bondage slut' look. Because, obviously, that didn't go to plan. In fact I totally wasted my money, because in the end it turned out sex wasn't his main obsession at all. And call me tight, but even if I'm single and give absolutely *no* fucks about looking sexy, after the humungous amount it cost me and how comfy it is, I'm damn well going to get my wear out of this stuff.

As I pull myself to my feet, there's a lilt to his lips. 'So I take it from the way you came upstairs like an Olympic sprinter, there's nothing wrong with your legs?' Another comment we could do without.

'Nope.'

'You do realise you can't be too careful about accidental bumps? You're sure you didn't knock your head on the wall?' As he peers at me, his face is so close to mine I can feel the heat coming off him.

'Nope.' With this many questions, it's almost like being back in A&E. I'm also momentarily glad I never gave up on my three dabs of red Gucci Rush on my neck every morning, even though I can't smell it at all.

'So, in that case, shall we get on with the blind? Is this the window?'

'You don't *have* to do it.' It needs to be said.

'I know I don't *have* to.' He's staring straight into my eyes. 'I suspect we're both equally strong and independent, Edie, but sometimes you have to forget being stubborn and accept the help people want to give. Like I have with Cam.'

'Yes, but people love helping a child.' It's completely different from me accepting help. 'Especially one whose mum doesn't live with them.' Jeez knows why I let that slip out, or why I'm scouring his face to tell me more.

'Cam's mum died.'

It hits me like a body blow, but there's a strange sense of relief too. 'Shit, I'm so sorry. I had no idea you were a . . .' This is no time to lose the word.

'That's not quite how it is.' He pauses to breathe. 'Cam's parents were both killed in a boating accident, I'm his guardian, not his dad.'

'Oh shucks, poor Cam, that's so much worse.' As for all my 'bad father' judgements, in that one sentence the way I'm looking at him has been turned upside down. However much Cam looks like a mini version of him, Barney's a hero for stepping up, and he's possibly struggling as much as the rest of us. 'I'm sorry, that came out all wrong, but I had no idea.' I'm cringing that I've judged him at times.

'I didn't rush to tell you, it was great that for once someone saw Cam for himself, rather than the tragic child who lost his parents.' His face is lined with stress. 'But that's why I flounder, and why I grab all the support I can.'

'Right.' Even though I'm not the greatest talker at the best of times lately, at this moment I'm totally lost for words.

'I know it's hard, but life will be a whole lot easier if you stop fighting the help too, Edie Browne. It's a roller blind and four screws. It's not a big deal.' If the revelation about Cam wasn't enough, the pools of those deep brown eyes telling me he completely understands my reluctance are seriously disarming. 'So where would you like it?' He's moving this on, holding a bracket up to the window frame.

'I can choose?' I'm not sure I'm up to deciding.

'Actually no.' He wrinkles his nose. 'That was me trying to sound impressive, it's complete bullshit. Now I'm looking at it more closely, there's only one place it will fit.'

I'm not sure why I find that funny, but I laugh anyway. 'Best put it there, then.' Through the small panes of the window the sky is impossibly blue, and there's a shimmer of the sea in the distance, which has to explain why I'm suddenly feeling all light and airy.

I've worked on building sites for ever, I'm completely used to the sight of guys making holes in walls. So not being able to take my eyes off Barney wielding his level and marking out the places for the screws is crazy. And my eyes locking onto his tanned biceps as they flex under the sleeves of his T-shirt as he lines up his power tool is worse. The only explanation is it has to be the kind of artist's interest, that comes from staring at him for so long at life drawing. That need to know how the muscles work before you can draw a decent picture.

He's brushing away the curly bits of wood shavings with his finger. 'So do you have a lot of seizures then?'

'Sorry?' My gasp is so big if I hadn't been chewing hard on my thumb knuckle I might have inhaled my whole fist. It takes the tiniest part of a second for me to stop feeling guilty and start wondering why the hell he's sticking his nose in. Just because he's making holes in my bedroom window doesn't give him the right to ask about my most private stuff.

'You might have forgotten, but I was there on Sunday, I saw you go down.' He's still examining the holes. Lining up the brackets and winding the screws into place.

'I've only had one before.' It makes it easier because I'm talking to his back. As I scrape around my head for something else to tell him, even I'm surprised by what comes out next. 'Back in October.'

'It must be hard.'

'What?'

'It has to be tricky, not knowing when they're going to happen.' He's pulling on the brackets, testing them, then he goes back to winding the screws again. 'I mean, it was fine at the party, everyone was there to help. But what if I hadn't been there to catch you, or worse, what if you'd been at home on your own?'

Yes, yes, yes, yes. 'Actually, it's really . . .' Fucking scary. Mind-numbingly petrifying. Terrifying enough to send me into a cold sweat, to make me think about it every night when I wake up in the dark. '. . . difficult.'

He turns towards me. 'There you go, underplaying things again, Edie. It's okay, you don't have to hide it from me, that's pure fear I'm seeing in your eyes.'

'It's . . .' From somewhere I find a whisper and force it out. 'Actually, I hate it.' That's it, it's out there. He's the first person I've ever shared that with.

'The worst bit must be never being able to be by yourself. Josie's lovely, but sooner or later you'll both want your independence.' Somehow now he's turned back to the window he's seamlessly slipped back to sounding like a know-it-all again.

'Any suggestions, I'm happy to have them.' He won't have. I think about it every day, and I still haven't come up with an answer. When we do get the house sold and Aunty Jo moves on I'll have to find someone else to live with. Or most likely, move back to

Mum and Dad. I try not to think that I'll never be able to be on my own.

'Leave it with me, I'm working on it.'

'What the hell does that mean?' I'm kicking myself for sounding like it matters so much.

'I don't want to get your hopes up for nothing, so I'll only tell you if it works out.'

'That would be a biggie. But there's no such thing as a free sandwich.' That's not right. 'A free picnic.'

'I think the word you're looking for is "lunch", Edie Browne, but I like both of yours better.' As he turns around to me again, his eyes are dancing.

'So, what do you want that's not lunch, to pay you back in case it does work out?' This has to be the guilt talking too, but I have to warn him. 'I can't do hard stuff.'

'You're the one with the good ideas around here.' This time there's no mistaking. He definitely laughs. 'Seriously, you do enough for Cam, but if you ever have a flash of business inspiration to pass my way, I won't say no.'

Shepherd's huts are really not my thing, but I'm already pondering over his, with their dull wooden insides, how they'd surely be so much more saleable if they were painted.

He hands me the end of the tape and points to the bracket. 'Just hold this here for me, then I'll measure and we'll cut the blind to size.'

He's still laughing, but as I stare at the tape what I see is enough to block his laughter out.

'Edie?' His voice tightens. 'You are okay . . . is the room spinning?'

'No, it's not that.' My eyes are locked on the metal strip. 'It's the numbers.' Suddenly my heart's surging in my chest.

'Yes, if they weren't there it wouldn't be a tape.' He's nodding patiently, but he isn't getting it.

'The numbers . . .' I can't quite believe what I'm saying. '. . . I *know* them. I've been pretty good lately when Aunty Jo's pointed to them on the fridge, but this is the first time I've come across them in real life and they've actually meant something to me.' I run my finger backwards and forwards along the tape. 'Three, seven, five, nine, one.' I stare up at him.

'I reckon you've got that all the way to a hundred there.'

'To where?' I feel like Dad when politics comes on TV. Sometimes you can't help zoning out.

'You know, ten, twenty, thirty, forty . . .'

Thirty? At last there's something I can lock onto again. I smile at him. 'I'm Edie Browne and I'm thirty-two.' It all comes out together, because it's one of the first things Mum taught me to remember. 'Born 29th November 1985.'

'We'll have a party when the time comes for your birthday.'

Except we won't, because I'll be well gone by then. But before I can think about getting back to work, I'm going to need my numbers to be way better than they are.

He's staring at me expectantly.

'With the tape I thought I was doing okay, but I'm not at all.' My heart was whooshing with excitement, but now I've realised how much I still don't know my insides feel like someone stamped on them.

'Edie, it's a few figures, it doesn't matter.'

'But it does to me.' I swallow the saliva that's gathering in my throat, and curse myself for being so all over the place. Whenever this happens, the next thing I know, I'm crying.

Barney gives me a nudge as he rolls in the tape. 'Forget about measuring, you were going to tell me about my free lunch. That's way more important.'

It takes a moment for my head to move on from tangles of numbers, but I need to begin by being honest.

'I can't say I've ever personally hankered after a home on wheels.' Hopefully this covers that I couldn't be less of a fan, but at least thinking about making my excuses has dried up my tears. 'But when I first saw yours I was surprised – maybe even a little disappointed – to find they were just shells.'

Barney's face twists into a grimace. 'We call them shepherd's huts, but it's a well-kept secret, we basically sell wooden boxes.'

'And you're doing really well with that, but what about all the customers who don't have the vision to see what those wooden boxes could become? You're missing them completely.'

'You could be onto something there, Edie. So what are you saying?'

'Only that if you had a few pictures, or better still, a finished example, you'd broaden your appeal. I mean on every new development we do it's the show house that sells the rest of the homes.'

'I'm a carpenter with one favourite colour – battleship grey.'

'I noticed that.' I send him a grin. 'I'm not saying I'll be any better, but I could try some mood boards, work up some colours or maybe some themes?'

'Brilliant, let's give it a go.'

My smile fades as I remember. 'I'm not an expert, in my day job I mostly shout at builders.' There's no point not being honest, other people in the office have always done the designs.

'I'm looking at your pillows.' His lips twist into a grin as he nods towards the bed. 'Anyone who can write *And they slept . . .* on one pillow, and . . . *happily ever after* on the other has got a lot more idea about customer appeal than I do.'

'Arrrghh.' My silent groan comes out way too loud. I really didn't want him to notice my *Mr and Mrs* cushion try-outs, let alone read them. Worst of all, he might think they're my personal pillows of choice and assume that's what I'm looking for in life. 'They're not for me, I'm definitely not desperately seeking Mr Browne.'

'You already told me that the day you arrived and again when we went scrambling.' He laughs. As for the way that smile cuts straight through and belts me in the stomach, that wasn't part of the plan either. When his smile widens and he gets those slices in his cheeks, it makes everything *so* much worse. 'If you give me a few ideas to kick around, I'll even come and paint your bedroom for you, how about that?'

'What?' It comes out as another squeak.

'This wallpaper must play havoc with your brain. I've only been in here five minutes and my head's throbbing.' He's laughing properly now. 'If we're going to get you better, those giant flowers have to go, pretty much right away. And if you're supposed to be taking it easy, it makes sense for me to do the physical stuff, while you work on ideas for the shepherd's huts. I take it making me some mood boards or whatever it is you call them won't tire you out too much?'

In terms of things going downhill fast, I'm pretty much back on the bobsleigh. Giving the guy next door a free pass to my bedroom, and having a Tourette's moment and offering to help him make his poncy shepherd's huts look cool. Two things to take me right out of my comfortable place. And getting smacked in the face with the realisation of how far my maths needs to go. On balance, if I could wipe out where the last few minutes has taken my life, and stick with the curtains, I would.

And for the record, there's a number ten on my list. That smile. It's a total killer. All I can say is thank cupcakes it never gets used. If it did I'd have to shoot back to Bath. Straight away. On the next Uber.

Chapter 26

Epic Achievement: Dying of shame and living to make the tea.

Men in my personal space? I don't wholeheartedly recommend it, but if it's moving the cottage forward, I'll have to work with it.

'Tea, two sugars, and some shortbread.' It's just out of the oven. Still warm.

As I put the mug down on the table in my bedroom, I'm bracing myself to withstand any reaction.

Barney takes a slurp of tea, and as he takes a bite he unleashes a grin. 'Is this *Scottish* shortcake then? You do know the Scots prefer salt on their porridge instead of sugar?'

I saw that one coming, so I've already turned away. In the two weeks since Barney first came into my room, I've taken precautions in other areas too. All my clothes are safe in their drawers, and hidden another time by a layer of dust sheets. With the entire room swathed in Aunty Jo's flowery curtains from Happy-land, it feels a lot less like I'm a teenager luring boys back to my lair.

'Good work. Is it nearly ready?' I lean to the window to check the view. 'The sea is all green and jangly.' It's worth mentioning, because now the days are brighter, the sea changes every time I look.

'Another coat on those two walls, I'll be done. This serenity grey you've chosen has made the room a whole lot calmer.'

'It does what it says—'

His smile widens. '—on the tin.'

And I haven't held back on my side of the bargain either; I've been working on shepherd's hut ideas. First I got a whole load of different photos together on my laptop, then once I scrolled through them with Barney, it was obvious which ones he liked and hated from his groans and sniffs.

So I'm currently overlooking my shudders, channelling my inner shepherdess, and working up themes like Wriggly Tin Man, Scandi Weave, Anything That's Wool or Wood, and Gardens are Green (mostly, but sometimes they have bursts of flowers). As Bella and Tash both pointed out, it's not like I identify with the luxury flats we fit out. I'd never choose wall-to-wall marble for my own bathroom, but I'm happy to deliver them for work. If I think of the Dots, Stripes and Daisies shepherd's hut interior I'm dreaming up as a proper job and a step closer back into the workplace, I can see my brand-new soothing bedroom walls are simply a bonus.

Barney's not the only guy running round the cottage with a paint roller in his hand either. It took one morning of Malcolm sprucing up the lawn with his electric clippers for him to persuade us to let him carry on working inside. People who make things look like their best version are a rare find; not many guys would have transformed the garden to magazine-picture neat in between two cups of tea, and that's how fast he worked. Beth reckons that, unlike my dad, hers is meticulous about the edges and tidying up. Once he told us he came with his own garden vac *and* Weed and Feed, he was straight on the team.

One thing's certain, he wasn't joking about how much *he* needed feeding. In other words, I'm getting plenty of practice baking. With Malcolm here doing bits of decorating some part of most days, we get through so much cake, if we had to get it in town we'd have already blown the entire budget.

It's not only in the cottage that we're making progress. After I put up a card in Plum's gallery – beautifully written by Aunty Jo – we had loads of interest, and more of the stables are being painted out as the barn yard slowly fills up with people who are happy to find what we are careful to point out will be a 'home for a few weeks' max. When George was sorting out the informal letters for them to sign, he mentioned to Aunty Jo that properties sell best here in the summer, so that's what we're heading for.

As a wet nose snuffles against my ankle, I bend down to pat the dog. 'Does Robert want a drink?' However sniffy Aunty Jo is about dogs in the bedrooms, where Barney goes the dog goes too. It's not anything you'd argue about with either of them.

Barney smiles down at the little daxi. 'Thanks, but he's got some water over here.' He's looking up at me now. 'So you like dogs then?'

'Robert's cute.' As I tickle his ears and he rolls over onto his back, it's as if he heard. 'I always wanted a dog as a kid.' Tash and I were desperate but Mum always said it wasn't fair when she was out all day at work. And the growth of households with dogs wasn't a trend Marcus's mates had jumped on as yet, which I was sad about at the time. But if we were struggling over custody of the suitcases, I can't imagine how we'd have managed with a pet.

'And you're not allergic or anything?'

'I don't think so.'

'And would Aunty Jo take to a dog then?'

'She gets tetchy with me when I forget to leave my clean boots by the vegetable rack and swap into my slippers, so dog hairs and dirty paws might push her over the edge.'

He pulls a face at that. 'Robert's small, but in his head he's the size of a Great Dane. So long as I never raise my voice or my hopes when I ask him to do anything, we get along fine. He's really helped Cam settle in too.'

'It must be hard for Cam?'

'He's not doing so badly. Beth and Loella and the kids all look out for him, and he likes coming here.' His face relaxes again. 'He's got a very soft spot for you and Aunty Josie.'

'We've got soft spots for him too.' I'm wondering how long he's been here. 'He's six, remember?'

'I always forget that.' His lips twist.

'And next he'll be seven.'

Barney laughs. 'Now you're just showing off, Edie Browne.'

I'll take that, even though I know my counting should be better.

'One more thing while you're here, I couldn't help noticing when I went down for more paint before, you do *know* who Josie's talking to on her laptop?'

It sounds like a tricky question so I add *all* the details. 'She and my mum could talk for England, except right now she's at school, so it's probably Jean from Happy-land.' She's another big chatter.

Barney lifts an eyebrow. 'Unless your mum sounds like Dr Dre, I'd say it's not her.'

'Dr *who*?'

'He's a Californian rapper. It's definitely a guy with a strong American accent, probably the same one she was Skyping yesterday.'

That too? 'But she doesn't know any men – from *anywhere*.'

'It could be *completely* innocent, but you might want to check it out. There are random guys who befriend lonely women on

Facebook, with the prime intention of emptying their bank accounts.'

'Oh crap. So what do I do now?'

'She's only along the landing, why don't we just ask her?'

'You'll come?' Just for now, I mind his nosiness a lot less.

'It won't take long, we're only looking out for her.' He pushes his paint tray further onto the window sill.

In the few seconds it takes us to pad along the landing, the deep Yankee twang is unmistakable. As we reach the bedroom Barney taps on the door and I follow him straight in.

'Aunty Jo?'

If we were going for an ambush, we nailed it. She's sitting at her table with her laptop and as we breeze into the room her screen slams shut.

'Barnaby, Edie . . .' That's all that comes out, before her squeal comes to a halt.

Barney gets there before I do. 'Sorry, we didn't mean to butt in.'

Aunty Jo's opening and closing her mouth like a goldfish. 'No, you're absolutely not disturbing anything. Nothing at all. I was just sitting here . . . putting on my Dewdreamer. At my age beauty doesn't happen on its own, we have to put the hours in.'

I'm racking my brain as to how we wind this back to her Skyping unsuitable people from across the ocean.

But Barney gets there first again. 'Sorry, Josie.' He's still apologising. 'We could have sworn we heard you watching *Catastrophe* just before. There's this really funny American guy in it, he's so hilarious I told Edie she had to come in and see him for herself.'

I have to hand it to Barney. On balance he might be telling a little while lie, but that probably worked a whole lot better than, *Who the hell are you talking to? They're trying to screw you over and empty your bank account.*

'*Catastrophe?*' Repeating what's just been said says Aunty Jo's as guilty as they come. 'Well, I'm not sure I've ever heard of that one.' Her worried expression slides into dismay. 'And now Robert's here.'

Barney stoops down, scoops him up and tickles his head. 'Trouble's never far behind, are you, Robert? Great timing though, I've been wanting to ask, have you considered what good company a dog could be, Josie?'

'Absolutely not.' Aunty Jo pulls away as Robert's tongue comes towards her cheek. 'Mavis Baxter's Retriever pup ate so much underwear the vet had to operate. When they opened him up they found six pairs of mini bikinis and her two best Chantilly lace thongs. I couldn't cope with that at my age.'

I can't hold back my smile. 'I hope they gave her them back.' I've no idea why we're talking about dogs when we're here to uncover Facebook love rats, but at least Barney knows where Aunty Jo stands on puppies now.

Aunty Jo turns to me. 'You have put all your undies out of harm's way, Edie?'

Barney's grinning. 'Checking for choking hazards is the first thing I do when I come upstairs, I even look under the bed.'

I don't let him catch my eye there. Even if I *could* do snappy back chat I wouldn't be replying to that.

And he's still going. 'Another thing I've been meaning to ask, Josie, with all the room you've got here, have you thought of taking paying guests – or doing Airbnb?'

I don't believe he's gone so far off topic.

Aunty Jo's nose wrinkles even more than it did when she saw Robert. 'I don't like the idea of strangers in the house.' Except for Barney and Malcolm, obviously.

'In that case, maybe you should think about two or three shepherd's huts. You've got plenty of room in the field.'

'Barney!' Considering he was worried about her being exploited,

I hope my best 'wither the builder' look is enough to shut him up.

'What?' His voice goes high in protest. 'I'm trying to make suggestions to help Josie consolidate her real life, not her virtual one, and sort her income problems out at the same time. With those sea views, you'd cover your costs and be into profit in no time, I'd obviously give you a great discount.'

I'm wondering what part of 'making the property saleable to sell' he doesn't understand. I rush across the room and cover Aunty Jo's ears. 'Don't listen, he's being . . .'

'Sensible? Creative? Constructive?'

'No, the word I was looking for is "ridiculous".' And for the record, it has to be said. 'And stop finishing my sentences for me.'

'Sorry, I was only trying to be helpful.'

Aunty Jo's voice is bright. 'I appreciate your generous offer, Barnaby, but I'm afraid it's a "no" for now.' Her nostrils flare, then she clasps her hands together. 'But I have to confess, you were right earlier, I *was* talking to an American. Chester Charles was one of Harry's closest associates.'

I feel myself deflating. 'So he didn't ask for your cash?' Even if I only feel as big as the one on the tape measure, I will get my word in on this. Just to be sure he's not a hard-core fraudster from death row or anything.

She's blinking at me. 'Whyever would he do that? As far as I know, he's a millionaire, possibly even a billionaire.'

In which case, it doesn't matter. 'Good to know, then how about a cup of tea?'

Barney's laughing. 'Thanks, Edie, great idea, mine's two sugars, remember?' Talk about a tea tart – the mug I brought him before won't even be cold yet.

Chapter 27

Day 186: Sunday, 6th May
Bank Holiday Weekend at Periwinkle Cottage

Epic Achievement: Waking up as me – that's all.

When I drift into consciousness on Sunday, the early light is seeping through the muslin blind. For the first time ever, I don't screw up my face and think I'm how I was before the accident, then take an agonising amount of time slowly clawing my way back to remembering how different real life is from how it should be. Instead, as I slide into the day, I'm myself as I am now, and I'm loving the stillness and the quiet. Even better, when I open my eyes properly and stare across the snowy expanse of quilt to the pale silver walls, it feels like I'm waking up inside a cloud.

Less serene is me thinking about flinging my arms around broad shoulders in a soft denim jacket, to say thanks for all the help for giving me my perfect bedroom. It's only a fleeting thought, but realistically if it was a grateful hug, there would be no need at all to be hanging on for so long. I know I'm a bit all over the place, but I'm damn sure I'm right on this one.

What I was a lot less right about was barging in on Aunty Jo the other day. I know I only crept up on her because I was worried,

211

but I still haven't found the right moment to apologise. When I suggested we get her earning, I hadn't expected her to embrace the idea with so much enthusiasm. Ever since, Aunty Jo has been flat-out helping sew Loella's quilts, and when we're working together on the hen party pillows it's been more important to get the order finished than bring up my blunder over mistaken identity.

Barney seems to pop in a hundred times a day too. For the record, I've been working on my big numbers. A hundred is now lodged in my head as a large amount. Like *a lot more* times than you'd ideally like anyone to go up and downstairs doing final touching up to your paintwork. And Malcolm is here almost as much, bobbing in and out, planting things around the garden. Although for some reason, I mind that less.

But now it's Sunday, and apart from curling up with the book that just arrived, the whole day is free. *Looking for Poldark* is a quick reader, it's very skinny, and has been specially written to tempt adult learners to dip in. Marcus always reckoned if he'd been dark not blond he'd have been the spit of the guy who plays the lead in the TV series. I never saw the likeness myself, but at least the book sounds like a page-turner.

But first I have to make it up to Aunty Jo, so for one morning only I throw myself right into the meditation with none of my usual groans. Aunty Jo's adamant I'm going to get huge benefits as soon as I stop fighting and give myself up to it, so she's been reading me long lists of mantras in the hope I'll find something I can mutter without rolling my eyes every time I say it. Last night in front of the TV she read out *Ninety-nine Ways to a New You*. Instead of the usual *Om Dum Tiddly Hum* lines it was things like *'Every day is a second chance'* and *'When it rains, find a lemon under the rainbow and have a G&T'*. After that I realised anything goes so long as it works for you. In fact most of what is on my useful phrase list would do the job.

I was going to try mumbling '*Life's better with blueberry pie*', then I remembered they're black not blue, and even when I could taste I didn't really like them. So instead I went for '*I'm a strong independent woman, and I don't need a man*', because even though it's one of those things that are used too often that I can't immediately remember the name of, it was a good match for today. After saying that for long enough to get cramp in my ankle *and* my right bum cheek, I'd pretty much blasted all those misplaced feelings about getting too close to denim jackets.

I wait until Aunty Jo's put her spoon down from her porridge, then I burst in from the kitchen with a towel and a bowl of warm water, and launch into my plan to say sorry like I really mean it.

'Sooooo, time to dip your toes into my Bank Holiday Surprise Treat.'

'What's all this?'

'It's a pedi, Aunty Jo.' I hold up my bottle and a handful of cotton wool pads. 'First I'll take off your nail varnish.'

'That's nice.' She slips off her ballet slipper, holds out her foot and gives a little shiver as the cold liquid touches her toe. 'I always thought it would be exciting to work as a beautician.'

'Now you've started making cash, there's nothing to stop you branching out.' I look up at her from where I'm kneeling on the rug. 'It could be brill.' I'm talking as I rub. 'Imagine doing pedis for all your old friends?'

As she leans back she closes her eyes and lets out a sigh. 'I'm not sure I'll ever go back to Harpenden again, Sweetpea.' Which is way off the plan I understood, but whatever.

'Okay, next bit.' I slide her foot into the bowl, slap on a handful of scrub, take a breath and try to work out how to begin.

She grabs my quote sheet from the table and starts to fan herself. 'Could you open the French windows a crack, Chickpea? With my feet in this warm water, I'm overheating.'

I get up and do what she asks, then slide back onto the floor and get hold of her foot again. 'So, I'm really, *really* sorry for asking about your friend, Chester.'

She sinks further back into the sofa cushions. 'There's nothing to be sorry for, I *was* hiding it. But he's lost his wife too, and he's *such* a good listener.' Her chest heaves in a sigh. 'Once I thought about it more, me spending so much time Skyping him in New York does feel like a betrayal.'

I feel so mean for making her say that. 'It's not, not if it helps.'

'I probably won't be doing it so often in future.' She's biting her lip and as I go back to working on her other foot she wiggles her toes. 'I try not to show my feet too much, they're so bent and twisted from all those years of ballet.'

'Dancing did that?' It's a good way to move this on.

'It's not all tutus and pink ribbons, it wrecks your feet and your body. But you can't give in, the moment you falter there's someone else ready to take your place.'

'So that was your job, just like Margot?' After all our breakfasts together, her name slides out as easily as my own.

'For a while. And then I met Harry.' Her voice tails off, and we both know why. She gave everything up for him. That's what women did. And now he's gone.

I towel her feet dry and set to with the clippers and emery board. Then as I move on to scraping with the little stick, I can't keep it in.

'I chose work not Marcus.'

'You had to make a choice?' She sounds surprised.

'He wanted a baby, but I wasn't ready to give up on my career.' The genie's out of the bottle and I'm only on her first toe.

'But I thought you modern women had it all – couldn't you do both?' Her brows knit.

'With the new job there was lots of travelling, and a big

workload, but I wanted a couple of years to prove to myself I could do it.' I let out a sigh. 'Kids were next up on Marcus's life list, and he didn't want to wait. All he could see was that without a baby he was lagging behind his friends. All I could see was him being selfish and not considering me at all.'

'That's why you argued? Why you separated?'

I nod. When it's pared down to those few simple sentences, I can't understand how we couldn't find a compromise.

'And do you miss him?'

'Everything changed, so it's hard to say.' I've no way of telling if the ache in my chest is about losing myself or him. Or the shiny life we had together. So that's another to put in the 'pending' tray.

'It sounds strange to say, but Marcus might have had a point. If you don't have children when you're young and fit, you can be too old before you realise.'

I'm Edie Browne . . . 'I'm only thirty-two, surely there's loads of time?' Marcus can't have been right, can he?

'We put it off too long and by the time we tried it was too late. I'd hate you to be like us.'

'I'm so sorry.' I give her foot a squeeze and pat her knee.

'Eventually you accept it, but it's very hard at the time. You shouldn't be too hasty, if you want to be with Marcus, don't be too proud to reconsider.'

'Okay, I'll think about it.' It's strange, when we argued, kids were a lot more of an abstract concept than they are now. After seeing so many tumbling through the cottage, and how interesting and quirky they can be, I can see why so many people actually plan to have them. As I smooth on the foot balm with mint leaves on, I smile at her for being so kind. 'So what colour would you like?' I nod towards the basket of little bottles.

'I always choose peachy pink.' She's back to wiggling her toes. 'But Harry liked dark red.'

'Maybe that, then?' The one I pick up is the colour of red wine. As I shake it, I'm searching for her fingers in the crack between the sofa cushions, and I give her hand a squeeze. 'Harry wouldn't mind, you have to let yourself live again.'

Her eyes are shining as she swallows. 'You do too, Edie.'

I'm nodding, but for a time my throat's too tight to talk. As I slide the silky colour onto her toenails I count in my head to take my mind off feeling weepy. I'm on the second coat and I've counted to fourteen when there's a knock on the window.

It takes me a moment to arrange my bare-faced smile into a state to face 'the world'. But by the time I'm ready to shake back my bed-hair, the pair of boots I'm staring at definitely aren't Barney's.

'Malcolm!' Aunty Jo reacts first. 'Don't look at my gnarly feet, we're just doing a bit of pampering.'

'And having some of that girly chat too.' He pulls a face. 'I popped up to water the hollyhocks, I'm sorry, I couldn't help overhearing.'

'Oh dear.' Aunty Jo goes pale.

Malcolm laughs. 'Don't worry, your secrets are safe with me. But for what it's worth, a long-distance relationship?' He's tutting. 'Totally unsatisfactory.' He turns to me. 'And children are great, don't let anyone tell you otherwise.'

'Thank you for sharing that.' If I glare at him the way Beth does, hopefully he'll close down before he upsets Aunty Jo any more.

Malcolm's looking over the stack of old wood he's carrying, oblivious. 'Anyway, how about tomorrow's Bank Holiday Monday gardeners' outing to take your minds off things? We're visiting a couple of lovely cottage gardens in Rosehill village, then we're having a rollicking' on the beach on the way home.'

'A what?'

He laughs. 'A rollicking good time – it just means a bit of fun. And it's certainly better for you both than staying home, fretting over absent . . . er . . . friends.'

'Maybe when we start to drive we'll come.' We'll be long gone by the time we do, but it's the perfect excuse. And then I catch a glimpse of Aunty Jo, and take in how bereft she looks. 'Unless you'd like to drive us, Malcolm? We could always take the Mini?'

Malcolm's smile widens. 'Great minds, Edie, I came to offer my services. I promise I'll bring you home whenever you're ready.'

He's a retired paramedic. We couldn't be in better hands. I'm actually watching those hands as he lowers the planks he's carrying and heaps them onto the coffee table, along with a pot of paint and a coil of rope.

'Malcolm! What *are* you doing?' Anyone else would have set Aunty Jo's sawdust alarm off a lot sooner.

'They came from the barns, I've cut them to size and drilled holes in the corners. All Edie has to do is paint whatever will fit on from her list, then attach some rope handles. It's an order from a shop on the quayside – they got back to Loella – and they'll pick them up this evening.' He takes in Aunty Jo's astonished expression. 'Don't worry, Edie negotiated a top price.'

I'm jumping in to explain. 'Loella and I dropped in a few shops with a sample sign on the off-chance, I had no idea they'd come back so fast.'

'First the hen party pillows, now this.' Aunty Jo's beaming. 'We could be cooking on gas after all.'

Malcolm's eyes slide off the rather big wood pile and onto my book. 'You'll have to look for Poldark another time. He isn't *that* good-looking in real life, it's all down to camera angles, you do know that?'

'Rubbish, Beth's dad, you're only jealous.' If it comes out easily it's because I'm bouncing inside. To anyone else it might seem like nothing. But making signs is something I can actually do, with a bit of help from Aunty Jo, and now someone wants to pay me to do it. And I almost got the orders myself. On this day in my life, it doesn't get any better. Okay, it's only a few letters on bits of old board. But it means I'm wanted and I'm useful. When I've been totally useless for so long, there's no better feeling.

He's backing towards the door. If he's got any sense he'll leave before Aunty Jo sends him to get his vac.

'Eleven sharp tomorrow, okay? I'll be in my best car, so be ready.'

I'm laughing. 'Can't wait.' And just this once I mean it.

Chapter 28

Day 187: Monday, 7th May
Bank Holiday Weekend Outing to Rosehill

Epic Achievement: Whooping it up with the gardening club. (Just please don't tell anyone.)

Painting the signs was a great opportunity to let my mind wander. Once I'd looked down my list and chosen my shortest sayings, I concentrated really hard and roughed them out in chalk on the planks. As soon as Aunty Jo had checked them over for mistakes, I began to paint the letters using the brushes I'd bought to make a sign for the cottage.

'Stay wild', 'Boom!', 'Salty but Sweet', 'You Can', 'Sparkle & Shine', 'Expect AMAZING'.

Somehow it seemed important that they weren't just any old words, that they were mine, from my heart. But best of all, this time I was able to read the words enough to pick the phrases out myself.

'Shhhhhhhh', 'Grow cactus' – complete with a picture of the cutest little spiky plants – 'Dream BIG', '. . . and chill', 'Make waves', 'As free as . . .', 'Doing this for me', 'Never or now?'

Aunty Jo pointed out that the last one wasn't in the order you'd expect. But in the end we decided it worked better that way because it makes you think more.

As I painted there was space to ponder what we had talked about over the pedi. And I have to come clean. When I say I never thought about having kids, it's not completely true. At times when I lived with Marcus there were rogue thoughts that came out of nowhere, stayed for a moment, then left just as fast. Sometimes when I was passing his games room, in my head for a few fleeting seconds I'd try out what it would be like if it was a nursery. If instead of the cries of FIFA commentators, how it would be if I was standing on the landing listening to the regular breathing of a small sleeping person.

Obviously this was going to be at some very non-definite point in the future, and – obviously, absolutely, crucially – I never said anything to Marcus. I probably didn't actually admit it to myself either. But one day when I accidentally came across the most adorable pale grey fabric with tiny white stars on – it was a given that Marcus would be having a son, he was one of those guys who you just know don't waste their efforts making female sperms – before I even realised what I was doing, I'd noted down the supplier, and taken a snippet. All without it being *in any way* significant. I'd got as far as knowing that was what I'd be using for a blind, if ever it happened, that was all. Saving these things when you see them sidesteps so much frustration if you can't find them later.

It was on the same kind of half-conscious level as the way I daydreamed about the invitation courses at Paper Moon. There wasn't any rush. I wasn't in any way desperate to get proposed to, the images were hazy and distant, as if I were seeing them through layers of floating chiffon. But the point is, they were definitely there. I have had those thoughts. Somehow they simply existed as part of the certainty of my future with Marcus. Like so much else back then, before I got my promotion, before we argued, I'd taken it as a given that, as the cogs turned, everything would fall into place for us, when the time was right. Quite how I missed that Marcus had it all mapped out in his head and wanted the baby part 'now' is a mystery. I certainly never came across *him* standing on the landing looking dreamy. And then everything got turned upside down, and now none of it matters anyway. Apart from what Aunty Jo said yesterday making me think a little bit.

So much for planning for the future. I certainly never thought I'd be out with a gardening club any time before I was Dad's age, but here I am. Getting transported in the back of Beth's dad's Ford Granada, which is almost as old as Beth.

Rosehill isn't far away, and as we head between the hedges and fields away from the more crowded coast, Beth's dad lets us listen to his *Dad's Jukebox* CD. You know what dads are like, turning up the volume when they like a song. We have to put our hands over our ears in *All Right Now,* then my dad's favourite, Razorlight's *America* comes on. Beth's dad is just as insistent as mine about us all joining in, and don't ask me how, but I still know all the words and he's having so much fun he flips it back and plays it through twice more. So before we know it, we're pulling up and getting out on the sweetest village green surrounded by the most picturesque rows of stone cottages and houses, to find all the usual crowd are there too. Not only are there picture book clouds scudding across the bright sky, it's also suddenly baking hot. As we wander past the small paned windows and pretty doorsteps along the main street, despite peeling off my sweatshirt and rolling up my jeans, I'm still having to flap my *Love Saves the Day* T-shirt to stay cool. It's one I bought before I argued with Marcus, and the slogan is bittersweet because that particular day, love didn't save anything at all. If I was buying it again now I'd definitely choose the T-shirt with stars on instead. Just saying. For the record.

Once the tour gets underway, the first gardens we visit are

teensy but immaculate, and crammed between the sweetest higgledy-piggledy stone houses behind wobbly garden walls. As we peep into really neat greenhouses, crammed with trays full of seedlings, Beth is behind us, telling us all the plant names. We pick our way along paths between swathes of tulips and bluebells, gasp at flower-studded camellias, and peer at stripy hostas in shady corners.

She points up at a cascade of tiny blue flowers tumbling over a random stone wall. 'That's a clematis alpina, they're great because they love shade and they flower all through spring.'

'Amazing.' I'm so enthusiastic I'm even surprising myself here. 'The gardens are so pretty, like rooms but outside.'

'Growing things is easier than you'd think, it's very good for inner wellbeing, you should try it some time.' She pauses to send me one of her significant stares, which is completely lost on me because as someone whose Brownie Guide sunflower seeds never made it out of the packet, I have no idea what the hell she's alluding to. 'You'll probably like the next one even better, Edie, it's where we're having refreshments.'

Then we all go to someone's really lovely pale lavender summerhouse, flanked by flowering cherries in full bloom, and spill out across a petal-covered lawn for the kind of cream tea that Cornwall is legendary for. The scones are huge, fluffy and warm, and come on large white china plates, with a dollop of cream and individual jars of homemade strawberry jam, and the tea is strong and delivered in chunky blue and white striped mugs.

Loella gives me a nudge as she kneels down on the checkered wool rug next to me and nods at the fabulous wooden building. 'That's one of Barney's, by the way, painted by the customer.'

'Cool.' It's actually much more than that, so I take a few photos to use on my mood boards. Now she's mentioned him, I might as well ask. 'Where is he, anyway?'

'He was very mysterious, off on some top-secret mission, apparently.' She scratches her nose, then she picks up her scone and turns to the rest of the garden. 'So, remind me, which is the *right* way, jam first with cream on top, or cream first and then jam?'

From her half wink at me she knows it's going to be a controversial question. My stomach's rumbling too much to wait until everyone's had their say, so I quietly get on with the job and compromise by sliding jam under my cream *and* over it. Then Mia spots what I'm doing and copies me, then Tally and all the other kids insist on doing the same.

And when we've all come to the end – some of us for a second time – and we're picking up the last crumbs off our plates on our fingertips, Loella claps her hands for quiet. 'This radical and ultimate variation of jam-cream-jam is going to go down in history as the Edie Browne Cornish Cream Tea, as discovered on the St Aidan Cottage Gardeners' May Bank Holiday Monday outing.'

I know she's only messing about, but it still leaves me grinning, and glowing like the afternoon sunshine on the inside. Although I can't help wondering what Edie from Bath and Bristol would have made of it. I'm not sure she'd have understood at all. Perhaps she'd have been shocked that my life had become so small that that was enough to make me happy? Then it hits me. She wouldn't have been looking round gardens in the first place, so she'd have missed it anyway.

By the time we wind our way back towards the sea again it's late afternoon and, although the sun is still glinting off the pale blue water, the crowds of Bank Holiday visitors are beginning to thin out. We find a spot on the beach at the far end of the bay, away from the town, where the sand is dented and choppy from a day of footfall. We throw down the rugs again, and while the adults dip into the cool box for beers and cans of Coke, the kids dance off and begin to make a castle. Then Loella, Beth's dad and

I wander off along the tideline to find driftwood, and by the time we stomp back along the sand with aching ankles and arms, someone has strung a net across the beach. So while Beth and Morgan make a fire and cook sausages, the rest of us dive around playing that thing where you knock a football in the air with your hands, while the sea behind us rolls in and out and comes closer up the beach as the tide rolls in. Although like everything else in St Aidan, there are apparently no rules, and somehow everyone ends up feeling like they're on the winning team.

I'm back down on the rug again, chatting to Aunty Jo, biting into my hot dog bun, busy trying not to drop ketchup on my jeans, when I feel a poke in my ribs from Loella.

'Barney's here now, there's no hiding his surprise, is there?'

As I look up, I see exactly what she means. Cam is walking along with Robert scampering beside him, at times almost lost in the sand drifts, his usual little brown perky self. But the animal Barney's hanging onto is close to the size of a small pony, and judging by his smile being as wide as the bay, I'd say he's pleased about it.

'You got a new dog?' As I take in what looks like a dirty white floor mop on four gangly legs, its tail wagging wildly in the wind, I'm suddenly doubting my snap judgement. Then it bounds towards me, lets out a woof, and starts to lick my face.

'I was going to say, "Edie, meet Dustin", but I think he just introduced himself.'

'He likes tomato.' I whisk my hot dog out of the way and swipe my hand across my chin, hoping between us we've sorted the sauce smears.

As the dog flops down on the rug beside me, Aunty Jo leaps across to the next blanket and Barney, Cam and Robert shuffle into the space she's left.

Aunty Jo pulls even further back. 'Do tell me you won't be

bringing him to Periwinkle, Barney, my Dyson won't cope with paws that huge and sandy.'

'I feel like I've seen him somewhere before.' As I rub his ears and look into the deep pools of those brown doggy eyes, there's something very familiar about his soft white furry face.

'He's the spit of the singing dog on the Flash advert, you probably recognise him from there, right down to the way he shakes mud over the house.' He cocks an eyebrow at Aunty Jo. 'Don't worry, he'll only come to splatter your walls if you ask him to.'

'I love that advert.' Beth breaks into song. '*Where the hell has all the mud gone . . .? Flash, ah-ha, it works miracles . . .*' and I lead the 'Me too' echoes.

'So what is Dustin, where's he come from, and what the hell are you doing with him?' Loella's doing her bit to bring St Aidan up to speed on this.

'If you're asking about his family tree, his mum was a standard poodle and his dad was an Old English Sheepdog. And his full name is Dustin Welly Boots, but he's fine with just Dustin.'

'A designer hybrid then?' Beth likes her definitions.

'I'd say he was more of a happy accident. As for the rest, he's an assistance dog, but his owner's ill, so he's staying with Cam and I until they can both go home again.'

'You mean the ones that wash up, answer the phone, and pick up socks?' I've seen them on daytime TV, they do stuff like emptying the dishwasher, and bringing your post if you're in a wheelchair.

'If he helps that much, pass him our way.' Loella and Beth are nodding at each other.

'Sorry, help dogs are all individually tailored to match their owner's needs. You'll have to carry on with your own chores. Dustin doesn't do cleaning.' Barney shoots Beth a grin. 'I've got a friend who works as a trainer with one of the charities in Exeter, he's come to us through her.'

'So what does he do?' As he rests his head on my knee it's hard to imagine him doing anything more strenuous than cosying up on the sofa.

'Dustin's special talent is alerting people if his owner needs help, say if she falls. But mostly he's just good company.'

I'm suddenly taking a lot more notice. 'If I had a dog like that, I'd be so much less worried about being on my own.' I can't think why I didn't think of it before. It was probably because I was thinking about so many other things too.

The way Barney's eyes lock with mine, it's like he's reading my mind. 'That's right, Edie, if you hang out with Dustin while he's here, you'll get a better idea. But I'd say a dog like him might be great for you.'

'Guy Barnaby, whichever hat you've pulled this rabbit out of, brilliant work.' Loella reaches across and punches his arm

'Hang out?' I'm staring at Barney.

'I was hoping you might be able to take him out for walks while he's staying? Or visit him at ours when we're out. He's used to a lot more exercise than Cam and I can give him on our own.' Barney's smile is warm. 'Once you get to know each other better, it might give you a chance to try going out by yourself again on the beach. Better still, it'll give poor Josie a rest. I've seen you dragging her along the seafront, you practically walk her legs off.' It's good he's managed to turn this away from me.

Cam's tapping my arm. 'Robert and me want to come too, Barney says we can all go walking on the beach every day when we've done our reading.'

'That's a date then?' I'm smiling down at him, still rubbing Dustin's shaggy head.

'Tomorrow. After school.'

'Defo.'

'So how about a hot dog? Please tell me we haven't missed them.' Barney's moving onto more pressing matters.

Which leaves me holding onto Dustin, and sounding out the words on the sauce bottles with Cam, and puzzling over where the hell 'Heinz' comes into all this. I'm just warning him that hot mustard will make his tongue burn when someone brings a guitar over. It's only when I hear Barney's groan that I realise it's meant for him.

'Strumming by the camp fire, Edie's going to think I'm such a cliché.'

Too right. Going out with the gardeners was already a stretch. If he starts playing *Streets of London* I'll have to jump in Beth's dad's taxi before I die of shame. Hot dogs and hand ball on the beach are one thing. Yes, I do festivals with big stages, but mass singing in small groups in public is way too much for any version of Edie I know. Even the sun sliding down towards the sea, washing the whole beach in a soft golden light, doesn't make it acceptable.

'Okay, it's a school day tomorrow, there's only time for a couple.' He slings the guitar strap over his head, pulls a piece of plastic out of his pocket and runs his thumb across the strings. 'I'm taking requests . . .'

Everybody shouts at once.

'Okay, we'll leave *Mamma Mia* for when we have an Abba night.' He's fiddling, tightening the strings. 'Let's start with Loella's favourite.'

A second later he launches into *American Pie*, and from the way the kids go wild it's not the first time they've heard it. There's an original version which lasts for ages, and an extended one. But the St Aidan version, as played by Barney here, has to be the longest in the world ever, and it ends up getting faster and faster. Then before I even realise he's finished, he's moved straight into a perfect little rendition of *A Crazy Little Thing Called Love*. By the time he gets onto *Breakfast at Tiffany's*, I've given up rolling my eyes and I'm just marvelling at how natural and relaxed he is. I look around to check on Aunty Jo, but she's next to Beth's dad and they're both nodding along. As I tap on Dustin's back, I'm trying to make sense of who exactly Barney is. Decorator, stand-in dad, dog whisperer, then he gets his kit off for the life drawing, and now he's this busker working the crowd with some beaten up guitar and the kind of deep undertones in his voice that are giving me goosebumps.

'Okay, last one.' He looks across at me. 'Not *too* much of a cliché, Edie Browne?'

What can I say? In the end I decide it's best to be honest. 'It's more happy-by-the-sea.'

'I'll take that, even if it does sound like it came straight off your list.'

'No, I promise it didn't.' But I will put it on as soon as I get home.

'So, one last song for all of us here in Happy-by-the-Sea.' Everyone starts shouting again, but he recrosses his ankles and shakes his head. 'This one's mine.'

If he starts playing Dire Straits' *Romeo and Juliet* I might just start to cry. But I'm in luck because he doesn't. As the first slow, laid-back notes drift across the bay, and he raises an eyebrow at me, I already know the tune.

Just a perfect day,
Drink Sangria in the park
And then later
When it gets dark, we go home . . .'

It probably is every bit of the cliché he said I'd say it was, but I forgive him for that. However overdone this one is, I love it anyway, and from the smiles on everyone else's faces, so do they.

'*Oh it's such a perfect day,*

228

I'm glad I spent it with you . . .'

For the smallest fraction of a second it's like he's singing this just for me. That he somehow senses the warm fuzzy feeling that seems to have inexplicably wrapped itself around me like a blanket some time around my third hot dog. It's complete bollocks anyway, because he wasn't even here for most of the day, he only rolled up recently, and it's nothing to do with him anyway. The perfect part is definitely mine. The kind of perfect that's down to an afternoon of flowers and laughing. This one snatched moment, sitting watching the sun slide down towards the sea, with the soft sand giving underneath me as I shift, the frill of the water as it sidles up the beach. Me, but not just me on my own; this is me sitting in the middle of people who all care for each other and only want the best for people. A freckle-faced little boy with his hand on one of my knees, and a dog snoring on my other. One of those moments where you wish the world would stop turning, because for this split second I wouldn't want to be anywhere else, or any other way. Because I'm truly and utterly . . .

Then to my complete horror/shock/mortification, I slide back into real life and realise I'm singing along too.

Chapter 29

Epic Achievement: Rationalising the randomness. (And embracing it, for now.)

As places go, sleepy St Aidan with its handful of shops and hotchpotch of cottages that slide down to the sea, couldn't be more different from the hum and buzz of the cities I left behind. In Bath and Bristol, even though there are parks and trees, mostly it's an undulating ocean of roofs and chimneys and walls and windows, with roads and noise that go on forever. Out of season, in a tiny seaside ghost town where most of the houses aren't lived in anyway, I was expecting the kind of emptiness where I could ease my way back to normality against a backdrop of waves rushing up the beach and the cry of seagulls, with the only excitement being the occasional treat from an evening-opening chippy. But if I was counting on my days here being calm and serene and coherent, I couldn't have been more wrong.

I'm trying to put my finger on the difference between before and now, because in theory, juggling a house, a partner and a full-time job, which is what I did for years up until I moved out of Marcus's, life should have been frantic. But actually I feel way busier now. Back then everything I did was mapped out as far into the future as I could see, and further. Projects were forecasted, holidays and weekends away were pencilled in. My detailed monthly planners were filled up ages ahead with meetings and – less so – fun and relaxation. Then every day was broken up into boxes, short bites of time that were perfectly synchronised so activities flowed easily from one to the next. There were a huge number of people in my life then too, but because they all popped up in the right squares, somehow they fitted in seamlessly.

Even though I maybe wasn't naturally organised to start with, by the end I was so on top of my game we even knew what we'd be eating for dinner weeks before we ate it. On the surface I was still my original, slightly ditsy, smiley self. But if you bothered to look underneath it was a whole neater and tidier story.

Once I'd learned the trick of ruling out surprises, I came to rely on how certain life was. I have to admit, I got to like how reassuring it is to know things aren't going to go tits up at any moment. Until the day Marcus dropped his kiddie bombshell, the only unpredictable bits of my life were the songs coming up on the radio, and the odd site crisis. When the worst I had to deal with was the wrong kind of door closers getting fitted to kitchen cupboards, or the odd hammer getting dropped into a bath so we had to sanction a new one – well, I'd say that super-busy had been realigned into wonderfully manageable.

Then I think of now . . . when there are hardly any people and barely any tasks – and yet life is completely chaotic. Hardly anyone goes out to office jobs, people spend so much more time chatting, doing things together, popping in and out of each other's houses and gardens. Everyone's looking out for everyone else, but in some ways that's exhausting. It's like coping with a family the size of a town.

Once I get to thinking about it, it's lovely that everyone in St Aidan is so welcoming. It's amazing that they're all so involved, and reaching out so much to help us. But no one plans more than a day or two ahead, and that's if you're lucky. Most times they don't look further than the next cup of tea. People have ideas, then they do them *immediately*. What happens from one second to the next depends on the latest brainwave. Every single event, from egg hunts to impromptu singalongs, rolls straight out. It's all very well being spontaneous, but when I'm so used to order it can feel overwhelming. And my other difficulty here is that I still haven't completely got to grips with time yet. I know light and dark, and meals, but in between time is silky; however hard I try to anchor it down, the knots still slip.

As Aunty Jo said when we were poring over her calendar together this morning, I've already been here over two months now. After so much anything-could-happen randomness, I'm wondering how it will feel when I finally get back to Bath and my safe, reliable little boxes.

St Aidan might have been empty when I arrived but it certainly isn't now the season's getting going. There's no hope of a parking space at weekends – not that parking bothers us for now – but the businesses are buzzing. The good part is my plank signs are selling by the stack, and they've ordered more. Loella and Beth helped me choose some of my calligraphy doodles and then had them printed as postcards. Plum has given me my own little rack to sell them at the gallery, and I've framed some as little pictures too. And the orders for cushions keep pinging in, so there's always something to do.

Now the visitors are coming, Plum's using the gallery space for exhibitions, and the classes were going to stop. In passing I mentioned to Loella that it seemed a shame when Aunty Jo's barn is standing empty, and the same afternoon Morgan arrived with some really pretty tables and chairs that were going begging up at The Harbourside Hotel. So it's official, the workshops will move up here until Aunty Jo sells, or the end of the season.

As if life wasn't full enough, now we've added in dog walks too. All it takes for those to happen is Barney knocking on the door with Dustin. With my slippery timescale, whenever he's ready works better for me too. If we had set arrangements I'd spend all my time worrying when they were going to be. At first when Dustin arrived last week we took him for walks with Robert, but he settled in really fast. Seeing as his legs are so much longer, he's getting extra walks on his own now too.

The best walks are the ones when Robert comes too and Cam is there to do the talking. Luckily Dustin loves playing football, so when it's just Barney, Dustin and me, I end up getting all athletic and running twice the distance booting the ball up and down the beach. My small talk's not brilliant at the best of times, but somehow lately when I'm out with just Barney it's like my tongue's glued to the roof of my mouth. But as Barney keeps saying, at least it means I get my miles in and it saves Aunty Jo the trouble. Unless there's a gardening club outing, she refuses to set foot on the sand, and she's not the world's most enthusiastic walker even when we restrict ourselves to cobbles and pavements.

This morning when Barney wanders into view he's got both dogs in tow. As it's already baking in the garden room, where we're finishing our coffee, I grab a cardi and a scarf and hurry outside before Aunty Jo gets too nervy about what Dustin might do to her freshly painted cottage walls.

Before we go anywhere I get the kind of exuberant 'good morning' greeting of licks and jumps and barks from Dustin that makes my heart want to burst, then bob down and get a smaller version from Robert. As I follow Barney out onto the lane, he hands me Dustin's lead.

'Poor old Dustin, Josie's not warming, is she?'

'You thought she would?' I'm not sure why it matters. I'm moving my legs extra fast to put some distance between us along the lane, trying to make it look like it's Dustin's idea.

'Everyone's smitten by Dustin, I had hoped she'd fall a lot more in love than she has.' He and Robert break into a run to catch me. 'Hang on, some of us back here have only got short legs.'

'Sorry, Dustin's pulling.' And some people's legs go all the way up to their armpits. Just saying. Obviously not Robert's.

'Dustin never pulls, he's trained to walk to heel, Edie Browne. You're never going to get the most out of the morning if you're marching.'

I'm hurling out the excuses. 'I'm used to going fast with Aunty Jo.' It's her way of getting it over. 'We all know how wound up she is.'

He's straight back at me. 'What, and you're not?'

My voice rises to a squeak. If I wasn't so incensed I'd mind more that we've hit the pavement now, and we're so close our shoulders are bumping. 'I'm the least uptight person I know. I've always been laid-back.'

He's coughing into his fist. 'And I'm an astronaut . . .'

It sounds like a distraction, but I can't actually remember. 'What do they do again?'

'They orbit the moon in rockets.' He's closing his eyes. 'This has nothing to do with spacemen, Edie, all I'm saying is if you dared to let go more you might surprise yourself.'

Which is rich coming from someone who barely cracked a smile for weeks, and makes me want to run back to the comfort of my well ordered life-boxes faster than ever. But I'm saved an argument when we run straight into one of Dustin's many admirers. Dustin's so much of a waggy bear, not many people pass us on the streets without stopping for a word and a pat, so once I'm down in the village I'm spared getting all self-conscious and tongue-tied.

Another thing now the days are brighter is how much I'm loving being on the beach itself. When I'm up at the cottage I'm always looking out to see what shade the sea is, trying to catch the reflections of its mood, whether it's wild and dishevelled and unpredictable, or serene and calm. On our way down, I long for every new glimpse, framed between the cottages as we wind down through the town, loving the moment when we get down to the quayside and see the whole bay shining in front of us like it is now.

As soon as we cross the harbour we let the dogs off the leads, and they shoot off across the dunes and leap down onto the beach, followed by Barney. I'm teetering on the edge of the last tuft of reeds, working out if I can jump down onto the sand or if I need to edge down on my bottom when Barney turns.

'Need a hand?'

It's the same as the day we went sailing. It's not actually a question because the next moment my feet are flying through the air, only instead of landing in a puddle in the bottom of the boat, this time when I land I'm standing, my boobs crushed against his ribs. I wait for him to take a step back, but he doesn't. He just stares right on down at me, except at close range those dark brown eyes are softer. And I'm stuck there, listening to the rush of the surf falling over the sand, and the bang of his heart – or possibly it's mine. It's one of those moments where the world seems to stop turning – there's enough time for me to watch his mouth part, his head tilt slightly, and for my stomach to leave my body entirely as his wrist lands on my shoulder.

His voice is low. 'We've almost got the beach to ourselves.'

Then his eyes blur out of focus, and for one crazy second I swear he's going to snog me. And the worst thing of all, my lips are parting, ready, and I'm already anticipating the softness and the warmth.

Then he blows out a breath, takes a step back. 'Sorry, I was miles away there.'

I spin, run across the soft sand, down to where the zigzags carved by the waves are like whale bones and the water stretches to infinity. Somehow the bluster of the wind beating on my ears and the incredible curve of the shore stretching in both directions around the curl of the bay isn't covering up how badly I misread that. As I turn around I'm gushing to move this on. 'It's only a few steps down from the promenade, but it's so much more wonderful to be down on the beach, with the sea thundering up on the sand, and my feet pounding towards the waves.'

As he catches me up a few strides later I'm kicking myself for not being able to wrench my eyes away from his throat as he swallows. 'So I take it we've converted you?'

I let my eyes fall to the foam sucking backwards, leaving the shiny expanse of wet sand. Not that I'm overcompensating, but I'm filling the space with anything so there isn't the tiniest crack for my embarrassment. 'I love that the tide just keeps tumbling in then runs back out again, day after day. How the water's got navy blue dapples today when it was bright turquoise yesterday. The way it seems like time's standing still, and yet with so much power it feels like it could go on forever.'

'I'll take that as a "yes" then.'

'I guess you can. And the longer I'm here, the more questions there are.' My strides are so long my breath is coming in little bursts. 'I mean, where does all that splashy foam come from . . . and why are there white horses dancing some days and not others . . . and how come periwinkle shells are so twisty?'

You can tell from the gush how hard I'm trying here. We're a good way along the bay when I look over my shoulder and realise I'm talking to myself, and that Barney stopped walking way back.

'Come on, snails.' He's so far behind I'm having to yell.

He's calling back. 'You keep going as far as the rock pile, Robert and I will wait for you here.'

I'm not going to grumble. Instead I throw another stick for Dustin, rub the sand off the shell I just picked up. As we carry on along the beach I'm forcing the last five minutes out of my head in the hope I'll never think of it again. Put it this way, some moments are best shared because laughing them off diminishes them. But me getting this so wrong makes it too witheringly awful to mention, even to Bella. As for how up for it I was, that's too embarrassing to admit, even to myself.

There's a cool breeze snatching at my hair and making my raggy ponytail even more messy. But the mottled colours of the sea and the warmth of the sun on my back reminds me of all the summers when Marcus and I used to go down to Devon. His family had rented the same rambling seaside house for the same two weeks in summer since he was a kid, and we always came along at some point to join in. It was all very *Swallows and Amazons*, nothing like my semi-detached childhood at all. There was a boat house, and a dinghy with brown sails, and a housekeeper, and lobster, and they cooked whole fish in the embers in a fire pit in the garden. And there was a thing called a fish kettle that his mum actually knew how to use, and the Prosecco came out of the boot in wooden boxes from the wine merchants instead of from the supermarket. Even though they always seemed really pleased to see us, and laughed instead of minding when I didn't want to eat oysters, I always felt like I'd made a mistake with the front door I'd knocked on, and accidentally arrived at the wrong party. It was the same feeling I had when we went to their proper house in the country too. The year Tiddlywink was born, Marcus's parents finally invited me to theirs for a big Christmas with all the frills. Bella was like, 'Yes, you're in, girl, bring on the log fires and canapés from Waitrose', but I was cacking it so much I had to say Tash was desperate for me to help at hers, and so we went there instead. That could have been my biggest mistake. Letting a guy smell a newborn close up can go either way, and in my case it turned out to be the wrong one. That's the trouble, once you start looking back on a relationship, the cracks hadn't just happened. Once you remember what you're looking for, and start doing the kind of deep thinking you can only do when you're walking on your own along an – almost – empty beach it's surprising how far back you can trace them.

By the time I reach the rocks and turn, Barney is so far away he looks really small, sitting on the sand resting his elbows on his knees. But I know he's watching us all the way back, because every time I lift my hand and waggle Dustin's stick in the air and try to act as if I didn't just make the biggest mistake of my life to date, he waves back at us. Eventually we pick up the pace and jog the rest of the way along the beach. As we arrive back, Dustin bounds up and sticks his nose in Barney's ear then gives it a good washing, then checks that Robert's still smelling the same. By the time he's finished, Dustin's tongue is lolling, and I'm warm and gasping, but I force myself to ask, because why wouldn't I?

'Is everything okay, why didn't you come?'

'We're fine, I wanted you and Dustin to try walking by yourselves. How was it?'

'Good, he chased sticks, mostly.'

'I was meaning for you, not him.' There's a twist to Barney's lips. 'Were you okay out there on your own?'

'I wasn't on my own.' Having the empty thinking space was delicious. Whatever anyone says, it's hard to drift off completely when there's someone – anyone – walking beside you.

'That's exactly what I hoped you'd feel, we'll do the same again tomorrow. When I organised for Dustin to stay I didn't dare hope you'd bond as you have, but if you had a dog of your own who was specifically trained to look after you, you'd feel even more secure.'

'So you actually got him for me?'

'Well er . . . yes . . . and . . . er . . . no.' The hesitation is the giveaway.

'But why?'

'You're young, and vibrant and alive, if there's a way of getting you your freedom back, we have to explore it.' That's so kind and so full of hope it's making me warm and shivery all at the same time. But it wasn't what I meant.

'But you hardly know me.'

'Yes, I do.' The lines on his face deepen. 'In any case, I reckon as humans we're hardwired to help, whether we know each other or not. It's part of our instinct, it's what makes us survive.' He lets out a sigh. 'When I was having a rough time when I first had Cam, people came through for me, and now it's my turn. Helping out isn't about reciprocating or paying back, it's more about paying on. Then, next time, you'll be there for someone else. Well, you already are with Cam, but you know what I mean.'

'You're so full of thoughts.' I'm sucking away the spit that's pooling under my tongue, and he's still shrugging this off.

'Don't overstate what I'm doing here, you went a few yards on your own with someone else's dog, while I watched out for you. I simply wanted to show you, however bad things seem for you, living with the threat of seizures, there will be a way, that's all.'

'Whatever the reason, thank you.' Any moment now I'm going to be wailing. But then Dustin bounds over, whacks me in the leg with his stick, then comes in for more fuss. By the time I've buried my nose in the top of his silky head, I'm more myself again.

Then Barney jumps to his feet, and this time, as we meander back towards the blue and white railings and the seafront, I'm so grateful I'm not wanting to hurry ahead or beat myself up for earlier. As we reach the broad stone steps that lead away from the beach, I stop to pick up another shell. He springs up onto the cobbles ahead of me and turns.

'There is something else I'm hoping you could help me with.'

'And?' If he wants me to pop round to give Dustin his dinner while he and Cam are out tonight, that's fine.

'I want to take your ideas a step further. I was so wrapped up in getting the shells right and the business off the ground, I missed the bloomin' obvious. The way people have reacted to your pictures, having a show hut or two would definitely help sales.'

'Cool, that's fine by me, you'd definitely ace it if you decorated a couple.' It's actually so satisfying I feel like punching the air, but I manage to hold back. 'You don't have to stop at show huts, you know.'

'Go on?'

'You already do made-to-measure shells, but if you did bespoke hut interiors and offered a tailored design service, you'd really add value.' I'm astonishing myself at how much of the jargon is still there to pull out, and I'm on a roll here. 'I mean, why stop at the insides? You could design the outside spaces too. Better still, you could have a corner of one of your barns full of quirky bits and pieces for people to choose from to put in their huts.'

'Whoever said you were a creative genius was seriously under-stating. You've just consolidated my business plan for years to come.'

I roll my eyes at him. 'Bollocks, Barney person, it's common sense.' Maybe with a bit of beachy magic thrown in.

'However much it was staring me in the face, I still managed to miss it all this time.' He's shaking his head. 'More important than ever now, I'd like to offer you some work.'

'Work, like a job?' My jaw has dropped because it's so far away from what I was expecting.

His lips are twitching. 'How would you feel about turning these ideas of yours into reality? Part-time hours, you can begin with an hour here and there. You could start with a show hut?'

'So, painting?' As I nod, my tummy's done a triple flip at the thought of real, actual employment.

'Yep, the areas are small so they're fiddly but they shouldn't be too tiring.' His eyes are shining. 'If we're going down the fancy route, I'd need your help with accessories too. With your latest brainwave, they'll be for inside *and* outside.'

I'm feeling too weak to reply.

He takes in how far my jaw has dropped and back-pedals. 'Sorry, that's me getting carried away, the last thing I wanted was to overwhelm you.'

'Over *what*?' If he was planning to scare me shitless, he couldn't have done a better job. My legs have frozen halfway up the steps.

'Okay, Edie Browne, breathe.' He's managing to smile and burst with kindness all at the same time. 'Let me start again – could you spare me an hour on Monday morning to roll some very pretty paint onto a very tiny wall?'

Put like that . . . 'Yes, I could.' My mind is jumping ahead to everything I should be asking. 'What time, when?' What to wear. The music they'll be listening to. If I need to bring my own sand-wiches.

'Let's stay relaxed about this. After we've taken Dustin and Robert out, the paint of your choice will be waiting, I'll be there all day. So I'll get the biscuits in, and whenever you feel ready, you just turn up with your smile and your overalls.'

Sounds like he's covered most bases. Which is just as well because I went out for a walk and apparently I've come back with a new career. It's like the guy who climbed a hill and came back down a mountain. Well, not quite, but you get the idea. However huge my excitement rush, I decide, on balance, not to throw my arms around him and smack kisses all over his cheeks. I only hope I don't disappoint him.

Chapter 30

Day 212: Friday, 1st June
At Periwinkle Cottage

Epic Achievement: Filling up my work wardrobe (just not in the way I'd hoped.)

If the last two weeks have shown me anything, it's that nothing in life is predictable. There I was expecting to be painting the cottage and the stables, and instead I'm messing around with shepherd's huts and falling over the children, who are suddenly all on half-term. I mean, when do they actually learn anything, because they're hardly ever at school? I'm putting the hours in – weekdays, weekends *and* holidays – and I've got my work cut out to catch up with what they already know.

When I'm down at the barns with Barney the first week it leaves Aunty Jo free to go to *all* the classes, as well as the over sixties lunches, which are completely not what the name implies, because they seem to go on all day. And at Periwinkle the work is still progressing even though I'm not there. Thanks to Malcolm bringing in a couple of his mates from the Silver Surfers Club, cake consumption has gone through the roof, but space by space, the cottage is being transformed. As the paper is peeled off, the rooms left behind are light and airy, but best of all, they're looking very neutral and wonderfully marketable.

I'm still arguing over colour schemes with Aunty Jo. Her going big on bubblegum and neon rainbows is not helpful, not at this point or any other, come to that. We're rolling up the old carpets, painting the worst floorboards, scrubbing the best ones, mostly painting the walls white with an occasional hint of whisper grey, and little by little we're getting there with that airy beach hut feel.

As for me, going out to *actual* work, even for a short time every day, leaves me feeling slightly stunned and a lot more exhausted than I expect, considering the tiny amounts I'm doing. But it's also *so* good to break free from being at home all day, and any job with all-you-can eat Jammy Dodgers – a great choice, thank you, Barney – can't be so bad.

Having the dogs on hand at the barns to watch and cheer me on makes up for my attention span being painfully short. Barney must either be very desperate or some kind of saint, because if I were an employer I wouldn't give myself a job. It's funny how things like not being able to concentrate aren't obvious when you're pottering around the house, but when you're at work there's no place to hide. If I'm supposed to be painting, it's pretty damned obvious if I break off to wander round the orchard to see how the apples are coming on – nicely, in fact, a lot of the trees are laden. The first couple of days are the worst. I spend an inordinate amount of time marvelling at the kind of patterns the apple green leaves make against the velvet blue of the sky, and watching the seagull crowds that follow the fishing boats as they chug back towards the harbour. But after a few days I get into a better rhythm, and I learn to break up my short bursts of painting with outings to search for accessories to bring the huts to life.

We begin with the Wriggly Tin Man hut, where the outside is exactly what it says and which Barney has already painted the colour of a stormy sky, which kept him close enough to his comfort zone, with the windows picked out in cream. Inside I start by painting the walls creamy white, then add in shades of light grey for the feature areas, with darker grey on the flat cupboard fronts, and chunky timber on the tops.

I find some lovely grey and white geometric prints in Loella's fabric piles which Aunty Jo makes into cushion covers, along with some plain yellow ones too. For the furnishings we decided that reclaimed would be more in line with the feel and be more cost-effective than new, at least until we actually get some firm orders in, so I head off around everyone's houses to see what I can steal. Barney lets me have a soft petrol blue quilt cover which is grey enough to work, I borrow a couple of teak fifties-style sling chairs from Aunty Jo, that used to be in Harry's study in Happy-town, and I take a coffee table from Beth's dad's garage that Barney tops with rough-hewn planks. A couple of vintage storm lanterns come from Aunty Jo's barn, and Beth lets me borrow some of her tall candle lanterns for inside, and some stumpy ones to go up the steps. Then her dad lends me an old book on tin mines, and I get some copies of some of the old black and white pictures of miners from there and put them in some mismatched frames. By the time I've added in a couple of black and white stripe deckchairs outside and attached a string of solar light bulbs to poles around the sitting area, it's almost there. Two old milk churns with Malcolm's white flowers tumbling down the sides, and a little hanging plank sign saying *Tin Men live here*, and Barney's happy. Considering I'm not a fan, I'm surprisingly pleased with myself. It's a long way off Zinc Inc standards, I know, but the dappled light of the pear trees and the sea shimmering in the distance somehow make up for that.

When the post comes on Friday morning at the end of my second week, Aunty Jo and I have finished our Oat So Lovely and are lingering over coffee in the sunshine at the table out in the courtyard, waiting for today's influx of children. As I catch a glimpse of the familiar logo on the mini-catalogue the postman hands me, my heart lifts.

'Leah Lemon – I've missed these clothes so much.' I'm reading and remembering at the same time, and as I tear off the plastic, this arriving at the end of my first two weeks back at part-time work feels particularly auspicious.

'Your nice slacks come from there, don't they? And your tops.' Aunty Jo leans across. 'Ten per cent off too, Sweetpea, that means the clothes cost less than normal.'

'That's good then.' It gives me even more of an excuse to treat myself after so long without shopping.

'It's probably because you haven't bought any for a while, they're trying to tempt you back.'

'You can never have enough capri pants.' That's my mantra for the day as I flip through the pages. Ditto to summer chinos. Especially when the next size up from the ones I have upstairs would give me just that little bit more breathing space. When I come to the page with the lightweight tailored jacket and trousers, my tummy does the kind of flip you get from seeing your boyfriend when you're a teenager. 'That's what I'm really looking for.' I've never done suits for work, but I picked this one out last year as perfect for those days with tricky meetings. It's grown up enough to send out the message that you can't be messed around, without making you look like you take yourself too seriously. Sadly, by the time I got my fancy new title to go with the suit they'd sold out of their summer lines in my size, but I promised myself I'd buy one as soon as they came in again.

'A *work* suit?'

I've got no idea why Aunty Jo's sounding so doubtful; the way my time here is flying by, I'll be back in Bath before we know it. But there's no time to ask because Dustin is bounding towards me, and by the time he's finished saying 'Good morning' he's practically sitting on my knee.

'Work clothes? For goodness' sake don't go ordering any more overalls unless you want to melt, there's a heatwave coming.' It's typical of Barney to join in as he saunters across the gravel, but he's usually closer to the mark than that. 'I've been meaning to say, I've got loads of Levi's with ripped knees at home, if you'd like some to make into cut-offs for painting, just give a shout.'

'That would be lovely, thank you, Barney. Bermudas and T-shirts will be much cooler for Edie than those synthetic boiler suits.'

'I reckon they'll fit you okay.'

Don't you just hate it when tall guys take the same size as you in jeans? As if it's not bad enough having Aunty Jo accepting the offer, now I've got to squirm while Barney stares at my thighs to check.

'I'll bring you some T-shirts too.'

'Great, I'll look forward to that.' I can't wait. Cast-offs from down the lane don't quite cut it when I had my heart set on a Leah L suit.

'There you go, Sweetpea, summer shorts will be much more useful than office clothes for now. Does Lily Lemon do beachwear? Maybe you could order some of that?'

'Or maybe I'll leave it for now.' I try to ignore how deflated that's making me feel. At this rate Leah Lemon will be crossing me off her mailing list, so I'm not writing this off entirely. I'll have another look *after work*. It's funny how those two little words make me feel like I'm giving a secret, silent cheer. As if I'm almost human again.

'So now Tin Man's finished, which hut are we going onto next?' Barney picks up on Robert's hard stare. 'That's after the dog walk, obviously.' Having seen the first hut finished, he now wants to do a hut for every theme so far, but we'll see how that goes.

'We'll wait to do Dots and Daisies.' I chose some wallpaper samples from the internet, and Aunty Jo organised for the entire pub at the over sixties lunch to send off for the same ones, so I can get enough bits of paper to cover a whole wall of the hut in a random patchwork of flowery prints. But we're still waiting for those to come.

'We could do a beach one next, seeing it's so warm? The Seaside Stripes, or She Sells Sea Shells.' Barney's rubbing his hands.

'The stripy fabric's here.' As I smile at Aunty Jo she's already nodding. 'If you have time to sew it?'

Barney's tilting his head. 'So what about the furniture for that? It's fine ransacking everyone's garden sheds, but we've pretty much exhausted the supply along the lane. We might need to go shopping.'

'That's my line, Barney.' And I just made a sassy comeback, even without my suit. Except this far I'd done everything I could to avoid saying it, hence the begging and borrowing. 'What about the internet place with the happy endings and the bids?' I watch his eyes cloud and clear again.

'You mean eBay?' He pulls a face. 'Sorry, but I haven't got time to run around the county for that, we'll try some real shops first.'

'So do you know somewhere?' If we were in Bristol, I'd know the exact places to get interesting pieces to upcycle without getting ripped off. But we're not. And it's obvious any shopping around here will mean leaving St Aidan. I've actually got used to pottering around Barney's yard, but I'm really not ready for a long trip out of town with him, even if the entire gardening club comes along too.

'I get mate's rates at Junkyard Warehouse in Falmouth – we could try there? And Cam's gone off with Loella for the day, so I'm free.'

'Falmouth?' I might have been fast with my last comeback, but there's more to take in here. I always relied on that thing in my car to tell me where places were, but I'm sure it's not near.

'No need to look so appalled, Edie Browne. We're not going to the moon, it's only forty-five minutes away.'

'About like Bristol to Bath, Sweetpea.' Aunty Jo translating for me is almost automatic these days. It's not the distance I'm bothered about.

He gives a low laugh. 'Definitely no sailing or tree climbing. If we shoot straight off after the walk, we'll easily be back for when Cam comes home.'

'An all day trip then?'

'That depends on your definition of day.' He laughs. 'And how long you take over lunch. But if we're doing it, we'd better get going, those shepherd's huts aren't going to fill themselves.' Yet again he's talking complete sense. This has to be done. Some of us will have to grit our teeth and get on with it. The sooner it's done, the sooner it's over.

'Great. Got you.' This is a working day, I'm entirely used to keeping everything professional, there's no need to look at it as anything else. Get in the car, source what we need, drive back home again. How hard can it be? I know Marcus and I used to search for months before we found the perfect pieces for his place, but it's so much less agonising to choose when it's for anyone else than for yourself. If anyone knows why my '*Happy Friday*' sign's flashing up in my brain as I take Dustin's lead from Barney, please let me know. Answers on a postcard to Edie Browne, Periwinkle Cottage. Because I'm damned sure I don't know myself.

Chapter 31

Day 212: Friday, 1st June
Gone Shopping

Epic Achievement: Getting déjà vu – I'm guessing that's a good thing.
(Even if it's only to do with chairs.)

However tiny my new job is, having a day out for it is another box to tick on my way back to normality, so I should be whooping. But work trips are like everything else around here – there's a rest-of-the-world version, and then there's the St Aidan sort. First off is the transport – not the truck itself, more that Barney has to move a heap of Cam's felt pens, a couple of empty muffin papers, Robert's Christmas dog jumper, and a whole pile of shed sketches before I can even see the seat. Then as I climb in, he slides up the volume on his phone.

'So what's the music?' That's the first rule for successful work trips – negotiate what you're listening to and how loud the second you get in the car if you want to avoid all-day Shania. Not that I'm grumbling. But when I'm bumping down the lane in a double row cab with a pick-up on the back that would make a builders' van seem luxurious, I can't help a little pang for my own shiny work car complete with the Advanced Technology speaker upgrade.

'The soundtrack from *Bridget Jones*.'

'Er . . . *really?*'

'Malcolm's suggestion, on shuffle to keep an element of surprise. Apparently every woman loves it, so it should be relaxing.' He shoots me a sideways grin. 'You have to admit, there are a lot of similarities.' The points he got for saying woman not girl are scrubbed out in an instant.

'You're saying I'm like Bridget?'

'Not the posh bit, because your West Country burr is really strong when you swear.'

'And eff you too, Barney Barn.' That's the one bit I wouldn't have minded.

'I know your hair's darker, but think about the rest – sunnies on your head, being hot and having no idea, both being accident prone and full of unrealised potential, your penchant for bunny ears. Enough said? You even wrinkle your noses the same.'

There's so much there to argue with, I'm not even going to try. What's more, I'm not sure if it's good or bad that he's so familiar with BJ he can make the comparison.

'But Bridget wasn't ill.' I never pull the illness card, but just this once I'll make an exception if it means I can shut him up. And if he's skipped over the glaringly obvious, like us both being single, similarly wide, and our trousers being at least three sizes larger than we'd ideally like, I'm not going to flag those up either.

'That's how you define yourself, isn't it? The stroke *really* is all you see.' As he blows out his cheeks and lets out a long breath, his laugh has flipped to accusing disbelief. 'No one else even gives that a second thought. Yes, we're considerate, and we care, but when we look at you we see everything you can do, not what you can't. You know the biggest reason you're like Bridget? Because you're frigging amazing, and exactly like her, you can't even see that.'

'Is that it?' Somehow I manage to close my gaping jaw enough to get that out. 'Are you done?'

'Not quite.' He's drumming his fingers on the steering wheel. 'From now on, please let's concentrate on the stuff you're good at and forget the rest. Is that a deal?'

'I s'pose.' To be honest, I'm too shocked to say anything else. No one's ever been that insensitive or harsh enough to speak to me like this before. Worse still, I'm torn. I'm blazing that he's had the cheek to wade in. But when I stop to think harder, along with the angry protest he's dishing out compliments by the shedload.

'Great. In that case we'll let Robbie sing a bit louder.'

As the music fills the cab I sit back against the scuffed plastic of my seat and let *Me and Mrs Jones* wash over me. Bella will be jumping up and down when I tell her about this later, I can hear her now, screaming 'hot like Bridget Jones' is workplace harassment'. Whereas Tash might see the wood through the trees – or is it the trees through the wood? She'll focus on giving him the benefit of the doubt. Or is benefit something to do with make-up?

Whatever, it seems like now Barney's said his piece and I've agreed terms. We're moving on, so I brace myself. I've spent the whole beach walk gearing up for serious discussions on subjects like *Are milk churns the limit of our twee-ness?* – heaven help me if they're not – and *Does he see his client base as essentially coming down on the side of ditsy print, gypsy jewels or hewn slate?* But there's absolutely no chance for me to impress anyone with my conversational gems because he keeps up a running commentary of every village we drive past. And as if travelling with the talking version of Cornwall's *Lonely Planet* guide wasn't enough, we've got the dogs along too. Dustin's sticking his nose in my ear over the back of the seat and dribbling on my shoulder, but this is the one bit I'm pleased about.

As we finally chug our way into Falmouth the streets are clogged with traffic. By the time we emerge onto the waterfront the sun's washing over the stone cobbles and, despite the open windows, I'm baking because the truck windscreen is acting like a green-house. The quayside here is every bit as picturesque and mismatched as St Aidan, but somehow much bigger and taller and wider with industrial echoes around the edges. I take in the mix of pink and white and stone houses that are just as colourful as the ones I'm familiar with, but the expanse of jade water crowded with bobbing boats and masts seems to stretch forever. It might be the light sparkling on the harbour or it could be the upbeat tempo of *It's Raining Men*, but whatever it is, I'm less cross than I was.

Barney seems to know where he's going with no help from the woman on the satnav who tells you what lane to get into, and he winds his way between the buildings and pulls up behind what looks like a weathered yet very bulky shed. I'm squinting at the sign, but Barney gets there first.

'*Four floors of beautiful rubbish. Welcome to The Junkyard.*' He's looking pleased with himself as he jumps down from the truck and opens the back door. Then he whistles to Dustin and carefully lifts Robert down from the seat and lets him scamper off across the gravel car park. 'We should find the right combo of kitsch, stylish and battered here.'

I slide my sunnies onto the top of my head as we head towards the entrance. 'Do you think there's a toilet?'

'Behind the office, first on the left.' He holds the door open for us all, and points me towards the ladies.

By the time I come out again, I'm reassured my foundation hasn't slithered off my face and onto my shell top. As I make my way across a huge room stacked with rows of furniture piled high to where Barney is chatting to a guy with major muscles and a bushy beard, it's probably too dim for anyone to notice quite how long I've spent getting my lippy back to perfect. But at least it's light enough for me to immediately spot a couple of quirky little pieces that would fit nicely into a shepherd's hut.

'Edie Browne, come and meet Greg, he's just made his first sale.'

'What's that?' Being from St Aidan, I wasn't expecting him to start this fast.

'I've bought a job lot of two hundred seafront deckchairs.'

'Are you *sure* about that?' Four more huts, two chairs each. Even if he decides to do five, I'm sure that's still way too many.

'It's possibly a hundred and ninety-two more than we need straight away, but as the old saying goes, "They're too good to leave in the shop". Greg will deliver and there's plenty of room to store them upstairs at mine.

'Ok-a-a-a-a-y.'

'Once you paint some witty words on them they'll sell like hot cakes for ten times what I'm paying, I can already see customers asleep in chairs with lines of zeds on. Our second joint venture, if we carry on like this we'll be relocating to a tax haven in the Cayman Islands in no time.' His lips are twisting. 'Now back to the real business, can you see anything you'd like for the huts?'

As if one joint venture wasn't enough already. As it is, another chance for me to earn should make me feel like laughing not groaning. Then as I begin to scour the nearby piles, there's something about the dust floating in the sunlight shafts than takes me back to all the Saturdays Marcus and I went hunting in Bristol for those perfect reclaimed pieces for his house. We once drove all the way to Glasgow for two designer leather chairs I'd bought on eBay for a snip. I can still remember how good the super-sized ice-cool Cokes tasted when we stopped at Burger King on the way home. Looking back on that person biting into her Whopper Meal Deal Double Decker and fries, it's hard to think how excited I was for that future with Marcus. How naive I was to be *so* cheery and hopeful when it was all going to come crashing down within a few years. Back then we were still a team. Marcus was always the one who muscled in to open negotiations in the reclamation warehouses. But I was the one who chipped away and whittled and wheedled until the owners came down to something we could afford.

If I hadn't made the deal with Barney about looking forwards not back, I might be cursing that I've lost that edge. Kicking myself for not being able to work out what the price tickets say, let along get in there to bargain and argue. But as it is, for one time only, I'm going to let it go. Let's face it, any guy who just bought a barn full of deckchairs doesn't need my help with haggling.

However great it was rushing around the country being carefree and clueless, I'm not wholly sure I'd swap back to that, even if I could. Would I rather be wildly over-optimistic, with everything ahead of me to lose? Or is it better to have lost it already and be coming through the other side? It's funny to think I'm still looking for chairs. But deep down it's a relief to be doing it from a more grounded, realistic place. Rock-bottom wouldn't be the destination of choice for a lot of people. But when you actually arrive there, there's a reassuring firmness and solidity that no one tells you about. There's something peculiarly okay about being in a shit place where the smallest improvement can seem like great news.

As I look up I realise Barney's watching me.

'You look like you do this a lot.'

'With my ex, for that house I once told you about.'

Barney's brow wrinkles. 'So what did you do at work?'

'I told you that too, I shouted at builders.'

'And what were they building?'

'Lately I mostly oversaw large developments of exclusive flats.'

'Jeez, I can see why patchwork didn't exactly hit the spot after that.' He's blinking at me. 'And why I'm extra lucky to have you picking out gems for the huts. So is there anything here that would work?'

As I realise Barney's staring at me expectantly, I turn my mind back to the job in hand.

'How about this?' The cupboard I'm pointing to is plain, but best of all, it's not too deep. 'It will paint up very nicely. But there again so would this – and this – and this – and this – and this.' As I move along the rows I'm picking out shelves and chests of drawers and tables that would be insignificant in a larger house, but would be perfect for where we want to use them. As Barney moves behind me, nodding, Greg's sticking red 'sold' stickers on the fronts, and making notes of the numbers on their price tickets.

'Everything all right, Edie?'

'You're putting on sold stickers, but we haven't made up our minds.' Somehow I thought we'd be considering everything suitable, Barney would scratch his head, agonise about the prices, and then we'd be choosing the best ones. 'Do you want *all* of them?'

'It saves coming back again.'

'That's true.' I'll go with that.

'Actually, I need to come clean. I'm not just buying for the huts you're working on. I'm taking your other suggestion to heart, buying stock to sell on.'

'You're making a shop after all?'

'There are still a couple of stables left in the barn yard at Periwinkle. Just supposing I rent those and you take charge of styling . . .?' His eyes are bright as they lock with mine. 'We'll have an instant interior design centre for garden buildings.'

'You do know they're only temporary?'

'Obviously we can't stay there forever, but for the price of the paint we'd get an idea of whether it was workable. You could put your signs and the deckchairs in there too, and Beth's lanterns, and Loella's quilts and Josie's cushions, along with anything else you sourced.' He seems to have covered the lot, right down to the sweeteners.

'Browne and Barnaby then?' I'm being ironic.

'It's got a nice ring to it.'

My eyes are open so wide I think they're going to burst, but my throat has closed because that was the last thing he was supposed to say. 'Tell me you're joking.'

'The great thing is, this is just the beginning – these wooden boxes don't only have to go on axles and wheels or concrete plinths, we could explore the tree house aesthetic too.' He's sounding so excited, but someone has to bring him down to earth again.

'But how many people actually use their tree houses?' I can't believe I thought shepherd's huts were as bad as it could get. If we're talking useless toys for rich people, tree houses are so much worse. When I made suggestions, I wasn't bargaining on getting heavily involved.

'If they're properly constructed and designed, people love pods at tree level. With your vision and my timber skills, we make a crack team. All you need to do is say the word, Edie Browne. I can sense how reluctant you are to exploit your talent, but I'm not letting you give up on this one.'

'Great.' It comes out a lot more squeaky than I planned because it's so far from the truth. If ever I needed motivation to get back to Zinc Inc, the civilisation of Bath, and the blissful comfort zone of retirement flats, it's the threat of building shepherd's huts in the sky.

'Anyway, we'd better get on.' He gives my elbow a nudge with his. 'There's the whole of this floor to look through, then the easy chairs and wood-burners are upstairs, and then there's an outdoor section too. And we could call in at a chandlery or two while we're here.'

'Right.' My knees are feeling as weak as my croak. As morning's go, this one has been one of those times there are no words wide enough to express the size of the disaster area that sprung out of nowhere. As a measure of how uncomfortable it's been, I'd have swapped it for a patchwork class in a heartbeat. If this is what happens when I think out loud, next time I need to keep my mouth shut. Having ideas is one thing, getting embroiled is something else entirely.

'I'll get Greg to send out for some coffee and sandwiches, you look like you need an early lunch.'

Which has to be the best news I've had since I left St Aidan.

Chapter 32

Epic Thought: Life is made up of billions of infinitesimal fragments, most of which are exceedingly ordinary, because that's just how things are. But once or twice in a lifetime you can look back and identify one of those minuscule slivers of time as being extraordinary, having a significance that completely outweighs its tiny size. A moment where your world shifts, and the tilt changes the direction of your life forever.

The strange thing was, when Barney suggested I should stop worrying about the things I couldn't do, I only agreed to shut him up. I only ever meant to pretend to do it, and only for that day until he forgot about it. Inside my secret self, I think I was scared to let go. Terrified that if I stopped remembering how I used to be, I'd never get back there. That forgetting would be like throwing away the map that showed me the way back to myself. As if letting go would be like waving off the spaceship and deciding to stay on an alien planet.

But what I accidentally discovered that day was that it was possible to give myself a temporary break from the torment without giving up on the bigger picture. When I blanked out what I wanted to do but couldn't, initially it was only for a few seconds when I made myself stop remembering the deals I used to strike. But those few breaths when I stopped beating myself up for what I couldn't do were bliss. Better still, when I tried it for longer I had so much energy left over, I could concentrate better. But most of all, I felt lighter. And so much more free.

So I'm still just as determined to get back to who I was, but letting go of the frustration means that I'm more able to focus on doing that. Best of all, it's freed me up to make better progress. Thanks to Barney I'm fast-forwarding to my destination instead of going in slow-mo. As Aunty Jo pointed out, this is what she's been telling me to do since the day I got here. And once I stopped to think about it, this does tie in with all her 'All you need is wheat grass juice and a finger post pointing in the right direction' and 'Dance your best dance, no one gives a stuff if you fall over' mantras. But if you're not ready it's hard to listen, and even more impossible to hear.

The day we went to Falmouth, Barney must have struck it lucky. Since then I've expanded the approach. Doing all the things I'm good at for now, and forgetting about the rest is like finding the secret motorway back to where I began. But when I finally get back to Zinc Inc, however much I have remastered, I won't ever be quite be the same person. I'll certainly never take anything for granted again.

So when we came to planning the bathroom makeovers for the cottage, I helped choose the tiles, but I didn't let it bother me that I couldn't do sketches for how the tiles should fit. Like the latest decorators, the tiler came from the over-sixties lunches, which seem to be bursting with retired tradesmen looking for jobs to keep their hands in. If only I'd been old enough to go there myself when I first arrived, we'd have got this quest up and running a whole lot faster.

I never did manage to make a proper list of work at Periwinkle, and with my new rules and the fact that a lot of the work is already done, I probably won't be bothering now. As Aunty Jo says, we seem to be getting on fine without it. In any case, no one in St Aidan takes much notice of lists or instructions, they just turn up on the day and get on and do what needs doing.

To show how much progress we're making, Aunty Jo made a map of all the rooms in the cottage, and as each one is decorated I colour it in. She also made a barn yard map too, but this has the colours and the names of the people in the stables, also written by me. Loella ended up with her last 'l' and 'a' on another line. When she saw it she didn't seem to mind – far from it, she was actually thrilled. And with my new 'let it go' attitude I tried to give no fucks either. Actually, strangely for something so unimportant, I did give some fucks, but I made sure it wasn't too many. And with Barney taking the last two stables for his showroom, the barn yard is completely coloured in.

The day he started with the whitewash, Beth turned up with some alcohol-free Prosecco, Malcolm took away some of the metal buckets we'd bought in bulk in Falmouth and brought them back planted with cascades of blue and pink flowers, and Loella made a special bunting garland out of a strand of rope with matching felt flags to go over the doors. Then Barney put some of the Falmouth chairs around a huge trestle table he brought into the courtyard in front of the stables, and everyone from the barn yard shared their picnic lunches and had fizz in the sun.

As for the weather, last week's baking has turned to scorching. When Barney's leftover jeans arrived they were in a soft, tall, ironed pile and Aunty Jo said they smelled of the same apple blossom Lenor she swears by. When I finally decided I'd expire if I wore overalls another day, I chopped the first pair off just above my knees. By lunchtime I'd cut another couple of chunks off, but I'd stopped expiring from shock every time I caught a glimpse of my legs. By Friday they were so short my over-sized T-shirt was just skimming them, and I'd given up giving a damn about showing my thighs. This week I took the scissors to the T-shirts and hacked them into vests. As I put the final coat of paint on the cupboards I'm painting in the shade of Barney's open-fronted workshop, I'm finally cool.

'When did you get freckles on your nose, Edie Browne?'

I'm pleased it's Cam who's asking rather than Barney, because since the Bridget Jones day Bella's been on his case like the workplace police. As Cam shuffles beside me, hitching up his school bag, I can't help noticing his own freckles are even cuter since the sun brought more out.

'Shall I tell you something no one knows?'

'A secret?' His eyes light up.

'I always had freckles but they were under my make-up.' I might be selling a few customised deckchairs on Etsy, but I'm not rich enough to waste luminous Laura Geller when it's so hot it slides straight off. After a week battling foundation streaks and sweat rivers I decided to go bare until the freakish hot weather turns colder again. It's the same as having my legs out in public – once the sun goes in, I'll go back to caring. For now it's just too boiling to give any damns.

'What's make-up?' It's easy to forget it's all guys at his house.

As Barney appears in the doorway I won't mind if he joins in with an answer. 'It's like paint for your face, mostly used by girls, but it's fine if boys use it too.' That's one answer Bella couldn't argue with.

'When it was Mia's party my face was stripy.' Cam's nodding like he's an expert.

'That's because you were a tiger. Edie's face paint was more the colour of rosy cheeks, it's what grown-ups use to look extra pretty.'

Barney's grin in my direction is also him checking he hasn't made any blunders.

'And today I'm going to be a pirate.'

Barney's nod backs him up. 'That's why he's back early, we're off to see a special boat.'

'So can Edie Browne come with us?'

There's a beat of silence. 'She can if she'd like to.' If he was momentarily thrown, as Barney turns to me he's found his inner chill again. 'Cam's dad was working on this one for years before . . .' He tails off, then picks up again. 'It's a good chance to show Cam when it's moored up nearby.'

'Then we're going bodyboarding in the sea because I got my twenty-five metre swimming badge.'

Barney's looking bemused. 'Another rite of passage which is news to me! Apparently there's a beach with age-appropriate waves, so we'll call in there on the way home.' He grins at Cam again. 'Not forgetting Friday ice creams at the Surf Shack. As trips go, this one's hard to refuse?'

There's a gap where my reply should be, but the space is loaded with how much he's expecting me to come through on this. And I'm not forgetting how much I owe him. It's only thanks to Barney's straight talking that I'm getting on better. But I'm weighing all that against wanting to minimise the time I spend around him. He still makes me feel as if I'd rather not hang out with him until there's a way better version of me on offer.

'My best part will be the ice cream.' That's Cam cutting in.

'We all love those surfie sundaes.' I'm throwing out an excuse for him.

'It would be good for you to understand, that's all.' The stare Barney sends me over Cam's head is enough to make up my mind. 'I could do with the backup.'

'How long have I got to get ready?'

'Rub the paint splashes off your forehead and you'll be good to go.'

'Is it Dress Down Friday then?' My mind flashes to the last time I went on a boat trip with Barney. 'We're not wearing buoyancy aids?' As I stare down at my ragged vest and shorts, remembering casual Fridays is a giant leap back towards the office world.

'It's Penzance not Monte Carlo, best not go to too much trouble.' He takes in my puzzled frown. 'And we won't be setting off to sea this time.'

'Got you.'

Which is why I end up throwing away my last scrap of pride and leaving town pretty much as I am. As I clamber into the truck I'm in a cleaner version of what I was wearing before, with a dash of nude lippy and the flip-flops I got for one of those two-pound coins from the shed by the harbour so I didn't wreck my Roxy ones working. My hot tip for summers kicking around Cornwall in cut-offs – if you put your feet up on the dashboard to travel, your legs don't stick to the van seats *and* your thighs look way narrower when they're hanging down instead of spreading out. Any resemblance to similar musings Bridget Jones may have made is entirely accidental and nothing to do with us being alike in any way, or the fact that Barney's still sticking to the same soundtrack. Singing along to *All by Myself* very loudly with Cam as we bowl along the roads means I get to the end of it for the first time in forever without tears streaming down my face. But I can't help thinking a Captain Jack Sparrow soundtrack might have been better.

As we leave the car and whistle the dogs across the quayside in Penzance, with its proud stone buildings and neat, colourwashed houses reflecting in the glossy dark brown harbour water, Barney's lips are twitching into a smile. 'So what do you think?'

'Tell me what I'm looking at, I'll let you know.' I'm staring at rows of little boats like the one we went out on last time, all bobbing about along the pontoons. As we get closer to where the harbour edge drops off to the inky water, I reach for Cam's hand and clasp it tight.

'This is the one.' As Barney comes to a halt in front of a huge boat moored against the quayside Cam and I exchange disbelieving glances.

Cam's eyes are shining. 'But it's a *real* pirate ship.'

'And it's enormous . . . and magnificent.' Not that I'm an expert. But with its immense masts not only could it have sailed straight in from a period drama, it also dwarfs every other boat in this part of the harbour.

Barney shrugs. 'It's a sixty-foot ketch.'

Cam's joining in. 'But where are the sails?'

'They're rolled up when the boat's in the harbour, otherwise the wind would catch them and blow the boat out to sea.'

If I was puzzled before, now I'm confused. 'Can we have some back story on this please, Barney?'

'When Cam was smaller, his dad and I built and fitted out boats. Mostly they were more modern, but this one was what Cam's dad spent all his spare time working on before Cam came along.'

I'm struggling to take it in. 'Sorry, *where* was this?' Back in the day doesn't really cover it.

'In the boatyard we owned, further down the coast.' He smiles down at Cam. 'Do you remember Arnold and Barnaby's yard? The one with the big stone gateposts with lions on.'

Cam's nose wrinkles. 'I was scared of the lions.'

For the moment I hold in my astonishment that I'm not the only one here to have had a complete other life, and turn to the boat. Even without the sails the boat is impressive, with its timber top cabin and dark blue painted sides, and the masts stretching high into the air, with the rigging criss-crossing down to the deck.

Barney nudges Cam. 'And can you see what the writing on the side says?'

Cam's voice goes high. 'Cameron? It's got the same name as me.'

My heart's dissolving in my chest. 'How special is that?'

Barney gives Cam's shoulder a gentle squeeze. '*Cameron's Star* is the name of the boat, it's where your mum and dad found your name.' He looks over Cam's head to me. 'It's not always easy to find a meaningful way for Cam to connect with the past.'

I'm swallowing hard. 'I think you nailed it this time.'

Cam's hopping up and down, tugging Barney's T-shirt. 'How do we get onto it?'

I'm staring down at a ridiculously long narrow and wonky gangplank. 'Surely not?'

Barney's got a determined note to his voice. 'We hold onto the side ropes, look straight ahead, and we'll be fine.'

I let out a groan. 'You might as well tell me to jump straight into the harbour. Make sure you hang onto Dustin and Robert.'

He laughs. 'Think yourself lucky. If she was anchored further out you'd have to climb on board up a rope ladder from a dinghy.'

Cam's stretching out his hand. 'Come on, Edie, hold on to me, it's too exciting not to.'

'And when we get on board, there are stars your dad carved.' He turns from Cam to me. 'A thousand stars, that's way too good to miss, Edie.'

And he's right. Once we get onto the solid timber deck, they're all over the boat. Spiraling up the mast in clusters, on the handles on the ship's wheel, carved into the panelling on the side of the stairs that plunge below deck. And in the cabins they're like the Milky Way, stretching across the ceilings over the bunks.

Barney's smiling down at Cam. 'I remember when your mum

was waiting for you to be born. Your dad was so excited, all he'd think about was carving the stars on your boat, and planning the adventures you'd have together when you were older.' He points at the dark blue quilt covers covered with gold stars. 'And your mum made these too.'

When Barney said 'special', I had no idea he meant this much.

His smile is tinged with sadness as he watches Cam clambering on the bed, and peering out through the star-shaped porthole surround. 'Your dad's friends and I are taking care of it for now, but one day when you're old enough, *Cameron's Star* will be yours, just like your dad meant it to be. You'll be able to sail off for pirate trips of your own, how good will that be?'

Cam's eyes are huge as he stands on the edge of the bed. 'You and Edie *will* come with me?'

'If you want me on your crew, Cam, I'm in.' I'm thinking of Tiddlywink and Wilf, how their bedrooms are so colourful and rammed that Tash has to follow storage bloggers on Instagram so she can get tips to tame the chaos. How Cam should have had all that too with his mum and dad, and how they aren't here to pass on all the hopes and dreams they had for him.

As I see how exposed and pale and vulnerable the nape of his neck looks above his lopsided T-shirt, my chest is aching for him. Simply because he's one little person, who's so small, but surely deserves so much more than he's had, I want to put my arms around him and hug him and not let go. As he turns I can't stop myself holding out my hands. 'Shall I lift you down?' He comes towards me, and for a moment he puts his hands around my neck. As I pick him up he's warm but almost weightless in my arms. Then I turn and carefully stand him back on the polished wood floor.

And when he runs off back to the galley I don't follow him until I've got every wrinkle out of the starry quilt cover, and blown my nose, and looked out to imagine how his mum must have felt as she sewed those curtains. By the time I get back to them, Cam and Barney are waiting by the stairs.

'So are we all up for bodyboarding?' Barney's staring at me expectantly as Cam bounds upwards onto the deck. 'There's a towel and a wetsuit in the car, and changing rooms at the beach.'

'But you know I hate water?'

'That's why you're perfect to swim with Cam. It's great for him to have someone to show off to.'

'So I'm here because I'm shit?'

'But best of all, you laugh about it.' He's rubbing his forehead. 'Only joking, we had to bring you. We smile a lot more when we're with you than when we're not.'

With compliments like that, who needs insults? But deep down, it's actually good to be wanted. And somehow Barney was right. Seeing *Cameron's Star* had let me understand more, but knowing what Cam should have had makes my heart break even more for him.

Chapter 33

Day 226: Friday, 15th June
Back in St Aidan

Epic Achievement: Beginning to understand.

When we finally get back to St Aidan the seafront is busy so Barney drives around and parks at the end of the harbour. Cam and the dogs jump down from the truck and hurtle along the path that winds past the house with balconies on the front and down to the beach. As Barney and I follow I have to admit something.

'I need a Friday sugar rescue after that.' He probably thinks I mean the hour of hurling myself into the sea and being tumbled off my board by waves which turned out to be a lot more fun than I'd expected. If I'd known how warm wetsuits made you, I might have gone in the sea before. But needing a pick-up is more about how wrung out my heart feels.

Barney sighs. 'Cam came to the Surf Shack every Friday with his mum and dad. It was Rach and Bobbie's ritual, and we've always carried on.'

My stomach contracts again. 'So what happened?'

He's shaking his head. 'They'd both sailed since they were Cam's age, so they knew what they were doing. Then one afternoon they took a racer out from the yard to test some new rigging we'd done. The weather turned, Rach hadn't clipped on and she went overboard. Bobbie went in to save her, and we lost them both.'

'Oh my.'

'Like most accidents, it was senseless. Bobbie and I were best mates at school. We bought the boatyard as a wreck when we left, and spent every waking hour for the next fifteen years building it back up again. I considered keeping it on after the accident, but it was too much, with Cam to look after too. So when someone made a good offer, I accepted.'

'You lost your best friend and your business.' I'm kicking myself here. 'I'm so sorry.' Of course he knows about hurting, the anguish in his eyes is making my chest ache for him.

'It was tough. Bobbie and Rach didn't have any family left so when Cam was born I agreed to be his guardian if anything happened to either of them, never thinking it would.' He's watching Dustin chasing the foam on the breakers, splashing as the tide froths up the beach. 'Letting go of everything we'd worked so hard for was a killer. One minute we were running a thriving boat-building and repair business, the next I was up the lane with a three-year-old, a few wrecked barns, and only my carpentry skills to fall back on.'

'You didn't want to stay with boats?'

'After what we'd lost I couldn't even bear to look at one, let alone work on them.' He pulls a face. 'I'd already started to renovate the buildings along the lane so we moved in there and worked on them full-time. Then one day Beth and Loella dropped by with a photo of a shepherd's hut, and what I liked most was that you couldn't sail in it. That push gave me a new direction I needed, and the rest, as they say, is history. But it was never easy, I went to hell and back along the way.'

'While caring for Cam too.' No wonder Beth and Loella always implied he'd done well. 'Did you have anyone close to help?'

He pulls a face. 'I was seeing someone at the time of the accident, but she didn't stick around. Cam was always my priority, it wasn't fair on either of us to think about anyone new.' He kicks at the sand. 'Sometimes Cam kicks off, others he withdraws, but however many counsellors we see, they're never going to be able to bring his parents back.'

'It's so hard on him.' I can't help feeling wretched about how I misjudged Barney to begin with when he's been so willing to put himself on the line for Cam.

'It's not what any of us would have chosen, but I try to do my best for Cam. I might be a guy on my own without the first clue how to parent, but I'm going to do my damnedest to make sure he gets all the love and care and stability I can give him.' He kicks at a stone. 'When your world's turned upside down like Cam's has been, there's no knowing where you'll find your comfort or who's going to help you. I mean, no one could have predicted he'd find a Bridget Jones lookalike next door who would make him believe he could read and write just as well as everyone else, and had a never-ending supply of Unicorn cakes. No one's ever made him feel *that* special or wanted before. I couldn't be more grateful to you for being there these last few months and making his life so much better.'

My mouth's full of saliva, my throat too choked to swallow, and I haven't even got a sleeve to wipe my nose on, so I sniff and swipe my wrist across my eyes to clear away the tears. Just when I thought I was getting my emotions under control, now they're all over the place again. Except this time I'm not crying for myself, and I'm not crying for no reason. I'm crying for everything Cam has had taken away from him, and for this beautiful man with the huge, huge heart, who's trying so desperately to give him what he needs.

All I can hope is that Cam settles in and finds someone else to lean on and be his friend before I leave. Because that really isn't too far away. Which I'll have to remind Barney about soon too, just not now.

'No problem, any time.' I finally manage to squeeze the words out. 'Did you say ice cream?'

Chapter 34

Epic Achievement: Working up to something huge – watch this space!

'The last time we all went for sundaes on a Friday night it was dark and the beach was deserted.'

Walking along the sand towards the Surf Shack we've come closer together now, and as Barney reminisces – or tells it like it is, depending on who you are and how rosy your view of the world is – the sky is still bright and the cries of people grouped around the outdoor tables are blowing our way on the wind.

'And you were writing on the sand with a stick, Edie Browne.' That's Cam chiming in, his voice loaded with disapproval.

'And you were too.' I'm laughing at how judgmental kids can be. Looking back, for me it was another one of those significant moments where I accidentally cut the ropes that were tying me down. With the whole beach to write on I stopped trying so hard and after that writing became easier. Fun even. It's funny to think of a time when the beach was new, now I come here every day and it feels so much like *my* place.

As Dustin gallops up, he collides with my knees and showers

me with wet sand and I lean forward and take the stick out of his mouth. I'm about to fling it towards the shiny part of the beach by the water when Barney sweeps it upwards out of my hand.

'Hang on, don't throw the pen away until we've had a go.'

'For old times' sake?' It's a measure of how long I've been here. Or maybe it's not so long at all and we're just clinging on, trying to make traditions where there are none, because in our own ways, we're all alone. All wishing we were in some other place, with someone different.

'Come on, let's all write our names in the sand.' He passes the stick to Cam. 'You go first.'

'All of it? Cameron Michael Arnold?'

'If you're hoping for ice cream this side of midnight, you could just put Cam?'

'It is what we call you.' I'm backing Barney up here. 'If you write it all it might be dark again.'

'C-a-m.' His lips are sounding out the letters as he concentrates and drags the stick hard enough to make the marks, then he stands back, grinning. 'There.'

Barney thrusts the stick at me. 'You next, Edie – you don't have to put Browne, there aren't *that* many more Edie's around St Aidan.'

Barney's looking thoughtful. 'I think you're really more of an Edie B. Come to think of it, you should sign that on the shepherd's huts you paint and your signs and pictures.'

'Thanks, I like that. So in a long line, or below?'

'Underneath, I'd say.'

'Great.' I scrape my letters below Cam's in my best joined-up writing, and hand the stick back to Barney. 'Okay, Dustin, no need to steal the ball from Robert, it's not long to wait now.'

Barney writes his in big bold big letters, then stands back and nods. 'Not bad.'

'One thing.' I take back the stick and draw a couple more lines.

'A cactus? Is that because you're prickly or so on-trend?' Barney's laughing. 'Draw a guitar for me – it's a shame I haven't got mine with me, knowing how much you townies love a song on the sand, Edie B.'

I make sure he sees how hard I'm shaking my head at that. 'Cam, what drawing are you having?'

'An ice cream cone with strawberry sauce, like on my first picture. You do it.'

'No surprise there.' Barney takes back the stick then traces a line all the way around the edge, then he hurls the stick into the surf. As Dustin dives in after it, Cam and I pick up random stones and lay them along the lines. By the time they're done, Barney's pulled his phone out of his pocket and he's holding it in the air.

'Okay, bunch up here, say cheesy pizza, we'll have a selfie.'

'Cheesy *what?*'

'Pizza – another secret of St Aidan, that way it makes you laugh too.'

'Jeez, weird or what?' I'm trying to flap my hands around to hang onto my hair at the same time the gust of wind comes and tries to blow it off my head. All that and get Dustin and Robert, and hold onto them with one hand and put my arm around Cam too. And then there's this knot in my chest because we're all hugging together to fit in the frame.

It's over in a breath. And when Barney flips the phone screen towards me, there we are, all shorts and suntans and freckles and flapping T-shirts, wrapped up in an out-of-focus fuzz of laughter. Three people on a little patch of sand, three seconds of happiness before the wind snatches it away again. But for me there's a little bit more, because this is me getting to the end of another day where, even if I'm not in the exact place I should be, I'm actually glad I'm myself. Although as we jump and leap our way off up the beach again, my mind keeps spinning me back to *Cameron's Star*, and the parents who will never get to see Cam grow up. And my stomach's also clenching at the thought of that little patch of sand I've left behind. Of my name, framed between Cam and Barney's. And how long it's got to stay there until the tide rushes forwards over it, then slides backwards again sucking away every mark. And how soon it will be before the pounding water tumbles the sand grains back to their new smooth watery shine, obliterating every trace that we were ever here.

As we stride up the broad sleeper steps onto the deck at the Surf Shack the daylight must be fading because the strands of light bulbs swinging in the wind are already glowing yellow. Cam and I pull up some chairs, the dogs flop down on the planks, and Barney looks at Cam.

'Are you having your latest usual then?'

'What's that?'

When he really smiles there are dimples in his cheeks. 'The Unicorn Special because it's better than the Spiderman – it's strawberry, cherry and blue marshmallow ice cream with squirty cream and a raspberry horn. Please, Barney. And two spoons in case I drop one.' Once he's nailed the detail he beams at me. 'You should have the same.'

'Make that two Unicorns then, with extra napkins, please.' I'm so totally up for this, it's even funnier to think that last time I was desperate to get away. If they'd told me there were Unicorn sundaes on the menu I'd have made damn sure I came back sooner than now.

Barney waits inside while they make up the order, and when he sets down the glasses they're just as huge and crammed as when I've been here with Aunty Jo. But the Unicorn versions are so pretty, with their pink and purple and turquoise swirls, rainbow sprinkles and barley twist horn, when I see mine I actually let out a squeak that's way more girlie than I'd intended.

With sundaes this big you have to give them every bit of your attention, or you don't make any impression at all. So for a while there's only the sound of munching and the occasional groan of pleasure from me as I hit the unexpected crunch of the pastel-coloured meringue. After the heat of the day it's a novelty to be shivering as the freezing ice cream slides down my throat. It's only when I eventually stop and look up I notice the ice cream Barney's digging into is shades of sludge.

'So what the hell is yours?'

'It's a mix from the Guy-Zone freezer.' He ignores my eye roll. 'Indian pale ale, chilli chocolate, quadruple espresso, rocky road and root beer.'

'Wow, very macho.'

'I order it when I want my voice to go deeper.' He laughs. 'No, that's a joke, it's actually great for waking you up. Have a try.' He loads up his spoon and holds it out. 'Or dip in for yourself if you'd rather.'

Refusing his spoon would make a lot more of it than it is. So I lean in, grab it and push the ice cream lump into my mouth and slurp. 'Woahhh.'

'Not liking the tough-boy choice?'

'That's *totally* disgusting.' I'm clutching at my tongue. 'What *the hell* is it?'

'That's root beer, one of the most delicious flavours known to man . . . or woman.' The more I shudder, the more he laughs. 'Made from liquorice, wintergreen, saspirilla and aniseed, among other things.'

But as his grin widens I can feel my eyes widening until they're almost popping out of my head.

'Edie? Is something wrong? Shit, you're not allergic, are you, tell me you haven't gone into anaphylactic shock?'

I'm shaking my head wildly in answer because the words are locked in my throat. When they finally come out they're half rasp, half sob. 'I tasted it.'

'Edie can't taste *anything* because she broke her head.' Cam's jumping up and down. 'That's why she made salty cakes and fell over at her party.'

'All that time.' However much I'm dabbing them with my serviette, my eyes won't stop leaking.

'When I said it would wake you up I was joking. I'm so happy for you.' If Barney's pulling me into a hug I hope he knows it's the fast way to get a soaking T-shirt. Two arms, I'm still not getting the fabric conditioner smell, let alone any of the rest. For this one time only, it could be a good thing I lost my sense of smell.

'So does she get to taste *all* the ice cream now?' Cam's gone back to his sundae, and he's got a spoon in each hand.

'I guess she'll have to.'

Cam's eyes are shining. 'I like going out with you, Edie B.'

'Me too with you, Cameron Michael Arnold.' How's that for total recall?

277

Chapter 35

Epic Achievement: I'm guessing no one else ever tried EVERY flavour ice cream from the Plank Place at ONE sitting – putting myself forward, as this has to be some kind of St Aidan record? Whatever, it was totally epic in every sense of the word.
(Just saying.)(In case anyone missed it.)

It's true what they say about watching pots – if you're waiting for something it can take forever to happen. But if you forget about it – or in my case concentrate on something else – what you're aching for tends to happen so much faster. The same holds true whether you're cooking or stalking your inbox. The minute I mentally left 'the office' and stopped pressing refresh, my email pinged in.

As flavours go, root beer's not exactly subtle or delicate, in fact, as Bella said, I might easily have got the same effect from swigging toilet cleaner. But however it happened, it took that intensity to wake me up to the potential that I could taste again, and that kick-start reminded me not to give up trying. You can't argue, dream-come-true excuses to take a spoonful from every ice cream flavour in the ice cream shop freezer don't come along every day. And once I tried all of them, I could taste others too. To be honest, on balance I've always preferred cupcakes to smoky barbecue sauce, take me to a bar and I'll be downing syrupy cocktails not beer. But if no other options open up, given time and effort, I might yet get to like all those boy-zone flavours. As Tash always reminds me, some patients have reported improvements up to twenty-three years after their strokes, so the doc who said to be patient and travel with hope definitely knew what he was talking about.

This sudden leap of progress spurs me on in other areas too. I finally finish my Quick Read –spoiler alert: they don't ever find Poldark himself, but I give it five stars because all the characters find their own happy endings, which is actually better. Then I order another one from the same series called *Dead End Street*, which is billed as a 'murder mystery to make you smile and shiver'. So far I've read enough to know it's set on one of those roads you can't get out of like our close, but I haven't come to any scary bits or laughed yet.

Then Aunty Jo ropes in Malcolm to help with a whole new raft of sticky signs around the house. As if those *cushion/sofa/fridge* labels weren't already enough, she's now gone all technical with words like *beams* and *balustrades* and *stud partitions* and *sash cords* and *splashbacks* and *thresholds* and *double glazed fenestration units*. As a measure of how thorough she's been, the night she does it I go to clean my teeth and end up with the labels for *tile grout*, *Jack and Jill bathroom* and *toughened glass shower screen* sticking to my pyjama top, all because I accidentally leaned up against the wall to recover from the horrific shock of the Euthymol toothpaste Barney bought me.

In a way the last few months have been like passing through a series of rooms. There was the first room, where I was bewildered and home with Mum or at the hospital, and it was such a big step to leave that behind. Then, when I first arrived here, every day was centred around the garden room at Periwinkle Cottage. But now it's as if that door has closed, and I've moved forwards again. The new room is bigger, and all about the orchard, and the shepherd's huts and the showroom in the barn yard. With so many people there, and the carpenters, it's a lot more like being back on the building sites. Better still, rather than tying Aunty Jo down to being with me, she's free to go off on jaunts with Malcolm and the over sixties, because there's always someone around at Barney's to call on if I need help.

I'm not the only one making bounds of progress either. Malcolm has got Aunty Jo driving again. He started by taking her down the B&Q car park in the evenings when I was painting at Barney's, and now she can go all the way from the harbour back to here. Okay, he still has to sit and talk her through it, but if she can get back behind the wheel, realistically, there's hope for all of us. Me and my beautiful little slate grey car may yet be on the road. I'm pausing for a silent fist squeeze, and to send wishes across the universe to catch any passing unicorns or fairy godmothers. *Please, please, please. Let me be able to drive again.* There was once a time I doubted it would ever happen, but with the roll we're on I've finally convinced myself; so long as you believe in yourself enough, anything is possible.

With the shepherd's huts, the Seaside Stripe variation is done all the way down to the rope-festooned blue and white life belt ring hanging next to the door. And under the shade of the reclaimed sail suspended from the apple trees there are the first of the deckchairs, with *Sail away* and *Captain's Chair* painted in lovely wavy letters on the canvas. And just to add a touch of extra authenticity, there's a pile of lobster pots and a washing line with stripy beach towels pegged on it.

Which leaves me on my root beer wave of euphoria, moving

onto the next hut. Barney's already painted it a wonderful shade of dusky pink on the outside, and because this is the ditsy print one we strung some pretty bunting all around where the roof meets the wall. Inside I've painted the plank walls the colour of clotted cream, and picked out some comfy chairs with red checked linen covers which are still up at the showroom. Today as I dip under the boughs in the dappled shade of the apple trees, and pause for a moment because the sea is the most wonderful shade of pale turquoise, I'm armed with a small bucket of paste I've scrounged from the decorator at Periwinkle and my pile of wallpaper samples, and I'm loving the quiet.

Even though I'm out in the orchard, I'm still close enough for Barney to keep an eye out from the courtyard, and I'm not quite on my own, because thanks to Barney's idea of me giving Dustin his meals, the only time Dustin lets me out of his sight is after I've given him his dinner last thing in the evening. After he eats it, then he goes and lies down on the rug by the door. For the rest of the day, at best he's like a shadow padding behind me, but mostly he's so close he's slobbering on my shorts. It's funny because at times he seems so bright I almost expect him to come out with a sentence. But even though his dinnertime never varies, he doesn't seem to be able to get past the idea that I may be about to whip out his bowl of biscuits and lean steak mince at any moment in the day. So when I talk about peace, that's obviously overlaid with Dustin's snorts and sniffs. In fact some of his sighs and grunts are so heartfelt it's hard to believe he's a dog not a human.

As I leaf through my pile of pinks and yellows and red wallpaper prints and snip them into smaller pieces, I'm hugging myself with excitement. I pick up my brush, slide on a slug of paste using one of Aunty Jo's trays as a pasting table. Then starting at the top, I begin to stick them on the end wall of the hut. I'm having such fun as the pattern grows that I miss hearing the creak of the timber entrance steps. The first inkling I have that Barney's standing in the doorway is when Dustin lets out a half-woof greeting.

'Are you busy?'

'Only working on my sticky wall.'

'You do know they're all different?' There's a lilt around his lips. 'No, actually it's already looking really cool.'

'Thanks.' As I stare up at the patchwork of roses and rampant flowers and polka dots randomly repeating across the hut, I can't help a flutter in my chest, because it's striking yet pretty at the same time. 'So how can I help?'

'I just had a call from a couple who'd love you to talk them through this theme. I suggested they looked at the huts we've already finished, but apparently only pink will do.'

'So long as they don't mind glue, that's fine with me.' I grin and wave my brush at him. At Zinc Inc demanding clients went with the high-end territory, and Jake was laid-back and patient enough to handle them, which took the pressure off the rest of us. We all vied to have our own worst nightmare customer story, but I hadn't expected to meet any here in St Aidan.

'You could run them around the showrooms too?'

He's making those sound way more upmarket than they are as well, because we've literally thrown them together in between other jobs the last few weeks. But there's one that looks very like a smaller version of The Junkyard, with items ripe for restoration, and another that's bursting with style and ideas with restored pieces that are ready to go.

'Great, just send them along whenever they get here.' There's no need to worry, these people have to be time wasters or he'd be seeing them himself.

'You could sound more—'

'More what?'

'Enthusiastic. Up for it. Like you actually believed in the product you're creating.'

'Really?' It comes out as a squeak because I'm so close to being found out here.

He's frowning as he rubs his head. 'I don't know why when you do it so well, but sometimes I get the feeling you don't actually like shepherd's huts.'

My gulp's so big I almost swallow my tongue, and next thing the glue brush is splattering across the hut. 'Sh-i-i-i-i-t . . .'

'Is that "shit" for the paste on the floor, or "shit" because, excuse the cliché, I finally hit the nail on the head?' His stare is so hard as he passes the brush back it's turning me inside out.

I might as well come out with it. 'Where I come from shepherd's huts mean rich townies faking the simple life.' Having to expand on my 'more money than sense' objections, I'm understanding them better myself. 'It's all about pretence, and people with their heads up their bums; it's not the best scene.'

'Objecting on Marie Antoinette grounds? That's an interesting take, from Planet Bath and Bristol.'

'So how's it different here? It's still people trying to buy happiness, and you flogging them dreams that won't come true.' Put like that, I can hardly believe I've been working for the cause. But painting them is one thing, selling them's another entirely.

'Edie Browne, you make me sound like a charlatan and a cheat.' From his breaking grin, my arguments seem to be amusing him more than upsetting him. 'Maybe people here have less money, but I don't feel they have unrealistic expectations for what the product will deliver. Let's face it, people in St Aidan take responsibility for making their own happiness.'

'Okay.' I still can't help pulling my sceptical face.

'Sure, they're spending money, but in a creative way. Most of our customers are simply buying space that will make their lives better.' Put like that it's almost acceptable.

'I'll save that one for Mr and Mrs Pink, then.'

'You won't have long to wait.' He squints over his shoulder. 'They're here now.'

'Crap shit bollocks, you might have said.' I'm tugging at my saggy cut-offs, wishing I hadn't skimped on the statement lippy. 'What about the teensy problem of me looking like shit?' Smart and presentable is a million miles off his radar.

'Don't worry, you're fine. In any case, that vest is the perfect mix of rebellion and stylish wit.'

'Why, what does it say?' When I pulled it on after the walk on the beach I was in too much of a rush to hang around to read the logo.

'*Luxure, Fierté, Gloutonnerie . . .*' There are crinkles at the corners of his eyes again. '*Lust, pride, gluttony* – it's the seven deadly sins, in French.'

'That's good for *workplace uniform?*' There's not even time to put it on back-to-front.

'It works for me.' As he turns back to the orchard he's laughing properly. 'Come on, I'll introduce you.'

As I follow Barney down the steps, the couple tiptoeing across the grass look completely unsure and a lot like how I expect my mum and dad will look ten years' from now. As my smile widens with no effort from me, I'm scrubbing out all my ideas about picky clients.

'Mary and Jim have *both* their elderly mums living with them, which is why they're looking for a garden retreat to escape to.' Barney turns to me. 'This is Edie. She'll show you how far we've got with the Spots and Pots hut you liked the sound of and then she'll run you up to the barn yard to give you more idea of what will be going in it.'

'Hi there, lovely to meet you.' I give a cough. 'And I think Barney means Daisies and Dots or Dots and Daisies even.' What hope is there when neither of us can even get the name right? 'It's this way.' I'm heading back up the steps, but Mary's hanging back.

'Does it come with bunting?'

'It can come with anything you like.'

'There you are, Jim, you can't argue with that.' The way Mary smiles at me first, then shakes her head at Jim's back reminds me of my mum when she's trying to make improvements around our house. If Jim's anything like as set in his ways as my dad, they won't be buying for years, which takes the pressure off me. Mary's already sold on this, but I already know nothing I do will help persuade Jim.

As I whisk them in, first we have to stop to say hello to Dustin, then we get down to business. I'm so sad to hear Mary sighing over the patchwork wall, knowing there's no chance Jim's going to let her have one, I completely forget to worry about my words drying up. Later, when we all go up to the barn yard showrooms and she tries out the red checked armchairs I've chosen, and nods at the pale blue blind fabric, and reaches out to touch the polka dot cushions I've picked out, my heart is squishing for her. By the time she opens and closes the cupboards I've put to one side and lingers over the petal-shaped cut-outs on the bookcase, I'm almost reaching for my hanky.

In the end she chooses one of Beth's lanterns and some scented candles, and I take them back so they can pay Barney for those, and they're still there waving as Dustin and I wander back into the orchard. If all the customers were as nice as those two, I'd happily show them round all day every day – but obviously Barney would go broke because no one would be buying.

It only takes a few more pieces on my patchwork wall for me to realise I'm running out of glue. As I head back to Periwinkle for a paste top-up and wave my bucket at Barney across the court-yard to let him know where Dustin and I are going, Jim and Mary are still with him. I have time to mix my paste, and have a good chat to the decorator, and they're still only just driving off down the lane. As we arrive back at the shepherd's huts, Dustin's sniffing the tree trunks and I'm swinging my much bigger, very full bucket, and it's a surprise to see Barney's already there waiting for us, sitting on the steps of the pink hut.

'More customers?' At this rate the patchwork's going to take days.

'Better than that, Edie B.' As he stands up his palm is raised and as I inadvertently raise mine he high fives me, then whooshes Dustin into a hug. 'Congratulations, you just made your first sale.'

'I *WHAT*?' I take a step backwards so I can see his face better and decide if he's serious.

'Mary and Jim just bought a—' As I stare at them his eyes go wide. 'Watch out, Edie—'

By the time I realise he's telling me to look out for the log behind me it's too late. My feet have already collided with it, my balance has gone and I'm catapulting backwards. Worse still, as my arms flail wildly my bucket lifts. As it traces a huge arc, the paste shoots out and takes on a life of its own, flying upwards like a splurge of wild ectoplasm against the sky. Then as I thud backwards onto the grass the paste falls faster, landing in one huge unceremonious splat that somehow covers most of my body.

'Holeeeeee sh-i-i-i-i-t.' I'm scraping the gunk out of my eyes and blowing it out of my mouth, and there's something furry and warm wriggling under my head. 'Dustin, what the hell?' As I put out my hand his body writhes underneath my fingers and I can't hold in my howl. 'Noooooooo, I fell on Dustin.' I'm scrabbling in the dirt, desperately trying to take my weight off him. 'Did I kill him?' But the moment I manage to lift my head and push myself up onto my elbows, there's a flash of white fur, a whole new splash of paste splatters, and Dustin's wriggled free and is dashing between Barney and me, barking frantically.

'Good lad, Dustin, settle down. Edie's okay, you've done your job.' As Barney stoops down beside me, the racket subsides. 'Thank you, well done, Dustin, that was brilliant.' He looks down at me. 'On balance I'd say he's way too noisy to be dead.'

'Thank Christmas for that.' I'm rubbing Dustin's head, and as his nose comes in to find my ear I hook my arm around his neck and pull his panting body against mine.

'You didn't crush Dustin, he was actually in front of you when you fell. What you felt there was him making sure you didn't bang your head when you fell by cushioning your head with his body.'

'Oh my.' I'm swallowing back my tears at the thought that he'd do that.

Barney's hand is on my shoulder and he's smiling down at me. 'He was trained to rescue his owner if she had a seizure. Once you sat up and he sensed you weren't fitting he came to attract my attention so I'd come to help.'

'Wow, that's amazing.'

'It seemed wrong to put it to the test when he's not your dog, but it's good to accidentally find out he'll be there to help you if ever you need it.' Barney's biting back his smile. 'Obviously if we'd tried it ourselves earlier, we could have done it without the paste explosion.'

Despite the paste, I'm still burying my face in Dustin's side. 'After this Aunty Jo will have to let him in next door.'

'You'll both need a shower before either of you are allowed anywhere near Periwinkle. I reckon Dustin's had his sights set on your bed since he arrived, him getting all heroic is his way of sealing the deal.' As Barney unpeels his hand from my arm he starts to laugh. 'Jeez, you couldn't be any more sticky . . . Wait there, I'll grab you a towel from the line.'

'Sorry to wreck the display.'

'Wreck as many as you like, you just sold a Ditsy Spot. That's what we were talking about when you tripped.'

'A pink one?'

'Fully decorated, with enough extras to fill an entire garden.'

'Shucks.' Even I know that's major. 'But how?'

'Mary and Jim loved what you showed them, but they liked that you weren't pushy.'

'I really didn't think Jim was up for it.'

'He wasn't at all – but you showed him life would be better with a hut to retreat to.'

I can't take credit here. 'But I stole that from you.'

'You only used what we talked about earlier to make them see that truth – a hut will be wonderful in their situation. I watched you walking around, you're great at making people feel at ease, and getting them to listen.' There's a light in his eyes I haven't seen before. 'With me talking to them about the construction, and you dealing with the interiors, I reckon that's our blueprint for the future.'

If he were Jake in one of those appraisal meetings we have, he'd be praising me for my fabulous customer communication skills, but I seriously doubt there's any such thing in St Aidan. I'm about to gush back – as best I can – but the last word stops me dead. If 'the future' sounds big and permanent, that's only because it is. But much more importantly, for me the future isn't here, it's somewhere else entirely. This bit is just another one of those rooms I'm moving through, and I'll be shutting the door on this one very soon. Lately, when I get out my calendar timeline, the part that's left in St Aidan is looking tiny.

The funny thing is, for a time after I arrived I had this doubt that I'd ever make it back to the beginning again. I had this sagging feeling deep inside that I'd never be good enough again. But lately, mostly thanks to Barney, I'm smashing it. I know it was the last thing I wanted when he suggested it, but working on the huts is what has pushed me forwards. It's given me confidence that so long as I do things in my own way, I'll get there. He's let me dabble in the design side I've always hankered after trying, I've found out I'm way more creative than I thought, I still notice all the picky details that Jake relied on me for. And today has made me realise, I may have less control over my words and my banter might be scarily non-existent, but somehow I can still make that connection with people. I can still say enough of what's important. Basically, what's missing is the froth, the bit that didn't matter anyway. Hell, if I can sell a shepherd's hut to a man who had no intention of buying one, I'm well on my way. Not that I'm one to big myself up, but this morning may have sealed my ticket back to Bath and Bristol. And the more it sinks in, the more I feel like I'm flying.

'You do know I'm only here for the summer.'

'Summer's barely begun.' He sniffs. 'If you think St Aidan's crowded now, just wait. When the summer rush *really* gets underway, you'll know what rammed means.'

'Then I'm going home.' This has always been the plan. First it's my mum's birthday, and I'm going back for her party, and soon after that is when my leave from work comes to an end.

'It's always summer in St Aidan, Edie Browne.' He frowns. 'That sounds like a line from a song.'

'Please not your guitar.'

'Sorry, but selling a hut has to be the best excuse.' He gives a low laugh. 'I'll take requests?'

'You're way too sticky to play.' I can't help thinking back to that first day on the beach when Dustin arrived. How Barney's laid-back voice and the words of *Perfect Day* did make the little bubble of the moment the kind of perfect that would never happen again. It would be wrong even to hope to recreate it. Then I slide back to reality. Of course I don't want to listen to bloody guitar strumming, why the hell would I even waver on that? The faster I get out of here, the better.

'It's your loss.' He gets up, grabs a towel and tosses it down to me. 'You know, crazy as it sounds, Cam and I were kind of hoping you'd want to stay forever.'

There's a second when my stomach drops so fast every bit of air leaves my chest cavity. Then I fill my lungs again, and get hold of myself. 'But I have to go, I belong somewhere else. It's an accident I was ever here at all.' However much I've fallen in love with the shimmer of the sea, and the certainty that those wonderful waves will always keep on rolling in up the beach, St Aidan is the last place I'd have ended up if I hadn't been ill. It's ironic that it's Barney's help, with all the long walks, and the work challenges, that made me up my game. Without those I'd be so far behind where I am now. As it is I feel more and more like a normal, functioning human every day. He gave me the key to unlock my prison, and the minute the door opens far enough I'll be up and away.

And then Aunty Jo will be heading out of town too. I couldn't have stayed on without her, and the cottage is closing in on finished. It won't be long before we'll be calling the agents in, and with my quest complete it's onto the next thing. Hopefully I'll be back to the start. Or near enough that no one will notice the difference when I slip back into my place in Bath again. With a few St Aidan cheats to carry me on my way, and my new-found talent for taking the long way around but getting there in the end, I'll surely be – what's that old saying? A-okay.

'Sorry, I shouldn't be laying this on you. It's fine, we'll man up, we're tough.' Barney holds out his hand and hauls me to my feet the lines on his face makes him look anything but. 'Come on, it's the hose for you two.'

As I stand by the tap in the courtyard with Dustin, as the water rains down on us in a spray of diamond drops in the sunlight, turning my skin to ice and forcing every bit of breath out of my body, there are two things that are needling me. First, a few minutes ago I was soaring. But now I'm like a hot air balloon that's lost its hot air and collapsed in a bundle. Second, I'm thinking of home. How far away it feels. And what a huge change it's going to be when I jump back there. Which has to explain why, when I glimpse a figure passing on the lane, I'm somehow imagining it looks like Marcus. Because when I go back home, he won't be figuring at all.

Chapter 36

Epic Achievement: Shampooing Dustin
(He is such a wriggling reluctant client, reminding me
why I will never be looking for work in a doggy grooming salon.)

'So how many deadly sins T-shirts have you got?'

When I went back to Periwinkle Cottage to grab a proper shower and new clothes and looked more closely further down my pile of clean vests, I found faded blue and khaki versions with exactly the same logo. So now I'm back in the orchard, complete with a new paste supply, but before I pick up where I left off on the pink hut, I might as well clear this question up.

'Maybe six. Or even more?' Barney gives an embarrassed shrug. 'Actually seven makes sense. It was Beth and Loella's idea of a joke a couple of Christmases ago, their very unsubtle way of encouraging me to be more wild and out there. Every parcel I opened from around the tree was the same logo on a different colour T-shirt.'

'You have Christmas *together* with *presents* from *everyone?*'

'And you don't?'

I do, but obviously Christmas with Mum and Dad and Tash and Brian and Tiddlywink and Wilf – and sometimes Marcus, when we were together – is a very different deal from a free-for-all gift-fest here on the lane. It's not just the shock that that's how he celebrates, I actually can't believe the Secret Santa thing hasn't reached St Aidan. But taking in his bemused stare, I decide to skip the details of how that one works. 'So did you take the advice?'

'What do *you* think?' There's a teasing laziness about his half smile. 'I'd hardly be *this* wicked if I hadn't.'

Bella would undoubtedly swap sexy for lazy and slam Barney for inappropriate body language in the workplace, but – shit, crap and bollocky stuff – I was the one who actually began this, so I need to move things on.

'Anyw-a-a-a-y I better get started.'

'About that.' As he clears his throat he's sounding more cryptic than I do. 'I meant to say, Mary and Jim are in a hurry.'

'They stayed a long time if they were rushing.' Just saying, he's surely got that wrong.

'That's why we were talking so long, they offered to pay a premium for immediate delivery. Would you be up for helping them with that?'

'Delivery?' I'm frowning because I don't get it. 'Of what?'

'Well, if we really cracked on we could finish this hut by early next week and let them have it. They'd like to come and see you tomorrow to finalise the exact bits they'd like to add in, and get your advice on colours.'

'You want to sell the display?'

'So long as you agree. They're such a lovely couple, and it's the fastest way to get them their hut. Don't worry, we'll soon make you another and paint that one pink too.' Incredible. What was I saying about making it up as he goes along?

'Great.' It isn't at all. 'In that case I really do need to get on.'

'Would you be up for some extra furniture painting over the weekend to make this happen?' He's still there, looking suitably sheepish, then his face splits into a grin. 'Double pay, *and* I'll make sure there's cake on Sunday, Edie B.'

'You frigging well better.'

As I swing my bucket up the steps to get on with my patchwork wall I'm more happy with myself for that fast comeback than annoyed. They're Barney's huts. As for which ones he chooses to sell, there's more important stuff for me to give my fucks about. And I am happy Mary and Jim will be getting what they want.

But so long as you overlook that I'm a sucker for unicorns and flamingoes, I'm not normally a pink person. I mean, hell, I'd take urban industrial over pansy petals any day. But now I'm up in the hut again, there's something about the tiny glimpse of a triangle of sea from the window framed through the apple tree's branches. I know that they're totally moveable, and the view isn't part of the hut anyway, so I'm being ridiculous here. But the way the light plays inside this one is kind of calm yet clear, and somehow the mismatch of patterns gives the sweetness an edge.

So what am I saying here? Only that as I sit with my pasting brush and the shadows of leaves in the breeze flickering over me, the vintage radio tuned into Pirate FM playing Everything Eighties, sticking my paper rectangles to the wall, and thinking of how pretty the cupboards would look if we painted them apple green – or even the palest shade of dusty rose – I'm completely relaxed. Worse still, for someone who would have avoided this like a dose of chickenpox back in March, I have to admit that for this one tiny moment I'm enjoying myself. However unlikely it seems, Edie Browne is feeling the love here. And please don't ask me which version of myself that is, because with every day that passes the edges are getting more and more blurred.

I'm on my knees, trimming my pieces for the last row, when

Dustin's tail starts to thump on the lightly polished floorboards. As he looks up from where he's lying in the doorway I can hear the sound of Aunty Jo's chatting getting closer as she wanders across the grass. As her face appears in the doorway, her smile's even brighter than usual and it's funny to think there was a time when she didn't smile at all.

'There's someone special here to see you, Sweetpea.' There's nothing unusual in this. She pops in several times a week to show off the huts to her new friends from the lunch club or the barn classes, and whoever they are, she always gives them the same build-up.

'Lovely, come up and see.' As I push my paste out of the way I know she'll be as excited as I am when she sees where all those wallpaper samples she collected for me have ended up.

'You might like to close your eyes, this is quite a big surprise.' It's a slightly odd variation, but I can tell from the low growl in Dustin's throat that it's a guy, and one he's not totally sure of.

'I'm probably okay.' If she's brought round some celebrity relation from the lunch club, I only hope I recognise them. I'd manage Ant or Dec, or Piers Morgan, or Graham Norton, otherwise I'll be struggling. I mean, people say Simon Cowell's tiny in real life. Not recognising people who think they're famous is the most embarrassing thing, so as I turn around I'm screwing myself up for the biggest cringe moment ever.

'Hello, Edie . . .'

There's a slight lurch as they step up into the hut, and in the moment before Dustin goes wild those two deep resonating words coming from behind Aunty Jo are enough to make my stomach drop through the floor.

'M-m-marcus . . .?' The triple flip my heart just did is making me feel like I'm about to throw up. *Of all the fucks.* For a minute the world stops turning. Even though we're apart now, if only for all the happy years we spent together, I should already have leapt to my feet, thrown my arms around him and been pulled into a huge hug. But instead I'm frozen, glued to the white painted floor planks because the trauma of him turning up out of literally nowhere has sent my leg muscles into some kind of spasm. The whole point of spontaneous hugs is they're impulsive, they work because you can't hold them back. If you delay to consider they become impossibly laboured and awkward. By the time I shake myself back into the present enough to get hold of Dustin's collar, the moment's gone, and it's too late. For both of us. Instead of a wild enthusiastic outpouring of waving arms and clashing bodies, it's as if an invisible chasm has opened up in the hut floor.

'What the hell happened to you?' Marcus is running his fingers through his hair, even though it's always so impeccably groomed and cut it only ever falls in the right place. 'From what Bella said I was ready for a touch of Bohemian, not full-blown hippy-dippy native. You do know pale skin is the way forward, tans are well off-trend. I've got some great free samples of Heliocare factor 90 lying around at the office – if I'd known you were going to let yourself go this badly, I'd have sent sun block supplies.'

'Lovely to see you too.' I'd forgotten how full-on an onslaught from Marcus can be, and if I'm honest, as I finally manage to scramble to my feet and pull Dustin next to me to quieten him, the shock is two-way. Even in head to toe casuals, Marcus's navy J. Crew shorts and matching maroon stripe polo are a lot more starchy than I remember. Now I'm more certain I'm not going to immediately bring up my lunch, I might as well ask. 'What are you doing . . .' I don't want to sound like I'm assuming he's here to see me. '. . . in St Aidan?'

'You remember Devon?' He's flashing me his best charming smile, and even though I'm not picking it up, I know he'll be doused in his favourite Christian Dior Sauvage body spray and smelling delectable. 'I'm down for the usual week with "the olds".'

'Oh, that.' I nod hard, and hope he doesn't notice my shiver as I flashback to the annual rent-a-mansion-and-a-creek and think of all the seafood they'll be chugging through. Even so, there's a nostalgic twang in my middle for those nights we used to lie on the beach, just the two of us, the salt spray tangling our hair, our skin smelling of summer, trying to count the billion stars scattered across the sky.

'They've chartered an ocean-goer this time. We've been out every day since Saturday, but the forecast for today was a bit blustery so I thought I'd drop by and catch up with you instead.'

He's been down for ages, he's only here today because he couldn't go out on his bloody yacht. It would have been a total waste to be sick, and my banging heart would do well to wake up to that message too, although I'm sure that's more nerves than anything else. Then there's another lurch of the steps, Dustin's tail bangs against my legs, as guess who appears in the doorway.

'I heard Dustin going bonkers.' As Barney comes right on into the hut there's sawdust in the dark waves of his hair and dust smears across his folded forearms. Next to the straight lines of Marcus's sideburns, he's looking achingly rough and rugged, and in the glint in his eye there's a hint of that wicked we were talking about earlier. 'Is everything okay in here?'

'Barney, don't worry, Edie's fine, and isn't this cosy?' Aunty Jo beams, but as both guys seem to be taking up a ridiculously large amount of space, extremely crowded or horribly cramped would have been a better way of putting it. 'This is Marcus, one of Edie's friends from home. He arrived unexpectedly so I brought him across, I hope you don't mind us disturbing Edie at work.'

For some reason I'm pleased she's making Marcus sound less significant than he once was and making it damned clear he's turned up uninvited.

'What the heck are you doing messing around in a shepherd's hut of all places, Edes, we all know there's only one thing you despise more in life, and that's tree houses.' Marcus wrinkles his nose as he stares around. 'All these florals too, it's like Edie's body has been taken over by an alien force. Is this personality transplant down to the illness then, or did you get attacked by Cornish zombies?'

So that's what having all your secrets splurged in one breath feels like. It's a relief I got that one out of the way earlier or Barney might be looking even more gobsmacked. As it is, I know I haven't been the biggest fan, but now my Dots and Daisies are under fire, the back of my neck is prickling and I'm coming over like a mama bear defending her cub. I know I might once have agreed with him wholeheartedly, but right now I'd happily claw Marcus's face off for being so mean.

'Sure, it's a different area of the market to my usual one.' I've no idea how that came out when what I meant to say was, *And fuck you too, Marcus*. 'But at least I'm doing it with integrity.'

Far from backing off, Marcus's face lights up. 'That's my Edie, halting maybe, but still just as feisty.' As he turns to look at Barney he's crossed the invisible chasm and arrived in my personal space and, before I know it, he's sliding his arm around me. 'When we did up our house together, it was industrial all the way, she wouldn't go within a mile of a flower. Good on her for coming up with the goods in a place that's light years behind the cutting edge.'

I've no idea why I feel like I'm dying here when Marcus is only telling the truth about the past. I'd rather not be lumped in with the insults though, or squished quite this tightly under his arm.

Barney's wrinkling his nose. 'What can I smell?' As a random way to show that Marcus's barbs about St Aidan are completely flowing over him, it's a great reply.

I shrug. 'No point asking me.'

Aunty Jo sniffs too, then beams. 'If you mean the man perfume, it's very like my favourite one of Malcolm's, Le Male by Jean Paul Gaultier. The bottle's shaped like a body. Own up, who's wearing it?' It's one of those questions we all know the answer to already. If Barney was the one asking it's not going to be him.

'Guilty as charged.' Marcus puts his hands up.

So not the Dior after all. This is the one that's supposedly great for getting laid, so I could take that either way. Although it's typical of upside-down-St Aidan that Malcolm uses it too. And, even stranger, Aunty Jo knows what the bottle looks like.

'Malcolm is my friend's dad. He's in the over sixties club.' It's worth adding that last bit to see how far Marcus's eyebrows shoot up in horror.

'The surprises just keep coming today. First you working on cutesy caravans of all things, Edie, and now pensioners splashing on the Jean Paul G.' Marcus is shaking his head, and laughing. 'Well, we can't stand here all day admiring polka dots and discussing male grooming, or you could break off early, Edie. I was hoping we'd find a better vibe further down the coast so I could take you out for dinner. I must admit I didn't know you'd be working, I was hoping I could steal you away for the whole weekend.'

I'm looking up at Barney and his face looks like a thundercloud just passed across it.

'It's your call, Edie. Whatever you decide, it's fine with me.'

'We could pull in some spa treatments, get you back in shape again.' Marcus is staring down at me, and wearing his persuasive smile. Then, in the space where I'm thinking what the hell to say, some very familiar notes come from the radio, and as his smile melts to another level he turns to Barney. 'Coldplay, *Viva la Vida* – they're playing our song, Edie.'

'Funny.' There's that wicked gleam in Barney's eye again. 'It just shows how wrong you can be. For months we've been thinking Edie's favourite was *All by Myself*.'

'Surely Edie must have told you about her Chris Martin crush by now, it's all his fault she goes for blond and gaunt.' Marcus glances at his wrist then back at me. 'So are we good to go, Edes?'

There's a certainty about the way he's just assuming I'll agree. Who knows why, but all I can think of, as he taps the face of his latest Rolex, is his watch collection. How many rows of them he has, in special boxes. How we had to put a special lockable section in the wardrobe to keep them safe. And how I used to find it funny that he was always convinced he was the spit of Chris Martin, when he isn't at all.

'Don't worry about Dustin, Sweetpea. I can always cover your walks.' Aunty Jo is nodding, but her eyes are wide enough for her significant stare to be boring into me 'You and Marcus have *so much* to catch up on.'

'The dog's *yours?*' Marcus's smile has flipped to high-pitched shock. 'Since when did you want *a dog?*'

'It's a long story. Things change.' What's more, it's wrong of him to roll up here thinking we can pick up where we left off without any seams. If he'd called ahead or arrived one conversation earlier, I'd have been completely free to go. As it is, whatever Barney says about letting me off, if I disappear for the weekend, Mary and Jim won't get their delivery and it's his reputation on the line. My loyalties are here. 'And I'm sorry, Marcus, I can't come with you, there's a deadline.'

'You *are* joking?' It was worth saying if only to hear his shriek of disbelief. 'You're sticking *pictures* in a *shepherd's hut*, where's the urgency in that?'

'I've got a client meeting, then an order to finish.' And the way he's reacting I'm even more decided, that's what I'd rather do.

'So you're saying you can't fit in a coffee between now and

Sunday? There are important things I want to talk to you about.'

'Probably best to leave it until I'm back home.' I'm not meeting Aunty Jo's eye because I know she'll think I'm being stubborn to turn him down, that Marcus turning up could be serendipity offering me a second chance to grab a happy ever after, and I'm throwing it away. It's not that I haven't thought about what she said a while ago. But Marcus is a lot nicer on his own ground. Being all sneery and trying to play the macho man for Barney's benefit is not the best look for him. And if he's seriously got something significant to say, he'll be prepared to wait a few weeks for me.

It's not lost on me – if he'd been willing to be even a tiny bit flexible at the time, the course of our lives might have been completely different. Not that I'm blaming him in any way, because I'm not. But if we hadn't split up, I'd never have got to do the skydive to prove to the world – and possibly to him too – how great I was on my own.

'Great, have it your own way, I'll see you in Bath, then.' Marcus is halfway down the steps when he hesitates, and turns. 'Am I missing something here? When did you ever turn down dinner, Edie, let alone a weekend in a spa hotel, what are you not telling me?'

'What . . . *what?*'

'Thrown together, confined spaces, hearts and flowers . . . I should have known. You two, you're an item, aren't you?'

'Hell, no.' He couldn't be more wrong. I'm glaring at Barney, then poking him on the arm because it might be helpful for him to back me up here instead of gazing vacantly out at the sea.

'Absolutely not. I have no idea where you got that . . . er . . . idea, but it's completely not true.'

Marcus's eyes narrow. 'So what's with the matching shirts then?'

'Matching what?' As I screw my head around and see what Barney's wearing my gut collapses.

'Work uniform.' Barney's expression is inscrutable. 'You do know what the logos are? The seven deadly sins, in French. They're ironic, by the way.'

'Of course I bloody know, my Masters is in Modern European Languages for Chrissakes.' However much of a dick he's sounding, Marcus is determined to get the last word in here. 'Way too sophisticated for a fishing village, and fuck all to do with caravans. If you and Poldark here decide to take some proper creative marketing advice, Edie, you know where I am.'

We're all still watching Marcus as he wrestles his way past the pear tree and back out onto the lane.

'Well, thanks for that, Edie B. You giving up three days of luxury to stay here and work, means a lot. Mary and Jim will be very grateful.' Barney's clearing his throat. 'In fact, we all are.'

'Any time.' I'd committed, I'm a professional, I couldn't have made any other choice. I just hope everyone knows it's for no reason other than because I want to finish the hut. I'm opening and closing my mouth, wondering how the hell to clear that one up, when there are more familiar notes on the radio.

'*It's Raining Men.*' Aunty Jo is beaming at me. 'How funny is that? They're playing *all* your songs today, aren't they Edie?' She turns to Barney. 'And you have to admit, it doesn't get any better than being compared to Poldark, does it?'

Somehow the hut is still vibrating as I turn to Barney. 'Workplace . . . *uniform?*'

'What?' Barney's grin is the width of St Aidan Bay. 'There are seven of the damn things, we're bound to turn up in the same ones some days, it's the law of averages.'

'Averages my arse.'

As for holding my own with workplace comebacks, I reckon I'm pretty close to being back in the game.

Chapter 37

Day 292: Monday, 20th August
A night away . . .

Epic Achievement: The last box.

The next few weeks go by in blur, partly down to the heat haze, but mostly due to the fog on my sunnies. It's a lovely change that everyone's wearing them, not just me, but however much I wipe them my lenses steam up with a mix of sweat, sand grains, suncream and doughnut sugar. And mostly all four at the same time. The lotion is thanks to Marcus, who sent *all* the factors in a huge Jiffy bag the second he got back home, along with a note. The writing on his company compliments' slip was so scribbly you didn't need the Express Delivery sticker to tell he was in a major hurry. Everyone pitched in to help decipher the scrawl, but in the end not even the calligraphy experts could make out the words, so I'm none the wiser about what the message said, or the sentiments behind it.

If we're talking handwriting, it's very encouraging that mine is *way* better than his. When I sent a postcard back, I made sure my *Thanks for the factors, lovely to catch up again, Edie x* note was super neat. These days I dash off the lettering on my signs without a second thought, but this took loads of tries before it was the kind of perfect that I wanted. It's a good thing Plum gives me mates' rates on her views of the bay. Loella insisted I should have sent him one of my own cards, but I didn't want to lay myself open to being accused of stinting, or being too hippy-dippy or whatever it was he called me.

As for the doughnut sugar, that's down to the explosion of new stalls I have to pass along the village streets and the quayside on my dog walking route, all offering free tasters to first timers and locals. Basically, whether it's Dizzy Doughberries, Fat Bottoms' Sugar Shed, Heavenly Holes or any of the other delicious-sounding assortment of names, I'm powerless to walk past empty-handed.

Summer wouldn't be summer without the echoes of tennis either. Aunty Jo is a huge fan and so long as she's not out for lunch, the rhythmic thud of balls being whacked around the courts at Wimbledon drifts across the courtyard from the open French windows of the day room. As the first wave of carpet fitters move in we're coming painfully close to the end of her tiny budget.

And then the school holidays begin, and suddenly we're getting what all the crowd jokes have been about. Before it was mainly at weekends when you needed a tin opener to get across the beachside car parks, but now it's all day, every day. On the busiest days it's sometimes hard to spot any sand at all between the beach towels.

All the children from nearby come down with us for a dip in the sea when we go for our early morning dog walks. Then once we get home from the beach the kids are like a sea swell, and spend all day swirling between the orchard and the barn yard and Aunty Jo's. All except for Cam that is. He mostly follows Dustin around, who, in turn, rarely moves out of slobbering distance of my T-shirt.

With Periwinkle and 'the quest' it's one of those times when all the ends pull together at once. One day it's looking like it's still a million miles away from done. Aunty Jo is buffing up all the new bathroom tiles and polishing the taps until they're more gleaming than the ones on the Flash advert. The kitchen doors are still up in the barn getting their final coat of makeover paint, we're shunting the last of the Happy Valley furniture out of the house to store at Barney's, falling over the second wave of carpet fitters as we move in the pieces I've borrowed from the shepherd's hut showroom.

Before I know it, Aunty Jo is putting out all her specially made cushions on the sofas and chairs we've brought in, I'm rushing around, adding in little touches like driftwood and ropes of hanging shells and my beachy notices, and Barney is drilling to hang up my specially made Periwinkle Cottage sign. And up in the barn yard Beth and Loella have put extra strings of bunting over all the doorways to make it look extra twee there too.

Back in the cottage garden Malcolm couldn't be spending any more time sprinkling and trimming the grass and nurturing his borders, and the pots of flowers are exploding with colour. This is the only living lawn in St Aidan to have survived the scorching summer and still be so green it looks like it's fake not real.

Then late one afternoon, just as we're on course to finish, Loella rocks up with the news that her friend with a luxury hideaway has had a last-minute already-paid-for cancellation, so we've got the offer of a handful of tipis for a night of free beachside glamping, a few miles up the coast. To everyone else, it's a no-brainer. To me, however seductive, it's a typical St Aidan last-minute hitch I could do without.

Loella's looking at her phone. 'It's already teatime. I promise we'll have you back before breakfast, Edie B.' She's tweaking the cushions on Aunty Jo's sofa and wagging her finger at me. 'Bring your swimmers and your toothbrush – and your lippy if you must – pick you up in ten, you're bunking in with us.'

Not long later, we're a few headlands along the coast, and we're wandering between the most picturesque encampment of pale brown tipis decked with unlit fairy lights, and out onto the pale sand of a tiny private bay.

Loella has every right to look delighted. 'See, Edie, it's every bit as gorgeous as I told you?'

I have to hand it to her. 'It is, I'd forgotten how amazing it feels to be on an empty beach.'

'That's the trouble with living in a holiday destination, it's too easy to forget to go away.'

I'm about to point out I'm only days away from disappearing to my mum's for her party, but Cam comes and pulls on my hand, so with Dustin bounding along beside us we make our way down to the sea.

We swim and splash in the shallows on our bodyboards, explore the rock pools nestling at the edge of the bay, then we pull in a game of beach volleyball while the guys cook dinner on the gas barbie up by the tents. Then, thanks to a supremely civilised 'no noise, no fires' rule, the campfire singalong is replaced with burying Barney, and then we all lie around on luxury sun loungers and watch the sun go down. The first stars come like pricks of light in the smoky blue of the evening and we're still gazing upwards trying to count them when the sky has turned black and is splashed with a trillion spots of light and the moon slides up so high its reflections are shimmering in the sea.

Beth is the first one to stir. 'Well, that's the last of the bubbly.' They've downed quite a few bottles since we arrived. 'We might as well see if those gorgeous beds are as comfy as they look.'

I leave them to get the younger kids settled down and nip across to the toilet block with Mia for a quick shower. By the time we wander back to the tipi with our toothbrushes, the children's cries have mostly died down and Loella dips into view through the tipi flaps.

Her voice is low. 'Hey, I hope you don't mind, there's a tiny change of plan.'

'What's that?'

'Cam wanted to sleep in with my lot, he snuck into your bed.'

'Great, so . . .?'

'If you wouldn't mind swapping to Cam's bed instead?'

Sleeping with BARNEY? Somehow I manage *not* to swallow my tongue. 'Fine.' It comes out as a rasp, but I'm hoping she's too sozzled to notice. I can't make more of this than it is. We're all adults here, why wouldn't I sleep in a tent with a friend? So long as I can get my lustful thoughts under strict control . . .

She squeezes my hand. 'Thanks, I know Barney would be really grateful. Cam's never wanted to do a sleepover before, so if he's ready to do it on his own we don't want to hold him back.'

I've noticed the same with Tash. Once the responsibility of being a parent kicks in, those kiddie worries are so overwhelming they override everything else. There's apparently very little room for the normal adult behaviour that created the kids in the first place. The real wonder is that anyone has more than one child. And seeing that Barney is even more oppressed by being an unexpected surrogate parent, I'll be completely safe from his side. He's going to be beside himself worrying about Cam. Even Bella would see that. So I have nothing to stress about here.

I tiptoe between the swinging light strings, and when I get to Barney's tipi he smiles up at me in the half light from where he's lounging on some stripy rugs in the entrance.

'Thanks for this.' He glances into the tent behind him. 'We actually got some amazing beds, but Cam and I decided we'd rather sleep out here, under the stars.'

'He was mad to swap, I had a wartime camp bed.' I laugh as I peer past him to two huge vintage beds, covered in pillows. 'Anywhere's good for me, I'm knackered.' I was, but I'm not now. In fact, I've never felt more awake.

'Sit down.' He pats the ground at the side of him, although to be fair he's lying more than sitting. 'So, you're almost done at the cottage, you've finished the shepherd's huts. I reckon you're due a rest.'

'Maybe.' We're on reassuringly neutral ground with this. As I flop down onto the soft rug I make out his T-shirt, his bleached low-slung jeans turned up at the bottom. 'So long as there's any furniture left to paint, when I come back from the Bath trip I'll carry on with that.' Being busy takes my mind off the uncertainty of what's coming next. 'Now it's almost here, I'm really nervous about going back.'

'You've got no need to worry, the way you handle customers, you'll smash your way back into Zinc Inc.'

'I hope so.' Meeting Jake next week is the big test I'm working up to.

'Not many people know what it's like to lose what you've poured your whole life into.' His voice is desolate. 'Or the guts it takes to start over, and claw your way back.'

My heart's going out to him. 'You know from losing the boat-yard. But you've come back from that so well.'

'It's your help that made my business finally come together.' He nods. 'But this is your moment, not mine. Now you believe in yourself again, whatever you put your mind to, you'll be able to do it. Your talent will take you wherever you want to go.' He lets out a sigh. 'When I think of how you were when you arrived on the lane, you've come so far.'

'It's all thanks to you. I took your advice to stop worrying, tried the new direction you suggested. There's only one box on my to-do list I haven't ticked . . .' And damn that that slipped out into the darkness. As Bella's constantly reminding me, I still haven't had a snog, let alone slept with anyone. I'm guessing from the somersaulting tummy I get around Barney that everything in that department is still in working order, but she keeps pushing me to find out.

'So what's left?' He sounds intrigued.

'Swimming with dolphins.' I'm pleased how fast it comes out considering I'm making it up.

'That's bollocks, you used to hate water. I could take all night to guess, although I have a *pretty good* idea . . .' There's laughter in his voice as he nudges me with his elbow. 'If you're a princess looking for a frog to kiss, just say the word. I'll be more than happy to help.'

'You *would?*' I've imagined this so many times, now he's here for the taking it's almost unreal.

'I'm not claiming to be an expert, I've been out of the game longer that you. But I'd do my best to step up to any challenge you throw at me.'

My heart's banging against my chest wall so hard I'm blurting. 'I'll have to do it with someone . . . at some stage . . . obviously . . . and it would help if there was . . . er – chemistry . . .'

'We'd be okay there.' He runs his finger down my arm and watches my shiver. 'I think the problem would be knowing when to stop. But it's one night, it's been handed to us. We could think of it as a gift?'

I can feel the heat of his thigh pressing against mine. 'One time only . . .' I'm leaning against him, running my finger over the shadows of his forearm, up the muscles of his biceps and under his T-shirt. 'We'd never mention it again . . .' my palm is around the back of his head, my fingers are locking in his hair, and as I'm pulling him towards me I feel like a total tart, but I don't even care '. . . not to anyone . . . not even to each other . . .'

His breath is warm on my lips. 'Stop talking, Edie B, and try this . . .'

As his lips touch mine I stop breathing and lean into the soft, sweet warmth of his mouth. Then my body explodes, and even though my eyes are tight shut, I'm still seeing stars, bright and white, shooting against a dark velvet sky. The distant fall of the waves on the beach come and go, the warm night air is soft on our skin and there's the sense of falling into a time slip. And then, slowly, our lips are parting.

'So . . . ' Barney's voice is low and gritty. 'How's that for fireworks? You *are* getting those sparks?'

If I'd stuck my fingers in a plug socket my body wouldn't be fizzing this much, but it's too good to stop now. 'Maybe we could try that one more time . . . just to make sure . . .?'

*

It's one of those nights that falls out of nowhere and feels like heaven. At six I wake up bursting for a pee, and it hits me that the glam in glamping stops short of en suites. So I stagger off to the loo block, and when I get back minutes later Cam's crawling under the rug next to Barney.

Chapter 38

Day 297: Saturday, 25th August
In Saltings Lane

Epic Achievement: Fitting an entire garden's worth of bunting into a teensy suitcase – have flags, will travel! – and feeling like a living, breathing pop-up party. (After all this effort I so hope the buffet is good because I am majorly looking forward to that bit.)
Woo-hoo! Bring on the birthday cake and profiteroles – just saying.
Not that I'm excited about going home, but waaahhhhh . . .

And then we're back. And Loella was right, we were away such a short time, it's as though glamping never happened. And Barney's been as good as his word. So much so, it sometimes feels like I dreamed the whole thing, although I rerun it in my head a hundred times an hour. At least.

And then suddenly the cottage is done done. Everyone from the barn yard is wiping their bare feet on the brand-new door mat, padding around the house, admiring the light and airy spaces, and gasping at how expensive the light grey newly painted kitchen units look under the new hardwood work surfaces. And even though they all know a buyer will definitely spell the end of the road for their temporary homes in the stables they still manage to smile and say what an awesome transformation it's been and hug us and wish Aunty Jo all the luck in the world with her sale.

And before we know it, all our friends have melted away, and the estate agent is there making notes and snapping pictures on his iPad.

All the time the final push to finish the cottage has been going on, I've been getting Facebook messages from Jake at Zinc Inc. They started with close-up photos. A detail from a super slick bathroom cabinet. Kitchen drawer sides made from glass. Some funky toilet cubicles from a bar revamp in town. All the things he knows would literally make my heart beat faster, because they're so well designed and executed. And it's scary how well he knows me; he's not wrong once.

Seeing as this is work I want to be my best self, so with the kids' help I make a long list of suitable words to pick from to speed up my replies. *Awesome, wow, sick, brill, on point, fabuloso, effing amazing.* Then, just for fun, and because Beth has trained me never to let an idea go before I've squeezed every creative drop out of it, I paint a load of signs saying the same thing. Before I know it, Plum's given me my own *Exclamations!* hat-stand to hang signs on at the gallery, and they're also selling like hot cakes at the shed on the quayside, and on Etsy too. In fact they're rivalling my other current best-sellers – deckchairs saying *Cat nap* and *Dog tired* with stencils of a curled up cat and a Robert-dog on. Beth and Aunty Jo are keeping track of sales because apparently there's a box on the tax return form we have to fill in when the time comes. And I know we're in the middle of the tourist rush hour, and it's a long way from any amount that would make Marcus raise an eyebrow, but I'm still excited by how much cash is mounting up from some old bits of wood, some worn-out deck-chairs and a few painted words.

Jake's picture messages keep on coming, and when he adds in

a few lines of writing I barely notice because it's hidden among so many photos. When he sends the bones of a pitch he's done for flats in a mill conversion, my shiver is pure fear, but the afterglow is excitement. And the teasing goes on, all the way through July. By the time we're into August, I'm itching to get back to my real job in a proper office. But the best part of all is that now summer is almost over and it's nearly time for me to go back to where I came from, probably all thanks to Barney's last push to reassure me, I feel ready for it in a way I never imagined I could.

*

'Well, we did it.'

Aunty Jo and I are out on the lane, and as we wait for our early morning ride out of town, after the rush of getting ready, I'm pulling her into yet another celebration hug. There were times back in the spring when the tasks ahead seemed insurmountable, and it was impossible to think we'd ever get to this point. But here we are. With the cottage on the market and looking wonderful, Aunty Jo is one buyer away from a secure future wherever she chooses to make it. And here I am, mended and almost ready to close the circle and pick up my old life where I left off.

'We have to admit the sea air has worked for both of us along the way.'

'It certainly did, Sweetpea.' Apart from her signature coral-pink lippy, Aunty Jo couldn't look more different from the person who answered the door the day I arrived. It's not only that she laughs and smiles, and wears proper clothes instead of Harry's pyjamas. Thanks to the two-for-one deals and the delectable sticky toffee puddings down at the Yellow Canary, she also no longer looks like she's going to snap in the middle.

It's not just the sea air, though – it's the people here who've helped us make our journeys. And however much I'm longing to get back home, and however much this was only ever meant to be for a short time, there has to be a sadness about leaving a place and the friends who have played such a big part in helping us put our broken selves back together again.

But we aren't saying 'goodbye' for good just yet. It's true, we are standing beside our pull-along cases waiting for Malcolm to arrive in his Ford Granada and whisk us off to Bath but it's just a short visit for my Mum's sixtieth party. My stomach flutters with excitement though, when I think of picking up where I left off, and wandering down those wide, elegant streets to the office. It's only when I get a warmth in my chest as I think about the beautiful, familiar, pale stone vistas that I know how much I've missed them. Malcolm and Aunty Jo are coming for a night or two over the Bank Holiday, but I'm staying on a bit longer. I'll catch up with Jake, pull in a hospital appointment, and grab a fleeting taste of the city vibe I know I'll be longing to get back to, and then get the train back down for a last couple of weeks with Aunty Jo.

Barney and Loella are already down on the beach with the dogs and the kids, so we're leaving without a wave-off committee. Ever since Dustin came to my rescue even though I didn't need rescuing, he's been sleeping in the crook of my knees, and in the day Cam has been with us too. Standing here without either of them for the first time in ages, every time I look down at the gap by my hip where they should be, there's a horrible lurch in my chest as if I've lost something.

Some things never change though. I'm still just as embarrassed by the neon print on Mum's wacky luggage as I was the last time it was out on this lane. If anything, it's worse today because the sun's so much brighter and my case is huge because it's bursting with enough borrowed bunting to fill my parents' back garden.

But it doesn't matter, it's not as if there's anyone around to see. Other than Reggie the postman, obviously, who's skidding to a halt in front of us now.

'Mind your toes, ladies, here you go.' He hands the letters to us through the open window of his little red post van. 'It says Bradleys on the back of the envelope, so these will likely be your sales details, Josie. I've looked you up on Rightmove, you've certainly done wonders in there. You should have a fair few viewers this weekend.' He frowns at the suitcases. 'You're not going away *today*, are you?'

'It's fine.' Aunty Jo brushes away his horror. 'The agents are doing viewings while we're up in Bath.'

'Good luck anyway and travel safe.' He laughs and crashes the van into gear. 'The way the roads are today, it wouldn't surprise me if you'd sold before you get there.'

'Thanks, and see you soon.' Watching the dust rise from the tyres as the van bounces off along the lane to Barney's, I'm trying to remember what it was like having letters delivered by someone who didn't care about every last detail of our lives. Maybe I'm being unfair; Tony the postman at Zinc Inc came for a chat most days but we knew that was mainly an excuse to hit up Sadie's sweetie drawer. But there's no time to think of more because the City Link van is bumping our way.

'Hi, Seth.' This time I get in first as he jumps down, parcel in hand.

'That's one suitcase I'm not going to run over in a hurry.' He pulls a face at my luggage. 'Signature here, please.'

I do a zigzag on his little screen with my fingernail, Aunty Jo steps forward and takes the parcel, and as the van turns in the barn yard she's looking as if her eyes are about to pop.

'Everything okay, Aunty Jo?'

'It will be when you've opened this.' She's pushing the package into my hands. 'I thought it wasn't going to arrive in time . . . don't look at the label.'

'But . . .' For a moment my heart stops. 'It's Leah Lemon.'

'I said not to look, but never mind that now. This is just a little . . .'

'It's not little, it's big.' Even as I'm pulling the tape off, opening the wide, flat box, I'm biting on my lip. Then, as I pull back the tissue paper and run my fingers over the wonderfully soft fabric inside, I can't say anything at all because my chest implodes.

'No present in the world would be big enough to say thank you properly for everything you've done for me, Greenbean. But I hope you'll find this useful.' Despite my yowls, Aunty Jo's carrying on. 'It's for when you go back to work.'

I pull her towards me, juddering as I sob. 'It's the suit – the one I wanted – isn't it?'

'Yes, it is.' She's nodding and sniffling and we're standing on the lane, clinging onto each other, tears washing down our cheeks, until eventually she dips in her pocket 'What are we like?' She passes out a hanky each and we both blow our noses.

'Thank you so much, I've never had a better present.' I'm half laughing, half crying. 'I only hope our *Glamlash* is tear-proof.'

That makes Aunty Jo laugh too. 'The day the catalogue first came I really didn't believe you'd make it back to your job. But now I do.' She gives another loud sniff. 'It's not just everything you've done for me, I'm so proud of everything you've achieved and overcome, Edie. I couldn't be happier to buy it for you.'

There's no time to say any more because yet another van pulls up in the lane, and as the driver flings open the back doors and pulls out a length of wood and a mallet my stomach drops.

'Look, Aunty Jo, he's putting up the sign.'

I'm half waiting for Barney to come out and tell him not to block the lane but he doesn't because he's on the beach. We watch in silence as the driver hammers in the stake and attaches the classy dark blue For Sale sign. Then he taps on a second smaller one.

I'm working my way down it. '... *Cottage* ... *4 beds* ... *sea views* ... *barns* ... *huge po - po – po* ...'

'Huge *potential*, Sweetpea.'

'Of course.' It's as if the sign makes it real for the first time. Real, and *very* final. As I clasp her fingers I can feel her shaking. 'Are you okay?'

'I have to be.' She lets out a faltering breath. 'I can't possibly manage a place this size on my own, quite apart from everything else.'

Somehow in our rush for the finish line, and the latest plan – for Aunty Josie to move closer to my mum – I'd lost sight of how upsetting letting go this last link to Harry might be. How much like home it feels here. How much I love the sea, even if she doesn't.

'New beginnings for both of us,' I say. Except that's total crap because she's uprooting for a second time and I'm going back to what I've been missing for months, so it's way easier for me. 'Don't worry, we'll all be there to help you.'

Then as the door slams and the van turns and drives off towards town, in my head I can hear the door on the room of the orchard and Barney's barns inching shut. Very soon that door's going to be clanging closed behind me too. I know exactly how wobbly Aunty Jo feels because, for a tiny fragment of time, I want to wrench the door open and dive back inside too. Stay where it's safe. Which is completely ridiculous, considering everything I've worked for over the last few months is so I can leave.

I dip into my bag and pull out my mirror. 'Lippy?'

We're still doing the running repairs to our faces when Malcolm's car trundles along the lane. He pulls to a halt in front of us, gets out onto the verge and runs straight into the sign. But all he does as he moves around to open the boot is to shake his head very slowly.

Once we're all on board, he turns the car around, and it's only when we get to the lane end that he takes his hands off the steering wheel and rubs his hands together.

'Right, Bath here we come.' For someone beginning a weekend away, he couldn't sound less enthusiastic. And we get all the way to Bodmin before he asks us if we'd like to listen to Beth's special *Dad's Jukebox* CD.

'Ooh, Lynyrd Skynyrd, *Free Bird*, that's nice.' Aunty Jo recognises the first track straight away. She turns round and hands me the fat envelope. 'Now the road's winding less, see what you think of these, Chickpea.'

As I close my eyes and listen to the twangy notes and song lines that are all about someone having to leave, the picture stuck on the insides of my eyelids is Barney. Sitting on the top step of a hut, with his beaten-up guitar resting on his ripped jeans, the stubble shadows playing across his cheekbones, Cam a little further down.

And I'm *so* hoping that I haven't taken too much from them. That while I've been soaking up all the benefits in the orchard, I've done well enough by him and Cam too. Because I know I'm leaving him with an orchard full of beautifully decorated huts, and more orders than he'd ever dreamed was possible. But there's still this nagging feeling that I'm leaving a job half done. There's an awful sinking, doubting pain deep inside my chest that's telling me I could have – should have – somehow done more.

Then *Good Old Fashioned Lover Boy* comes on, followed by Razorlight, and *America*, and it's as if I've landed in Dad's car, not Malcolm's. I lean back against the velour seat, pull out the brochure Aunty Jo gave me, and leaf through the sharp edges of the paper.

The neat black writing is the same kind Sadie used to do on the Zinc Inc documents and I'm staring at the print so hard it goes wobbly. It's funny because all the letters look like old friends, but we get all the way to the road where all the cars go really fast and I'm still stumbling over the first few words. Even though I'm sounding out the bits like Cam and I have done a million times, I manage the first few, but after that my head won't work at all.

We're seeing signs to Bristol when Aunty Jo's mobile rings, and it's the estate agent telling her she's got an asking price offer on the cottage and they want to buy the contents too. So I probably don't need to look at the details too carefully after all.

Chapter 39

Day 298: Sunday, 26th August
Back in Bath

Epic Achievement: Finding my way home (finally.) Just that.

As we got closer to my parents' house the swathes of green fields gave way to the mottled blue sprawl of the outskirts of town, and as we sped past heavy lorries and the warehouses and factories I hadn't seen for months I could already feel the thrum of the city vibrating through me. Then we left the fast road and looped around the streets of Bath where the pale stone terraces with their tall repeating windows and the rolling vistas of grey slate roofs broken by tall church spires were achingly familiar. At first, after the cosy patchwork of St Aidan's higgledy cottages, everything looked huge and oversized. But by the time we turned the corner into Mum and Dad's close the houses were more homely again, little brick boxes cosying up with their neat gardens, double garages and driveways. And by the time we pulled up outside number twenty-six it was almost like I'd never been away.

Mum was extra shiny, and hugged us in through the front door instead of through the porch at the back. I'm not sure if her hairdresser's blow dry, Joules T-shirt and new pale pink lippy were down to the fact she would be adding a zero onto her age or the pressure of Aunty Jo turning up with her own driver. It took Dad approximately three seconds to get a beer in Malcolm's hand and whisk him off to his shed. Which left Mum free to bring us women up to speed on the party food lists – there were pages of the damn things – and give Aunty Jo a rundown of places nearby she might want to move to. This is Mum, she'd checked out all the new developments within a ten-minute drive and booked viewings for later in the day.

It's funny when you go home for celebrations and the place is unrecognisable. I just hope Dad gave Malcolm the heads-up that we aren't always this tidy or he might have the wrong impression entirely. Mum and Dad had been in overdrive; all the furniture indoors was pushed back against the walls, and outside the back garden was bursting with borrowed garden chairs. Apart from a break to see the flats with Aunty Jo and to go out to pick up the giant 'death by chocolate' birthday cake, we just got sucked into helping with the preparations. By the time we're having our Thai takeaway on the patio that evening, the garden is festooned with bunting. As we relax on an exotic array of other people's sun loungers, everyone except me is already getting stuck into the party alcohol and Aunty Jo is pretty much sold on a flat around the corner. What with a balcony overlooking the park, dado rails on the landings, *and* being next to a row of shops with a veggie shop which is so on-trend you can't buy anything unless you take your own bags, what's not to like?

As Mum and I said – as we high fived each other before bed – 'Our work here is done'.

The upside of being alcohol free is not having hangovers. When I wake next morning, even if the light isn't quite as luminous as I'm used to, for the first few seconds it's kind of wonderful that in place of the distant crash of the waves I'm listening to the rumble of buses and the whine of next door's lawnmower. I have time to sit in my little grey room, breathing deeply and muttering,

'I'll soon be back, it's going to be awesome, bring on the cake, work will be fab.' I say it quite a few times before I hear Dad groaning his way along to the bathroom.

Once we go downstairs I astonish Mum by making everyone Oat so Lovely for breakfast, which she very sweetly says is her best birthday present ever. Suffice it to say, no one else looks in any state to make their own porridge. Then, after a couple of green teas, Aunty Jo puts the oven on and starts cooking vol-au-vents, Malcolm counts out the candles and I cram them onto the cake, and a singing fireman birthday telegram comes to the door, sent as a joke from Mum's mates at her 'Bums and Tums' class. Then Tash, Brian, Tiddlywink and Wilf arrive with armfuls of flowers, and homemade cards with the glue still wet that somehow accidentally get stuck to Dad's new M&S sweatshirt, and that kicks the party off.

It's one of those afternoons that goes by in a blur while I eat my own body weight in Brie and cranberry puffs and mini cheese soufflés. The garden is heaving, and there are so many of Mum's friends I haven't seen in ages I'm spending so much time mingling and chatting I'm seriously neglecting the sweet table. It's only after the cake and the toasts – I'm sticking firmly to cans of elderflower fizz so there's no mistakes here – that I finally manage to load up a dish with strawberries and profiteroles and double chocolate mousse for Tiddlywink and me, and we flop down on the grass beside Malcolm, Mum and Aunty Jo to eat them.

'It's a great way to kick-start your new social life, Aunty Jo.' As I grin at her and hand Tiddlywink a strawberry, I'm wishing Malcolm was enjoying himself more, but I can see why he'd be overwhelmed by the city.

'I've already been asked to join the book group.' Aunty Jo pretends to flick a crumb off her dress, but she's secretly looking very pleased. 'And Tums and Bums and the Rachmaninov Society.'

'You don't have to join them all.' I send her a wink. 'Remember to save time for life drawing.'

'It would be a shame to waste those easels.' She's smiling at me. 'If you like we can go to that together, Sweetpea. And if ever you want a break from your mum and dad, you can always come and stay with me. Two bathrooms – we could have one each.'

'Thanks, Aunty Jo.' I reach over and give her hand a squeeze. She's so full of thoughts, but she's also got a point. In the long-term it might be easier to live with her than here.

'Actually . . .' My mum's clearing her throat and looking unusually tentative. 'Thinking about that, I've been meaning to tell you. I said Marcus could come this afternoon, so he might be popping in later.'

'You did . . . *WHAT?!*' I'm rubbing the lump in my throat where I swallowed my profiterole whole, checking Tiddlywink's okay after my sudden lurch, and wondering how exactly my mum made the jump from Aunty Jo's flat to my ex. 'Why the hell did you do that?'

'He came round on Friday with flowers for my birthday. It seemed mean not to invite him.'

How does he do it? Well, her birthday was probably programmed into his phone from before, but the rest? I don't remember him ever bringing me flowers, but the hard bit is, I'm not completely sure if that's because he never did or because it got lost in one of my mind holes.

'Well, you're going to have to *un*-invite him.' At least I'm sure about that bit.

'Don't be silly, Edie, that would be rude.'

'And asking my ex to your party *isn't?*'

'I know you're not together any more but he's like part of the family. He's often popped round with roses the last few months, he still cares about how you're doing.' My mum's somehow missing that we need to stop living in the past and move on. 'In any case, he pretty much asked himself.'

'That figures.' I can see Tash eyeballing me from where she's scraping chocolate icing out of Wilf's ears with a napkin.

'Don't worry, Edie, you know what he's like, if he isn't here by now, he's probably had a better offer.' Tash gets to her feet, and slides her feet into her flip-flops. 'If you've got a minute, I could do with a hand changing Wilf?'

'Back soon, Tiddlywink.' We both know Tash is completely capable of doing this herself and just trying to get me out of the way to smooth things over here. I'm not that happy about leaving my pudding either, but there's still lots left on the table so I hand the dish to Mum and follow Tash towards the back porch.

We're making our way past the coat hooks and Tash has her hand on the door to the kitchen when she pulls up, looking towards the open front door. 'Talk about bad timing, that's all we bloody need.'

'What . . . why?'

'There's no good way of saying this. It's Marcus. He's just getting out of his car.' She's frowning as she releases her grip on me. 'Do you want me to send him away? Give me five seconds, he'll be gone.'

'It's okay.'

Part of me wants to hide in the cupboard, and yet I also know I need to get this over. I go to the door and look across at that familiar blond hair, more the colour of dirty sand now I know the beach so well. Then I call out, 'Marcus!' I watch him twist around.

'Edes, shall I come in?'

'No, stay there, I'll come out.'

'Are you sure?' Tash is next to me, her voice low. 'Do you need a wingman?'

I shake my head.

'I'll be here by the window. If you want backup, Edie, wave and I'll come.'

'Thanks.' I squeeze her hand. Numb is okay. It could be the best way to be to handle this.

By the time I get to the end of the drive, Marcus has still got his boot lid up. As I arrive on the pavement he's holding out a can.

'Fancy a cold beer?'

'I'm an alcohol free zone now.'

'My bad, I didn't think.' He's using the same vintage Coca-Cola icebox I bought him for parties and he grabs us a couple of bottles of cola then closes the boot lid. 'Do you mind if we have a quick chat here, before we join the others?'

'Fine.' I choose a spot on the garden wall between the bushes with red and purple flowers we used to pop when we were kids, and ease my bum onto the sun-warmed stone coping. This was our favourite place to sit back in the day, only then we had bubblegum and rollerskates and annoyed my mum by writing on the pavement with the purple crab apples from the tree.

'So, how's it going?' Marcus arrives in the gap next to me. 'Is it good to be home?'

'Great, thanks.' It's a lot easier talking to him here on familiar ground. 'Next visit I'll be going back to work.'

'So you *are* returning?' He's scouring my face for clues. 'Meaning, there isn't anyone else in the frame to keep you away?'

'Yes, I am. And it's definitely still just me.' There's a flutter as I think of my test drive with Barney, but that was all it was. I have to let it go and move on.

'So, how are you really – once we strip away those rose-tinted gypsy caravans, the foreign language T-shirts and the never-ending views of the beach?' I watch his Adam's apple bulge as he swallows. 'You can be honest here, Edes, this is me you're talking to.'

'Sometimes it's hard.' I give a shrug and wonder how he knows to push this. Reading Aunty Jo's house details in between party

325

preps has taken way longer than a Dead End Murder book. 'All those pesky long words.'

'So nothing new there then?' As he gives my ribs a gentle nudge with his elbow he's laughing. 'You were never the world's best speller – anything longer than a five letter word, you had to Google it. It sounds to me like it's just business as usual.'

'Jeez, Marcus.'

'We might as well tell it like it is.' His arm comes around my shoulder and he pulls me into a squeeze. 'Don't look so hurt, it's not important. Everyone always loved you for your wonderful puddings and the way you pulled us up on the bullshit, it wasn't ever for your intellectual conversation.' He blows out his cheeks. 'Do you know, being home alone playing FIFA is every guy's dream for a week, but any longer is hell. I've really missed you, Edes.'

I'm shaking my head.

'This is where I leave a gap, and you say you missed me too.' His brow wrinkles into a frown. 'You *have* missed me?'

'Well, yes . . .' And no. I can hardly tell him, when I think back carefully, the biggest pangs I can remember were for the house. 'Sometimes . . .' I take in his appalled expression. 'I've had a lot to think about.'

'I'm sorry, I know you have.' He's pursing his lips. 'But, given how much we've missed each other, I've been thinking we could give it another go.'

Nothing's completely straightforward with Marcus, so it's best to ask. 'So how would that work?'

He's smiling like it's a no-brainer. 'Well, you're obviously not up to your high-flying job, so we could drop straight back to Plan B?'

'Plan *what?*'

'The family. I mean, Kate and Wills have got three now, we're already miles behind them. It's perfect timing for you to take a career break.'

'You're making a lot of . . .' And dammit because if ever I needed to think of the word it's now.

'A lot of what, assumptions?' He shrugs as he takes in my nod. 'Not at all. I'm simply being creative, that's what I'm good at, remember?'

'Of course.' I should do, he reminds everyone often enough.

'You could look after the children and pick up your career again later. Hell, I'll even wait until you get your career sorted out, if you insist.'

'I-I-I don't know what to say.' I know I've toyed with the idea in my head, but coming out of nowhere it's knocked me off-balance.

'You could try saying what a brilliant idea it is? Think of our house, bursting with kids, even a dog or two if you must. It's a wonderful image.'

'It is.' I saw the same picture once in the dark after that chat with Aunty Jo. And a whole summer with the children on the lane has shown me how much I like being around kids.

Marcus cuts off my thought train. 'We'd obviously upsize, maybe even move to the country.'

'Hang on, you'll be promising me a pony next.'

'If that's what's going to make our kids happy, why the hell not?' And the funny thing is, he sounds so enthusiastic and genuine he's almost carrying me along.

'But . . .' There's something holding me back.

'I know you want this too, Edes. Look what I found.' He dips into his pocket and holds out a tiny scrap of grey fabric, and my stomach drops. 'Tucked behind the mirror in my gaming room – I take it the nursery prints weren't there to help my *Call of Duty* skills?'

'Okay.' I'm putting my hands up on my head, I can't pretend here. If I didn't want him finding my private daydreams I should have been more careful where I left them. 'The stars are mine.'

327

'See, we *are* realigned.' He's punching the air. 'I know you'll never be how you used to be, but I'll accept that.'

'R-r-right.'

'So that's a "yes"?' His arm's around me again, and this time it's squeezing me tighter than ever. 'Why not move straight back in? Let's get this family on the road.'

'Actually . . .'

'Don't say anything more, take as long as you need.' He swoops down and briefly brushes my lips with his. 'Slow-mo's how it's got to be from now on, but I'm good with that. I'll be in Bulgaria anyway.'

'*Bulgaria?*'

'Two weeks offline, off toxins, off grid. It's a super-pure creative conference experience, my latest freebie. I'll be back practically before I've gone.' He glances at his latest watch. 'Hey, how's that for a timekeeper? If it was any more slender it would actually cease to exist.' Then he pulls a face. 'Where's your watch?'

As I stare at my empty wrist my heart drops to somewhere around my knees. 'Oh, I left it in the bathroom.' At Aunty Jo's, and it was months ago, but he doesn't have to know that.

'Well, that's good. It cost a packet, I'd hate you to have lost it.' He grins at me, then looks back at his own watch again. 'Jeez, if I don't give your mum her crate of champagne and run, I'm going to miss my plane.'

As he jumps up and dives into the back seat of his car, I turn and see Tash coming out of the drive, Wilf in her arms, Tiddlywink lurching from foot to foot, jumping along beside her.

'Everything okay down here? You waved, then I saw Marcus go in for a snog . . .' Her eyes are wide with query.

'It was more of a peck.' Seeing how little it challenged my lippy, it might have even been an air kiss.

'We're more than okay.' Marcus swings across the pavement

towards us, a Moët crate in the crook of his arm. 'Edes and I had a very constructive chat, so *watch this space*. Expect to see a lot more of me *very* soon.' His one enigmatic raised eyebrow is completely inappropriate seeing as he has already pretty much given the game away. Then he turns to me again and holds up the box. 'Okay, take me to the birthday girl, then I'm gone.'

As I stare up at him it all locks into place. I know he's smart and good-looking, and successful. And he's everything I used to love before. But I also know if I go back to him now, I'll be selling myself short. Even if we had those children he's aching for, his love comes with so many clauses and conditions, I'll always feel like his consolation prize.

But in the split second that I take all that in something more important hits me – me not wanting to start a family wasn't about the job at all. My cold feet then *and* now are because Marcus isn't the right person.

'I know you're in a rush, but before you go—' I take a huge breath, then let the words out slowly, to make sure he gets them. 'I won't be moving back in with you.'

He turns to me accusingly, putting down the crate of champagne. 'But you haven't had time to decide.'

I'm not sure I've ever seen Marcus panicked before. 'I would like kids, Marcus, but when I have them I want it to be with someone who loves me as I am, not someone who wishes I was different.'

'Jeez, Edes, where are you getting these ideas? This is real life, not the sodding summer of sixty-nine.' As his voice rises, his leg takes a swing at the car, and his foot bounces off the back tyre.

'So, just to be clear, it's thanks but no thanks to getting back together.'

His eyes narrow. 'This is about you wanting kids with that ironic Aidan Turner lookalike, thinking he'll be a better dad than me?'

'You're totally wrong.' I don't remember Marcus ever being *this* perceptive, but however close to the truth he is today, I refuse to admit any of it. To him or myself.

He's shaking his head at me as he flings open the car door. 'Fine. Call me when you come to your senses, and we'll talk again.'

'I won't—' He's slammed the door, and he's already roaring off down the close, so as my words tail off I'm left talking to myself. '—won't be calling . . . or changing my mind.'

'Go, Edie!' Tash gives me a play punch, then, as she slides her arm around my shoulders, she's looking down at me with admiration. 'However well you did, he always managed to undermine you, so well done for putting him straight.'

I grin at Tiddlywink and lean over to pop a flower bud. 'He was always big on the "What the hell, Edie?" looks. I don't want that any more.'

Tash is smiling as she nods. 'You've changed.'

'And what does that mean?'

'Only that you'd never have had the balls to do that before you went to Cornwall.'

I have to remind her. 'I had left him.'

'But we all thought if he asked, you'd be straight back.' She raises her eyebrows and her smile widens as she takes in the crate of champagne still on the kerb. 'Impeccable planning though. You got the champagne, *and* you told him where to get off.' She sends me a wink. 'It's lovely to see my little sister's finally got her shit together.'

I have no idea why she's saying that now, but it's a first so I'm happy to take it.

Chapter 40

Day 300: Tuesday, 28th August
In the city

Epic Achievement: Squaring the circle when I meant to close it.
(Obviously being ironic here about the achievement bit – do I even
know what squaring the circle means? Probably not. Did I ever?
Probably not that either. Doughnuts were involved – they're circles
too.) (Just saying.)

When you've had the adrenalin burst of a big sunny event, it's only natural that the days that follow might feel less sparkly when the weather turns. After the thrill of coming home again – then the party and the shuddering thrill of standing up to Marcus for a second time – as Bella drives me into town on Tuesday lunchtime I'm being reminded how dismal soaking city streets can be when the rain clouds close in overhead. Put it this way, if I was looking for promising signs for my return, I wouldn't be finding any, so it's a good thing I'm not. Once we're out of the car we dash along the shiny pavements, dodge the wall of water splashing up as a bus hits a puddle, and head for the traffic lights next to our favourite lunchtime hangout.

'It's been baking hot for months, and it buckets down the day you're back.' Bella links her arm through mine and she's shouting over the roar of engines. 'Don't worry, it's only a shower. The sun will soon be out again and it's a good excuse to use your pretty flamingo brolly. Are you okay?'

As the cars rumble past, I shrink under my umbrella and wish I could put my hands over my ears.

'It's very noisy.' Comparing it to the crash of the waves is a slippery slope. They're louder than thunderclaps when it's stormy, but I'm totally determined not to become a Cornwall bore. What happened in St Aidan stays there, end of. Even though I'm yelling here and my words are drowned out I'm still bubbling inside with the thrill of it all. 'But it's good to be back.'

'Great that you're here, come on.' She yanks me out into the road. 'That green man up there means we can go.'

'And the red man means stop.' As I make a leap for the kerb I still know that much, even if it's taking a while to get my head around the rest. I feel like I did the first time we went to London on our own when we were teenagers and the only reason we got our courage up to cross Oxford Street was because we could see Topshop on the other side. I laugh at her. 'I'm pleased you're here to hang onto.' It's actually a relief Jake suggested meeting at the coffee shop later so we can go back to the Zinc Inc office together.

'Any time.' Bella's grinning at me. 'Wet lunchtimes are always crazy, and the place is still heaving with tourists too.'

As we scurry for the shelter of the Sugar Sugar Coffee Emporium and the water squelches between my bare toes, I'm cursing for not swapping my slip-on mules for ankle boots. We run past the stretch of deserted outdoor tables, then I sigh as I take in the tall plate glass shop windows, with the boxy gold leaf writing.

'No sitting outside today.'

'As a big favour, they're saving us our favourite table in the window. It's your "welcome back" treat.' Bella's right to look pleased with herself because lunchtime reservations at Sugar Sugar are unknown. We shake out our umbrellas at the door and walk on past the queue of customers waiting for seats and sit down at the one empty table covered in a blue checked cloth. 'Realistically, takings probably plummeted when you stopped coming in, so they'll be more than delighted to have you back. Today's on me – are you having your usual?'

'If you're sure?' I take in her nod.

'So two large lattes, two extra large pecan pastries, please.' She smiles at the waitress who had slid over, notepad in hand, then turns back to me. 'You will still be here on Friday? We'll keep things low-key, have a quiet after-work drink with the gang and ease you back into city life.'

It's very tempting, and she's right again; it would be good to catch up with all the people I've not seen for so long. I know there's no rush to get back to St Aidan, but I'm torn. I have a lifetime ahead of me to go out with the girl crew, but barely any Friday nights left to go to the Plank Place with Cam. Even thinking about it now, there's a twang in my chest. I dip into my bag to touch up my lippy before the coffee comes, and pick up my sunnies too. This has to be the first time in months I'm not wearing them. But while I'd happily go out with them propped on my head in St Aidan when the rain was sluicing down, that's the kind of thing people in Bath give more damns about, so I pushed them into my bag instead. Before I wouldn't have given any damn myself either way, but I'm feeling a bit like the new girl at school here, really desperate to fit back in.

'Sunnies?' Bella notices them on the cloth immediately as I patch up my mouth. 'I love how optimistic you are.'

'I'm hoping the pie will be dazzling.' I'm always straight with Bella, but it's hard to say why I'm putting them on when the slice of sky we can see above the street is the colour of coal.

'You won't have long to wait.' She grins at me as the waitress sweeps our way and unloads her tray. As the woman leaves, Bella leans forward and drops her voice. 'And while we're eating you can tell me how our favourite party gatecrasher, Marcus, is.'

It takes a few bites of delectably flaky pastry and toffee bread-crumbs for me to work out my reply.

'Lonely, otherwise much the same.'

'Hot, hunky, having occasional dickhead moments which we always forgive him for, and perpetually on his way somewhere more on-trend then?' She's laughing at me because we both know how perfectly that sums him up.

'Only now he's suggesting we get back together and have a baby.'

'Seriously, is that what you want?'

I let out a groan. 'I've *so* missed our kitchen . . .'

'Edie Browne, that's no kind of a reason, and you know it.'

I push a flake of pastry into my mouth. 'I shocked myself, I actually I told him where to stick his offer – as nicely as I could.'

'Phew, I'm pleased to hear it.'

'He was always telling me to "keep up" when we lived together before, so I'd never make the pace now. I had this vision, him rushing ahead and me staring after him looking at a little speck in the distance where the land meets the sky.'

The corners of her mouth pull downwards. 'It's sad, but he was never the greatest at building your confidence. It's great that you held out.'

'I told him I wasn't a consolation prize, I didn't want him accepting second best. But the more I think about it, *I* settled for second best with *him*. For all those years, I did everything he asked. Our life looked wonderful in the Instagram shots, but I wasn't ever completely what he wanted.'

'We deserve to be adored as we are, Edie. Anything less, it's not worth the trouble.'

'Too damn right.'

'So, I take it Marcus didn't stand up to comparison?' There's a wicked glint in her eye as she scours my face. 'Your naughty night in the yurt did ruin you, after all.'

'Shit, Bella, it's not like that. Anyway, it was more of a tipi.'

'Forget the frigging tent, it's the principle I'm talking about – once you've had Hendrick's, you wouldn't want to go back to bog-standard gin.'

'Well, it doesn't matter. I won't be drinking either.'

'Surely you *have* to – wasn't "spectacular" the word you used?'

'It's not just Bath, people in Cornwall have one-night stands too.'

'Really?' Bella looks genuinely taken aback. 'But what about those pictures you drew?'

'He's very drawable, but he hasn't space in his life for a relationship, and we both knew that. It's about much more than me being here, and him there. Cornwall's crazy. I've come back to sanity, my planner and my new beginning.'

'And that's it?'

'So long as Jake will have me.'

As I brush the crumbs off my newly pressed white shirt, the fizz of excitement in my chest at being out in town is turning to a flutter of nerves about work. Now I'm so close to getting back, however worried I am about my reading, I mustn't panic. So long as I stay cool, I can nail this.

'Jake loves whatever you do, he always has.' Bella wrinkles her nose. 'I can't see that altering, he'll ease you back in.' Her eyes narrow. 'So long as that's what you want?'

'Why wouldn't I? Leaving all my friends and family here to go and live on the edge of nowhere in St Aidan, spending every waking hour focusing on my recovery – that was all so I could get to this point. I'm minutes away from my last big step, meeting up with Jake today is me closing my circle.'

'What you've been through hasn't altered you then?' She gives a shrug. 'Tough times often give you a new perspective. People come out afterwards with very different priorities. Even if you're in denial about your hunky shepherd, I thought you might have fallen in love with the sea?'

It's not the first pang I've had thinking about how much I'm missing looking out at the line where the ocean smudges into the sky, the crash of the waves tumbling up the beach. The twitter of finches on Mum's bird feeder aren't any substitute for the seagull cries echoing around the bay.

I let out a sigh. 'It's an amazing place, but it was only ever an interlude. It's done its work, and now I'm back where I should be. Where I *want* to be.' There's no room for change or doubt, so I make sure I sound certain. 'I do like chatting to kids more now.' If she's thinking about how my time away has changed me, I can't let it go without flagging that one up. As I think of the freckles on Cam's nose there's a familiar squish in my chest. 'With my tan I can wear less make-up . . .'

'You definitely look different. More relaxed, maybe happier?' Bella's smile widens behind her pie as she takes in my appalled stare. 'Different, but still fab. You really suit your hair longer.'

'There's no spare cash for haircuts in St Aidan.' I take a swig of coffee, then swipe away my foam moustache, and remind myself I need a complete makeover before I come back for good. As my less-than-perfect nails show, it's been too easy to slip into bad habits and let my standards drop. I'm blaming it on the steaming summer, but I've seriously neglected my beauty regime lately and got sloppy with my clothes. Months of hanging around the beach, I'm like an embodiment of my own 'Let it all hang loose' signs. I just hope Jake is less observant than Bella.

As I look around the café as the lunchtime chatter gets louder, it's odd to see everyone dressed as if they've really tried, in clean, new, stylish outfits, their glossy hair sharp enough for a magazine shoot. I know I'm keeping Aunty Jo's suit for later. But in my last-year's shirt and with my tailored slacks, no one in St Aidan would give a flying fig if my capri pants were a few inches too long for this autumn, although they might think I'd gone over the top with this understated silk shirt. But somehow I'm not really cutting it in Bath. I mean, when did the bare ankle thing get so big? I've been away months not years, but everyone's trousers seem to have shrunk hugely. And that's before we get to all those wide legged ones.

I look outside to give myself a rest from the flurry of waitresses and me feeling so off-trend in the fashion stakes. Beyond the smart people dashing past out on the pavement, the traffic is a blur. If I'd realised how overwhelming the constant movement was going to be, I'd have made sure Bella tucked us away in a dark corner so I could nudge myself back into the bustle more gently. We'd usually fight for this view, sitting at the centre of the action is pretty mind-blowing, but today it's in an uncomfortable way not a buzzy one. I've been outside all summer, where the space is airy and the sounds drift away. Being confined with all the crashing of plates and the scraping of chairs on the concrete floor is making my head vibrate.

Don't get me wrong. I'm beyond pleased to be here, I can't wait to start soaking up the atmosphere of the city bars and the wide open squares and rediscovering the menus at the pavement cafés. It's just going to take a teensy bit of getting used to the excitement levels, that's all. Right now it would be blissful to take time out, dive under the table, hide in the tent of the tablecloth, and go through a few of Aunty Jo's mantras. If this was St Aidan, no one would give me a second glance. If I did it here I'd most likely get blue-lighted away. So instead I close my eyes tight, and mutter them silently in my head. *Eat more strawberry ice cream . . . Good things take time . . . You can never have too many waffles . . . I'm doing this for me . . . May every day be sunny . . . Please, please, please let me get back to Zinc Inc . . .*

'Edie?' Bella's reaching across the table, tapping my arm. 'It's Jake, he's here now.'

'A little bit early. I hope I'm not interrupting your catchup?'

I snap my eyes open as I hear the familiar resonance and the laughter in Jake's voice. There's just enough time to take a gulp of air before he sweeps me onto my feet and into one of his bear hugs. As I unstick my cheek from his jacket I notice he's got his own dedicated waitress in tow, which is a measure of how often he's here and the shedloads he spends on their cake.

'I got us another round of coffees, and I hope you're hungry for doughnuts.' He nods at the plate the waitress is unloading onto the table, which is stacked with the things, then smiles at me as he slides into the chair with his back to the window. 'No pressure. We don't have to eat all twelve now, we can take a couple back to the office for later.' He picks up a doughnut that's dripping with dark chocolate and nuts and puts a file down on the table. 'Don't worry, that's our latest successful bid. I thought you might like to look over it later, but let's cover the important stuff first. You're looking great, Edie, so tell me how you've been and what kind of doughnut are you having?'

'I'm good, *really* good, thanks.' I make a grab for the nearest sticky icing, thinking how well it goes with whatever's left of my lippy.

'Straight for the pink.' As Jake rubs his hands across his number two cut, his grin widens. 'Well done, you passed your first test. I was worried Cornwall might have changed you, it's a big relief to see it hasn't.'

'Test?' *Shit.* I seriously hadn't thought. Then I catch his eye. 'You're joking me, aren't you?'

'You have no idea how pleased I am to see you, or you wouldn't be asking that.'

The file's upside down, but I peer across the table and try to see if I can make out the words on the front. T-H-E . . . The. Thank shizzle it starts with one I know. My chest is tight as I look at the letters, because the second word is so long. W-A-T-E-R-F-R-O-N-T. What the hell's going to happen if I can't tell what it says? However much he's joking about and plying me with cake, I *am* on trial here. If I can't even read the front of his file, there's no chance of getting 'my job back.

'How auspicious is this, Edie? First a doughnut mountain, now it's stopped raining. Any minute now the sun will be out again.' Bella's laughing across the table and pointing at the street. 'Welcome homes don't get any better than this.'

As I crane my head to look up, the sky above Jake is still grey. Then, as I watch, the clouds crack open and a sun shaft breaks through and hits a puddle. In an instant the water on the pavement turns from shiny brown to a brilliant glare. I'm busy blinking, trying to clear the black hole the light's made in my eye when I notice a rainbow shimmer around Jake's head. I stretch out my hand to reach for my sunnies, but somehow I can't seem to reach them.

'Everything okay, Edie?' Bella's hand lands on mine, but when I turn to look at her, beyond the black splodges in my eye, she's got her own rainbow shimmer too. 'Do you need your sunglasses?'

'Edie?' Jakes voice echoes, as if it's coming from very far away.

'Water, it says water . . .' Suddenly it's clear in my head. 'Water, then something else.' Water, water, water. 'Waterfront – that's it.'

And then the room is spinning, and the ceiling is tilting. If I know the water part, it may be enough to save me. And as the concrete floor rushes towards my face all I can think of is how much it's going to hurt, and how I wish Dustin were here to put his head under mine.

Chapter 41

Day 304: Saturday, 1st September
In my mum's living room

Epic Achievement: Quoting Dracula – yes really.

As my dad always says, 'We learn from failure, not success', and as a driving instructor, he should know. Although borrowing quotes from a book about vampires is a bit of a twisted way of cheering up his unsuccessful pupils. For me, there are two ways of looking at the last few days. If I'm learning from my mistakes, I should be way more knowledgeable now than I was at the start of the week. But, at the same time, after everything I've been through – truly, I should have known better. I should have taken more care.

Life can be tricky like that. Everyone knows the more you look forward to an event, the less likely you are to enjoy it. I've been aching to get back to Bath, but when you give something a big build up, how often does it come up to expectations? Even so, me passing out in Sugar Sugar in front of the boss I was trying to prove myself to was beyond an epic fail. What's more, it's entirely my own fault. I should have known to ease myself back in. The problem was, I assumed I'd storm back into town and pick up without a hitch. If I'd been less urgent and eager, I'd have known to take baby steps. As it was I took a giant jump and landed flat on my face. Again.

If the last few months has taught me anything, it's that I know how to pick myself up. I'm not upset, I'm not mortified. I'm just shaking myself down and getting on with it.

In a way it was a good time to have a hospital appointment. Sliding along those lino-clad corridors, sitting in waiting bays, seeing so many ill people, even though they tweaked my meds and told me I wouldn't be driving any time soon, there were no real surprises. But, unlike last year, this time I knew for sure I didn't belong there. I was only passing through, then getting the hell out.

I didn't make it back to St Aidan on Friday, and I didn't go out with the girls either. But I'm taking my own advice, doing things slowly, taking more care, which means I'm staying with Mum and Dad a few more days. Tying up my loose ends. Facing up to getting fired. Which is why Mum has just shown Jake into their living room, and put a large mug of tea in his hand.

'So, according to the consultant, all Edie did at the café was faint due to feeling overstressed.' My mum's loading Jake's plate up with a huge slice of jam and cream sponge and helpfully getting the explanations out of the way on my behalf. 'They seemed happy that it wasn't anything that would happen too regularly.'

'Nothing at all to do with doughnuts.' I throw that in to remind my mum I *am* actually here.

'Phew, it's all good news then.' Jake sits back against Mum's latest stripy cushions and grins at me from the end of the other leather sofa. 'I'm pleased you're okay, that's the main thing.'

'And thank you for bringing Edie the lovely flowers.' Mum's smiling at Jake and heading for the kitchen door. When she says flowers she's talking half a shop rather than a bunch. 'If you don't need me here, I'll go and get them into water.'

I wait until she's quietly pulled closed the door behind her, then I tuck my legs up and begin. 'So, I never got a chance to ask – how's everyone at the office?'

Jake pulls one of his 'anything might happen' faces. 'Pretty much the same. We've got loads on, there's a new apprentice called Jack, and Sadie's finally had a date with Tony, the postman.'

'If it's the same Tony who used to hit on her chocolate drawer, that's amazing.'

'Yes, it took twenty months and four hundred mini Mars bars, but she got him in the end.'

'But does she *like* him?' I know how fussy she is when it comes to men.

'Enough to go for a second date and get a Brazilian.' Jake considers as he takes a bite of cake. 'She's got very high standards.'

'I've *so* missed you all.' My heart's aching for all the office quirks I haven't been around.

'Which brings me back to why I'm here. It's not only to spend Saturday afternoon eating my way through your mum's cupboards until I find the flapjack tin.' Toffee is another of Jake's weaknesses I'd momentarily forgotten.

'You're here for the car.' It's been seriously kind of him to let me keep it this long, but with no chance of me getting behind the wheel we all know it's got to go.

'Mostly I want to talk about finding stress-free ways for you to ease yourself back to work.' He breaks off to grin at me. 'No pressure, obviously, but did you enjoy The Waterfront proposals?'

The file he gave me is sitting on the table, and as I stare down at it I can feel my confidence ebbing away. I blow out a breath. 'They scared the bejesus out of me, Jake. Honestly, I could barely understand a word.' That's why I know this is hopeless.

He frowns. 'Shit, please tell me you didn't try to read them? I only gave you them because I was hoping the photos would remind you how much you missed us.'

I let out a groan. 'Now you tell me. I've been beating myself up about that all week.'

His smile is guilty, but he's rubbing his hands together like he means business. 'There's nothing to be scared of. We'll start with an hour at a time, then build up. It'll be the same as when you first started, we'll see what you enjoy best, and go from there. But the main thing will be to keep everything low-key for the first few months.'

'Okay.' My mouth might be agreeing but my head's still screaming 'Noooooooo'.

'We're all behind you. Sadie's offered to drive you in every day, and she's going to run you anywhere you need to go, and be on hand to help. We're taking your car today so she can get used to it.'

Now I'm the one frowning. 'So you're not sending it back?'

He pulls a face. 'Why would we? You'll be coming to work in it.' His face slides into a grin, and he slaps a magazine down on the coffee table. 'Apparently your first job is to get up to speed with this.'

More technical words? For a minute I think I'm going to be sick. Then I look again and see Cheryl's face smiling out at me. '*Closer?*'

He nods. 'If you get in that car on the first day without knowing every last bit of goss on every member of the Beckham household, and armed with enough Twix bars to fill the glove box, Sadie has offered to mash me.'

And this is why I love Zinc Inc so much. 'So as long as I load up with chocolate and know where Katie Price and Ant and Dec are detoxing, I'm all good?'

'It's as easy as that. You've kept me sane for close to fifteen years. Whatever it takes to get you back, I'm willing to do it.' His left eyebrow goes up. 'I suspect we may be branching out into shepherd's hut interiors.'

Crap. 'Who the eff told you about them?'

'Your mother may have mentioned, purely in passing.' He rolls his eyes towards the kitchen door. 'It's a big growth area. Why wouldn't we follow that up now you've made such a cracking start?'

I can't believe I'm hearing this. 'Because . . . because . . . because . . .' Because it's like two parallel universes colliding. That's the whole point about parallel; it means they never meet. As for the words Barnaby and Browne tugging at the back of my mind, that was never real anyway.

'I'm not saying you have to, I'm simply saying I'm completely confident Zinc Inc will find a way to use your current talents to the full.' He's got a twinkle in his eyes. 'Forget Project Manager, Creative Director suits you much better.'

I'm squeaking with horror. 'Creative Director *of what?*'

'Our new Garden Buildings section, of course. Don't be fooled, they're only wooden boxes, it's only what you've been doing in Cornwall for months.' He grins at me. 'I always knew you'd be great working with clients and design. I'm furious I wasn't the one who thought of it first. And Sadie can't wait.'

I'm shaking my head hard to hide how I'm remembering Barney saying exactly the same thing about the boxes. 'Sometimes you're unbelievable, Jake, you do know that?'

'Unbelievable, but impossible to refuse, I hope.' He lets out a sigh. 'No one's quite got your eye for detail and the builders don't work as well for anyone else. We can't let you go, you've got to come back.'

Put like that, I can hardly refuse. 'Okay, I'll give it a try.'

To think I've been making such a huge deal about getting back to Zinc Inc, and in the end it's no more complicated than Scarlett Moffatt and a few Mars bars.

But shepherd's huts? That's yet another thing I have to thank Cornwall for. When I talked about closing my circle, I had no clue it would be with those.

Chapter 42

Day 308: Wednesday, 5th September
Back in St Aidan

Epic Achievement: This gap is spectacularly blank. In other words, zilch.

'It's bound to feel different, Edie, the holidays are over.'

As Aunty Jo and I sit in the day room the morning after I come back, it's about more than a chilly edge to the wind, the lane being empty and the sea looking like it's made from brushed steel. With the kids back at school, the mums are all at home clearing up six weeks' worth of chaos, so the barn yard is deserted too.

'I missed everything here more than I expected – the way the sea changes colour, the huge skies, the clouds, the light making everything luminous . . .' Even after ten days in Bath, I was still waking up listening for the sound of the waves.

Aunty Jo nods. 'Don't worry, we can always visit.'

I let out a sigh. 'If we come back again next year, we'll be tourists. It'll be a disappointment, because nothing will feel the same.' Every time I see the 'sold' sign through the window, my tummy disintegrates because it feels so final. We're both on our way to where we've wanted to go all year, and I've got the extra boost of knowing there's a place for me at Zinc Inc, but that doesn't stop this part being heart-wrenchingly sad in a way I'd never foreseen. And I'm aching for a blast on the beach while I can still have one. 'Have you seen Barney today?' I was secretly hoping he would burst in with the dogs for a walk at breakfast.

'He actually came by before you got up.' She shifts and stares hard at her pumps. 'He said there's nothing for you to paint because they'll be clearing the units soon. He's keeping Dustin away so he doesn't spoil the carpets, and Cam's booked into an after-school club, so he won't be visiting either.'

'You're right about the change.' I try to ignore that I feel like I've had a boot in the stomach.

'Barney and Cam both seemed a bit lost without you at first, Sweetpea.'

I can't help snapping. 'Well, it's good they got over it so fast.' I know it's hard for Cam, but it feels like the space I occupied has already sealed over. The only good side is this way I sidestep any lingering awkwardness after the glamping night. 'Anyway, where's Malcolm?' At least we can rely on him to be a permanent fixture.

Aunty Jo sniffs. 'Since your mum's party, I've barely seen him.' She looks up and pulls a face. 'He's done the garden, but he hasn't been in for cake. Or out for lunch.'

'Did Dad overdo the beer?'

'It wasn't that. Malcolm's not a city person, I was silly to take him.' She's bunching up her lips and frowning hard. 'It's completely normal, it was the same in Harpenden. When you're moving on, some people drop you like a hot potato.'

It's not that I'm doubting her. I just hadn't got Malcolm down as a dropper, that's all. Or Barney. They're actually two of the few people I'd trust to hold my chips. And, unless I'm mistaken, Malcolm took *us* to Bath, not the other way around.

'So, it's just you and me, then.' However hurt and put-out I feel, I refuse to waste my last days of freedom sitting around moping. 'How about we think about some ideas for the living room in your next place?'

She brightens. 'The cottage is beautiful now, but it's never truly felt like home.'

'We'll make sure your new flat does.' I plump down next to her and pass over her laptop. 'Let's look at some sofas.'

She's staring at me proudly. 'I've never had a room designed by a Creative Director before.'

I laugh. 'I'm not "in post" yet.' And I already know smart city clients are going to be a lot more exacting than the ones around here.

'But you will be, one day soon. That's what counts.' She pats my hand. 'Everyone's over the moon for you.'

'They all know?' I'm not sure why I bothered to ask that.

'Why wouldn't they?'

It's another one of those times when a laptop knows what you're wanting to buy before you do. Within seconds of her opening it up, the perfect sofa pops up on her screen. Dusky pink velvet. Bang on trend. With the squishiest cushions. And an *end of summer sale* tag that makes it completely irresistible.

'That's it!' Her eyes are shining. 'I'm smitten.'

'Great price, lovely fabric, it's very "now". The windows of the Neptune shop in Bath were full of grey and blush.'

She's tense with excitement. 'There's an extra discount for immediate delivery. If I order now, it'll be here this time tomorrow.' This is Aunty Jo. Saving it for the new flat was never going to work. I'll have to accept her new decor is going to be sofa-led.

'Order some Farrow and Ball Sulking Room Pink too. You've still got a few weeks here, let's make you a room you can truly enjoy until you move.'

'Thanks, Chickpea, this is so much better than being quiet.' She's straight onto Google. 'What are we searching for next?'

If I have on eye on the screen and the other on the French windows, it's only because I'm so used to people dropping in. Well, Cam. But obviously he doesn't.

So that was Wednesday.

Chapter 43

Epic Achievement: Does a pink sofa count?
(I didn't actually choose it, but it's certainly epically beautiful.)

On Thursday the sofa arrives. However beautiful it looked in the picture, in real life it's better.

The second we've ripped off the cardboard and pushed it into position, Aunty Jo closes her eyes and sinks down onto it. 'This is so comfy, I might just stay here all day.' Then she stretches out her arms and rubs the velvet.

'Great choice, Aunty Jo, it's gorgeous.' It's the kind of sofa that's so lovely you'd probably want two of them, but I don't risk saying that.

She pushes her nose up in the air. 'It's a shame no one else is here to help us test it.'

However much I agree, I'm not going to say it out loud.

'Why not see how *Swan Lake* looks from there?' I'm on a winner, she's never yet refused.

But she only frowns. 'You know, Chicken, it's the people, isn't it? The people are what's important, not the places. Or the rubbish

350

you watch on TV to pass the time.' The sigh she lets out goes on for ages, and when she looks back from gazing out of the window her expression is wistful. 'Being content is a funny thing. And other times you don't realise you were happy until you're not.'

I'm thinking of what I can add to that to give a positive spin to her move. 'That's why, if there's a chance to be happy, you have to grab it and not let go.'

She's dabbing her nose with a tissue. 'You're right. I'll make sure I remember that.'

'You can't beat good friends or fabulous sofas.' I don't want her getting all teary, so I find *Giselle*, slide it into the DVD player and press play. 'We'll go along and choose some bits from the barn yard later, we'll be sure to bump into someone to admire your sofa.'

But when we go to the barn yard there's no one there, and it's one of Barney's guys who carries round the little square cabinet Aunty Jo chooses for me to paint.

*

By Friday afternoon it's had three coats, and the pink is reminding Aunty Jo of her old ballet shoes so much she goes upstairs and finds them, and we hang them on the wall and tie their satin ribbons in ragged bows. Meanwhile I'm thinking about Bella and co, going around the pavement bars in Bath after work, while I'm here. When I opted for Unicorn Specials in St Aidan over a night out with the girls, I was obviously taking too much for granted.

'Do you fancy a Friday evening trip to the Plank Place?'

Aunty Jo looks up from the corner of the sofa where she's curled up with a book. 'That used to be your usual, didn't it?' How can ten tiny days away have changed things so much? I hate how it already sounds like it's in the past, and how miserable Aunty Jo's looking.

'The ice creams are on me tonight.' I find a piece of paper, scribble those same words, draw a teensy cactus and a sundae glass piled full, and fold it in two. 'I've got barely any time left here, I'm not staying home. I don't want to upset Cam, so I'll drop this note in next door, let Barney decide if they want to come.' I'm pushing my luck here. 'You could drop one in for Malcolm too?'

'I don't know about that.'

By the time I get out on the lane I'm almost losing my nerve, so I run like the wind and I'm back before Aunty Jo has turned her page. As she's still firmly on the sofa, she's obviously less desperate than me.

'Don't you have some long floaty *Swan Lake* ballet dresses?' I'm trying to keep my mind off the invitation that's lying outside Barney's big glass doors, wedged under one of Beth's lanterns.

Aunty Jo looks up. 'Only two, they're in the wardrobe, but they're very tattered.'

'Go and get them, and bring those old programmes out of your desk too.' Whatever it takes to cheer her up, I'm going for it. 'The buyers are committed, so bugger neutral, you and Periwinkle deserve a dance-themed makeover.'

As I rush off to see what else pink and grey I can find around the barn yard, I've practically forgotten the note. Well, that's not completely true, but I'm only thinking about it every other second, not all the time. So when I'm rearranging the cushions in the easy chair for the umpteenth time and hear a familiar low voice behind me, there's no wonder I jump so hard I end up throwing them across the room.

Barney's holding Robert in the crook of his arm, but he stoops to pick up the sheepskin one that landed on his boot. 'I thought you'd finished here?'

As I look at the shadow of stubble on his jaw, I try not to think how it felt against my palm, or how much gaunter and drawn he looks than when I left.

'We're having a change. embracing blush and bigging up the grey.'

The edges of his eyes crinkle as he frowns. 'What's Miss Havisham's wedding dress doing on the wall?'

'It's Aunty Jo's Dying Swan frock, to make it feel more homely.' As I lean in to give Robert a tickle he tries to make a lunge for me, but Barney holds him firm. 'Have a seat, be the first visitor to try the new sofa.' If he's going to make a crack about dead birds, he can take a running jump. But then I catch the wounded look in his eyes and know that he's not.

'I can't stay.' He drops Robert's lead onto the coffee table, sits down, still hugging Robert, and holds up my note between his fingers. 'There are a few things I need to clear up.'

'Right.' My mouth's gone dry. 'So the Plank Place is off?'

'I'm sorry, Edie, but Cam's losing another person he cares about. I've agonised over this. Now he's getting used to you not being around, it's better we keep our distance.'

'Okay.' It's not at all. I feel like he's put an axe through my heart, but I can see where he's coming from. 'And the rest?'

'About the glamping . . .'

'Oh, that.' My chest's imploding as I wait for him to carry on.

'It was a great night.'

I can't argue. 'Best ever.'

'But that's all it was, I'm not expecting more.'

'I'm . . . pleased to hear it.'

'I mean, neither of us is in a position . . .'

It's a relief he left it at that. 'We certainly aren't. Good call, if you hadn't got in first, I would have.' I have no idea why my chest is aching. 'So if that's all . . . I'll let you go?'

He's up and across the room faster than you can say 'Run for the hills', but he stops at the French window. 'That's one very comfy sofa.' He lets out a wistful sigh. 'It's a shame. Sugar Plum Fairy would have been great for a shepherd's hut theme.' Then, just before he goes, he pauses and pulls a face. 'But dead birds and the feel-good factor, how does that work? Make sure you call in and say goodbye before you leave.'

And then he's gone, and Aunty Jo's bustling through. 'Was that Barney? He can't go yet, he hasn't tried the settee.'

'He gave it five stars.'

'Are you okay?' Aunty Jo doesn't wait for my reply, instead she swoops on the table. 'Why on earth did he rush off without taking Robert's lead?'

'I'm not sure.' It's the same answer for both questions.

'Well, you'd best get it back to him quickly. He's going to need it.'

'Can't you take it?'

She snatches up her book. 'It's best if you do it, I'm finishing my chapter.'

'Fine.' It really isn't. He couldn't have made it any clearer, he doesn't want me anywhere near.

'Grab a cardi and pop along now, Sweetpea, you'll be back before you know you've gone.'

It's that funny thing about being told what to do by someone you knew as a child; if it's your aunty, sometimes your body overrides your mind. This is me, now. I'm out on the lane, with the wind whipping straight through my knitted sleeves, when I should still be in the house arguing my corner. So long as I do this at a run, I might not even notice I left, although it might help if the man I'm looking for hadn't left the area entirely. As I pass the end of the barn yard I finally spot Loella in her doorway, and slow my pace for a stride.

'Seen Barney?'

She jerks her thumb over her shoulder and grins. 'Down at his.'

I hare on down the lane, and as I round the corner and slide into Barney's courtyard, he's standing by the huge outdoor table. As I race towards him he turns around, so I wave the lead and skid to a halt next to him, panting.

'You left this.'

'So I did. Thanks for bringing it.' He takes the lead from me and holds it up. 'We'd have missed this, wouldn't we, Robert?'

There's a beat of time when the world stands still, and I know I should spin straight around and head for the lane. In a few gasps of air I'd be all the way back to the cottage. But the beat passes, and instead of running, I'm still here. Staring at the fruit tree boughs as they groan under the weight of the crop, marvelling at how the apples have turned from green to dark red. That the sea is solid and grey. How the streaks of foam across the water look like painted white lines.

Then, a moment later, Robert trots out of the open door, nose in the air, tail held high, heading straight for his lead. He takes a few strides towards Barney's hand, then as he catches sight of me he veers off, breaks into a gallop, and dashes towards me. I'm bracing myself, bending down to catch the weight of a dachshund in full flight, when there's a loud yap, and a bolt of whiteness comes haring from the doorway.

'Dustin?'

In two bounds he's cleared the space between me and the house, then, as the gravel flies, he slides to a halt in front of me. He waits until I catch Robert and sit backwards on my bum, then he dives into my arms too, but in a very gentle way, snuffling around my ears and rubbing his silky furry head against mine. Then, as I stretch out my legs in front of me, he plonks his bum on my thighs, sits down, and throws his full weight against my body.

'I missed you, Dustin.' I'm burying my face in his neck and hugging him, wiping the tears from the corners of my eyes, and giving extra pats to Robert, who's dipping in then haring around us in circles, barking.

Then there's another, louder howl, cutting through the afternoon sunshine.

'Edie Browne? Edie Browne! EDIE BROWNE!!!!' Cam's dashing across the courtyard and throwing himself past Dustin and as he lands on my chest he's pummelling my shoulder with his fists and shouting. 'It's you, you're here, you've come back!'

I pull him into a hug and hold him tight against me so he can't see my mouth distorting. When I finally let go, I'm laughing as much as I'm crying, and we end up in a heap. And somewhere in the scramble of dog claws and squirming bodies and wagging tails there's so much love and warmth that when I finally stand up I'm limp and wobbly.

Barney's shaking his head as he holds up Robert's lead. 'Well, if you're all done with rolling on the floor, is anyone up for a walk?'

'I thought you didn't want . . .?'

'It's a bit late for that now. Only two more weeks, you'd best enjoy it while you can.'

'Too right.' My mind's racing. It's not that I'm a schemer, but I'm thinking of Aunty Jo here too. Time's precious, we can't be shut out again. I turn as I hear a shout and see Loella wandering towards us, her zebra-print harem pants billowing in the breeze.

'Hey, how's our favourite wanderer, are the streets in Bath really paved with gold? And what the hell did you do to Malcolm while he was there? Since he got back he's as antsy as an elephant with eczema, yet we can't get him out at all.' She throws an arm around my shoulder and pulls me into a hug. 'Any plans for the rest of your stay?'

'Now you mention it . . .' I'm winging it here. 'How does a Barn Yard Festival in two Saturdays' time grab you?' It's my last-but-one day here, but I'll skip over that. 'A huge celebration of St Aidan's crafters to round off the season, as a thank you for all the help you've given us.'

Loella's hand closes tighter on my shoulder. 'Edie B, I like your thinking.'

'A festival, that's amazing! And the town will still be full of September visitors too.' It's Beth, and she's hurrying to join us. 'Will there be beer?'

'Why not? It can be whatever we want to make it.'

Beth blows. 'It's going to take a lot to get my dad out of the house, but this might just work.'

Loella's already bouncing. 'Edie B, your genius streak has struck again! We'll go and spread the word.'

My mouth got the better of my sense again. But after two days of silence in the barn yard, the thought of everyone moving out, drifting away one by one, is too depressing. It might be selfish, but at least this way we keep it buzzing for as long as we can. We can sit around feeling weepy or we can go out with a bang. And I know which I'd rather do.

But first things first, we're off to the beach. And if I'm really, really lucky, some ice cream too.

Chapter 44

Day 324: Friday, 21st September
Back in St Aidan

Epic Achievement: Dangling from a rope. It has to be that, doesn't it?

'So are you going to explain why I'm hanging in mid-air, halfway down a cliff face?'

This is me, and I'm talking to Barney. But first I need to cover what happened in the meantime.

In the rest of the world a Crafters' Festival would take months to roll out, but in St Aidan, spontaneous capital of the universe, two weeks is more than enough. As usual, Beth and Loella are on the job spectacularly fast, signing up stallholders. Before we know it there's a Barn Yard Festival Facebook page, the kids have made posters and flyers, and we're all over town. We make it into a feature in the local paper, and Beth and Loella even snatch a spot on Pirate FM.

The grand festival plan is that all the barn yard units will be open, with craft stalls around the yard too. Then across in the big barn we're having yet more stalls and serving afternoon teas. Barney's having his show huts in the field behind the barn, and

Roaring Waves brewery will be serving locally brewed craft ales from one of their gazebos. Some of Barney's farmer mates have brought in a trailer-load of bales to sit on, and the bunting last seen at my mum's party, plus a whole lot more, is zigzagging across the sky.

If I'm treading carefully with Barney and Cam, it's nothing to the eggshells we're all walking on with Malcolm. It's only when Aunty Jo insists on masterminding the afternoon teas that we finally coax him out to take her to the over sixties lunch to get helpers. It helped that the Yellow Canary had moved on to their autumn special menu. After three bowls of treacle tart and caramelised apple crumble, Malcolm softened enough to sign up for an afternoon of table clearing, and to take a tiny step towards forgiving Aunty Jo for what she can't help – moving away.

We all know how he feels about long-distance relationships, and those two do seem happier hanging out together than apart. It would be a shame if they can't sort out their differences and find some kind of compromise, but when neither of them are willing to talk about it to each other or anyone else, it's hard to help.

I have to admit, I know where they're coming from because I'm struggling too, with Barney. He's had me in bits ever since that first day on the lane, but there's a world of difference between knowing someone's hot, that they fill the room with static every time they walk in, and finding out they are an amazingly kind and deep and wonderful person you can't help having feelings for. There's another watershed, when you discover you love hanging out with them, then another still when you find when they're not there there's this huge hole. Then all mixed in there's that lust, and the whole fascination and fantasy of wanting them. But at the same time, deep in your heart, you know you'll never be able to have them, because they're so out of reach. And you train yourself to accept that, and make the most of the bits you can have.

And then the unthinkable happens and the whole shebang gets blown out of the water. Until I actually snogged him it was manageable. Now it's agony, knowing better what I can't have. Because he's always been clear; Cam's his priority, a huge responsibility, that he can't compromise with a relationship.

And I know in a couple of days it's going to break my heart to tear myself away from here. But as I feel now it would be impossible to stay and see Barney, and know I couldn't have him. If I hadn't been rushing around helping with the festival preparations, the last few days would have been even worse.

Yet, having said all that, I'm still a sucker. When Barney rolls up in the barn yard the day before the festival and says, 'Hey, Edie B, if I promise there's no bodyboarding or going in boats, can I borrow you?' I don't even bother to ask, I just follow like a proverbial bloody lemming. And this is where it's got me.

*

'Okay, feet on the rock, lean backwards on the rope. Find your balance point, Edie.'

'Shut the eff up about balance points, Barney, and tell me what the proper point of all this is?' As for how the hell he still looks smoking in a climbing harness and hard hat, that's another of life's mysteries.

He's laughing next to me. 'There isn't only *one* point. I brought you for loads of reasons. It seemed a good way to prove how far you've come.'

'What? You throw me off a cliff to prove that?'

'I didn't throw you, you pushed off yourself.'

I have to remind him. 'I screamed.' The creases that slice down his cheeks when he sends me that ironic smile are killing me.

'It was more of a whoop, and then you aced it.' He gives me the benefit of the full-frontal grin as he turns. 'I just wanted to bring you up here so you would remember the day at the creek, then look at yourself now.'

'Jeez, if you make me shudder, I might freeze again. That was *so* awful.'

'But you got there in the end. The interesting thing is, as your confidence has come back, you've rediscovered your courage too.' He's hugely overestimating.

'I'm abseiling, Barney. We're side by side, you're telling me what to do. We're just dangling, inching all the way down to the ground, we're not seconds away from tumbling into a sodding gorge with a river gushing in the bottom that would carry us out to sea.' I have to say, 'This is actually how I'd have been if a helicopter had winched me off that tree.'

'Okay, Edie, you win on that, but you do make me laugh.'

'You make me laugh too.' I don't mean the jokes, it's more this strange bubbly feeling that pops inside me whenever he's near.

He gives me that weird sideways look he does. 'Mostly I brought you here for the view of the sea.'

As we twist around, the stretch we're looking out onto is wide and deep and the colour of topaz, and I have to agree, it's spectacular. 'The blue is so solid today, like cobalt in the paintbox.'

'I want this to be the view you remember . . . so you'll want to come back.'

'You want me to come back?' My voice is high with surprise.

'You weren't planning to forget about us entirely?' He shoots me a 'what-the-hell?' glance. 'It sounds awful, but I was secretly hoping you wouldn't make it back to Zinc Inc.'

'Really?' It's higher still.

'Pure selfishness. I had this ridiculous thought that if you didn't you might want to come and stay with Cam and me. There's plenty of room, I've always been big on space and short on people to fill it. Do the Barnaby and Browne thing.'

'Christmas.' As my knees give way I lose my balance and my cool and end up twisting into the rock, and bouncing back out again.

'Are you okay there?' He pulls a face. 'No, you're completely right. You staying with us is the last thing you'd want, it's a dreadful idea, my worst this week, forget I ever mentioned it.' He shakes his head. 'But we've missed you, we *are* going to miss you. A lot.'

'I missed you too.' It's out there. '*Both* of you.'

He reaches across and squeezes my hand. 'I know the effort you put in to get back to Zinc Inc. And you're the queen of shepherd's huts, you're going to ace it up there with garden rooms.'

There's so much love in those deep brown eyes of his, my throat is constricting. 'I couldn't have done it without you, Barney.'

'Rubbish, the success is all yours, don't knock it.' He readjusts his helmet. 'There's something I wanted to ask . . .'

My stomach does a somersault. 'Yes . . .?' Mostly I'm packed, but if he's building up to asking me to stay, I'll agree in a heartbeat.

'Can Cam and I take you back to Bath?'

'S-sure.' My bursting chest has collapsed so fast I'm in danger of slipping through my harness.

'I know your family's coming down for the festival, but this way Cam can see where you're going. Somehow it's easier if he leaves you, rather than you leaving him.'

'Great.' I should have known he'd work out the best way for Cam. If I'd been a bigger person and less concerned with myself and my own problems I'd have thought of that too.

'And maybe we could come up to visit some time?'

I'm still clinging onto his fingers. 'T-totally.'

'So shall we go down, get you back on terra firma?'

I feel like I've hit the ground already. Even if he hadn't withdrawn his invitation practically even before he made it, I couldn't possibly stay here. Feeling like I was about to throw up every time he turned around? That wouldn't work at all. As far as my queasiness goes, the sooner I'm back in Bath, the better.

Chapter 45

Day 325: Saturday, 22nd September
The Barn Yard Festival

Epic Achievement: This one is all Aunty Jo's.

'We can thank my mum for the blue sky, she's never seen Cornwall any other way.' I'm chatting to Loella at her table outside her barn yard door on Saturday morning, and every time I remember this is my last full day here, my stomach turns to jelly. If I didn't have a million things to do, and Cam and Dustin to keep me distracted, I'd be bawling my eyes out.

Loella looks up from the rainbow-coloured pile of patchwork fabrics she's tidying. 'Your mum and Josie are like two peas.'

I watch them laughing further along the yard. 'My whole life I've never seen them as alike, but now Aunty Jo's got more curves, you're right. It's actually mind-blowing having the family from Bath wandering around here too.'

Beth's looking out from behind her stack of lanterns. 'Malcolm's taken your dad off, they're already doing a great job clearing tables outside the big barn and sampling the Roaring Waves beers. They've got most of the kids helping them too, so we're in for a blissfully quiet day.' She sends me a wink. 'How about you? I hear Barney's been trying to thrill you again.'

Loella's giving me a sideways look. 'The lengths that poor lamb goes to – will you please just go out with him?'

'That's not what he wants.'

Loella's doing a huge fake cough into her hand. 'Says *who*?'

'He thinks girlfriends aren't fair on Cam.'

'You're not any old girl, you're Edie B.' She's tilting her head to where Cam's sitting on the floor, building a pirate lair out of gravel and sticks watched closely by Dustin. 'I mean, Cam's with you, and so are both Barney's dogs. I rest my case.'

Whatever they think, I'm not going to get any special dispensa-tions. 'It came up twice since I got back, both times he shut me down. In any case, I'm about to disappear to Bath, that's as final as falling off a cliff. But don't worry, I've helped to make Barney's units look cool for today, then handed over.' We've let the prettiest pieces spill outside, and everything's been priced up with Loella's eldest and her bestie taking charge of sales, and coming to find Barney or me if there are any queries. 'And Barney's filled the field with huts and disappeared back to the office, so I'm off to have a look around.'

Beth's wagging her finger at me. 'When you find the fudge stall in the barn, ask for the mint and eucalyptus flavour.'

'I will, but first I'm going to sit at the table and take it all in. I can't believe how beautiful it is.' Down the middle of the court-yard there's a line of tables with a wooden framework overhead, with chairs to either side. But best of all, along the centre of the tables there's a row of jars filled with vibrant pink and purple and orange and yellow flowers, all donated by Malcolm's allotment holder friends.

Loella's nodding. 'You certainly excelled yourself with this one, Edie B.'

365

I laugh at her. 'I'd say you two went above and beyond yourselves.'

Beth's calling after me. 'And don't forget there's dancing later.'

'I won't.' I may just have to go and zip up my bags when that happens.

*

It's late afternoon when Aunty Jo pulls me aside. 'Sweetpea, I need a word.' She thrusts a raspberry muffin the size of our heads into my hand, shushes Dustin, and then pulls me out into the field and pushes me down on a bale.

'If it's about the sand Dustin dropped in the garden room, I promise to sweep it up before I go.'

'Stuff the sand, Edie.' She can't mean that. 'I just wanted to thank you for today, tell you how wonderful everything is.'

The straw bale is warm to the touch, and it's the first time I've sat down all day; every time I was going to, I ended up rushing off to somewhere else.

'You were right when you said it's the people who are important, Aunty Jo. Everyone's certainly pulled together to make today amazing.' Every time someone sends me a cheery wave or sweeps me into a hug, the sad ache in my chest is overlaid with a warm glow. And the festival is so alive. There are the distant notes of a guitar, and the crowds who have arrived haven't left, they've just moved through into the barn for Aunty Jo's tea and delicious Little Cornish Kitchen cakes, and on into the field to flop on the grass and bask in the warmth of the September sun while sipping drinks from the beer tent.

Aunty Jo clears her throat. 'You see, I've actually changed my mind. St Aidan does feel like home after all.' She crosses her legs, smooths her striped apron and fiddles with one of her glittery pumps. 'Your makeover in the day room worked wonders.'

I smile at her. 'Don't worry, we'll make your next place just as cosy.'

'No, Chicken, you don't understand.' She's staring at me and her hand lands on my arm. 'What I'm saying is, I don't want to move to Bath after all. I've decided to stay here.'

It takes a moment to pick up my sagging jaw. 'How's that going to work?'

'I definitely want to keep the cottage.' She's beaming at me as if she hadn't just totally wiped out everything we've both been aiming for since I arrived. 'I was hoping you'd know what to do for the rest. You're the one with the good ideas.'

'Right.'

She gives a little cough. 'And Malcolm's agreed to move in with me.'

My gasp is so big I almost choke. 'Did *he* suggest that?'

'No, I did what you said, and asked him.'

'Excuse me?'

'You definitely told me women do the asking these days, so I took a leaf out of your book. It was very empowering.'

'Shucks.' Since when did Aunty Jo listen to me?

She's watching me as my eyes turn to the beer gazebo. 'His answer was nothing to do with beer goggles either. It was earlier this morning, *before* the Roaring Waves tent arrived.'

My eyes are popping out of my head for every reason. 'Well done for that! Go, Aunty Jo!'

Her smile fades slightly. 'You do think Harry would be okay with it?'

As I nod I'm aching for her. 'I'm sure he'd understand, but most of all, I think he'd like that you were staying.'

'I already rang the agents to tell them the sale's off.' She's smiling again. 'I took your other advice too, you see.'

'How is this my fault?' The only advice I can remember dishing out is when I said the dado in Bath would suit her down to the ground, and that was more of a joke.

'You told me if there was a chance to be happy, I had to go for it.'

Fuck. 'That's true.'

'So I did . . . I have . . . I am. I can honestly recommend it. You should try it for yourself, Sweetpea.'

It's hard not to be right behind her when her eyes are shining. 'Well, George will be the best person to guide you.'

'But . . .?' She's pushing me.

'I'd maybe think of B&B in the cottage. We mentioned that once before.'

'And . . .?'

Now my eyes are the ones that are shining. 'You could carry on with the barn yard as it is . . .' it's dawning on me this isn't only huge for her, it's massive for everyone else too '. . . then no one will have to leave, and everything can carry on the same. I know we did swaps to start with, but now it's getting established the income will be more secure, especially after today. You could get Loella and Beth to run it, they could even start a crafting cooperative.' I sweep her into a hug. 'That would be so amazing for everyone, and for you too.'

'I like the sound of that.'

I do too. 'Then you could possibly look for the right person to buy the big barn so you release some cash.' Flicking my eyes around our rent-by-the-week crafters, I'm not sure there's anyone here with that kind of money. I give her arm a nudge. 'But you know what, this is St Aidan – it'll all work out, because everything always does. And Malcolm's a great man, you'll be wonderful for each other.'

As I pull her into another hug I'm really happy for her. But there's also a part of me that wishes I was getting to stay too. And how the hell has Aunty Jo had the guts to sort out her future when I'm feeling so confused about mine?

'Thank you, I knew you'd know what to do for the best. Now we've got a plan I can go and find Malcolm, and we can tell Beth and your mum.'

'I'll eat my cake here, and catch you up.'

And as I munch my way through the raspberry muffin, I know it'll be approximately two breaths before the 'confidential' news spreads all around the barn yard. I can't help being amazed that one pink sofa has changed so much more than Aunty Jo's living room.

Chapter 46

Day 325: Saturday, 22nd September
The Festival After-Party

Epic Achievement: Watching Aunty Jo grab her own happy ending.
And asking Barney to dance.

There's never a point when the festival finishes. A few people drift away, but most people sit around in the field looking out over the sea. As the sky turns turquoise then smoky pink then orange, the lights on the swinging strings begin to shine. Mum and Dad are with Tash and Malcolm's leading all the children around, lighting the candles in the lanterns, with Aunty Jo following hanging onto Tiddlywink and Wilf. The huge outdoor barbie is already glowing, the barn has been cleared for the dancing, and as the music begins to waft across the air I'm easing towards the lane when Loella catches me.

'And where do you think you're going, Mrs?'

'I've some packing to finish.' The only thing left out are my jeans and a Seven Sins T-shirt for the morning, but it's the best I can come up with.

'Nice try.' She's not buying it. 'We've ordered soft lighting, it won't be too loud, we've got the cheesiest party bangers for you to dance to.' She starts to sound desperate. 'Anyway, you *can't* leave now. There's something special for you later.'

Then Cam and Mia dash up and, as the other children dance around us, they hang off our arms and pull us back towards the barn. As we go in through the massive open doors, I take in the walls, washed with pastel lights, and Morgan gently twirling Beth around the floor to the twangy sound of *Baby I Love You*.

I pull a face at Loella. 'My dad's going to be in his element.'

'St Aidan discos aren't for wimps, you'll need double meds for this next bit.' She gives me a shove in the ribs then her grin widens. 'Come on, time to dance, and when we can't stand up any more we'll get some food.'

As the first few beats of the next song ring out I stop to listen. 'It isn't . . .?'

'What kind of disco would it be without *Let's do the Time Warp?* And then it'll be *Bohemian Rhapsody*, and we obviously all join in the words to that, and then we'll go crazy to *Jump*, and *Common People*, obviously, and I hope you're ready for S Club 7's entire playlist.' She's laughing at me now. 'So, are you ready to party?'

It turns out that's another one of those questions that don't need an answer. What happens next turns out to be the most fun I've had since . . . well, who knows?

My mum and dad come in with Malcolm and Aunty Jo. As he takes her hand and leads her off to a space on the dance floor I can't help thinking that I'm actually watching her walk into her new beginning. It's not that she'll ever stop missing Uncle Harry, but she and Malcolm both have too much to give to be on their own. Now they've found each other, they deserve to enjoy life together. But there's no time to get teary because *There's a Ghost in My House* comes on and everyone in the barn literally goes bonkers and starts to leap around. Malcolm and Aunty Jo are shouting the words, and punching the air along with everyone else.

It's one of those nights where all I do is dance and grin and bounce around, where everyone I look around at is someone I know, and they're all smiling too. The kids are all going wild, and every time a track comes to an end my legs feel so tired I know I'll have to sit down. Then the next tune begins and I know I have to dance this one too. And we're all just in this kind of never-ending bubble of dancing euphoria. Okay, I'll admit it. It could be the best time I've had, ever. Just please don't tell anyone.

All the time – well not quite *all* the time (I'm not that sad) – I'm keeping an eye out for Barney. By the time I've hit the point of exhaustion plus a huge amount, I've decided not everyone loves the dance floor as much as we do. The crowd outside around the barbie wouldn't be anything like as big if they did. He's obviously not a dancer. End of. I'm scraping the sweat out of my eyes, peeling my hair off my dripping forehead, gasping for breath after *Smells Like Teen Spirit* ends, when I realise the dance floor has emptied, and Cam's tapping me on the elbow.

'You've got to come outside now – it's time for your surprise.'

Barney wanders in behind him. 'We've all put something together we'd like you to watch, although, with the latest news, I've had to update it. That's where I've been.'

'What . . .?' I'm frantically blowing sideways to cool my cheeks because they have to be crimson, and running my fingers through my sweat-streaked hair to try to give it a lift.

Then, as we step back into the pale light outside the barn, the music fades to nothing and I forget all about fluffing my hair. In the centre of the field there's a screen. Aunty Jo and Mum and Dad are sitting in front of it on one of her garden benches, surrounded by people either standing or sitting on the grass on rugs, or in deckchairs. As we reach the bench she smiles up at me and pats the space beside her.

'Come on, Sweetpea, time to sit down.'

As Cam slides in beside me, and Dustin sidles in to jam his body up against my leg and rest his head on my knee, Barney steps to the front and clears his throat.

'So, Edie B, you turned up here a few months ago, and you made an instant impression. Let's face it, no one else has given the headmaster a nosebleed by booting him in the face with a football before.'

He stops and everyone laughs, and Loella and Beth give a few whoops, and across the field Mr Wagstaff does a mock dive.

Then Barney begins again. 'You've changed a lot since you arrived, Edie, but thanks to those legendary brainwaves of yours, you've shaken us up too. The barn yard has given a lot of us the chance to spread our wings, and dare to take those leaps we might not have done otherwise. And it's wonderful news that the barn yard will be carrying on.' He's staring straight at me now. 'You transformed my shepherd's huts and filled my order book to bursting point, Edie. But most of all, you've touched us all with your love and laughter and that amazing smile.

'So, to remind you of what you've been doing these last few months, and as our way of saying "thank you", we've made you a little montage of your best bits.' He pauses to raise an eyebrow. 'And Beth has insisted it might be worth mentioning before we begin – the photos are from everyone, but the backing track is all down to Malcolm.'

As Freddie Mercury starts to sing *Good Old Fashioned Lover Boy* Beth catches my eye and shakes her head. Then as the titles come up on the screen, Aunty Jo's hand finds mine and squeezes me hard.

EDIE BROWNE (with an 'e') and her EPIC ACHIEVEMENTS in ST AIDAN

Then suddenly there I am, up on the screen, with much shorter hair, wearing *so much* lippy, getting blown away on the beach. And that cuts to me sitting on Aunty Jo's sofa in front of her jungle-print walls, watching *Swan Lake* on the TV.

'Jeez, I'd forgotten how awful that paper was.' Loella's behind us, saying what we're all thinking. Then we cut to a picture of Aunty Jo and me tucking into huge muffins behind the ink pots at the calligraphy class, and so it goes on. It's like every moment of our time here is up there, good and bad. I'm wiping mud out of my eyes on the football pitch, we're running around the barn yard in our Easter rabbit suits, drinking strawberry punch that first day we saw Barney's barns. We're looking at the climbing plants at Rosehill with the garden club, stripping wallpaper in our Tyvek suits. When we come to one of Cam and me poring over our reading books, eating our Unicorn cakes, he digs me in the ribs and grins at me. Then we all laugh as there's a picture of Loella pulling a face eating my awful cupcakes. And did I really look that dreamy, watching Barney playing his guitar by the campfire on the beach? As the music changes to *I Love to Boogie*, there's Aunty Jo and me with our easels at the life drawing class, then we're in the garden room with all the kids. And as the pictures flick past, the first mix of shock and surprise moves onto an awe that people have got together to share so many of their pictures. And overlaid with that, there's this feeling of being wrapped up in so much love and warmth it makes me want to burst.

There's what feels like so many more photos, then Aunty Jo's car jammed up against the house, with Aunty Jo looking like a model perched on the bonnet in her shimmery pumps. Then the stables in the barn yard, summer barbecues, dog walks with the kids around the bay. Somewhere along the line the music changes, to Razorlite and *America*, and Beth pulls a face at me again. And then we're looking at the shepherd's huts, the lovely spaces in the orchard, shiny new bathrooms, the kitchen at Periwinkle, with Malcolm watering the flowers in the garden. Mary and Jim in front of their shepherd's hut in their garden at home, Barney and me on the steps of the Beside the Seaside hut, me looking at furniture at The Junkyard, me grinning as I put the final touches to the showroom displays. And still they're going on. Cam and me on *Cameron's Star*, at the Surf Shack with sundaes as big as we are, then there's another dig in the ribs and a grin from Cam as Cam, me and Barney flash onto the screen on the beach when we wrote our names and did our selfie. Then we cut to Aunty Jo and me with very sad faces, out on the lane, looking at the Sold sign, then me dangling from the cliff, lots of shots of the Festival and, as the music finally ends, Dustin and I are sitting together on the screen in a slice of sunlight on the steps of the shepherd's hut. Then someone must have pressed reset, because it starts all over again.

'So, when you look at it like that, it turns out your time here's been pretty epic for everyone.' Barney's grinning. As he walks around in front of us and drops a bottle of Goofy Foot alcohol-free beer into my lap, Aunty Jo squeezes my hand, then gives me a half wink, and whisks my mum and dad away.

Loella leans in from behind. 'I'll go and get you some hot dogs.'

As I scrape away my tears and try to get some words together, my heart feels like it's going to explode. But something else is shifting too. Watching those pictures, I know – this is my place now, this is where I'm happy. But much more importantly, I have to screw up my courage and tell Barney how I feel. If Aunty Jo did it for herself, I can too.

'I need a word, Barney barn person.'

'Here, have my jacket.' As he slides it round my shoulders it's soft and warm, and as his hip lands next to mine I hear him draw in a breath. 'And?'

'So, you don't dance?' I have to start somewhere.

'That would be telling.' He glances at the photos, still flipping across the screen, then he sends me a wicked grin. 'I was loading up the slide show earlier, but I'm saving myself for the slow tunes. They play them at the end.'

'Got you.' I swallow so hard I can hear the gulp.

'So, what's new?'

I draw in a huge breath, think of my *Never or now* sign, and fire. 'I know you don't do girlfriends, and I know I forced you to sleep with me . . .' I also know I'm blurting, but I can't stop. 'But I told Aunty Jo if we accidentally find something good we have to grab it by the balls and not let go, and it's worked for her, so it would be completely hypocritical of me to wuss out and not man up . . .'

His hand lands on my leg. 'Slow down . . .'

'And I know I'm supposed to be leaving . . .'

'Hang on. As I remember, I wasn't forced, I was more than willing. And who said I don't do girlfriends?'

'But you don't.'

'I could make an exception for the right person.'

'So you're telling me this *now*?'

He's got those slices in his cheeks. 'It's as good a time as any, you never seemed available before.'

'But I *jumped* you. At the glamping – you haven't forgotten that?'

He shrugs. 'I'm not sure that's how I remember it. But whoever did what, you said it was a one-off.'

'The thing is . . .' Getting back to the job in hand. 'Watching your lovely slide show, the pictures showed me more than ever that I belong here. And in case there's any chance you feel the same way, I need to seize the happiness with two hands before it disappears.' And I still haven't come out with it.

'Edie B . . .'

'If it's the last thing I do before I go, I have to tell you – I'm not sure when, and I'm not sure how, but I've fallen in love with you, Barney.'

He lets out a sigh. 'I can't tell you how pleased I am to hear that.'

'You are?'

'You just made my wildest, most impossible dream come true.' He pulls down the corners of his mouth. 'If this is confession time, it's my turn – I've loved you since the first day I saw you on the lane.'

Shit. '*Really?*'

'Whatever you think, I don't rush up ladders to help everyone when they're stuck in windows, or gatecrash their wallpaper stripping, or whisk them off across the bay in boats. But I couldn't help it. However much I thought I should, I couldn't stay away from you.' His arm's sliding around my shoulder, pulling me against his chest. 'I have to say, when it comes to women friends, Cam's got excellent taste. And the more I got to know you, the more time I wanted to spend with you.'

'So you and Cam might have space for me in your life?'

'We could give it a try.' He lets out a low laugh, then he sounds more serious. 'Truly, Edie, Cam and I would love you to be with us, but it has to be right for you too.'

'But the whole thing is . . . it hit me while I was watching the slide show . . . St Aidan is absolutely where I want to be. It's beautiful here, especially seen from halfway up a cliff . . .' I stop to grin up at him, and end up rubbing my hand on his cheek.

'I'm pleased you appreciated that.' He returns the grin, then leans in and kisses my palm.

'But it's more than the pretty cottages and the wonderful sea and the walks on the beach. I love the people here. They get me, I get them – I have no idea how I didn't see that until now. But most of all, I want to be with you and Cam.' As I'm looking up into his eyes, they're turning my insides to syrup. 'So if you're looking for a girlfriend after all, I'd like to apply for the position.'

His lips are twitching, and he's rubbing his cheek on my temple. 'Edie B, you are the most amazing woman, and I love you to pieces.'

'Not half as amazing as you.'

As he takes in a breath I feel his ribs expand against me. 'But . . . and there is a big but here . . . you've spent the last six months reaching for the impossible and achieved it, and now you've got the promise of a brilliant job. What kind of a guy would want to stop you doing that?'

'One who loved me and wanted to be with me?' It was meant to come out all strong, and ballsy, but instead it's embarrassingly weedy.

He's shaking his head again. 'You're amazing Edie, I already said that – that's why you earned your chance to shine. The least you deserve is to go back to your job, and Bath, and see how you like it. Anything less is selling yourself short.'

My voice is high, because I can't believe what I'm hearing. 'So you're telling me to go back to Zinc Inc?'

However irate I sound, Barney's staying patient. 'You used to love your life at Zinc Inc. Staying here now might seem like a choice, but it's more like a default. Ducking out now would be like catching the train to London and getting off at Reading. Years down the line you might regret taking the easy option. To be fair to all of us, you must go back to Bath, see how you like it – and *then* make your choice.'

I blow out a sigh. 'That's harsh, Guy Barnaby, but I can see where you're coming from. It's wise advice.' Who the hell would get off at Reading?

'Cam and I will be here waiting. But if you don't choose us in the end, it's fine. It only means it wouldn't have been right for any of us.'

'So I suppose you're going to say you won't sleep with me again either.'

That makes him laugh loudly. 'I didn't say I wouldn't use every-thing in my power to sway your choice. Including my body.'

'So in that case . . .?'

'Maybe we should have that dance?' He's dipping towards me. 'But there's something more important I want to do first.'

Fleetingly I'm wondering if he's talking about whatever food Loella's bringing. Then his mouth hits mine, and his tongue is feathering my lips apart, and as the world stops spinning time stands still.

It's a long time later when we come up for air and he breathes into my ear. 'I'm treading a fine line here between being discreet in front of your parents and wanting to rip your clothes off.'

So in a way when Loella turns up with the hot dogs it's not bad timing. Although, for once, I do manage to eat mine without throwing it all over Barney, and afterwards I slide my hand over that delicious bare bit of skin between his jeans and his T-shirt and into his back pocket. When I've secretly lusted after something for so long, now I've got the go-ahead to get my hands on the goods I'm very reluctant to let go.

And then we hear the tempo change in the barn, as the slow tracks begin. Okay, if I was hoping for something quirky like Prince's *Purple Rain*, or cool like Adele's *Someone Like You,* or heartfelt like *All by Myself*, I was never going to get it. This is St Aidan, it had to be kitsch, loud and a little bit over-the-top. I mean, *Lady in Red* would have been so much worse. So really if Aerosmith's *I Don't Want to Miss a Thing* ends up being our forever song, I'm okay with that.

We're kind of nervous, and holding each other at arm's length at first, tripping over Dustin – who somehow is still here – smiling at Beth beyond Malcolm's shoulder, laughing down at Cam. I mean, waving at my dad is not what I expected to be doing in any first dance of mine. There are a few stumbling, self-conscious seconds, then the fluttering fizz I felt at life drawing turns into the turbo charge of lust from the glamping, and next thing I know I'm clamped against the most beautiful body in the south-west, if not the world.

I remember one time around freshers' week, Marcus and I stopped in a village in his open-top car to find a sign to tell us where we were, and there was a fully packed car in a drive, and a teenager by the front door howling because they didn't want to be taken away to uni. Afterwards I often wondered if they got to stay at home, or if they went and a day later were having a whale of a time at drunken parties in hall.

I think about that day as Barney and I sway around the dance floor in the soft apricot light, and I stand on tiptoe and try out talking into his ear. 'I don't want to go . . .' It's so quiet the words are almost not there, but in my head I'm howling as loudly as that unhappy fresher.

His answer is like the wind off the sea. 'Make sure you choose us and come back soon, then.'

*

As it turns out, I've had my last night at Periwinkle Cottage without even realising. I spend Saturday night with Barney in his wide double bed, with his battleship grey sheets, in his lofty battleship grey bedroom. And in the morning Cam comes in to read me a story, then we have a long, late, lazy breakfast by the open kitchen doors, looking down to the sea, listening to the cries of the seagulls wheeling far below. And then we load my yellow and purple bags into Barney's truck, say our last few goodbyes and set off for Bath.

Chapter 47

Day 360: Saturday, 27th October
Five miles east of Salisbury

Epic Achievement: Another skydive.

'It's official, we have to be crazy to do this again,' Bella's muttering, rolling her eyes at me as we bump our way backwards along the fuselage floor.

I let out a groan. 'At least we got carpet this time.' Twenty quid extra for the deluxe version seemed like a good idea, but it doesn't make it any less scary.

'Just close your eyes and think of your dogs.'

Bella's the only person who can put on a flying helmet and still look gorgeous. And this time it's not just for us. We've both got our Just Giving pages – Bella's jumping for young people who have strokes and I'm jumping for assistance dogs. There can never be too many Dustins in the world, even if right now I wish I was anywhere else.

Dan's tapping me on the shoulder. 'C'mon, Edie, let's do this.'

Whatever's on the floor, when I look around the space where the door used to be is like a yawning chasm. Then the backdraught hits us and we're sucked out into a vortex.

The air rush is wrenching my cheeks off my face, and the blow is so hard I can't breathe. I'm just falling and screaming. Screaming and falling. Somehow I get to stick my arms and legs out, but it's even more freezing then I remember and I'm screaming harder and harder. And choking. And the patchwork of fields below are hurtling towards us at a million miles an hour and we have to stop soon or we're going to die.

And then we start to turn, and from across the sky Bella is waving at me. Only this time around I know I look just as gruesome as she does with my cheeks flattened.

Last time I did this I loved my life, but now I love living. Every moment is precious, I'm grateful for every day. And for that alone, I wouldn't change a thing about the last year.

Then, just when it feels like it's never going to stop, there's a yank, the air rush halts and I'm hanging. Everything's slowed down, my screams have stopped, my face is still numb, but it isn't getting pulled off any more. As I glance up, high above us there's a broad blue parachute stretching across the sky. And I'm already anticipating the feel-good explosion I'll get as we lurch back to earth, that sense I'll be invincible forever.

But I also know that since last year my biggest leap has been on the ground: learning to believe in myself, to be strong, to be happy with who I am. With the support of people who love me, I can be anything I want to be. Do anything I choose to do. Be wherever I want to be. And as I float downwards it couldn't be clearer – the choice I'm making is right. It's the only one for me.

As we drift, there's time to look down at the silver snake of the road glittering in the sun, the little box of the headquarters. Loella's truck, slewn across the car park. Aunty Jo and Malcolm sitting on picnic chairs, next to Sadie and the crew from Zinc Inc. Tash and my mum and dad standing by the fizz gazebo, Tiddlywink and Wilf pointing up at me.

Then the ground is rushing towards us really fast and there's Dan's voice again, as his hand clamps my head onto his chest. 'Okay, lift up your legs – we're almost down.'

One massive bump later we're lurching forwards. Then my feet hit the ground too and guys are slapping me on the back as they run past to pick up the parachute. As I stagger I hear a whoop, and Bella's crashing back down to earth off to the side of me.

As Dan's unclipping me he gives me a wink. 'Same time next year then?'

'Too right.' But I'm already looking past him because Beth, Loella and the kids are stampeding across the grass and, out in front, there's Cam and Dustin. And as they hurl themselves at my thighs Cam's screaming. 'You did it, you *really* did, you *really, really* jumped out of a plane.'

Then there's a lower, more gentle voice. 'Good job, Edie B.'

And as Barney throws his arms around me and pulls me into the kind of hug that warms me right to my core, it flashes through my head that if Colin Firth had been here, I wouldn't even have looked at him.

And as Barney spins me around I know there's never been any doubt in my mind about where I should be.

Then he puts me down and I look up into his eyes, take his face between my hands and brush the curls back off his forehead. 'Good job yourself, Barney barn person. So when we're done here, will you take me home with you?'

As he laughs down at me there are crinkles at the corners of his eyes. 'To St Aidan?'

I grin up at him. 'My trial month is over, I know now I belong with you and Cam. If that's okay?'

His lips slide into that heart-crushing smile of his. 'It couldn't be better, Edie B.'

P.S.

When I began I was talking about beginnings, and how they're hard to pinpoint, and I was desperate to get back to where I'd started, so the rest of my life could begin. Even though I didn't realise it then, that first day I turned up looking for Periwinkle Cottage was the start of a whole new and different life. Which kind of proves the difficulty with beginnings.

As soon as I move back to St Aidan, Barney and I lose no time launching Barnaby and Browne. I brave the polished concrete and testosterone and move in with Cam and Barney, and Dustin's owner goes into a care home so he gets to stay on too – in the crook of my knees at night, and similarly close in the day.

Now Malcolm's at Aunty Jo's full-time, they've already added window boxes, and now the barn yard is permanent it opens for sales every Saturday. There's another happy twist when Cam's trustees buy the big barn from Aunty Jo, and Barnaby and Browne agree to rent it until he grows up. Even better, St Aidan becomes Zinc Inc's Cornish outpost; we design and build the first shepherd's hut for one of their clients, with the promise of many more orders to come.

And somewhere along the line, I'm not even sure when, I stop counting the days because they aren't important any more.

When I did my first skydive my happiness was careful and

ordered, heaped up in neat piles. But the kind of happy I've found in St Aidan with Barney and Cam is wilder, and more intense. It's unexpected, surprising, rich and random and chaotic. Huge like the ocean, and as certain as the tides. But most of all, it's real. And it's wonderful.

And I can't ask for a better beginning or end than that.

Acknowledgements

A big thank you . . . To my editor, Charlotte Ledger, for her inspiration, support, brilliance and all round loveliness. This is our tenth book together, it's been the most wonderful journey. To Kimberley Young and the team at HarperCollins for their fabulous covers and all round expertise and support. To my agent, Amanda Preston for her warmth and brilliance, her vision and encouragement, her sparkle and her super-fast responses. Whether I'm crying into my tea towel, dancing around the kitchen, or venturing out to events in London, she's always there for me.

To my writing friends across the world . . . To the fabulous book bloggers, who spread the word. To all my wonderful Facebook friends. And special thanks to Naomi Priestly for helping with the medical bits in between her shifts on the stroke ward.

To my wonderful readers . . . these books are all for you, thank you so much for enjoying them – I love hearing from you and meeting up with you.

And last of all, huge hugs to my family, for cheering me on all the way. And big love to my own hero, Phil . . . thank you for never letting me give up.

Also by Jane Linfoot

The Little Cornish Kitchen

**Christmas Promises at the
Little Wedding Shop by the Sea**

Summer at the Little Wedding Shop by the Sea

Christmas at the Little Wedding Shop by the Sea

The Little Wedding Shop by the Sea

The Vintage Cinema Club

High Heels & Bicycle Wheels

The Right Side of Mr Wrong

How to Win a Guy in 10 Dates

HELP US SHARE THE LOVE!

If you love this wonderful book as much as we do then please share your reviews online.

Leaving reviews makes a huge difference and helps our books reach even more readers.

So get reviewing and sharing, we want to hear what you think!

Love, HarperImpulse x

Please leave your reviews online!

 amazon.co.uk kobo goodreads L♥vereading iBooks

And on social!

f/HarperImpulse 🐦@harperimpulse
📷@HarperImpulse

LOVE BOOKS?

So do we! And we love nothing more than chatting about our books with you lovely readers.

If you'd like to find out about our latest titles, as well as exclusive competitions, author interviews, offers and lots more, join us on our Facebook page! Why not leave a note on our wall to tell us what you thought of this book or what you'd like to see us publish more of?

f/HarperImpulse

You can also tweet us 🐦@harperimpulse and see exclusively behind the scenes on our Instagram page www.instagram.com/harperimpulse

To be the first to know about upcoming books and events, sign up to our newsletter at: http://www.harperimpulseromance.com/